NED TURNED AND FACED THE SPANIARDS.

BY PIKE AND DYKE

A TALE OF THE RISE OF THE DUTCH REPUBLIC

BY

G. A. HENTY

ILLUSTRATED

NEW YORK
CHARLES SCRIBNER'S SONS
1923

PREFACE.

My dear Lads,

In all the pages of history there is no record of a struggle so unequal, so obstinately maintained, and so long contested as that by which the men of Holland and Zeeland won their right to worship God in their own way, and also —although this was but a secondary consideration with them—shook off the yoke of Spain and achieved their independence. The incidents of the contest were of a singularly dramatic character. Upon one side was the greatest power of the time, set in motion by a ruthless bigot, who was determined either to force his religion upon the people of the Netherlands, or to utterly exterminate them. Upon the other were a scanty people, fishermen, sailors, and agriculturalists, broken up into communities with but little bond of sympathy, and no communication, standing only on the defensive, and relying solely upon the justice of their cause, their own stout hearts, their noble Prince, and their one ally the ocean. Cruelty, persecution, and massacre had converted this race of peace-loving workers into heroes capable of the most sublime self-sacrifices. Women and children were imbued with a spirit equal to that of the men, fought as stoutly on the walls, and died as uncomplainingly from famine in the beleaguered towns. The struggle was such a long one that I have found it impossible to recount all the leading events in the space of a single volume; and, moreover, before the close, my hero, who began as a lad, would have grown into middle age, and it is an established canon in books for boys that the hero must himself be young. I have therefore terminated the

story at the murder of William of Orange, and hope in
another volume to continue the history, and to recount the
progress of the war, when England, after years of hesitation, threw herself into the fray, and joined Holland in
its struggle against the power that overshadowed all Europe, alike by its ambition and its bigotry.   There has
been no need to consult many authorities.   Motley in his
great work has exhausted the subject, and for all the his-
torical facts I have relied solely upon him.

Yours very sincerely,

G. A. HENTY.

CONTENTS.

ILLUSTRATIONS.

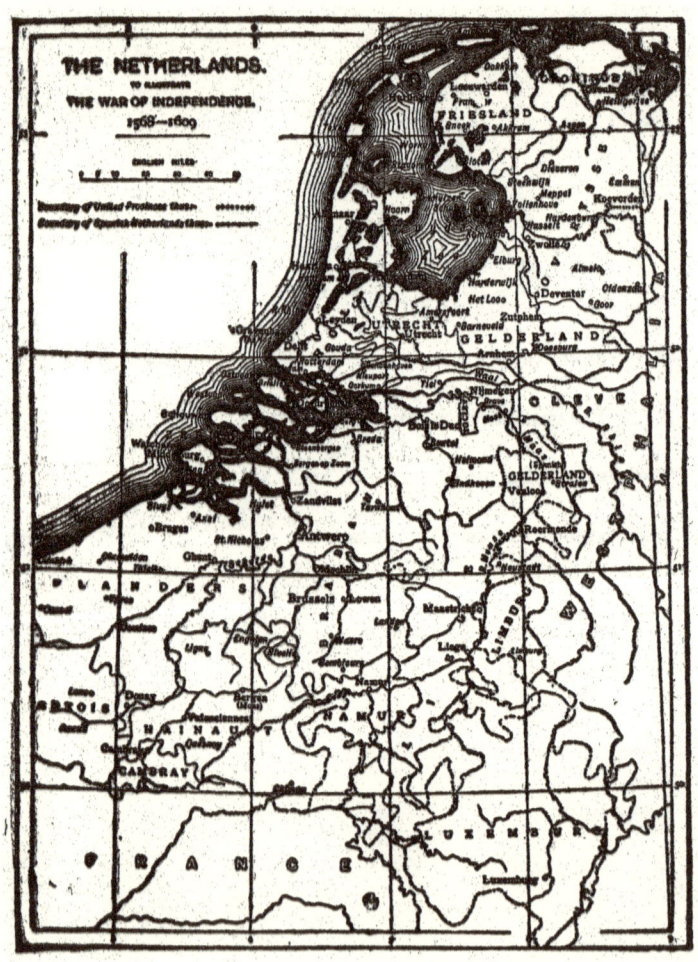

THE NETHERLANDS.
TO ILLUSTRATE
THE WAR OF INDEPENDENCE.
1568—1609

BY PIKE AND DYKE:

CHAPTER I.

THE "GOOD VENTURE."

ROTHERHITHE in the year of 1572 differed very widely from the Rotherhithe of to-day. It was then a scattered village, inhabited chiefly by a seafaring population. It was here that the captains of many of the ships that sailed from the port of London had their abode. Snug cottages with trim gardens lay thickly along the banks of the river, where their owners could sit and watch the vessels passing up and down or moored in the stream, and discourse with each other over the hedges as to the way in which they were handled, the smartness of their equipage, whence they had come, or where they were going. For the trade of London was comparatively small in those days, and the skippers as they chatted together could form a shrewd guess from the size and appearance of each ship as to the country with which she traded, or whether she was a coaster working the eastern or southern ports.

Most of the vessels, indeed, would be recognized and the captains known, and hats would be waved and welcomes or adieus shouted as the vessels passed. There was something that savoured of Holland in the appearance of Rotherhithe; for it was with he Low Countries that the chief trade of

England was carried on ; and the marines who spent their
lives in journeying to and fro between London and the
ports of Zeeland, Friesland, and Flanders, who for the
most part picked up the language of the country, and sometimes even brought home wives from across the sea, naturally learned something from their neighbours. Nowhere,
perhaps, in and about London were the houses so clean
and bright, and the gardens so trimly and neatly kept, as
in the village of Rotherhithe, and in all Rotherhithe not
one was brighter and more comfortable than the abode of
Captain William Martin.

It was low and solid in appearance ; the wooden framework was unusually massive, and there was much quaint
carving on the beams. The furniture was heavy and solid,
and polished with bees'-wax until it shone. The fireplaces
were lined with Dutch tiles ; the flooring was of oak, polished as brightly as the furniture. The appointments from
roof to floor were Dutch ; and no wonder that this was so,
for every inch of wood in its framework and beams, floor
and furniture, had been brought across from Friesland by
William Martin in his ship, the *Good Venture*. It had
been the dowry he received with his pretty, young wife,
Sophie Plomaert.

Sophie was the daughter of a well-to-do worker in wood
near Amsterdam. She was his only daughter, and although he had nothing to say against the English sailor
who had won her heart, and who was chief owner of the
ship he commanded, he grieved much that she should leave
her native land ; and he and her three brothers determined
that she should always bear her former home in her recollection. They therefore prepared as her wedding-gift
a facsimile of the home in which she had been born and
bred. The furniture and framework were similar in every

particular, and it needed only the insertion of the brick-work and plaster when it arrived. Two of her brothers made the voyage in the *Good Venture,* and themselves put the framework, beams and flooring together and saw to the completion of the house on the strip of ground that Wil-liam Martin had purchased on the bank of the river.

Even a large summer-house that stood at the end of the garden was a reproduction of that upon the bank of the canal at home; and when all was completed and William Martin brought over his bride she could almost fancy that she was still at home near Amsterdam. Ever since, she had once a year sailed over in her husband's ship, and spent a few weeks with her kinsfolk. When at home from sea the great sum-mer-house was a general rendezvous of William Martin's friends in Rotherhithe, all skippers like himself, some still on active service, others, who had retired on their savings; not all, however, were fortunate enough to have houses on the river bank; and the summer-house was therefore useful not only as place of meeting but as a look-out at passing ships.

It was a solidly built structure, inclosed on the land side but open towards the river, where, however, there were fold-ing shutters, so that in cold weather it could be partially closed up, though still affording a sight of the stream. A great Dutch stove stood in one corner, and in this in winter a roaring fire was kept up. There were few men in Rother-hithe so well endowed with this world's goods as Captain Martin. His father had been a trader in the city, but Wil-liam's tastes lay towards the sea rather than the shop, and as he was the youngest of three brothers he had his way in the matter. When he reached the age of twenty-three his father died, and with his portion of the savings William purchased the principal share of the *Good Venture,* which ship he had a few months before come to command.

When he married he had received not only his house but a round sum of money as Sophie's portion. With this he could had he liked have purchased the other shares of the *Good Venture;* but being, a thorough sailor, a prudent man, he did not like to put all his eggs into one basket, and accordingly bought with it a share in another ship.   Three children had been born to William and Sophie Martin—a boy and two girls.   Edward, who was the eldest, was at the time this story begins nearly sixteen.   He was an active well-built young fellow, and had for five years sailed with his father in the *Good Venture*.   That vessel was now lying in the stream a quarter of a mile higher up, having returned from a trip to Holland upon the previous day.

The first evening there had been no callers, for it was an understood thing at Rotherhithe that a captain on his return wanted the first evening at home alone with his wife and family; but on the evening of the second day, when William Martin had finished his work of seeing to the unloading of his ship, the visitors began to drop in fast, and the summer-house was well-nigh as full as it could hold.   Mistress Martin, who was now a comely matron of six-and-thirty, busied herself in seeing that the maid and her daughters, Constance and Janet, supplied the visitors with horns of home-brewed beer, or other strong waters brought from Holland for those who preferred them.

"You have been longer away than usual, Captain Martin," one of the visitors remarked.

"Yes," the skipper replied.   "Trade is but dull, and though the *Good Venture* bears a good repute for speed and safety, and is seldom kept lying at the wharves for a cargo, we were a week before she was chartered.   I know not what will be the end of it all.   I verily believe that no people have ever been so cruelly treated for their

conscience' sake since the world began; for you know
it is not against the King of Spain but against the
Inquisition that the opposition has been made. The
people of the Low Countries know well enough it would
be madness to contend against the power of the greatest country in Europe, and to this day they have borne, and are bearing, the cruelty to which they are exposed in quiet despair,
and without a thought of resistance to save their lives.
There may have been tumults in some of the towns, as in
Antwerp, where the lowest part of the mob went into the ca-
thedrals and churches and destroyed the shrines and images; but as to armed resistance to the Spaniards, there
has been none.

"The first expeditions that the Prince of Orange made
into the country were composed of German mercenaries,
with a small body of exiles. They were scarce joined by any
of the country-folk. Though, as you know, they gained one
little victory, they were nigh all killed and cut to pieces. So
horrible was the slaughter perpetrated by the soldiers of the
tyrannical Spanish governor Alva, that when the Prince of
Orange again marched into the country not a man joined
him, and he had to fall back without accomplishing anything. The people seemed stunned by despair. Has not the
Inquisition condemned the whole of the inhabitants of the
Netherlands—save only a few persons specially named—to
death as heretics? and has not Philip confirmed the decree,
and ordered it to be carried into instant execution without
regard to age or sex? Were three millions of men, women,
and children ever before sentenced to death by one stroke
of the pen, only because they refused to change their religion? Every day there are hundreds put to death by the
orders of Alva's Blood Council, as it is called, without even
the mockery of a trial."

There was a general murmur of rage and horror from the assembled party.

"Were I her queen's majesty," an old captain said, striking his fist on the table, "I would declare war with Philip of Spain to-morrow, and would send every man who could bear arms to the Netherlands to aid the people to free themselves from their tyrants.

"Ay, and there is not a Protestant in the land but would go willingly. To think of such cruelty makes the blood run through my veins as if I were a lad again. Why, in Mary's time there were two or three score burnt for their religion here in England, and we thought that a terrible thing. But three millions of people! Why, it is as many as we have got in all these islands! What think you of this, mates?"

"It is past understanding," another old sailor said. "It is too awful for us to take in."

"It is said," another put in, "that the King of France has leagued himself with Philip of Spain, and that the two have bound themselves to exterminate the Protestants in all their dominions, and as that includes Spain, France, Italy, the Low Countries, and most of Germany, it stands to reason as we who are Protestants ought to help our friends; for you may be sure, neighbours, that if Philip succeeds in the Low Countries he will never rest until he has tried to bring England under his rule also, and to plant the Inquisition with its bonfires and its racks and tortures here."

An angry murmur of assent ran round the circle.

"We would fight them, you may be sure," Captain Martin said, "to the last; but Spain is a mighty power, and all know that there are no soldiers in Europe can stand against their pikemen. If the Low Countries, which number as many souls as we, cannot make a stand against them with all their advantages of rivers, and swamps, and dykes, and fortified towns, what chance should we have who have none of these things? What I say, comrades, is this: we have got to fight Spain—you know the grudge Philip bears us—and it is far better that we should go over and fight the Spaniards in the Low Countries, side by side with the people there, and with all the advantages that their rivers and dykes give, and with the comfort that our wives and children are safe here at home, than wait till Spain has crushed down the Netherlands and exterminated the people, and is then able, with France as her ally, to turn her whole strength against us. That's what I say."

"And you say right, Captain Martin. If I were the queen's majesty I would send word to Philip to-morrow to call off his black crew of monks and inquisitors. The people of the Netherlands have no thought of resisting the rule of Spain, and would be, as they have been before, Philip's obedient subjects, if he would but leave their religion alone. It's the doings of the Inquisition that have driven them to despair. And when one hears what you are telling us, that the king has ordered the whole population to be exterminated—man, woman, and child—no wonder they are preparing to fight to the last; for it's better to die fighting a thousand times, than it is to be roasted alive with your wife and children!"

"I suppose the queen and her councillors see that if she were to meddle in this business it might cost her her kingdom, and us our liberty," another captain said. The Spaniards could put, they say, seventy or eighty thousand trained soldiers in the field, while, except the queen's own body-guard, there is not a soldier in England; while their navy is big enough to take the fifteen or twenty ships the queen has, and to break them up to burn their galley-fires "

" That is all true enough," Captain Martin agreed; "but our English men have fought well on the plains of France before now, and I don't believe we should fight worse to-day. We beat the French when they were ten to one against us over and over, and what our fathers did we can do. What you say about the navy is true also. They have a big fleet, and we have no vessels worth speaking about, but we are as good sailors as the Spaniards any day, and as good fighters; and though I am not saying we could stop their fleet if it came sailing up the Thames, I believe when they landed we should show them that we were as good men as they. They might bring seventy thousand soldiers, but there would be seven hundred thousand Englishmen to meet; and if we had but sticks and stones to fight with, they would not find that they would have an easy victory."

"Yes, that's what you think and I think, neighbour; but, you see, we have not got the responsibility of it. The queen has to think for us all. Though I for one would be right glad if she gave the word for war, she may well hesitate before she takes a step that might bring ruin, and worse than ruin, upon all her subjects. We must own, too, that much as we feel for the people of the Low Countries in their distress, they have not always acted wisely. That they should take up arms against these cruel tyrants, even if they had no chance of beating them, is what we all agree would be right and natural; but when the mob of Antwerp broke into the cathedral, and destroyed the altars and carvings, and tore up the vestments, and threw down the Maries and the saints, and then did the same in the other churches in the town and in the country round, they behaved worse than children, and showed themselves as intolerant and bigoted as the Spaniards themselves.

They angered Philip beyond hope of forgiveness, and gave him something like an excuse for his cruelties toward them."

"Ay, ay, that was a bad business," Captain Martin agreed; "a very bad business, comrade. And although these things were done by a mere handful of the scum of the town the respectable citizens raised no hand to stop it, although they can turn out the town guard readily enough to put a stop to a quarrel between the members of two of the guilds. There were plenty of men who have banded themselves together under the name of 'the beggars,' and sworn to fight for their religion, to have put these fellows down if they had chosen. They did not choose, and now Philip's vengeance will fall on them all alike."

"Well, what think you of this business, Ned?" one of the captains said, turning to the lad who was standing in a corner, remaining, as in duty bound, silent in the presence of his elders until addressed.

"Were I a Dutchman, and living under such a tyranny," Ned said passionately, "I would rise and fight to the death rather than see my family martyred. If none other would rise with me, I would take a sword and go out and slay the first Spaniard I met, and again another, until I was killed."

"Bravo, Ned! Well spoken, lad!" three or four of the captains said; but his father shook his head.

"Those are the words of hot youth, Ned; and were you living there you would do as others—keep quiet till the executioners came to drag you away, seeing that did you, as you say you would, use a knife against a Spaniard, it would give the butchers a pretext for the slaughtering of hundreds of innocent people."

The lad looked down abashed at the reproof, then he said:

"Well, father, if I could not rise in arms or slay a Spaniard and then be killed, I would leave my home and join the sea beggars under La Marck."

"There is more reason in that," his father replied; "though La Marck is a ferocious noble, and his followers make not very close inquiry whether the ships they attack are Spanish or those of other people. Still it is hard for a man to starve; and when time passes and they can light upon no Spanish merchantmen, one cannot blame them too sorely if they take what they require out of some other passing ship. But there is reason at the bottom of what you say. Did the men of the sea-coast, seeing that their lives and those of their families are now at the mercy of the Spaniards, take to their ships with those dear to them and continually harass the Spaniards, they could work them great harm, and it would need a large fleet to overpower them, and that with great difficulty, seeing that they know the coast and all the rivers and channels, and could take refuge in shallows where the Spaniards could not follow them. At present it seems to me the people are in such depths of despair, that they have not heart for any such enterprise. But I believe that some day or other the impulse will be given—some more wholesale butchery than usual will goad them to madness, or the words of some patriot wake them into action, and then they will rise as one man and fight until utterly destroyed, for that they can in the end triumph over Spain is more than any human being can hope."

"Then they must be speedy about it, friend Martin," another said. "They say that eighty thousand have been put to death one way or another since Alva came into his government. Another ten years and there will be scarce an able-bodied man remaining in the Low Country. By the way, you were talking of the beggars of the sea. Their fleet is lying at present at Dover, and it is said that the Spanish ambassador is making grave complaints to the queen on the part of his master against giving shelter to these men, whom he brands as not only enemies of Spain, but as pirates and robbers of the sea."

"I was talking with Master Sheepshanks," another mariner put in, "whose ships I sailed for thirty years, and who is an alderman and knows what is going on, and he told me that from what he hears it is like enough that the queen will yield to the Spanish request. So long as she chooses to remain friends with Spain openly, whatever her thoughts and opinions may be, she can scarcely allow her ports to be used by the enemies of Philip. It must go sorely against her high spirit; but till she and her council resolve that England shall brave the whole strength of Spain, she cannot disregard the remonstrances of Philip. It is a bad business, neighbours, a bad business; and the sooner it comes to an end the better. No one doubts that we shall have to fight Spain one of these days, and I say that it were better to fight while our brethren of the Low Countries can fight by our side, than to wait till Spain, having exterminated them, can turn the whole power against us."

There was a general chorus of assent, and then the subject changed to the rate of freight to the northern ports. The grievous need for the better marking of shallows and dangers, the rights, of seamen, wages, and other matters, were discussed until the assembly broke up. Ned's sisters joined him in the garden.

"I hear Constance," the boy said to the elder, "there has been no news from our grandfather and uncles since we have been away."

"No word whatever, Ned. Our mother does not say much, but I know she is greatly troubled and anxious about it."

"That she may well be, Constance, seeing that neither quiet conduct nor feebleness nor aught else avail to protect any from the rage of the Spaniards. You who stay at home here only hear general tales of the cruelties done across the sea, but if you heard the tales that we do at their ports they would drive you almost to madness. Not that we hear much, for we have to keep on board our ships, and may not land or mingle with the people; but we learn enough from the merchants who come on board to see about the landing of their goods to make our blood boil. They do right to prevent our landing; for so fired is the sailors' blood by these tales of massacre, that were they to go ashore they would, I am sure, be speedily embroiled with the Spaniards.

"You see how angered these friends of our father are who are Englishmen, and have no Dutch blood in their veins, and who feel only because they are touched by these cruelties, and because the people of the Low Country are Protestants; but with us it is different, our mother is one of these persecuted people, and we belong to them as much as to England. We have friends and relations they who may for aught we know have already fallen victims to the cruelty of the Spaniards. Had I my will I would join the beggars of the sea, or I would ship with Drake or Cavendish and fight the Spaniards in the Indian seas. They say that there Englishmen are proving themselves better men than these haughty dons."

"It is very sad," Constance said; "but what can be done?"

"Something must be done soon," Ned replied gloomily. "Things cannot go on as they are. So terrible is the state of things, so heavy the taxation, that in many towns all trade is suspended. In Brussels, I hear, Alva's own capital, the brewers have refused to brew, the bakers to bake, the tapsters to draw liquors. The city swarms with multitudes of men thrown out of employment. The Spanish soldiers themselves have long been without pay, for Alva thinks of nothing but bloodshed. Consequently they are insolent to their officers, care little for order, and insult and rob the citizens in the streets. Assuredly something must come of this ere long; and the people's despair will become a mad fury. If they rise, Constance, and my father does not say nay, I will assuredly join them and do my best.

"I do not believe that the queen will forbid her subjects to give their aid to the people of the Netherlands; for she allowed many to fight in France for Condé and the Protestants against the Guises, and she will surely do the same now, since the sufferings of our brothers in the Netherlands have touched the nation far more keenly than did those of the Huguenots in France. I am sixteen now, and my father says that in another year he will rate me as his second mate, and methinks that there are not many men on board who can pull more strongly a rope, or work more stoutly at the capstan when we heave our anchor. Besides, as we all talk Dutch as well as English, I should be of more use than men who know nought of the language of the country."

Constance shook her head. "I do not think, Ned, that our father would give you leave, at any rate not until you have grown up into a man. He looks to having you with him, and to your succeeding him some day in the command of the *Good Venture* while he remains quietly at home with our mother."

Ned agreed with a sigh. "I fear that you are right, Constance, and that I shall have to stick to my trade of sailoring; but if the people of the Netherlands rise against their tyrants, it would be hard to be sailing backwards and forwards doing a peaceful trade between London and Holland whilst our friends and relatives are battling for their lives."

A fortnight later, the *Good Venture* filled up her hold with a cargo for Brill, a port where the united Rhine, Waal, and Maas flow into the sea.   On the day before she sailed a proclamation was issued by the queen forbidding any of · her subjects to supply De la Marck and his sailors with meat, bread or beer. The passage down the river was slow, for the winds were contrary, and it was ten days afterwards, the 31st of March, when they entered the broad mouth of the river and dropped anchor off the town of Brill. It was late in the evening when they arrived. In the morning an officer came off to demand the usual papers and documents, and it was not until nearly two o'clock that a boat came out with the necessary permission for the ship to warp up to the wharves and discharge her cargo.

Just as Captain Martin was giving the order for the capstan bars to be manned, a fleet of some twenty-four ships suddenly appeared round the seaward point of the land.

"Wait a moment, lads," the captain said, "half an hour will make no great difference in our landing.   We may as well wait and see what is the meaning of this fleet. They do not look to me to be Spaniards, nor seem to be a mere trading fleet. I should not wonder if they are the beggars of the sea, who have been forced to leave Dover, starved out from the effect of the queen's proclamation, and have now come here to pick up any Spaniard they may meet sailing out."

The fleet dropped anchor at about half a mile from the town. Just as they did so, a ferryman named Koppelstok, who was carrying passengers across from the town of Maaslandluis, a town on the opposite bank a mile and a half away, was passing close by the *Good Venture*.

"What think you of yon ships?" the ferryman shouted to Captain Martin.

"I believe they must be the beggars of the sea," the captain replied. "An order had been issued before I left London that they were not to be supplied with provisions, and they would therefore have had to put out from Dover. This may well enough be them."

An exclamation of alarm broke from the passengers, for the sea beggars were almost as much feared by their own countrymen as by the Spaniards, the latter having spared no pains in spreading tales to their disadvantage. As soon as the ferryman had landed his passengers he rowed boldly out towards the fleet, having nothing of which he could be plundered, and being secretly well disposed towards the beggars. The first ship he hailed was that commanded by William de Blois, Lord of Treslong, who was well known at Brill, where his father had at one time been governor.

His brother had been executed by the Duke of Alva four years before, and he had himself fought by the side of Count Louis of Nassau, brother to the Prince of Orange, in the campaign that had terminated so disastrously, and though covered with wounds had been one of the few who had escaped from the terrible carnage that followed the defeat at Jemmingen. After that disaster he had taken to the sea, and was one of the most famous of the captains of De la Marck, who had received a commission of admiral from the Prince of Orange.

"We are starving, Koppelstok; can you inform us how we can get some food? We have picked up two Spanish traders on our way here from Dover, but our larders were emptied before we sailed, and we found but scant supply on board our prizes."

"There is plenty in the town of Brill," the ferryman

said; "but none that I know of elsewhere. That English brig lying there at anchor may have a few loaves on board.

"That will not be much," William de Blois replied, "among five hundred men, still it will be better than nothing. Will you row and ask them if they will sell to us?"

"You had best send a strongly armed crew," Koppelstok replied. "You know the English are well disposed towards us, and the captain would doubtless give you all the provisions he had to spare; but to do so would be to ruin him with the Spaniards, who might confiscate his ship. It were best that you should make a show of force, so that he could plead that he did but yield to necessity."

Accordingly a boat with ten men rowed to the brig, Koppelstok accompanying it. The latter climbed on to the deck.

"We mean you no harm, captain," he said; "but the men on board these ships are well nigh starving. The Sieur de Treslong has given me a purse to pay for all that you can sell us, but thinking that you might be blamed for having dealings with him by the authorities of the town, he sent these armed men with me in order that if questioned you could reply that they came forcibly on board."

"I will willingly let you have all the provisions I have on board," Captain Martin said; "though these will go but a little way among so many, seeing that I only carry stores sufficient for consumption on board during my voyages."

A cask of salt beef was hoisted up on deck, with a sack of biscuits, four cheeses, and a side of bacon. Captain Martin refused any payment.

"No," he said, "my wife comes from these parts, and my heart is with the patriots. Will you tell Sieur de Treslong that Captain Martin of the *Good Venture* is happy to do the best in his power for him and his brave followers.

That Ned," he observed, turning to his son as the boat rowed away, "is a stroke of good policy. The value of the goods is small, but just at this moment they are worth much to those to whom I have given them. In the first place, you see, we have given aid to the good cause, in the second we have earned the gratitude of the beggars of the sea, and I shall be much more comfortable if I run among them in the future than I should have done in the past. The freedom to come and go without molestation by the sea beggars is cheaply purchased at the price of provisions which do not cost many crowns."

On regaining the Sieur de Treslong's ship some of the provisions were at once served out among the men, and the rest sent off among other ships, and William de Blois took Koppelstok with him on board the admiral's vessel.

" Well, de Blois, what do you counsel in this extremity?" De la Marck asked.

"I advise," the Lord of Treslong replied, "that we at once send a message to the town demanding its surrender."

" Are you joking or mad, Treslong ?" the admiral asked in surprise. "Why we can scarce muster four hundred men, and the town is well walled and fortified."

"There are no Spanish troops here, admiral, and if we put a bold front on the matter we may frighten the burghers into submission. This man says he would be willing to carry the summons. He says the news as to who we are has already reached them by some passengers he landed before he came out, and he doubts not they are in a rare panic."

" Well, we can try," the admiral said laughing ; "it is clear we must eat, even if we have to fight for it ; and hungry as we all are, we do not want to wait."

Treslong gave his ring to Koppelstok to show as his authority, and the fisherman at once rowed ashore. Stating that the beggars of the sea were determined to take the town, he made his way through the crowd of inhabitants who had assembled at the landing-place, and then pushed on to the town-hall, where the magistrates were assembled. He informed them that he had been sent by the Admiral of the Fleet and the Lord of Treslong, who was well known to them, to demand that two commissioners should be sent out to them on behalf of the city to confer with him. The only object of those who sent him was to free the land from the crushing taxes, and to overthrow the tyranny of Alva and the Spaniards. He was asked by the magistrates what force De la Marck had at his disposal, and replied carelessly that he could not say exactly, but that there might be five thousand in all.

This statement completed the dismay that had been caused at the arrival of the fleet. The magistrates agreed that it would be madness to resist, and determined to fly at once. With much difficulty two of them were persuaded to go out to the ship as deputies, and as soon as they set off most of the leading burghers prepared instantly for flight. The deputies on arriving on board were assured that no injury was intended to the citizens or private property, but only the overthrow of Alva's government, and two hours were given them to decide upon the surrender of the town.

During this two hours almost all the inhabitants left the town, taking with them their most valuable property. At the expiration of the time the beggars landed. A few of those remaining in the city made a faint attempt at resistance; but Treslong forced an entrance by the southern gate, and De la Marck made a bonfire against the northern gate and then battered it down with the end of an old mast. Thus the patriots achieved the capture of the first town, and commenced the long war that was to end only with the establishment of the Free Republic of the Netherlands. No harm was done to such of the inhabitants of the town as remained. The conquerors established themselves in the best of the deserted houses; they then set to work to plunder the churches. The alters and images were all destroyed; the rich furniture, the sacred vessels, and the gorgeous vestments were appropriated to private use. Thirteen unfortunates, among them some priests who had been unable to effect their escape, were seized and put to death by De la Marck.

He had received the strictest orders from the Prince of Orange to respect the ships of all neutral nations, and to behave courteously and kindly to all captives he might take. Neither of these injunctions were obeyed. De la Marck was a wild and sanguinary noble; he had taken a vow upon hearing of the death of his relative, the Prince of Egmont, who had been executed by Alva, that he would neither cut his hair nor his beard until that murder should be revenged, and had sworn to wreak upon Alva and upon Popery the deep vengeance that the nobles and peoples of the Netherlands owed them. This vow he kept to the letter, and his ferocious conduct to all priests and Spaniards who fell into his hands deeply sullied the cause for which he fought.

Upon the day after the capture of the city, the *Good Venture* went into the port. The inhabitants, as soon as they learned that the beggars of the sea respected the life and property of the citizens, returned in large numbers, and trade was soon reestablished. Having taken the place, and secured the plunder of the churches and monasteries, De la Marck would have sailed away upon other excursions had not the Sieur de Treslong pointed out to him the importance of Brill to the cause, and persuaded him to hold the place until he heard from the Prince of Orange.

CHAPTER II.

A FEW days after Brill had been so boldly captured, Count Bossu advanced from Utrecht against it. The sea beggars, confident as they were as to their power of meeting the Spaniards on the seas, knew that on dry land they were no match for the well-trained pikemen; they therefore kept within the walls. A carpenter, however, belonging to the town, who had long been a secret partisan of the Prince of Orange, seized an axe, dashed into the water, and swam to the sluice and burst open the gates with a few sturdy blows. The sea poured in and speedily covered the land on the north side of the city.

The Spaniards advanced along the dyke to the southern gate, but the sea beggars had hastily moved most of the cannon on the wall to that point, and received the Spaniards with so hot a fire that they hesitated. In the meantime the Lord of Treslong and another officer had filled two boats with men and rowed out to the ships that had brought the enemy, cut some adrift, and set others on fire. The Spaniards at the southern gate lost heart; they were exposed to a hot fire, which they were unable to return. On one side they saw the water rapidly rising above the level of the dyke on which they stood, on the other they perceived their only means of retreat threatened. They turned, and in desperate haste retreated along the causeway now under water. In their haste many slipped off the road and were drowned, others fell and were smothered in the water, and the rest succeeded in reaching such of the vessels as were still untouched, and with all speed returned to Utrecht.

From the highest point of the masts to which they could climb, Captain Martin, Ned, and the crew watched the struggle. Ned had begged his father to let him go along the walls to the south gate to see the conflict, but Captain Martin refused.

"We know not what the upshot of the business may be," he said. "If the Spaniards, which is likely enough, take the place, they will slaughter all they meet, and will not trouble themselves with questioning anyone whether he is a combatant or a spectator. Besides, when they have once taken the town, they will question all here, and it would be well that I should be able to say that not only did we hold ourselves neutral in the affair, but that none of my equipage had set foot on shore to-day. Lastly, it is my purpose and hope if the Spaniards capture the place, to take advantage of the fact that all will be absorbed in the work of plunder, and to slip my hawsers and make off. Wind and tide are both favourable, and doubtless the crews of their ships will, for the most part, land to take part in the sack as soon as the town is taken."

However, as it turned out, there was no need of these precautions; the beggars were victorious and the Spaniards in full flight, and great was the rejoicing in Brill at this check which they had inflicted upon their oppressors.

Bossu, retiring from Brill, took his way towards Rotterdam. He found its gates closed; the authorities refused to submit to his demands or to admit a garrison. They declared they were perfectly loyal, and needed no body of

Spanish troops to keep them in order. Bossu requested permission for his troops to pass through the city without halting. This was granted by the magistrates on condition that only a corporal's company should be admitted at a time. Bossu signed an agreement to this effect. But throughout the whole trouble the Spaniards never once respected the conditions they had made and sworn to with the inhabitants, and no sooner were the gates opened than the whole force rushed in, and the usual work of slaughter, atrocity, and plunder commenced. Within a few minutes four hundred citizens were murdered, and countless outrages and cruelties perpetrated upon the inhabitants.

Captain Martin completed the discharging of his cargo two days after Bossu made his ineffectual attempt upon the town. A messenger had arrived that morning from Flushing, with news that as soon as the capture of Brill had become known in that seaport, the Seigneur de Herpt had excited the burghers to drive the small Spanish garrison from the town.

Scarcely had they done so when a large reinforcement of the enemy arrived before the walls, having been despatched there by Alva, to complete the fortress that had been commenced to secure the possession of this important port at the mouth of the Western Scheldt. Herpt persuaded the burghers that it was too late to draw back now. They had done enough to draw the vengeance of the Spaniards upon them; their only hope now was to resist to the last. A half-witted man in the crowd offered, if anyone would give him a pot of beer, to ascend the ramparts and fire two pieces of artillery at the Spanish ships.

The offer was accepted, and the man ran up to the ramparts and discharged the guns. A sudden panic seized the Spaniards, and the whole fleet sailed away at once in the direction of Middelburg.

The governor of the island next day arrived at Flushing and was at once admitted. He called the citizens together to the market-place and there addressed them, beseeching them to return to their allegiance, assuring them that if they did so the king, who was the best natured prince in all Christendom, would forget and forgive their offences. The effect of the governor's oratory was sadly marred by the interruptions of De Herpt and his adherents, who reminded the people of the fate that had befallen other towns that had revolted, and scoffed at such good nature as the king displayed in the scores of executions daily taking place throughout the country.

The governor, finding his efforts unavailing, had left the town, and as soon as he did so the messenger was sent off to Brill, saying that the inhabitants of Flushing were willing to provide arms and ammunition if they would send them men experienced in partisan warfare. Two hundred of the beggars, under the command of Treslong, accordingly started the next day for Flushing. The *Good Venture* threw off her hawsers from the wharf at about the same time that these were starting, and for some time kept company with them.

"Did one ever see such a wild crew?" Captain Martin said, shaking his head. "Never, I believe, did such a party set out upon a warlike adventure."

The appearance of Treslong's followers was indeed extraordinary. Every man was attired in the gorgeous vestments of the plundered churches—in gold and embroidered cassocks, glittering robes, or the sombre cowls and garments of Capuchin friars. As they sailed along their wild sea-songs rose in the air, mingled with shouts for vengeance on the Spaniards and the Papacy.

"One would not think that this ribald crew could fight,"

Captain Martin went on ; "but there is no doubt they will
do so. They must not be blamed altogether ; they are half
maddened by the miseries and cruelties endured by their
friends and relations at the hands of the Spaniards. I knew
that when at last the people rose the combat would be a
terrible one, and that they would answer cruelty by cruelty,
blood by blood. The Prince of Orange, as all men know,
is one of the most clement and gentle of rulers. All his
ordinances enjoin gentle treatment of prisoners, and he has
promised every one over and over again complete toleration in the exercise of religion ; but though he may forgive
and forget, the people will not.

"It is the Catholic church that has been their oppressor.
In its name tens of thousands have been murdered, and I
fear that the slaughter of those priests at Brill is but the
first of a series of bloody reprisals that will take place
wnerever the people get the upper hand."

A fresh instance of this was shown a few hours after the
Good Venture put into Flushing. A ship arrived in port,
bringing with it Pacheco, the Duke of Alva's chief engi-
neer, an architect of the highest reputation. He had been
despatched by the duke to take charge of the new works
that the soldiers had been sent to execute, and ignorant of
what had taken place he landed at the port. He was at
once seized by the mob. An officer, willing to save his
life, took him from their hands and conducted him to the
prison ; but the populace were clamorous for his blood, and
Treslong was willing enough to satisfy them and to avenge
upon Alva's favourite officer the murder of his brother by
Alva's orders. The unfortunate officer was therefore condemned to be hung, and the sentence was carried into
effect the same day.

A few days later an officer named Zeraerts arrived at

Flushing with a commission from the Prince of Orange as Governor of the Island of Walcheren. He was attended by a small body of French infantry, and the force under his command speedily increased ; for as soon as it was known in England that Brill and Flushing had thrown off the authority of the Spaniards, volunteers from England began to arrive in considerable numbers to aid their fellow-Protestants in the struggle before them.

The *Good Venture* had stayed only a few hours in Flushing. In the present condition of affairs there was no chance of obtaining a cargo there, and Captain Martin therefore thought it better not to waste time, but to proceed at once to England in order to learn the intentions of the merchants for whom he generally worked as to what could be done under the changed state of circumstances that had arisen.

Every day brought news of the extension of the rising. The Spanish troops lay for the most part in Flanders, and effectually deterred the citizens of the Flemish towns from revolting ; but throughout Holland, Zeeland, and Friesland the flame of revolt spread rapidly. The news that Brill and Flushing had thrown off the Spanish yoke fired every heart. It was the signal for which all had been so long waiting. They knew how desperately Spain would strive to regain her grip upon the Netherlands, how terrible would be her vengeance if she conquered ; but all felt that it was better to die sword in hand than to be murdered piecemeal. And accordingly town after town rose, expelled the authorities appointed by Spain and the small Spanish garrisons, and in three months after the rising of Brill the greater part of the maritime provinces were free. Some towns, however, still remained faithful to Spain. Prominent among these was Amsterdam, a great trading city, which feared the ruin that opposition to Alva might bring upon it, more than the shame of standing aloof when their fellow-countrymen were fighting for freedom and the right to worship God in their own way.

On the 23rd of May, Louis of Nassau, with a body of troops from France, captured the important town of Mons by surprise, but was at once beleaguered there by a Spanish army. In June the States of Holland assembled at Dort and formally renounced the authority of the Duke of Alva, and declared the Prince of Orange, the royally-appointed stadtholder, the only legal representative of the Spanish crown in their country; and in reply to an eloquent address of Sainte Aldegonde, the prince's representative, voted a considerable sum of money for the payment of the army the prince was raising in Germany. On the 19th of June a serious misfortune befell the patriot cause. A reinforcement of Huguenot troops, on the way to succour the garrison of Mons, were met and cut to pieces by the Spaniards, and Count Louis, who had been led by the French King to expect ample succour and assistance from him, was left to his fate.

On the 7th July the Prince of Orange crossed the Rhine with 14,000 foot and 7000 horse. He advanced but a short distance when the troops mutinied in consequence of their pay being in arrears, and he was detained four weeks until the cities of Holland guaranteed their payment for three months. A few cities opened their gates to him, but they were for the most part unimportant places, and Mechlin was the only large town that admitted his troops. Still he pressed on towards Mons, expecting daily to be joined by 12,000 French infantry and 3000 cavalry under the command of Admiral Coligny.

The prince, who seldom permitted himself to be sanguine, believed that the goal of his hopes was reached, and that he should now be able to drive the Spaniards from the Netherlands. But as he was marching forward he received tidings that showed him that all his plans were shattered, and that the prospects were darker than they had ever before been. While the King of France had throughout been encouraging the revolted Netherlands, and had authorized his minister to march with an army to their assistance, he was preparing for a deed that would be the blackest in history, were it not that its horrors are less appalling than those inflicted upon the captured cities of the Netherlands by Alva. On St. Bartholomew's Eve there was a general massacre of the Protestants in Paris, followed by similar massacres throughout France, the number of victims being variously estimated at from twenty-five to a hundred thousand.

Protestant Europe was filled with horror at this terrible crime. Philip of Spain was filled with equal delight. Not only was the danger that seemed to threaten him in the Netherlands at once and for ever, as he believed, at an end, but he saw in this destruction of the Protestants of France a great step in the direction he had so much at heart—the entire extirpation of heretics throughout Europe. He wrote letters of the warmest congratulation to the King of France, with whom he had formerly been at enmity ; while the Pope, accompanied by his cardinals, went to the church of St. Mark to render thanks to God for the grace thus singularly vouchsafed to the Holy See and to all Christendom.

To the Prince af Orange the news came as a thunder-clap. His troops wholly lost heart, and refused to keep the field. The prince himself almost lost his life at the hands of the mutineers, and at last, crossing the Rhine, he disbanded his army and went almost alone to Holland to share the fate of the provinces that adhered to him. He went there expecting and prepared to die. "There I will make my sepulchre," was his expression in the letter in which he announced his intention to his brother. Count Louis of Nassau had now nothing left before him but to surrender. His soldiers, almost entirely French, refused any longer to resist, now that the king had changed his intentions, and the city was surrendered, the garrison being allowed to retire with their weapons.

The terms of the capitulation were so far respected ; but instead of the terms respecting the towns-people being adhered to, a council of blood was set up, and for many months from ten to twenty of the inhabitants were hanged, burned, or beheaded every day. The news of the massacre of St. Bartholomew, of the treachery of the King of France towards the inhabitants of the Netherlands, and of the horrible cruelties perpetrated upon the inhabitants of Mechlin and other towns that had opened their gates to the Prince of Orange, excited the most intense indignation among the people of England.

The queen put on mourning, but was no more inclined than before to render any really efficient aid to the Netherlands. She allowed volunteers to pass over, furnished some meagre sums of money, but held aloof from any open participation in the war ; for if before, when France was supposed to be favourable to the Netherlands and hostile to Spain, she felt unequal to a war with the latter power, still less could she hope to cope with Spain when the deed of St. Bartholomew had reunited the two Catholic monarchs.

Captain Martin, married to a native of the Netherlands, and mixing constantly with the people in his trade, was naturally ardent, even beyond the majority of his country-men, in their cause, and over and over again declared that were he sailing by when a sea-fight was going on between the Dutch and the Spaniards, he would pull down his English flag, hoist that of Holland, and join in the fray ; and Ned, as was to be expected, shared to the utmost his father's feelings on the subject. Early in September the *Good Venture* started with a cargo for Amsterdam, a city that almost alone in Holland adhered to the Spanish cause.

Sophie Martin was pleased when she heard that this was the ship's destination ; for she was very anxious as to the safety of her father and brothers, from whom she had not heard for a long time. Postage was dear and mails irregular. Few letters were written or received by people in England, still more seldom letters sent across the sea. There would, therefore, under the ordinary circumstances, have been no cause whatever for uneasiness had years elapsed without news coming from Amsterdam; and,indeed, during her whole married life Sophie Martin had only received one or two letters by post from her former home, although many communications had been brought by friends of her husband's trading there. But as many weeks seldom passed without the *Good Venture* herself going into Amsterdam, for that town was one of the great trading centres of Holland, there was small occasion for letters to pass. It happened, however, that from one cause or another, eighteen months had passed since Captain Martin's business had taken him to that port, and no letter had come either by post or hand during that time.

None who had friends in the Netherlands could feel assured that these must, either from their station or qualities, be safe from the storm that was sweeping over the

country. The poor equally with the rich, the artisan
equally with the noble, was liable to become a victim of
Alva's Council of Blood. The net was drawn so as to catch
all classes and conditions ; and although it was upon the
Protestants that his fury chiefly fell, the Catholics suffered
too, for pretexts were always at hand upon which these
could also be condemned.

The Netherlands swarmed with spies and informers, and
a single unguarded expression of opinion was sufficient to
send a man to the block.   And, indeed, in a vast number
of cases, private animosity was the cause of the denunciation ; for any accusation could be safely made where there
was no trial, and the victims were often in complete ignorance as to the nature of the supposed crime for which they
were seized and dragged away to execution.

When the vessel sailed Sophie Martin gave her husband
a letter to her father and brothers, begging them to follow
the example of thousands of their countrymen, and to leave
the land where life and property were no longer safe, and
to come over to London.   They would have no difficulty
in procuring work there, and could establish themselves in
business and do as well as they had been doing at home.

They had, she knew, money laid by in London; for after
the troubles began her father had sold off the houses and
other property he had purchased with his savings, and had
transmitted the result to England by her husband, who
had intrusted it for investment to a leading citizen with
whom he did business.   As this represented not only her
father's accumulations but those of her brothers who
worked as partners with him, it amounted to a sum that
in those days was regarded as considerable.

" I feel anxious, Ned," Captain Martin said as he sailed
up the Zuider-Zee towards the city, " as to what has be-

fallen your grandfather and uncles. I have always made the best of the matter to your mother, but I cannot conceal from myself that harm may have befallen them. It is strange that no message has come to us through any of our friends trading with the town, for your uncles know many of my comrades and can see their names in the shipping lists when they arrive. They would have known how anxious your mother would be at the news of the devil's work that is going on here, and, being always tender and thoughtful for her, would surely have sent her news of them from time to time as they had a chance. I sorely fear that something must have happened. Your uncles are prudent men, going about their work and interfering with none; but they are men, too, who speak their mind, and would not, like many, make a false show of affection when they feel none.

"Well, well; we shall soon know. As soon as the ship is moored and my papers are declared in order, you and I will go over to Vordwyk and see how they are faring. I think not that they will follow your mother's advice and sail over with us; for it was but the last time I saw them that they spoke bitterly against the emigrants, and said that every man who could bear arms should, however great his danger, wait and bide the time until there was a chance to strike for his religion and country. They are sturdy men these Dutchmen, and not readily turned from an opinion they have taken up; and although I shall do my best to back up your mother's letter by my arguments, I have but small hope that I shall prevail with them."

In the evening they were moored alongside the quays of Amsterdam, at that time one of the busiest cities in Europe. Its trade was great, the wealth of its citizens immense. It contained a large number of monasteries, its authorities were all Catholics and devoted to the cause of Spain, and although there were a great many well-wishers to the cause of freedom within its walls, these were powerless to take action, and the movement which, after the capture of Brill and Flushing, had caused almost all the towns of Holland to declare for the Prince of Orange, found no echo in Amsterdam. The vessel anchored outside the port, and the next morning after their papers were examined and found in order she ranged up alongside the crowded tiers of shipping. Captain Martin went on shore with Ned, visited the merchants to whom his cargo was consigned, and told them that he should begin to unload the next day.

He then started with Ned to walk to Vordwyk, which lay two miles away. On reaching the village they stopped suddenly. The roof of the house they had so often visited was gone, its walls blackened by fire. After the first exclamation of surprise and regret they walked forward until opposite the ruin, and stood gazing at it. Then Captain Martin stepped up to a villager who was standing at the door of his shop, and asked him when did this happen, what had become of the old man Plomaert?

"You are his son-in-law, are you not?" the man asked in reply. "I have seen you here at various times." Captain Martin nodded. The man looked round cautiously to see that none were within sound of his voice.

"You have not heard then?" he said. "It was a terrible business, though we are growing used to it now. One day, it is some eight months since, a party of soldiers came from Amsterdam and hauled away my neighbour Plomaert and his three sons. They were denounced as having attended the field preaching a year ago, and you know what that means."

"And the villains murdered them?" Captain Martin asked in horror-stricken tones.

The man nodded. "They were hung together next day, together with Gertrude, the wife of the eldest brother. Johan was, as you know, unmarried. Elizabeth, the wife of Louis, lay ill at the time, or doubtless she would have fared the same as the rest. She has gone with her two daughters to Haarlem, where her family live. All their property was, of course, seized and confiscated, and the house burned down; for, as you know, they all lived together. Now, my friend, I will leave you. I dare not ask you in for I know not who may be watching us, and to entertain even the brother-in-law of men who have been sent to the gallows might well cost a man his life in our days."

Then Captain Martin's grief and passion found vent in words, and he roundly cursed the Spaniards and their works, regardless of who might hear him; then he entered the garden, visited the summer-house where he had so often talked with the old man and his sons, and then sat down and gave full vent to his grief. Ned felt almost stunned by the news; being so often away at sea he had never given the fact that so long a time had elapsed since his mother had received a letter from her family much thought. It had, indeed, been mentioned before him; but, knowing the disturbed state of the country, it had seemed to him natural enough that his uncles should have had much to think of and trouble them, and might well have no time for writing letters. His father's words the evening before had for the first time excited a feeling of real uneasiness about them, and the shock caused by the sight of the ruined house, and the news that his grandfather, his three uncles, and one of his aunts had been murdered by the Spaniards, completely overwhelmed him.

"Let us be going, Ned," his father said at last; "there is nothing for us to do here, let us get back to our ship. I am a peaceable man, Ned, but I feel now as if I could join the beggars of the sea, and go with them in slaying every Spaniard who fell into their hands. This will be terrible news for your mother, lad."

"It will indeed," Ned replied. "Oh, father, I wish you would let me stay here and join the prince's bands and fight for their freedom. There were English volunteers coming out to Brill and Flushing when we sailed from the Thames, and if they come to fight for Holland who have no tie in blood, why should not I who am Dutch by my mother's side and whose relations have been murdered?"

"We will talk of it later on, Ned," his father said. "You are young yet for such rough work as this, and this is no common war. There is no quarter given here, it is a fight to the death. The Spaniards slaughter the Protestants like wild beasts, and like wild beasts they will defend themselves. But if this war goes on till you have gained your full strength and sinew I will not say you nay. As you say, our people at home are ready to embark in a war for the cause of liberty and religion, did the queen but give the word ; and when others, fired solely by horror at the Spaniards' cruelty, are ready to come over here and throw in their lot with them, it seems to me that it will be but right that you, who are half Dutch and have had relatives murdered by these fiends, should come over and side with the oppressed. If there is fighting at sea, it may be that I myself will take part with them, and place the *Good Venture* at the service of the Prince of Orange. But of that we will talk later on, as also about yourself. When you are eighteen you will still be full young for such work."

As they talked they were walking fast towards Amsterdam. "We will go straight on board, Ned; and I will not put my foot ashore again before we sail. I do not think that I could trust myself to meet a Spaniard now, but should draw my knife and rush upon him. I have known that these things happened, we have heard of these daily butcherings, but it has not come home to me as now, when our own friends are the victims."

Entering the gate of the town they made their way straight down to the port, and were soon on board the *Good Venture* where Captain Martin retired to his cabin. Ned felt too restless and excited to go down at present; but he told the crew what had happened, and the exclamations of anger among the honest sailors were loud and deep. Most of them had sailed with Captain Martin ever since he had commanded the *Good Venture,* and had seen the Plomaerts when they had come on board whenever the vessel put in at Amsterdam. The fact that there was nothing to do, and no steps to take to revenge the murders, angered them all the more.

"I would we had twenty ships like our own, Master Ned," one of them said. "That would give us four hundred men, and with those we could go ashore and hang the magistrates and the councillors and all who had a hand in this foul business, and set their public buildings in a flame, and then fight our way back again to the port."

"I am afraid four hundred men would not be able to do it here as they did at Brill. There was no Spanish garrison there, and here they have a regiment; and though the Spaniards seem to have the hearts of devils rather than men, they can fight."

"Well, we would take our chance," the sailor replied. "If there was four hundred of us, and the captain gave the word, we would show them what English sailors could do, mates—wouldn't we?"

"Aye, that would we," the others growled in a chorus.

The next morning the work of unloading began. The sailors worked hard ; for, as one of them said, "This place seems to smell of blood—let's be out of it, mates, as soon as we can." At four in the afternoon a lad of about Ned's age came on board. He was the son of the merchant to whom the larger part of the cargo of the *Good Venture* was consigned.

"I have a letter that my father charged me to give into your hands, Captain Martin. He said that the matter was urgent, and begged me to give it you in your cabin. He also told me to ask when you think your hold will be empty, as he has goods for you for the return voyage."

"We shall be well nigh empty by to-morrow night," Captain Martin said, as he led the way to his cabin in the poop. "The men have been working faster than usual, for it generally takes us three days to unload."

"I do not think my father cared about that," the lad said when he entered the cabin ; "it was but an excuse for my coming down here, and he gave me the message before all the other clerks. But methinks that the letter is the real object of my coming."

Captain Martin opened the letter. Thanks to his preparation for taking his place in his father's business, he had learnt to read and write ; accomplishments by no means general among sea-captains of the time.

"It is important, indeed," he said, as he glanced through the letter. It ran as follows : "Captain Martin, —A friend of mine, who is one of the council here, has just told me that at the meeting this afternoon a denunciation was laid against you for having publicly, in the street of Vordwyk, cursed and abused his Majesty the King of Spain, the Duke of Alva, the Spaniards, and the Catholic religion. Some were of opinion that you should at once be arrested on board your ship, but others thought that it were better to wait and seize you the first time you came on shore, as it might cause trouble, were you taken from under the protection of the British flag. On shore, they urged, no question could arise, especially as many English have now, although the two nations are at peace, openly taken service under the Prince of Orange.

"I have sent to tell you this, though at no small risk to myself were it discovered that I had done so; but as we have had dealings for many years together, I think it right to warn you. I may say that the counsel of those who were for waiting prevailed; but if, after a day or two, they find that you do not come ashore, I fear they will not hesitate to arrest you on your own vessel. Please to destroy this letter at once after you have read it, and act as seems best to you under the circumstances. I send this to you by my son's hand, for there are spies everywhere, and in these days one can trust no one."

"I am much obliged to you, young sir, for bringing me this letter. Will you thank your father from me, and say that I feel deeply indebted to him, and will think over how I can best escape from this strait. Give him the message from me before others, that I shall be empty and ready to receive goods by noon on the day after to-morrow."

When the lad had left, Captain Martin called in Ned and William Peters, his first mate, and laid the case before them.

"It is an awkward business, Captain Martin," Peters said. "You sh'n't be arrested on board the *Good Venture*, as long as there is a man on board can wield a cutlass; but I don't know whether that would help you in the long run."

"Not at all, Peters. We might beat off the first party that came to take me, but it would not be long before they brought up a force against which we should stand no chance whatever. No, it is not by fighting that there is any chance of escape. It is evident by this that I am safe for to-morrow; they will wait at least a day to see if I go ashore, which indeed they will make certain I shall do sooner or later. As far as my own safety is concerned, and that of Ned here, who, as he was with me, is doubtless included in the denunciation, it is easy enough. We have only to get into the boat after dark, to muffle the oars, and to row for Haarlem, which lies but ten miles away, and has declared for the Prince of Orange. But I do not like to leave the ship, for if they found us gone they might seize and declare it confiscated. And although when we got back to England, we might lay a complaint before the queen, there would be no chance of our getting the ship or her value from the Spaniards. There are so many causes of complaint between the two nations, that the seizure of a brig would make no difference one way or another. The question is, could we get her out?"

"It would be no easy matter," Peters said, shaking his head. "That French ship that came in this afternoon has taken up a berth outside us, and there would be no getting out until she moved out of the way. If she were not there it might be tried, though it would be difficult to do so without attracting attention. As for the Spanish war vessels, of which there are four in the port, I should not fear them if we once got our sails up, for the *Venture* can sail faster than these lubberly Spaniards; but they would send row-boats after us, and unless the wind was strong these would speedily overhaul us."

"Well, I must think it over," Captain Martin said. "I

should be sorry indeed to lose my ship, which would be well nigh ruin to me, but if there is no other way we must make for Haarlem by boat."

The next day the work of unloading continued. In the afternoon the captain of the French ship lying outside them came on board. He had been in the habit of trading with Holland, and addressed Captain Martin in Dutch.

"Are you likely to be lying here long?" he asked "I want to get my vessel alongside the wharf as soon as I can, for it is slow work unloading into these lighters. There are one or two ships going out in the morning, but I would rather have got in somewhere about this point if I could, for the warehouses of Mynheer Strous, to whom my goods are consigned, lie just opposite."

"Will you come down into my cabin and have a glass of wine with me," Captain Martin said, "and then we can talk it over?"

Captain Martin discovered, without much trouble, that the French captain was a Huguenot, and that his sympathies were all with the people of the Netherlands.

"Now," he said, "I can speak freely to you. I was ashore the day before yesterday, and learnt that my wife's father, her three brothers and one of their wives have been murdered by the Spaniards. Well, you can understand that in my grief and rage I cursed the Spaniards and their doings. I have learnt that some spy has denounced me, and that they are only waiting for me to set foot on shore to arrest me, and you know what will come after that; for at present, owing to the volunteers that have come over to Brill and Flushing, the Spaniards are furious against the English. They would rather take me on shore than on board, but if they find that I do not land they will certainly come on board for me. They believe that I shall

not be unloaded until noon to-morrow, and doubtlessly expect that as soon as the cargo is out I shall land to arrange
for a freight to England. Therefore, until to-morrow
afternoon I am safe, but no longer. Now, I am thinking of trying to get out quietly to-night ; but to do so it is
necessary that you should shift your berth a ship's length
one way or the other. Will you do this for me ? "

"Certainly I will, with pleasure," the captain replied.
"I will give orders at once."

"No, that will never do," Captain Martin said. "They
are all the more easy about me because they know that as
long as your ship is there I cannot get out, but if they saw
you shifting your berth it would strike them at once that
I might be intending to slip away. You must wait until
it gets perfectly dark, and then throw off your warps and
slacken out your cable as silently as possible, and let her
drop down so as to leave me an easy passage. As soon as
it is dark I will grease all my blocks, and when everything
is quiet try to get her out. What wind there is is from the
south-west, which will take us well down the Zuider-Zee."

"I hope you may succeed," the French captain said.
"Once under sail you would be safe from their war-ships,
for you would be two or three miles away before they could
manage to get up their sails. The danger lies in their
row-boats and galleys."

"Well, well, we must risk it," Captain Martin said. "I
shall have a boat alongside, and if I find the case is desperate we will take to it and row to the shore, and make
our way to Haarlem, where we should be safe."

Ned, who had been keeping a sharp look-out all day, observed that two Spanish officials had taken up their station
on the wharf, not far from the ship. They appeared to
have nothing to do, and to be indifferent to what was go-

ing on. He told his father that he thought that they were watching. Presently the merchant himself came down to the wharf. He did not come on board, but spoke to Captain Martin as he stood on the deck of the vessel, so that all around could hear his words.

"How are you getting on, Captain Martin ?" he asked in Dutch.

"Fairly well," Captain Martin replied.   "I think if we push on we shall have her empty by noon to-morrow."

"I have a cargo to go back with you, you know," the merchant said, "and I shall want to see you at the office, if you will step round to-morrow after you have cleared."

"All right, Mynheer, you may expect me about two o'clock. But you won't see me," he added to himself.

The merchant waved his hand and walked away, and in a few minutes later the two officials also strolled off.

"That has thrown dust into their eyes," Captain Martin said, "and has made it safe for Strous. He will pretend to be as surprised as anyone when he hears I have gone."

CHAPTER III.

A FIGHT WITH THE SPANIARDS.

AS soon as it became dark, and the wharves were deserted, Captain Martin sent two sailors aloft with grease pots, with orders that every block was to be carefully greased to ensure its running without noise. A boat which rowed six oars was lowered noiselessly into the water, and flannel was bound round the oars. The men, who had been aware of the danger that threatened their captain, sharpened the pikes and axes, and declared to each other that whether the captain ordered it or not no Spaniard should set foot on board as long as one of them stood alive on the decks. The cook filled a great boiler with water and lighted a fire under it, and the carpenter heated a caldron of pitch without orders.

"What are you doing Thompson?" the captain asked, noticing the glow of the fire as he came out of his cabin.

The sailor came aft before he replied, "I am just cooking up a little hot sauce for the dons, captain. We don't ask them to come, you know; but if they do, it's only right that we should entertain them."

"I hope there will be no fighting, lad," the captain said.

"Well, your honour, that ain't exactly the wish of me and my mates. After what we have been hearing of, we feel as we sha'n't be happy until we have had a brush with them 'ere Spaniards. And as to fighting, your honour;

from what we have heard, Captain Hawkins and others
out in the Indian seas have been a-showing that though
they may swagger on land that they ain't no match for an
Englishman on the sea. Anyhow, your honour, we ain't
going to stand by and see you and Master Ned carried
away by these 'ere butchering Spaniards.

"We have all made up our minds that what happens to
you happens to all of us. We have sailed together in this
ship the *Good Venture* for the last seventeen or eighteen
years, and we means to swim or sink together. No disrespect to you, captain ; but that is the fixed intention of
all of us. It would be a nice thing for us to sail back to
the port of London and say as we stood by and saw our
captain and his son carried off to be hung or burnt or
what not by the Spaniards, and then sailed home to tell
the tale. We don't mean no disrespect, captain, I says
again ; but in this 'ere business we take our orders from
Mr. Peters, seeing that you being consarned as it were in
the affair ain't to be considered as having, so to speak, a
right judgment upon it."

"Well, well, we shall see if there is a chance of making
a successful fight," Captain Martin said, unable to resist a
smile from the sailor's way of putting it."

The night was dark, and the two or three oil lamps that
hung suspended from some of the houses facing the port
threw no ray of light which extended to the shipping. It
was difficult to make out against the sky the outline of the
masts of the French vessel lying some twenty yards away ;
but presently Ned's attention was called towards her by a
slight splash of her cable. Then he heard the low rumble
as the ropes ran out through the hawse-holes, and saw that
the masts were slowly moving. In two or three minutes
they had disappeared from his sight. He went into the cabin.

"The Frenchman has gone, father; and so noiselessly that I could hardly hear her. If we can get out as quietly there is but little fear of our being noticed."

"We cannot be as quiet as that, Ned. She has only to slack away her cables and drift with the tide that turned half an hour ago, we have got to tow out and set sail. However, the night is dark, the wind is off shore, and everything is in our favour. Do you see if there be any one about on the decks of the ships above and below us."

Ned went first on to the stern, and then to the bow. He could hear the voices of men talking and singing in the forecastles, but could hear no movement on the deck of either ship. He went down and reported to his father.

"Then, I think, we may as well start at once, Ned. There are still sounds and noises in the town, and any noise we may make is therefore less likely to be noticed than if we waited until everything was perfectly still."

The sailors were all ready. All were barefooted so as to move as noiselessly as possible. The four small cannon that the *Good Venture* carried had been loaded to the muzzle with bullets and pieces of iron. A search had been made below and several heavy lumps of stone, a part of the ballast carried on some former occasion, brought up and placed at intervals along the bulwarks. The pikes had been fastened by a loose lashing to the mast, and the axes leant in readiness against the cannon.

"Now, Peters," Captain Martin said, "let the boat be manned. Do you send a man ashore to cast off the hawser at the bow. Let him take a line ashore with him so as to ease the hawser off and not let the end fall in the water. The moment he has done that let him come to the stern and get on board there, and do you and he get the plank on board as noiselessly as you can. As soon as the bow-hawser is on

board I will give the men in the boat the word to row. Ned
will be on board her, and see that they row in the right
direction. The moment you have got the plank in get out
your knife and cut the stern warp half through, and directly
her head is out, and you feel the strain, sever it. The
stern is so close to the wharf that the end will not be able
to drop down into the water and make a splash."

Ned's orders were that as soon as the vessel's head pointed
seawards he was to steer rather to the right, so as to prevent
the stream, which, however, ran but feebly, from carrying
her down on to the bows of the French ship. Once beyond
the latter he was to go straight out, steering by the lights on
shore. The men were enjoined to drop their oars as quietly
as possible into the water at each stroke, and to row deeply,
as having the vessel in tow they would churn up the water
unless they did so. The boat rowed off a stroke or
two, and then, as the rope tightened, the men sat quiet until
Captain Martin was heard to give the order to row in a low
tone; then they bent to their oars. Peters had chosen the
six best rowers on board the ship for the purpose, and so
quietly did they dip their oars in the water that Captain
Martin could scarce hear the sound, and only knew by looking over the other side, and seeing that the shore was reced-
ing, that the ship was in motion. Two minutes later
Peters came forward.

"I have cut the warp, Captain Martin, and she is moving out. I have left Watson at the helm." Scarce a word
was spoken for the next five minutes. It was only by
looking at the lights ashore that they could judge the
progress they were making. Every one breathed more
freely now the first danger was over. They had got out
from their berth without attracting the slightest notice,
either from the shore or from the ships lying next to them.

Their next danger was from the ships lying at anchor off the port waiting their turn to come in. Were they to run against one of these, the sound of the collision, and perhaps the breaking of spars and the shouts of the crew, would certainly excite attention from the sentries on shore.

So far the boat had been rowing but a short distance in advance of the end of the bowsprit, but Captain Martin now made his way out to the end of that spar, and told Ned that he was going to give him a good deal more rope in order that he might keep well ahead, and that he was to keep a sharp lookout for craft at anchor. Another quarter of an hour passed, and Captain Martin thought that they must now be beyond the line of the outer shipping. They felt the wind more now that they were getting beyond the shelter of the town, and its effect upon the hull and spars made the work lighter for those in the boat ahead.

"Now, Peters, I think that we can safely spread the foresail and call them in from the boat."

The sail had been already loosed and was now let fall; it bellied out at once.

"Haul in the sheets, lads," Captain Martin said, and going forward gave a low whistle. A minute later the boat was alongside. "Let her drop astern, Peters," the captain said, as Ned and the rowers clambered on board; "we may want her presently. Hullo! what's that? It's one of the guard-boats, I do believe, and coming this way." The men heard the sound of coming oars, and silently stole to the mast and armed themselves with the pikes, put the axes in their belts, and ranged themselves along by the side of the ship towards which the boat was approaching. "Will she go ahead of us or astern?" Captain Martin whispered to the mate.

"I cannot tell yet, sir. By the sound she seems making pretty nearly straight for us."

"How unfortunate," Captain Martin murmured; "just as it seemed that we were getting safely away."

In another minute the mate whispered, "She will go astern of us, sir, but not by much."

"I trust that she will not see us," the captain said. "But now we are away from the town and the lights, it doesn't seem so dark, besides their eyes are accustomed to it."

There was dead silence in the ship as the boat approached. She was just passing the stern at the distance of about a ship's length, when there was a sudden exclamation, and a voice shouted, "What ship is that ? Where are you going?" Captain Martin replied in Dutch, "We are taking advantage of the wind to make to sea."

"Down with that sail, sir !" the officer shouted ; "this is against all regulations. No ship is permitted to leave the port between sunrise and sunset. Pull alongside, lads ; there is something strange about this !"

"Do not come alongside," Captain Martin said sternly. "We are peaceable traders who meddle with no one, but if you interfere with us it will be the worse for you."

"You insolent hound !" the officer exclaimed furiously, "do you dare to threaten me. Blow your matches, lads, and shoulder your arquebuses. There is treason and rebellion here."

Those on board saw six tiny sparks appear, two in the bow and four in the stern. A minute later the boat dashed alongside. As it did so three great pieces of stone were cast into it, knocking down two of the rowers.

"Fire !" the officer exclaimed as he sprang up to climb the ship's side. The six muskets were discharged, and the

men rose to follow their leader, when there was a cry
from the rowers " The boat is sinking ! She is staved in !"

At the same moment the officer fell back thrust through
with a pike.   Two of the soldiers were cut down with axes,
the others sprang back into the sinking boat, which at
once drifted astern.

" Up with her sails, lads!" Captain Martin shouted; " it
is a question of speed now.   The alarm is spread on shore
already."   The sentries on the various batteries were discharging their muskets and shouting, and the roll of a drum
was heard almost immediately.   The crew soon had every
stitch of sail set upon the brig.   She was moving steadily
through the water ; but the wind was still light, although
occasionally a stronger puff gave ground for hope that it
would ere long blow harder.

" They will be some time before they make out what it
is all about, Peters," Captain Martin said.   " The galleys
will be manned, and will row to the spot where the firing
was heard.   Some of the men in the boat are sure to be able
to swim, and will meet them as they come out and tell them
what has happened.   The wors of it is, the moon will be
up in a few minutes.   I forgot all about that.   That accounts for its being lighter.   However, we have got a good
start.   One or two guard-boats may be out here in a quarter of an hour, but it will take the galleys twice as long to
gather their crews and get out.   It all depends on the
wind.   It is lucky it is not light yet, or the batteries might
open on us ; I don't think now they will get sight of us
until we are fairly out of range."

Now that there was no longer occasion for silence on
board the *Good enture*, the crew laughed and joked at the
expense of the Spaniards.   They were in high spirits at
their success, and their only regret was that the brush with

their pursuers had not been a more serious one. It was evident from the talk that there was quite as much hope as fear in the glances that they cast astern, and that they would have been by no means sorry to see a foe of about their own strength in hot pursuit of them. A quarter of an hour after the shattered boat had dropped astern the moon rose on the starboard-bow. It was three-quarters full, and would assuredly reveal the ship to those on shore. Scarcely indeed did it show above the horizon when there was the boom of a gun astern, followed a second or two later by a heavy splash in the water close alongside.

" That was a good shot," Captain Martin said ; " but luck rather than skill I fancy. There is little chance of their hitting us at this distance. We must be a mile and a half away ; don't you think so, Peters ?"

" Quite that, captain ; and they must have given their gun a lot of elevation to carry so far. I almost wonder they wasted their powder."

" Of course they can't tell in the least who they are firing at," the captain said. " They cannot have learnt anything yet, and can have only known that there was firing off the port, and that a craft is making out. We may be one of the sea beggars' vessels for anything they know, and may have come in to carry off a prize from under their very noses."

" That is so," the mate replied ; " but the gun may have been fired as a signal as much as with any hope of hitting us."

" So it may, so it may, Peters ; I did not think of that. Certainly that is likely enough. We know they have several ships cruising in the Zuider-Zee keeping a look-out for the beggars. On a night like this, and with the wind astern, the sound will be heard miles away. We may have trouble yet. I was not much afraid of the galleys, for though the wind is so light we are running along famously. You see we have nothing in our hold; and that is all in our favour so long as we are dead before the wind. Besides, if the galleys did come up it would probably be singly, and we should be able to beat them off, for high out of water as we are they would find it difficult to climb the sides ; but if we fall in with any of their ships it is a different matter altogether."

Four or five more shots were fired, but they all fell astern ; and as they were fully two miles and a half away when the last gun was discharged, and the cannoners must have known that they were far out of range, Captain Martin felt sure that the mate's idea was a correct one, and that the cannon had been discharged rather as a signal than with any hope of reaching them.

"Ned, run up into the foretop," the captain said, "and keep a sharp look-out ahead.   The moon has given an advantage to those who are on our track behind, but it gives us an advantage as against any craft there may be ahead of us.   We shall see them long before they can see us."

Peters had been looking astern when the last gun was fired, and said that by its flash he believed that he had caught sight of three craft of some kind or other outside the ships moored off the port.

"Then we have two miles' start if those are their galleys," the captain said.   "We are stealing through the water at about the rate of four knots, and perhaps they may row six, so it will take them an hour to come up."

"Rather more than that, I should say, captain, for the wind at times freshens a little.   It is likely to be an hour and a half before they come up."

'All the better, Peters.   They will have learnt from those

they picked up from that boat that we are not a large craft, and that our crew probably does not exceed twenty men; therefore, as those galleys carry about twenty soldiers besides the twenty rowers, they will not think it necessary to keep together, but will each do his best to overtake us. one of them is sure to be faster than the others, and if they come up singly I think we shall be able to beat them off handsomely. It is no use discussing now whether it is wise to fight or not. By sinking that first boat we have all put our heads in a noose, and there is no drawing back. We have repulsed their officers with armed force, and their will be no mercy for any of us if we fall into their hands."

"We shall fight all the better for knowing that," Peters said grimly. "The Dutchmen are learning that, as the Spaniards are finding to their cost. There is nothing like making a man fight than the knowledge that there is a halter waiting for him if he is beaten."

"You had better get two of the guns astern, Peters, so as to fire down into them as they come up. You may leave the others, one on each side, for the present, and run one of them over when you see which side they are making for. Ah! that's a nice little puff. If it would but hold like that we should show them our heels altogether."

In two or three minutes the puff died out and the wind fell even lighter than before.

"I thought that we were going to have more of it," the captain said discontentedly; "It looked like it when the sun went down."

"I think we shall have more before morning," Peters agreed; "but I am afraid it wont come in time to help us much."

As the moon rose they were able to make out three craft

astern of them. Two were almost abreast of each other, the third some little distance behind.

"That is just what I expected, Peters; they are making a race of it. We shall have two of them on our hands at once; the other will be too far away by the time they come up to give them any assistance. They are about a mile astern now, I should say, and unless the wind freshens up a bit they will be alongside in about twenty minutes. I will give you three men here, Peters. As soon as we have fired load again, and then slew the guns round and run them forward to the edge of the poop, and point them down into the waist. If the Spaniards get on board and we find them too strong for us, those of us who can will take to the forecastle, the others will run up here. Then sweep the Spaniards with your guns, and directly you have fired charge down among them with pike and axe. We will do the same, and it is hard if we do not clear the deck of them."

Just at this moment Ned hailed them from the top. "There is a ship nearly ahead of us, sir; she is lying with her sails brailed up, evidently waiting."

"How far is she off, do you think, Ned?"

"I should say she is four miles away," Ned replied.

"Well we need not trouble about her for the present; there will be time to think about her when we have finished with these fellows behind. You can come down now, Ned."

In a few words the captain now explained his intentions to his men.

"I hope, lads, that we shall be able to prevent their getting a footing on the deck; but if they do, and we find we can't beat them back, as soon as I give the word you are to take either to the forecastle or to the poop. Mr. Peters will have the two guns there ready to sweep them with bullets. The moment he has fired give a cheer and rush down upon them from both sides. We will clear them off again, never fear. Ned, you will be in charge in the waist until I rejoin you. Get ready to run one of the guns over the instant I tell you on which side they are coming up. Depress them as much as you can. I shall take one gun and you take the other, and be sure you don't fire until you see a boat well under the muzzle of your gun. Mind it's the boat you are to aim at, and not the men."

Captain Martin again ascended to the poop and joined Peters. The two boats were now but a few hundred yards astern, and they could hear the officers cheering on the rowers to exert themselves to the utmost. The third boat was fully a quarter of a mile behind the leaders. When they approached within a hundred yards a fire of musketry was opened.

"Lie down under the bulwarks, men," Captain Martin said to the three sailors. "It is no use risking your lives unnecessarily. I expect one boat will come one side and one the other, Peters. If they do we will both take the one coming up on the port side. One of us may miss, and it is better to make sure of one boat if we can. I think we can make pretty sure of beating off the other. Yes, there they are separating. Now work your gun round a bit, so that it bears on a point about twenty yards astern and a boat's length on the port side. I will do the same. Have you done that?"

"Yes, I think I have about got it, sir."

"Very well then. Stoop down now, or we may get hit before it is time to fire."

The bulwarks round the poop were only about a foot high, but sitting back from them the captain and the mate

were protected from the bullets that were now singing
briskly over the stern of the ship.

"They are coming up, Peters," Captain Martin said.
"Now kneel up and look along your gun ; get your match
ready, and do not fire till you see right into the boat, then
clap on your match whether I fire or not."

The boat came racing along until, when within some
twenty yards of the stern, the cannons were discharged
almost simultaneously. The sound was succeeded by a
chorus of screams and yells ; the contents of both guns
had struck the boat fairly midships, and she sank almost
instantly. As soon as they had fired Captain Martin ran
forward and joined the crew in the waist. He had already
passed the word to Ned to get both guns over to the starboard side, and he at once took charge of one while Ned
stood at the other. The Spaniards had pushed straight
on without waiting to pick up their drowning comrades in
the other boat, and in a minute were alongside. So close
did the helmsman bring the boat to the side that the guns
could not be depressed so as to bear upon her, and a
moment later the Spaniards were climbing up the sides of
the vessel, the rowers dropping their oars and seizing axes
and joining the soldiers.

"Never mind the gun, Ned ; it is useless at present.
Now, lads, drive them back as they come up."

With pike and hatchet the sailors met the Spaniards as
they tried to climb up. The cook had brought his caldron
of boiling water to the bulwarks, and threw pailful after
pailful down into the boat, while the carpenter bailed over
boiling pitch with the great ladle. Terrible yells and
screams rose from the boat, and the soldiers in vain tried
to gain a footing upon the ship's deck. As they appeared
above the level of the bulwarks they were met either with

thrust of pike or with a crashing blow from an axe, and it was but three or four minutes from the moment that the fight began that the boat cast off and dropped behind, more than half those on board being either killed or disabled. A loud cheer broke from the crew.

"Shall I run the guns back to the stern again," Peters asked from above, "and give them a parting dose?"

"No, no," Captain Martin said, "let them go, Peters ; we are fighting to defend ourselves, and have done them mischief enough. See what the third boat is doing, though."

"They have stopped rowing," Peters said, after going to the stern. "I think they are picking up some swimmers from the boat we sank. There cannot be many of them, for most of the rowers would have been killed by our discharges, and the soldiers in their armour will have sunk at once."

Captain Martin now ascended to the poop. In a short time the boat joined that which had dropped astern, which was lying helpless in the water, no attempt having been made to man the oars, as most of the unwounded men were scalded more or less severely. Their report was evidently not encouraging, and the third boat made no attempt to pursue. Some of her oarsmen were shifted to the other boat, and together they turned and made back for Amsterdam.

"Now then for this vessel ahead," Captain Martin said ; "that is a much more serious business than the boats."

The vessel, which was some two miles ahead of them, had now set some of her sails, and was heading towards them.

"They can make us out now plainly enough, Peters, and the firing will of course have told them we are the vessel that they are in search of. I don't think that there is any getting away from them."

"I don't see that there is," the mate agreed. "Whichever way we edged off they could cut us off. The worst of it is no doubt she has got some big guns on board, and these little things of ours are of no good except at close quarters. It would be no use trying to make a running fight with her?"

"Not in the least, Peters. We had better sail straight at her."

"You don't mean to try and carry her by boarding?" Peters asked doubtfully. "She looks like a large ship, and has perhaps a hundred and fifty men on board; and though the Spaniards are no sailors they can fight on the decks of their ships."

"That is so, Peters. What I think of doing is to bear straight down upon her as if I intended to board. We shall have to stand one broadside as we come up, and then we shall be past her, and with our light draught we should run right away from her with this wind. There is more of it than there was, and we are slipping away fast. Unless she happens to knock away one of our masts we shall get away from her."

When they were within half a mile of the Spanish ship they saw her bows bear off.

"Lie down, lads." the captain ordered, "she is going to give us a broadside. When it is over start one of those sea-beggar songs you picked up at Brill; that will startle them, and they will think we are crowded with men and going to board them."

A minute later eight flashes of fire burst from the Spanish ship, now lying broadside to them. One shot crashed through the bulwarks, two others passed through the sails, the rest went wide of their mark. As soon as it was over the crew leapt to their feet and burst into one of the wild songs sung by the sea beggars.

"Keep our head straight towards her, Peters," Captain Martin said. "They will think we mean to run her down, and it will flurry and confuse them."

Loading was not quick work in those days, and the distance between the vessels was decreased by half before the guns were again fired. This time it was not a broadside ; the guns went off one by one as they were loaded, and the aim was hasty and inaccurate, for close as they were not a shot struck the hull of the *Good Venture,* though two or three went through the sails. In the bright moonlight men could be seen running about and officers waving their arms and giving orders on board the Spaniard, and then her head began to pay off.

"We have scared them," Captain Martin laughed. "They thought we were going to run them down. They know the sea beggars would be quite content to sink themselves if they could sink an enemy. Follow close in her wake, Peters, and then bear off a little as if you meant to pass them on their starboard side ; then when you get close give her the helm sharp and sweep across her stern. We will give her the guns as we pass, then bear off again and pass her on her port side; the chances are they will not have loaded again there."

The Spanish ship was little more than a hundred yards ahead. When she got before the wind again Captain Martin saw with satisfaction that the *Good Venture* sailed three feet to her two. The poop and stern galleries of the Spaniard were clustered with soldiers, who opened a fire with their muskets upon their pursuer. The men were all lying down now at their guns, which were loaded with musket balls to their muzzles.

"Elevate them as much as you can. She is much higher out of the water than we are. Now, Peters, you see to the guns, I will take the helm."

"I will keep the helm, sir," the mate replied.

"No you won't, Peters; my place is the place of danger. But if you like you can lie under the bulwark there after you have fired, and be ready to take my place if you see me drop. Now, lads, get ready."

So saying the captain put down the tiller. The *Good Venture* swept round under the stern of the Spaniard at a distance of some forty yards, and as she did so the guns loaded with bullets to the muzzle were fired one after the other. The effect was terrible, and the galleries and poop were swept by the leaden shower. Then the captain straightened the helm again. The crew burst into the wild yells and cries the beggars raised when going into battle. The Spaniards, confused by the terrible slaughter worked by the guns of their enemies, and believing that they were about to be boarded on the port side by a crowd of desperate foemen, hastily put up the tiller, and the ship bore away as the *Good Venture* swept up, presenting her stern instead of her broadside to them.

To the momentary relief of the Spaniards their assailant instead of imitating their manœuvres kept straight upon her course before the wind, and instead of the wild cries of the beggars a hearty English cheer was raised. As Captain Martin had expected, the guns on the port side had not been reloaded after the last discharge, and the *Good Venture* was two or three hundred yards away before the Spaniards recovered from their surprise at what seemed the incomprehensible manœuvre of their foes, and awoke to the fact that they had been tricked, and that instead of a ship crowded with beggars of the sea their supposed assailant had been an English trader that was trying to escape from them.

A dozen contradictory orders were shouted as soon as the

truth dawned upon them. The captain had been killed by the discharge of grape, and the first lieutenant severely wounded. The officer in command of the troops shouted to his men to load the guns, only to find when this was accomplished that the second lieutenant of the ship had turned her head in pursuit of the enemy, and that not a single gun would bear. There was a sharp altercation between the two authorities, but the military chief was of the highest rank.

" Don't you see," he said furiously, " that she is going away from us every foot. She was but a couple of hundred yards away when I gave the order to load, and now she is fully a quarter of a mile."

"If I put the helm down to bring her broadside on," the seaman said, "she will be half a mile ahead before we can straighten up and get in her wake again ; and unless you happen to cripple her she will get away to a certainty."

"She will get away anyhow," the soldier roared, "if we don't cripple her. Put your helm down instantly."

The order was given and the ship's head swayed round. There was a flapping of sails and a rattling of blocks, and then a broadside was fired ; but it is no easy matter for angry and excited men to hit a mast at the distance of nearly half a mile. One of the shots ploughed up the deck within a yard of the foot of the mainmast, another splintered a boat, three others added to the holes in the sails, but no damage of importance was done. By the time the Spaniard had borne round and was again in chase, the *Good Venture* was over half a mile ahead.

"It is all over now, captain," Peters said as he went aft. "Unless we light upon another of these fellows, which is not likely, we are safe."

"Are any of the men hit, Peters ?"

"The carpenter was knocked down and stunned by a splinter from the boat, sir; but I don't think it is serious."

"Thank God for that," the captain said. "Now, will you take the helm?" There was something in the voice that startled the mate.

"Is anything the matter, sir? Don't say you are hit."

"I am hit, Peters, and I fear rather badly; but that matters little now that the crew and ship are safe."

Peters caught the captain, for he saw that he could scarce stand, and called two men to his assistance. The captain was laid down on the deck.

"Where are you hit, sir?"

"Half-way between the knee and the hip," Captain Martin replied faintly. "If it hadn't been for the tiller 1 should have fallen, but with the aid of that I made shift to stand on the other leg. It was just before we fired, at the moment when I put the helm down."

"Why didn't you call me?" Peters said reproachfully.

"It was of no good getting two of us hit, Peters; and as long as I could stand to steer I was better there than you."

Ned came running aft as the news was passed along that the captain was wounded, and threw himself on his knees by his father's side.

"Bear up, Ned; bear up like a man," his father said. "I am hit hard, but I don't know that it is to death. But even if it is, it is ten thousand times better to die in battle with the Spaniards than to be hung like a dog, which would have befallen me and perhaps all of us if they had taken us."

By Peters' directions a mattress was now brought up, and the captain carried down to his cabin. There was no thought on board now of the pursuers astern, or of possible danger lying ahead. The news that Captain Martin was badly wounded damped all the feelings of triumph and enthusiasm which the crew had before been feeling at the success with which they had eluded the Spaniard while heavily punishing her. As soon as the captain was laid on a sofa Peters examined the wound. It was right in front of the leg, some four inches above the knee.

"There is nothing to be done for it," Captain Martin said. "It has smashed the bone, I am sure."

"I am afraid it has, captain," Peters said ruefully ; "and it is no use my saying that it has not. I think, sir, we had best put in at Enkhuizen. We are not above four or five miles from it now, and we shall find surgeons there who will do all they can for you."

"I think that will be the best plan, Peters."

The orders were given at once, and the ship's course altered, and half an hour later the lights of Enkhuizen were seen ahead.

CHAPTER IV.

WOUNDED.

THEY dropped anchor a short distance off the port, and then lit some torches and waved them.

"The firing is sure to have been heard," Peters said, "and they will be sending off to know what is going on, otherwise there would have been small chance of getting in to-night."

As the mate anticipated, the sound of oars was soon heard, and a large boat rowed out towards them. It stopped at a distance of a hundred yards, and there was a shout of "What ship is that?"

"The English brig *Good Venture*. We pray you to allow us to bring our captain, who has been sorely wounded by the Spaniards, on shore."

"What has been the firing we have heard? We could see the flashes across the water."

"We have been twice engaged," Peters shouted; "first with two Spanish galleys, and then with a large ship of war, which we beat off with heavy loss."

"Well done, Englishman!" the voice exclaimed, and the boat at once rowed out to the brig. "You cannot come in to-night," the Dutch official said, "for the chain is up across the harbour, and the rule is imperative and without exception; but I will gladly take your captain on shore, and he shall have, I promise you, the best surgical aid the town can give him. Is he the only one hurt?"

"One of the men has been injured with a splinter, but he needs but bandaging and laying up for a few days. We have had a shot or two through our bulwarks, and the sails are riddled. The captain's son is below with him ; he acts as second mate, and will tell you all about this affair into which we were forced."

"Very well; we will take him ashore with us then. There is quite an excitement there. The news that a sea-fight was going on brought all the citizens to the walls."

The mattress upon which Captain Martin was lying was brought out and lowered carefully into the stern of the boat. Ned took his seat beside it, and the boat pushed off. Having passed the forts they entered the port and rowed to the landing-place. A number of citizens, many of them carrying torches, were assembled here. "What is the news?" a voice asked as the boat approached.

"It is an English ship, burgomaster. She has been hotly engaged; first with Spanish galleys, and then with a war-ship, which was doubtless the one seen beating up this afternoon. She sank one of the galleys and beat off the ship." A loud cheer broke from the crowd. When it subsided the official went on: "I have the English captain and his son on board. The captain is sorely wounded, and I have promised him the best medical aid the town can give him."

"That he shall have," the burgomaster said. "Let him be carried to my house at once. Hans Leipart, do you hurry on and tell my wife to get a chamber prepared instantly. You have heard who it is, and why he is coming, and I warrant me she will do her best to make the brave Englishman comfortable. Do two others of you run to Doctors Zobel and Harreng, and pray them to hasten to my house. Let a stretcher be fetched instantly from the town hall."

As soon as the stretcher was brought the mattress was

placed on it, and six of the sailors carried it on shore. The crowd had by this time greatly increased, for the news had rapidly spread. Every head was bared in token of sympathy and respect as the litter was brought up. The crowd fell back and formed a lane, and, led by the burgomaster, the sailors carried the wounded man into the town. He was taken upstairs to the room prepared for him, and the surgeons were speedily in attendance. Medicine in those days was but a primitive science, but the surgery, though rough and rude, was far ahead of the sister art. Wars were of such constant occurrence that surgeons had ample opportunity for practice; and simple operations, such as the amputation of limbs, were matters of very common occurrence. It needed but a very short examination by the two surgeons to enable them to declare that the leg must at once be amputated.

"The bone appears to be completely smashed," one of them said. "Doubtless the ball was fired at a very short distance." A groan burst from Ned when he heard the decision.

"I knew that it would be so, Ned," his father said. "I never doubted it for a moment. It is well that I have been able to obtain aid so speedily. Better a limb than life, my boy. I did not wince when I was hit, and with God's help I can stand the pain now. Do you go away and tell the burgomaster how it all came about, and leave me with these gentlemen."

As soon as Ned had left the room, sobbing in spite of his efforts to appear manly, the captain said: "Now, gentlemen, since this must be done, I pray you to do it without loss of time. I will bear it as best I can, I promise you; and as three or four and twenty years at sea makes a man pretty hard and accustomed to rough usage, I expect I shall stand it as well as another."

The surgeons agreed that there was no advantage in delay, and indeed that it was far better to amputate it before fever set in. They therefore returned home at once for their instruments, the knives and saws, the irons that were to be heated white-hot to stop the bleeding, and the other appliances in use at the time. Had Ned been aware that the operation would have taken place so soon, he would have been unable to satisfy the curiosity of the burgomaster and citizens to know how it had happened that an English trader had come to blows with the Spaniards ; but he had no idea that it would take place that night, and thought that probably some days would elapse before the surgeons finally decided that it was necessary to amputate it.

One of the surgeons had, at the captain's request, called the burgomaster aside as he left the house, and begged him to keep the lad engaged in conversation until he heard from him that all was over. This the burgomaster willingly promised to do; and as many of the leading citizens were assembled in the parlour to hear the news, there was no chance of Ned's slipping away.

"Before you begin to tell us your story, young sir, we should be glad to know how it is that you speak our language so well; for indeed we could not tell by your accent that you are not a native of these parts, which is of course impossible, seeing that your father is an Englishman and captain of the ship lying off there."

" My mother comes from near here," Ned said. "She is the daughter of Mynheer Plomaert, who lived at Vordwyk, two miles from Amsterdam. She went over to England when she married my father, but when he was away on his voyages she always spoke her own language to us children, so that we grew to speak it naturally as we did English."

Ned then related the news that met them on their arrival

at his grandfather's home, and the exclamations of fury on the part of his father.

"It is a common enough story with us here," the burgomaster said, "for few of us but have lost friends or relatives at the hands of these murderous tyrants of ours. But to you, living in a free land, truly it must have been a dreadful shock; and I wonder not that your father's indignation betrayed him into words which, if overheard, might well cost a man his life in this country."

"They were overheard and reported," Ned said; and then proceeded to relate the warning they had received, the measures they had taken to get off unperceived, the accidental meeting with the guard-boat and the way in which it had been sunk, the pursuit by the galleys and the fight with them, and then the encounter with the Spanish ship of war.

"And you say your father never relaxed his hold of the tiller when struck !" the burgomaster said in surprise. "I should have thought he must needs have fallen headlong to the ground."

"He told me," Ned replied, "that at the moment he was hit he was pushing over the tiller, and had his weight partly on that and partly on his other leg. Had it been otherwise he would of course have gone down, for he said that for a moment he thought his leg had been shot off."

When Ned finished his narrative the burgomaster and magistrates were loud in their exclamations of admiration at the manner in which the little trader had both fought and deceived her powerful opponent.

"It was gallantly done indeed," the burgomaster said. "Truly it seems marvellous that a little ship with but twenty hands should have fought and got safely away from the *Don Pedro*, for that was the ship we saw pass this afternoon. We know her well, for she has often been in port here before we declared for the Prince of Orange a month ago. The beggars of the sea themselves could not have done better,— could they, my friends ? though we Dutchmen and Zeelanders believe that there are no sailors that can match our own.

The story had taken nearly an hour to tell, and Ned now said:

"With your permission, sir, I will now go up to my father again."

"You had best not go for the present," the burgomaster said. "The doctor asked me to keep you with me for a while, for that he wished his patient to be entirely undisturbed. He is by his bedside now, and will let me know at once if your father wishes to have you with him."

A quarter of an hour later a servant called the burgomaster out. The surgeon was waiting outside.

"It is finished," he said, "and he has borne it well. Scarce a groan escaped him, even when we applied the hot irons ; but he is utterly exhausted now, and we have given him an opiate, and hope that he will soon drop off to sleep. My colleague will remain with him for four hours, and then I will return and take his place. You had best say nothing to the lad about it. He would naturally want to see his father ; we would much rather that he should not. Therefore tell him, please, that his father is dropping off to sleep, and must not on any account be disturbed ; and that we are sitting up with him by turns, and will let him know at once should there be any occasion for his presence."

Ned was glad to hear that his father was likely to get off to sleep ; and although he would gladly have sat up with him, he knew that it was much better that he should have the surgeon beside him. The burgomaster's wife, a kind and motherly woman, took him aside into a little parlour, where a table was laid with a cold capon, some manchets of bread, and a flask of the burgomaster's best wine. As Ned had eaten nothing since the afternoon, and it was now past midnight, he was by no means sorry to partake of some refreshment. When he had finished he was conducted to a comfortable little chamber that had been prepared for him, and in spite of his anxiety about his father it was not long before he fell asleep.

The sun was high before he awoke. He dressed himself quickly and went downstairs, for he feared to go straight to his father's room lest he might be sleeping.

"You have slept well," the burgomaster's wife said with a smile ; "and no wonder, after your fatigues. The surgeon has just gone, and I was about to send up to wake you, for he told me to tell you that your father had passed a good night, and that you can now see him."

Ned ran upstairs, and turning the handle of the door very quietly entered his father's room. Captain Martin was looking very pale, but Ned thought that his face had not the drawn look that had marked it the evening before.

"How are you, my dear father ?"

"I am going on well, Ned ; at least so the doctors say. I feel I shall be but a battered old hulk when I get about again ; but your mother will not mind that, I know."

"And do the doctors still think that they must take the leg off ?" Ned asked hesitatingly.

"That was their opinion last night, Ned, and it was my opinion too; and so the matter was done off hand, and there is an end of it."

"Done off hand?" Ned repeated. "Do you mean"— and he hesitated.

"Do I mean that they have taken it off? Certainly I do, Ned. They took it off last night while you were downstairs in the burgomaster's parlour; but I thought it would be much better for you not to know anything about it until this morning. Yes, my boy, thank God, it is all over! I don't say that it wasn't pretty hard to bear ; but it had to be done, you know, and the sooner it was over the better. There is nothing worse than lying thinking about a thing.

Ned was too affected to speak; but with tears streaming down his cheeks, leant over and kissed his father. The news had come as a shock to him, but it seemed to have lifted a weight from his mind. The worst was over now ; and although it was terrible to think that his father had lost his leg, still this seemed a minor evil after the fear that perhaps his life might be sacrificed. Knowing that his father should not be excited, or even talk more than was absolutely necessary, Ned stayed but a few minutes with him, and then hurried off to the ship, where, however, he found that the news that the captain's leg had been amputated, and that the doctors hoped that he would go on well, had been known some hours before ; as Peters had come on shore with the first dawn of daylight for news, and heard from the burgomaster's servant that the amputation had taken place the evening before, and an hour later had learned from the lips of the doctor who had been watching by the captain's bedside, that he had passed a fairly good night, and might so far be considered to be doing well.

" What do you think we had better do, Master Ned? Of course it will be for the captain to decide ; but in these matters it is always best to take counsel beforehand. For although it is, of course, what he thinks in the matter will be done, still it may be that we might direct his thoughts; and the less thinking he does in his present state the better."

" What do you mean as to what is to be done, Peters?"

" Well, your father is like to be here many weeks ; in-

deed, if I said many months I don't suppose it would be
far from the truth.   Things never go on quite smooth.
There are sure to be inflammations, and fever keeps on
coming and going ; and if the doctor says three months,
like enough it is six."

" Of course I shall stay here and nurse him, Peters."

" Well, Master Ned, that will be one of the points for
the captain to settle.   I do not suppose he will want the
Good Venture to be lying idle all the time he is laid up;
and though I can sail the ship, the trading business is altogether out of my line.   You know all the merchants he
does business with, going ashore, as you most always do
with him ; I doubt not that you could fill his place and
deal with them just the same as if he was here."

" But I cannot leave him at present."

" No, no, Master Ned ; no one would think of it.   Now,
what I have been turning over in my mind is, that the
best thing for the captain and for you and your good
mother is that I should set sail in the *Venture* without the
loss of a day and fetch her over.   If the wind is reason-
able, and we have good luck, we may be back in ten days
or so.   By that time the captain may be well enough to
think where we had better go for a cargo, and what course
had best be taken about things in general."

" I think that would certainly be the best plan, Peters ;
and I will suggest it to my father at once.   He is much
more likely to go on well if my mother is with him, and
she would be worrying sadly at home were she not by
his side.   Besides, it will be well for her to have something to occupy her, for the news of what has befallen her
father and brothers will be a terrible blow to her. If I put
it in that way to him I doubt not that he will agree to the
plan ; otherwise, he might fear to bring her out here in

such troubled times, for there is no saying when the Spaniards will gather their army to recover the revolted cities, or against which they will first make their attempts. I will go back at once, and if he be awake I will tell him that you and I agree that it will be best for you to sail without loss of an hour to fetch my mother over, and that we can then put off talking about other matters until the ship returns."

Ned at once went back to his father's bed-room. He found the captain had just awoke from a short sleep.

"Father, I do not want to trouble you to think at present, but will tell you what Master Peters and I, who have been laying our heads together, concluded is best to be done. You are likely to be laid up here for some time, and it will be far the best plan for the *Good Venture* to sail over and fetch mother to nurse you."

"I shall get on well enough, Ned. They are kindly people here; and regarding our fight with the Spaniards as a sign of our friendship and good-will towards them, they will do all in their power for me."

"Yes, father, I hope, indeed, that you will go on well; and I am sure that the good people here will do their best in all ways for you, and of course I will nurse you to the best of my power, though, indeed, this is new work for me; but it was not so much you as mother that we were thinking of. It will be terrible for her when the news comes that her father and brothers are all killed, and that you are lying here sorely wounded. It will be well nigh enough to drive her distraught. But if she were to come over here at once she would, while busying about you, have less time to brood over her griefs; and, indeed, I see not why she should be told what has happened at Vordwyk until she is here with you, and you can break it to her. It will come better from your lips, and for your sake she will restrain her grief."

"There is a great deal in what you say Ned, and, indeed, I long greatly to have her with me; but Holland is no place at present to bring a woman to, and I suppose also that she would bring the girls, for she could not well leave them in a house alone. There are plenty of friends there who would be glad to take them in; but that she could decide upon herself. However, as she is a native here she will probably consider she may well run the same risks as the rest of our countrywomen. They remain with their fathers and husbands and endure what perils there may be, and she will see no reason why she should not do the same."

"What we propose is that the *Venture* should set sail at once and fetch my mother over, and the girls, if she sees fit to bring them. I shall of course stay here with you until the brig returns, and by that time you will, I hope, be strong enough to talk over what had best be done regarding the ship and business generally."

"Well, have your way, Ned. At present I cannot think over things and see what is best; so I will leave the matter in your hands, and truly I should be glad indeed to have your mother here with me."

Well content to have obtained the permission Ned hurried from the room.

"Has the burgomaster returned?" he asked when he reached the lower storey.

"He has just come in, and I was coming up to tell you that dinner is served."

"Is it eleven o'clock already?" Ned exclaimed. "I had no idea it was so late." He entered the room and bowed to the burgomaster and his wife.

"Worshipful sir," he said, "I have just obtained leave from my father to send our ship off to London to fetch hither my mother to come to nurse him. I trust that by the time she arrives he will be able to be moved, and then they will take lodgings elsewhere, so as not to trespass longer upon your great kindness and hospitality."

"I think that it is well that your mother should come over," the burgomaster said; "for a man who has had the greater part of his leg taken off cannot be expected to get round quickly. Besides, after what you told us last night about the misfortune that has befallen her family, it were best that she should be busied about her husband, and so have little time to brood over the matter. As to hospitality, it would be strange indeed if we should not do all that we could for a brave man who has been injured in fighting our common enemy. Send word to your mother that she will be as welcome as he is, and that we shall be ready in all respects to arrange whatever she may think most convenient and comfortable. And now you had best sit down and have your meal with us. As soon as it is over I will go down with you to the wharf, and will do what I can to hasten the sailing of your ship. I don't think," he went on, when they had taken their seats at table, "that there is much chance of her meeting another Spaniard on her way out to sea, for we have news this morning that some ships of the beggars have been seen cruising off the entrance, and the Spaniards will be getting under shelter of their batteries at Amsterdam. I hear they are expecting a fleet from Spain to arrive soon to aid in their operations against our ports. However, I have little fear that they will do much by sea against us. I would we could hold our own as well on the land as we can on the water."

Ned found the meal extremely long and tedious, for he

was fretting to be off to hasten the preparations on board
the *Good Venture,* and he was delighted when at last the
burgomaster said :

"Now, my young friend, we will go down to the wharf
together."

But although somewhat deliberate, the burgomaster -
proved a valuable assistant. When he had told Ned that he
would do what he could to expedite the sailing of the ship
the lad had regarded it as a mere form of words, for he
did not see how he could in any way expedite her sailing.
As soon, however, as they had gone on board, and Ned
had told Peters that the captain had given his consent to
his sailing at once, the burgomaster said: "You can scarce
set sail before the tide turns, Master Peters, for the wind
is so light that you would make but little progress if you
did.   From what Master Martin tells me you came off so
hurriedly from Amsterdam that you had no time to get
ballast on board.   It would be very venturesome to start
for a voyage to England unless with something in your
hold.   I will give orders that you shall be furnished at
once with sand-bags, otherwise you would have to wait
your turn with the other vessels lying here; for ballast is,
as you know, a rare commodity in Holland, and we do not
like parting even with our sand hills.   In the meantime,
as you have well nigh six hours before you get under way,
I will go round among my friends and see if I cannot procure you a little cargo that may pay some of the expenses
of your voyage."

Accordingly the burgomaster proceeded at once to visit
several of the principal merchants, and, representing that it
was the clear duty of the townsfolk to do what they could for
the men who had fought so bravely against the Spaniards,
he succeeded in obtaining from them a considerable quan-

tity of freight upon good terms; and so zealously did he push the business that in a very short time drays began to arrive alongside the *Good Venture*, and a number of men were speedily at work in transferring the contents to her hold, and before evening she had taken on board a goodly amount of cargo.

Ned wrote a letter to his mother telling her what had taken place, and saying that his father would be glad for her to come over to be with him, but that he left it to her to decide whether to bring the girls over or not. He said no word of the events at Vordwyk; but merely mentioned they had learned that a spy had denounced his father to the Spaniards as having used expressions hostile to the king and the religious persecutions, and that on this account he would have been arrested, had he not at once put to sea. Peters was charged to say nothing as to what he had heard about the Plomaerts unless she pressed him with questions. He was to report briefly that they were so busy with the unloading of the ship at Amsterdam that Captain Martin had only once been ashore, and leave it to be inferred that he only landed to see the merchants to whom the cargo was consigned.

" Of course, Peters, if my mother presses you as to whether any news has been received from Vordwyk, you must tell the truth; but if it can be concealed from her it will be much the best. She will have anxiety enough concerning my father."

" I will see," Peters said, " "what can be done. Doubtless at first she will be so filled with the thought of your father's danger that she will not think much of anything else; but on the voyage she will have time to turn her thoughts in other directions, and she is well nigh sure to ask about her father and brothers. I shall be guided in my

answers by her condition. Mistress Martin is a sensible
woman, and not a girl who will fly into hysterics and rave
like a madwoman.

"It may be too, she will feel the one blow less for being
so taken up with the other; however, I will do the best I can
in the matter, Master Ned. Truly your friend the burgomaster is doing us right good service. I had looked to lose
this voyage to England, and that the ten days I should be
away would be fairly lost time; but now, although we shall
not have a full hold, the freight will be ample to pay all
expenses and to leave a good profit beside.

As soon as the tide turned the hatches were put on, the
vessel was warped out from her berth, and a few minutes
later was under sail.

Ned had been busy helping to stow away the cargo
as fast as it came on board, twice running up to see how
his father was getting on. Each time he was told by the
woman whom the burgomaster had now engaged to act as
nurse, that he was sleeping quietly. When he returned after
seeing the *Good Venture* fairly under way he found on peep-
ing quietly into the room that Captain Martin had
just woke.

"I have had a nice sleep, Ned," he said, as the lad went
up to his bedside. "I see it is already getting dark. Has
the brig sailed?"

"She has just gone out of port, father. The wind is light
and it was no use starting until tide turned; although indeed,
the tides are of no great account in these inland waters.
Still, we had to take some ballast on board as our hold was
empty, and they might meet with storms on their way home;
so they had to wait for that. But, indeed, after all, they
took in but little ballast, for the burgomaster bestirred himself so warmly in our favour that the merchants sent down

goods as fast as we conld get them on board, and short as
the time was the main-hold was well nigh half full before
we put on the hatches; so that her voyage home will not be
without a good profit after all."

"That is good news, Ned; for although as far as I am
concerned the money is of no great consequence one way or
the other, I am but part owner, and the others might well
complain at my sending the ship home empty to fetch my
wife instead of attending to their interests."

"I am sure they would not have done that, father, seeing
how well you do for them, and what good money the *Venture* earns. Why, I have heard you say she returns her value
every two years. So that they might well have gone without a fortnight's earnings without murmuring."

"I don't suppose they would have murmured, Ned, for
they are all good friends of mine, and always seem well pleased with what I do for them. Still, in matters of business it
is always well to be strict and regular; and I should have
deemed it my duty to have calculated the usual earnings
of the ship for the time she was away, and to have paid
my partners their share as if she had been trading as usual.
It is not because the ship is half mine and that I and my
partners made good profit out of her, that I have a right to
divert her from her trade for my own purposes. As you
say, my partners might be well content to let me do so; but
that is not the question, I should not be content myself.

"We should always in business work with a good conscience, being more particular about the interests of those
who trust us than of our own. Indeed, on the bare ground
of expediency it is best to do so ; for then, if misfortune
happens, trade goes bad, or your vessel is cast away, they
will make good allowance for you, knowing that you are a
loser as well as they, and that at all times you have

thought as much of them as of yourself. Lay this always to heart, lad. It is unlikely that I shall go to sea much more, and ere long you will be in command of the *Good Venture*. Always think more of the interests of those who trust you than of your own.

"They have put their money into the ship, relying upon their partner's skill and honesty and courage. Even at a loss to yourself you should show them always that this confidence is not misplaced. Do your duty and a little more, lad. Most men do their duty. It is the little more that makes the difference between one man and the other. I have tried always to do a little more, and I have found my benefit from it in the confidence and trust of my partners in the ship, and of the merchants with whom I do business. However, I am right glad that the ship is not going back empty. I shall reckon how much we should have received for the freight that was promised me at Amsterdam, then you will give me an account of what is to be paid by the merchants here. The difference I shall make up, as is only right, seeing that it is entirely from my own imprudence in expressing my opinion upon affairs particular to myself, and in no way connected with the ship, that I was forced to leave without taking in that cargo."

Ned listened in silence to his father's words, and resolved to lay to heart the lessons they conveyed. He was proud of the high standing and estimation in which his father was held by all who knew him, and he now recognized fully for the first time how he had won that estimation. It was not only that he was a good sailor, but that in all things men were assured that his honour could be implicitly relied upon, and that he placed the interest of his employers beyond his own.

After the first day or two Ned could see but little change in his father's condition; he was very weak and low, and spoke but seldom. Doubtless his bodily condition was aggravated now by the thought that must be ever present to him—that his active career was terminated. He might, indeed, be able when once completely cured to go to sea again, but he would no longer be the active sailor he had been; able to set an example of energy to his men when the winds blew high and the ship was in danger. And unless fully conscious that he was equal to discharging all the duties of his position, Captain Martin was not the man to continue to hold it.

Ned longed anxiously for the return of the *Good Venture*. He knew that his mother's presence would do much for his father, and that whatever her own sorrows might be she would cheer him. Captain Martin never expressed any impatience for her coming; but when each morning he asked Ned, the first thing, which way the wind was blowing, his son knew well enough what he was thinking of. In the meantime Ned had been making inquiries, and had arranged for the hire of a comfortable house, whose inhabitants being Catholics, had, when Enkhuizen declared for the Prince of Orange, removed to Amsterdam. For although the Prince insisted most earnestly and vigorously that religious toleration should be extended to the Catholics, and that no one should suffer for their religion, all were not so tolerant; and when the news arrived of wholesale massacres of Protestants by Alva's troops, the lower class were apt to rise in riot, and to retaliate by the destruction of the property of the Catholics in their towns.

Ned had therefore no difficulty in obtaining the use of the house, on extremely moderate terms, from the agent in whose hands its owner had placed his affairs in Enkhuizen.

The burgomaster's wife had at his request engaged two female servants, and the nurse would of course accompany her patient. The burgomaster and his wife had both protested against any move being made; but Ned, although thanking them earnestly for their hospitable offer, pointed out that it might be a long time before his father could be about, that it was good for his mother to have the occupation of seeing to the affairs of the house to divert her thoughts from the sick-bed, and, as it was by no means improbable that she would bring his sisters with her, it would be better in all respects that they should have a house of their own. The doctors having been consulted, agreed that it would be better for the wounded man to be among his own people, and that no harm would come of removing him carefully to another house.

"A change, even a slight one, is often a benefit," they agreed; "and more than counterbalances any slight risk that there may be in a patient's removal from one place to another, providing that it be gently and carefully managed."

Therefore it was arranged that as soon as the *Good Venture* was seen approaching, Captain Martin should be carried to his new abode, where everything was kept prepared for him, and that his wife should go direct to him there.

CHAPTER V.

NED'S RESOLVE.

ON the ninth morning after the departure of the brig
Ned was up as soon as daylight appeared, and made
his way to the walls. The watchman there, with whom he
had had several talks during the last two days, said:

"There is a brig, hull down, seaward, and I should say
that she is about the size of the one you are looking for.
She looks, too, as if she were heading for this port."

"I think that is she," Ned said, gazing intently at the
distant vessel. "It seems to me that I can make out that
her jib is lighter in colour than the rest of her canvas. If
that is so I have no doubt about its being the *Good Venture*, for we blew our jib away in a storm off Ostend, and
had a new one about four months ago."

"That is her then, young master," the watchman said,
shading his eyes and looking intently at the brig. "Her
jib is surely of lighter colour than the rest of her canvas."

With this confirmation Ned at once ran round to the
house he had taken, and told the servants to have fires
lighted, and everything in readiness for the reception of the
party.

"My father," he said, "will be brought here in the
course of an hour or so. My mother will arrive a little
later."

Ned then went round to the doctor, who had promised
that he would personally superintend the removing of his

patient, and would bring four careful men and a litter for
his conveyance. He said that he would be round at the
burgomaster's in half an hour. Ned then went back to his
father. Captain Martin looked round eagerly as he entered.

" Yes, father," Ned said, answering the look; "there is a
brig in sight, which is, I am pretty sure, the *Good Venture*.
She will be in port in the course of a couple of hours. I
have just been round to Doctor Harreng, and he will be
here in half an hour with the litter to take you over to the
new house."

Captain Martin gave an exclamation of deep thankful-
ness, and then lay for some time with his eyes closed, and
spoke but little until the arrival of the doctor and the men
with the litter.

" You must first of all drink this broth that has just been
sent up for you," the surgeon said, "and then take a spoonful of cordial. It will be a fatigue, you know, however well
we manage it; and you must be looking as bright and well
as you can by the time your good wife arrives, else she will
have a very bad opinion of the doctors of Enkhuizen."

Captain Martin did as he was ordered. The men then
carefully raised the mattress with him upon it, and placed
it upon the litter.

" I think we will cover you up altogether," the doctor
said, "as we go along through the streets. The morning
air is a good deal keener than the atmosphere of this room,
and you won't want to look about."

The litter was therefore completely covered with a blanket,
and was then lifted and taken carefully down the broad
staircase and through the streets. The burgomaster's wife
had herself gone on before to see that everything was comfortably prepared, and when the bed was laid down on the
bedstead and the blanket turned back Captain Martin saw

a bright room with a fire burning on the hearth, and the burgomaster's wife and nurse beside him, while Ned and the doctor were at the foot of the bed.

"You have not suffered, I hope, in the moving, Captain Martin ?" the burgomaster's wife asked.

"Not at all," he said. "I felt somewhat faint at first, but the movement has been so easy that it soon passed off. I was glad my head was covered, for I do not think that I could have stood the sight of the passing objects."

"Now you must drink another spoonful of cordial," the doctor said, "and then lie quiet. I shall not let you see your wife when she arrives if your pulse is beating too rapidly. So far you have been going on fairly, and we must not have you thrown back."

"I shall not be excited," Captain Martin replied. "Now that I know the vessel is in sight I am contented enough; but I have been fearing lest the brig might fall in with a Spaniard as she came through the islands, and there would be small mercy for any on board had she been detected and captured. Now that I know she is coming to port safely, I can wait quietly enough. Now, Ned, you can be off down to the port."

The doctor went out with Ned and charged him strictly to impress upon his mother the necessity for self-restraint and quiet when she saw her husband.

"I am not over satisfied with his state," he said, "and much will depend on this meeting. If it passes off well and he is none the worse for it to-morrow, I shall look to see him mend rapidly; but if, on the other hand, he is agitated and excited, fever may set in at once, and in that case, weak as he is, his state will be very serious."

"I understand, sir, and will impress it upon my mother; but I do not think you need fear for her. What-

ever she feels she will, I am sure, carry out your instructions."

Ned went down to the port. He found that the brig was but
a quarter of a mile away. He could make out female figures
on board, and knew that, as he had rather expected would
be the case; his mother had brought his sisters with her.
Jumping into a boat he was rowed off to the vessel, and
climbing the side was at once in his mother's arms. Already
he had answered the question that Peters had shouted before he was half-way from the shore, and had replied that
his father was going on as well as could be expected. Thus
when Ned leapt on board his mother and the girls were in
tears at the relief to the anxiety that had oppressed them
during the voyage lest they should at its end find they had
arrived too late.

"And he is really better?" were Mrs. Martin's first
words as she released Ned from her embrace.

"I don't know that he is better, mother, but he is no
worse. He is terribly weak; but the doctor tells me that
if no harm comes to him from his agitation in meeting you,
he expects to see him mend rapidly. He has been rather
fretting about your safety, and I think that the knowledge
that you are at hand has already done him good. His
voice was stronger when he spoke just before I started
than it has been for some days. Only, above all things,
the doctor says you must restrain your feelings and be
calm and quiet when you first meet him. And now, girls,
how are you both?" he asked turning to them. Not very
well, I suppose; for I know you have always shown yourselves bad sailors when you have come over with mother."

"The sea has not been very rough," Janet said; "and
except when we first got out to sea we have not been ill."

"What are you going to do about the girls?" Mrs.

Martin asked. "Of course I must go where your father is, but I cannot presume upon the kindness of strangers so far as to quarter the girls upon them."

"That is all arranged, mother. Father agreed with me that it would not be pleasant for any of you being with strangers, and I have therefore taken a house; and he has just been moved there, so you will have him all to yourself."

"That is indeed good news," Mrs. Martin said. "However kind people are, one is never so comfortable as at home. One is afraid of giving trouble, and altogether it is different. I have heard all the news, my boy. Master Peters tried his best to conceal it from me, but I was sure by his manner that there was something wrong. It was better that I should know at once," she went on, wiping her eyes. "Terrible as it all is, I have scarce time to think about it now when my mind is taken up with your father's danger. And it hardly came upon me even as a surprise, for I have long felt that some evil must have befallen them or they would have assuredly managed to send me word of themselves before now."

By this time the *Good Venture* had entered the port, and had drawn up close beside one of the wharves. As soon as the sails were lowered and the warps made fast, Peters directed three of the seamen to bring up the boxes from the cabin, and to follow him. Ned then led the way to the new house.

"I will go up first, mother, and tell them that you have come."

Mrs. Martin quietly removed her hat and cloak, followed Ned upstairs, and entered her husband's room with a calm and composed face.

"Well, my dear husband," she said almost cheerfully, "I have come to nurse you. You see when you get into trouble it is us women that you men fall back upon after all."

The doctor, who had retired into the next room when he heard that Mrs. Martin had arrived, nodded his head with a satisfied air. " She will do," he said. " I have not much fear for my patient now."

Ned, knowing that he would not be wanted upstairs for some time, went out with Peters after the baggage had been set down in the lower room.

" So you had a fine voyage of it, Peters?"

" We should have been better for a little more wind, both coming and going," the mate said; " but there was nothing much to complain of."

" You could not have been long in the river then, Peters?"

" We were six and thirty hours in port. We got in at the top of tide on Monday morning, and went down with the ebb on Tuesday evening. First, as in duty bound, I went to see our good dame and give her your letter, and answer her questions. It was a hard business that, and I would as lief have gone before the queen herself to give her an account of things as to have gone to your mother. Of course I hoisted the flag as we passed up the river. I knew that some of them were sure to be on watch at Rotherhithe, and that they would run in and tell her that the *Good Venture* was in port again. I had rather hoped that our coming back so soon might lead her to think that something was wrong, for she would have known that we could scarce have gone to Amsterdam and discharged, loaded up again, and then back here, especially as the wind had been light ever since she sailed. And sure enough the thought had struck her; for when I caught sight of the garden-gate one of your sisters was there on the look-out, and directly she saw me she ran away in. I hurried on as fast as I could go then, for I knew that Mistress Martin would be sorely frightened when she heard that it was neither your father nor you. As I got there your mother was standing at the door. She was just as white as death. 'Cheer up, mistress,' I said as cheery as I could speak. 'I have bad news for you, but it might have been a deal worse. The captain's got a hurt, and Master Ned is stopping to nurse him.'

"She looked at me as if she would read me through. 'That's the truth as I am a Christian man, mistress,' I said. 'It has been a bad business, but it might have been a deal worse. The doctor said that he was doing well.' Then your mother gave a deep sigh, and I thought for a moment she was going to faint, and ran forward to catch her; but she seemed to make an effort and straighten herself up, just as I have seen the brig do when a heavy sea has flooded her decks and swept all before it.

"'Thanks be to the good God that he is not taken from me,' she said. 'Now I can bear anything. Now, Peters, tell me all about it.'

"'I ain't good at telling a story, Mistress Martin,' I said; 'but here is Master Ned's letter. When you have read that maybe I can answer questions as to matters of which he may not have written. I will stand off and on in the garden, ma'am, and then you can read it comfortable-like indoors, and hail me when you have got to the bottom of it.' It was not many minutes before one of your sisters called me in. They had all been crying, and I felt more uncomfortable than I did when those Spanish rascals gave us a broadside as I went in, for I was afraid she would so rake me with questions that she would get out of me that other sad business; and it could hardly be expected that even the stoutest ship should weather two such storms, one after the other.

" ' I don't understand it all, Master Peters,' she said, ' for my son gives no good reason why the Spaniards should thus have attacked an English ship; but we can talk of that afterwards. All that matters at present is, that my husband has been wounded and has lost his leg, and lies in some danger; for although Ned clearly makes the best of it, no man can suffer a hurt like that without great risk of life. He wishes me to go over at once. As to the girls, he says I can take them with me or leave them with a friend here. But they wish, as is natural, greatly to go; and it were better for all reasons that they did so. Were they left here they would be in anxiety about their father's state, and as it may be long before he can be moved I should not like to leave them in other charge than my own. When will you be ready to sail again ?'

" ' I shall be ready by to-morrow evening's tide, Mistress Martin," I said. 'I have cargo on board that I must discharge, and must have carpenters and sailmakers on board to repair some of the damages we suffered in the action. I do not think I can possibly be ready to drop down the river before high water to-morrow, which will be about six o'clock. I will send a boat to the stairs here at half-past five to take you and your trunks on board.'

" ' We shall be ready,' she said. 'As Ned says that my husband is well cared-for in the house of the burgomaster, and has every comfort and attention, there is nothing I need take over for him.' I said that I was sure he had all he could require, and that she need take no trouble on that score; and then said that with her permission I would go straight back on board again, seeing there was much to do, and that it all came on my shoulders just at present.

"I had left the bosun in charge, and told him to get the hatches off and begin to get up the cargo as soon as he had

stowed the sails and made all tidy; for I had not waited
for that, but had rowed ashore as soon as the anchor was
dropped. So without going back to the brig I crossed the
river and landed by the steps at the bridge, and took the
letters to the merchants for whom I had goods, and prayed
them to send off boats immediately, as it was urgent for
me to discharge as soon as possible; then I went to the
merchants whose names you had given me, and who ship
goods with us regularly, to tell them that the *Venture* was
in port but would sail again to-morrow evening, and would
take what cargo they could get on board for Enkhuizen or
any of the seaward ports, but not for Amsterdam or other
places still in the hands of the Spaniards.

"Then I went to the lord mayor and swore an information before him to lay before the queen and the council
that the Spaniards had wantonly, and without offence given,
attacked the *Good Venture* and inflicted much damage
upon her, and badly wounded her captain; and would have
sunk her had we not stoutly defended ourselves and beat
them off. I was glad when all that was over, Master Ned;
for, as you know, I know nought about writing. My business is to sail the ship under your father's orders; but as
to talking with merchants who press you with questions,
and seem to think that you have nought to do but to stand
and gossip, this is not in my way, and I wished sorely that
you had been with me, and could have taken all this business into your hands.

"Then I went down to the wharves, and soon got some
carpenters at work to mend the bulwarks and put some
fresh planks on the deck where the shot had ploughed it
up. Luckily enough I heard of a man who had some sails
that he had bought from the owners of a ship which was
cast away down near the mouth of the river. They were a

little large for the *Venture;* but I made a bargain with him in your father's name, and got them on board and set half a dozen sailmakers to work upon them, and they were ready by the next afternoon. The others will do again when they have got some new cloths in, and a few patches; but if we had gone out with a dozen holes in them the first Spaniard who saw us, and who had heard of our fight with the *Don Pedro,* would have known us at once.

"I was thankful, I can tell you, when I got on board again. Just as I did so some lighters came out, and we were hard at work till dusk getting out the cargo. The next morning at daylight fresh cargo began to come out to us, and things went on well, and would have gone better had not people come on board pestering me with questions about our fight with the Spaniards. And just at noon two of the queen's officers came down and must needs have the whole story from beginning to end ; and they had brought a clerk with them to write it down from my lips. They had said we had done right gallantly, and that no doubt I should be wanted next day at the royal council to answer other questions touching the affair. You may be sure I said no word about the fact than in six hours we should be dropping down the river; for like enough if I had they would have ordered me not to go, and as I should have gone whether they had or not—seeing that Captain Martin was looking for his wife, and that the mistress was anxious to be off—it might have led to trouble when I got back again.

"By the afternoon we had got some thirty tons of goods on board, and although that is but a third of what she would carry, I was well content that we had done so much. After the new sails had come on board I had put a gang to work to bend them, and had all ready and the anchor up just as the tide turned. We had not dropped down many hundred yards when the boat with Mistress Martin and your sisters came alongside ; and thankful I was when it came on dark and we were slipping down the river with a light south-westerly wind, for I had been on thorns all the afternoon lest some messenger might arrive from the council with orders for me to attend there. I did not speak much to your mother that evening, for it needs all a man's attention to work down the river at night.

" The next morning I had my breakfast brought up on deck instead of going down, for, as you may guess, I did not want to have your mother questioning me ; but presently your sister came up with a message to me that Mistress Martin would be glad to have a quarter of an hour's conversation with me as soon as duty would permit me to leave deck. So after a while I braced myself up and went below, but I tell you that I would rather have gone into action again with the *Don Pedro*. She began at once, without parley or courtesies, by firing a broadside right into me.

" ' I don't think, Master Peters, that you have told me yet all there is to be told.'

" That took me between wind and water, you see. However, I made a shift to bear up.

" ' Well, Mistress Martin,' says I, ' I don't say as I have given you all particulars. I don't know as I mentioned to you as Joe Wiggins was struck down by a splinter from the long-boat and was dazed for full two hours, but he came round again all right, and was fit for duty next day.'

" Mrs. Martin heard me quietly, and then she said :

" ' That will not do, John Peters ; you know well what I mean. You need not fear to tell me the news ; I have long been fearing it. My husband is not one to talk loosely

in the streets and to bring upon himself the anger of
the Spaniards. He must have had good cause before he said
words that spoken there would place his life in peril.
What has happened at Vordwyk ?

"Well, Master Ned, I stood there as one struck stupid.
What was there to say ? I am a truthful man, but I would
have told a lie if I had thought it would have been any
good. But there she was, looking quietly at me, and I
knew as she would see in a moment whether I was speaking
truth or not. She waited quiet ever so long, and at last I
said :

"'The matter is in this wise, Mistress Martin. My
orders was I was to hold my tongue about all business
not touching the captain or the affairs of this ship. When
you sees the captain it's for you to ask him questions, and
for him to answer if he sees right and good to do so.'

"She put her hand over her face and sat quiet for some
time, and when she looked up again her eyes were full of
tears and her cheeks wet ; then she said in a low tone:

"'All, Peters,—are they all gone?'

"Well, Master Ned, I was swabbing my own eyes ; for it
ain't in a man's nature to see a woman suffering like that,
and so quiet and brave, without feeling somehow as if all
the manliness had gone out of him. I could not say nothing. What could I say, knowing what the truth was?
Then she burst out a-crying and a-sobbing, and I steals
off without a word, and goes on deck and sets the men a-
hauling at the sheets and trimming the sails, till I know
there was not one of them but cussed me in his heart and
wished that the captain was back again.

"Mistress Martin did not say no word about it afterwards. She came up on deck a few times, and asked me
more about the captain, and how he looked, and what he

was doing when he got his wound. And of course I told her all about it, full and particular, and how he had made every one else lie down, and stood there at the tiller as we went under the stern of the Spaniard, and that none of us knew he was hit until it was all over; and how we had peppered them with our four carronades, and all about it. But mostly she stopped down below till we hauled our wind and headed up the Zuider-Zee towards Enkhuizen."

"Well, now it is all over, Peters," Ned said, "there is no doubt that it is better she should have heard the news from you instead of my father having to tell her."

"I don't deny that that may be so, Master Ned, now that it is all over and done; but never again will John Peters undertake a job where he is got to keep his mouth shut when a woman wants to get something out of him.   Lor' bless you, lad, they just see right through you ; and you feel that, twist and turn as you will, they will get it out of you sooner or later.   There, I started with my mind quite made up that orders was to be obeyed, and that your mother was to be kept in the dark about it till she got here ; and I had considered with myself that in such a case as this it would be no great weight upon my conscience if I had to make up some kind of a yarn that would satisfy her ; and yet in three minutes after she got me into that cabin she was at the bottom of it all."

"You see, she has been already very uneasy at not hearing for so long from her father and brothers, Peters ; and that and the fact that my father had spoken openly against the Spanish authorities set her upon the track, and enabled her to put the questions straightforwardly to you."

"I suppose that was it, sir. And now, has the captain said anything about what is going to be done with the ship till he gets well?"

"Nothing whatever, Peters. He has spoken very little upon any subject. I know he has been extremely anxious for my mother to arrive, though he has said but little about it. I fancy that for the last few days he has not thought that he should recover. But the doctor told me I must not be uneasy upon that ground, for that he was now extremely weak, and men, even the bravest and most resolute when in health, are apt to take a gloomy view when utterly weak and prostrate. His opinion was that my mother's coming would probably cheer him up and enable him to rally.

"I think, too, that he has been dreading having to tell her the terrible news about her father and brothers; and now he knows that she is aware of that it will be a load off his mind. Besides, I know that for his sake she will be cheerful and bright, and with her and the girls with him, he will feel as if at home. The doctor told me that the mind has a great influence over the body, and that a man with cheerful surroundings had five chances to one as against one amongst strangers, and with no one to brighten him up. I have no doubt that as soon as he gets a little stronger he will arrange what is to be done with the brig, but I am sure it will be a long time before he can take the command again himself."

" Ay, I fear it will be," Peters agreed. "It is a pity you are not four or five years older, Master Ned. I do not say that I couldn't bring the ship into any port in Holland; for, having been sailing backwards and forwards here, man and boy, for over thirty years, I could do so pretty nigh blindfold. But what is the good of bringing a ship to a port if you have not got the head to see about getting a cargo for her, and cannot read the bills of lading, or as much as sign your name to a custom's list.

" No, Master Ned, I am not fit for a captain, that is

quite certain. But though I would not mind serving under another till your father is fit to take charge again, I could not work on board the *Venture* under another for good. I have got a little money saved up, and would rather buy a share in a small coaster and be my own master there. After serving under your father for nigh twenty years, I know I should not get on with another skipper nohow."

"Well, Peters, it is no use talking it over now, because I have no idea what my father's decision will be. I hope above all things that he will be able to take command again, but I have great doubts in my mind whether he will ever do so. If he had lost the leg below the knee it would not so much have mattered; but as it is, with the whole leg stiff, he would have great difficulty in getting about, especially if the ship was rolling in a heavy sea."

John Peters shook his head gravely, for this was the very thing he had turned in his mind over and over again during the voyage to and from England.

"Your cargo is not all for this place, I suppose, Peters?"

"No, sir. Only two or three tons which are down in the forehold together are for Enkhuizen, the rest are for Leyden and the Hague. I told the merchants that if they put their goods on board I must sail past the ports and make straight on to Enkhuizen; for that first of all I must bring Mistress Martin to the captain, but that I would go round and discharge their goods as soon as I had brought her here. It was only on these terms I agreed to take the cargo."

"That will do very well, Peters. I will go on board with you at once, and see to whom your goods are consigned here, and warn them to receive them at once. You will get them on shore by to-night, and then to-morrow I will sail with you to Leyden and the Hague, and aid you in getting your cargo into the right hands there. Now that my mother and the girls are here my father will be able to spare me. We can be back here again in four or five days, and by that time I hope he will be so far recovered as to be able to think matters over, and come to some decision as to the future management of the brig. Of course if he wishes me to stay on board her I shall obey his orders, whether you or another are the captain."

"Why, of course, you will remain on board, Master Ned. What else should you do ? "

"Well, Peters, my own mind is set upon joining the Prince of Orange, and fighting against the Spaniards. Before I sailed from home I told my sisters that was what I was longing to do, for I could scarce sleep for thinking of all the cruelties and massacres that they carried out upon the people of the Netherlands, who are, by my mother's side, my kinsfolk. Since then I have scarce thought of aught else. They have murdered my grandfather and uncles and one of my aunts ; they have shot away my father's leg, and would have taken his life had he not escaped out of their hands ; so that what was before a longing is now a fixed idea, and if my father will but give me permission, assuredly I will carry it out.

"There are many English volunteers who have already crossed the sea to fight against these murderers, although unconnected by ties of blood as I am, and who have been brought here to fight solely from pity and horror, and because, as all know, Spain is the enemy of England as well as of the Netherlands, and would put down our freedom and abolish our religion as she has done here. I know that my wishes, in this as in all other matters, must give way to those of my father. Still I hope he may be moved to consent to them."

Ned thought it better to allow his father and mother to remain quietly together for some time, and did not therefore

return to the house until twelve o'clock, when he knew that
dinner would be prepared; for his mother was so methodical
in her ways that everything would go on just as at home
directly she took charge of the affairs of the house. He
went up for a few minutes before dinner, and was struck
with the change in the expression of his father's face. There
was a peaceful and contented look in his eyes, and it almost
seemed to Ned that his face was less hollow and drawn than
before. Ned told him that it would be necessary for the
brig to go round to Leyden and the Hague, and that Peters
had proposed that he should go with him to see the merchants, and arrange the business part of the affair.

"That will do very well," Captain Martin said. "You
are young, Ned, to begin having dealings with the Dutch
merchants, but when you tell them how it comes that I am
not able to call upon them myself, they will doubtless excuse your youth."

"Do you wish us to take any cargo there, father, if we
can get any?"

Captain Martin did not answer for some little time, then
he said:

"No, Ned, I think you had best return here in the ship.
By that time I shall, I hope, be capable of thinking matters
over, and deciding upon my arrangements for the future.
When is Peters thinking of sailing?"

"By to-morrow morning's tide, sir. He said that he could
be ready perhaps by this evening; but that unless you wished
it otherwise he would not start till to-morrow's tide, as he
will thereby avoid going out between the islands at night.

"That will be the best way, Ned. If the winds are fair
he will be at the Hague before nightfall."

The day after his return Ned took an opportunity of
speaking to his mother as to his wish to take service with the

Prince of Orange, and to aid in the efforts that the people of the Netherlands were making to free themselves from their persecutors. His mother, as he feared would be the case, expressed a strong opposition to his plan.

"You are altogether too young, Ned, even if it were a matter that concerned you?"

"It does concern me, mother. Are you not Dutch? And though I was born in England and a subject of the queen, it is natural I should feel warmly in the matter; besides we know that many English are already coming over here to help. Have not the Spanish killed my relations, and unless they are driven back they will altogether exterminate the Protestants of the Netherlands? Have they not already been doomed to death regardless of age and sex by Philip's proclamation? and do not the Spaniards whenever they capture a town slay well nigh all within it?"

"That is all true enough," his mother agreed; "but proves in no way that you are a fit age to meddle in the affair."

"I am sixteen, mother; and a boy of sixteen who has been years at sea is as strong as one of eighteen brought up on the land. You have told me yourself that I look two or three years older than I am, and methinks I have strength to handle pike and axe."

"That may be perfectly true," said Mrs. Martin, "but even supposing all other things were fitting, how could we spare you now when your father will be months before he can follow his trade on the sea again, even if he is ever able to do so?"

"That is the thing, mother, that weighs with me. I know not what my father's wishes may be in that respect, and of course if he holds that I can be of use to him I must give up my plan; but I want you to at any rate to mention it to him. And I pray you not to add your objections, but to let him decide on the matter according to his will."

"There will be no occasion for me to add objections, Ned. I do not think your father will listen to such a mad scheme for a moment."

It was not until three or four days later that Mrs. Martin, seeing that her husband was stronger and better, and was taking an interest in what passed in the house, fulfilled her promise to Ned by telling his father of his wishes.

"You must not be angry with him," she said when she had finished; "for he spoke beautifully, and expressed himself as perfectly willing to yield his wishes to yours in the matter. I told him, of course, that it was a mad-brained scheme, and not to be thought of. Still, as he was urgent I should lay it before you, I promised to do so."

Captain Martin did not, as his wife expected, instantly declare that such a plan was not to be thought of even for a moment, but lay for some time apparently turning it over in his mind.

"I know not quite what to say," he said at length.

"Not know what to say?" his wife repeated in surprise. "Why, husband, you surely cannot for a moment think of allowing Ned to embark in so wild a business."

"There are many English volunteers coming over; some of them not much older, and not so fit in bodily strength for the work as Ned. He has, too, the advantage of speaking the language, and can pass anywhere as a native. You are surprised, Sophie, at my thinking of this for a moment."

"But what would you do without him?" she exclaimed in astonishment.

"That is what I have been thinking as I lay here. I have been troubled what to do with Ned. He is too young yet to entrust with all the business of the ship, and the

merchants here and at home would hesitate in doing business with a lad.   Moreover, he is too young to be first
mate on board the brig.   Peters is a worthy man and a
good sailor, but he can neither read nor write and knows
nought of business ; and, therefore, until I am able, if I
ever shall be, to return to the *Good Venture,* I must have
a good seaman as first mate, and a supercargo to manage
the business affairs of the ship.   Were Ned four years older
he could be at once first mate, and supercargo.   There,
you see your objection that I need him falls to the ground.
As to other reasons I will think them over, and speak to
you another time."

CHAPTER VI.

THE PRINCE OF ORANGE.

MISTRESS MARTIN was much troubled in her mind by what seemed to her the unaccountable favour with which her husband had received Ned's proposal. She did not, however, allow any trace of this feeling to escape her, nor did she mention to Ned that she had as yet spoken as to his wishes to his father. The next day Captain Martin himself renewed the subject.

"I told you yesterday, Sophie, why in my opinion Ned would at present be of little aid to me in the matter of the brig, and may even go further in that respect and say that I think for a time it will be just as well that he were not on board. Having no established position there would be no special duties for him to perfom. Now, I have made a point of telling him all about the consignments and the rates of freight, and have encouraged him always to express his opinion freely on these matters in order that his intelligence might thereby be quickened; but if he so expressed himself to the supercargo the latter might well take offence and difficulties arise, therefore before you spoke to me I had quite resolved that it would be best he should sail no more in the *Good Venture* until old enough to come in and take the place of second mate and supercargo, but that I would place him with some captain of my acquaintance, under whom he would continue to learn his duty for the next three or four years."

" That is a good reason, doubtless, husband, why Ned should not sail in the *Venture*, but surely no reason at all why he should carry out this mad fancy of his."

" No reason, I grant you, wife; but it simply shows that it happens at this moment we can well spare him. As to the main question, it is a weighty one. Other young Englishmen have come out to fight for the Netherlands with far less cause than he has to mix themselves up in its affairs. Moreover, and this principally, it is borne strongly upon my mind that it may be that this boy of ours is called upon to do good service to Holland. It seems to me wife," he went on, in answer to the look of astonishment upon his wife's face, " that the hand of Providence is in this matter.

" I have always felt with you a hatred of the Spaniards and a deep horror at the cruelties they are perpetrating upon this unhappy people, and have thought that did the queen give the order for war against them I would gladly adventure my life and ship in such an enterprise; further than that I have not gone.   But upon that day when I heard the news of your father and brothers' murder I took a solemn oath to heaven of vengeance against their slayers, and resolved that on my return to England I would buy out my partners in the *Good Venture*, and with her join the beggars of the sea and wage war to the death against the Spaniards. It has been willed otherwise, wife. Within twenty-four hours of my taking that oath I was struck down and my fighting powers were gone forever.

" My oath was not accepted. I was not to be an instrument of God's vengeance upon these murderers. Now, our son, without word or consultation with me, feels called upon to take up the work I cannot perform. It happens strangely that he can for the next two or three years be well spared from his life at sea. That the boy will do great feats I do not suppose; but he is cool and courageous, for I marked his demeanor under fire the other day. And it may be that though he may do no great things in fighting he may be the means in saving some woman, some child, from the fury of the Spaniards. If he saved but one, the next three years of his life will not have been misspent."

" But he may fall—he may be killed by the Spaniards !" Mistress Martin said in great agitation.

" If it be the will of God, wife, not otherwise. He is exposed to danger every time he goes to sea. More than once since he first came on board, the *Venture* has been in dire peril; who can say that her next voyage may not be her last. However, I decide nothing now; to-morrow I will speak to the boy myself and gather from his words whether this is a mere passing fancy, natural enough to his age and to the times, or a deep longing to venture his life in the cause of a persecuted people whose blood runs in his veins, and who have a faith which is his own and ours.

Mrs. Martin said no more; her husband's will had, since she married, been in all matters of importance law to her, and was more so than ever now that he lay weak and helpless. His words and manner too had much impressed her. Her whole sympathies were passionately with her countrymen, and the heavy losses she had so recently sustained had added vastly to her hatred of the Spaniards. The suggestion, too, of her husband that though Ned might do no great deeds as a soldier he might be the means of saving some woman or child's life, appealed to her womanly feelings.

She had girls of her own, and the thought that one of like age might possibly be saved from the horrors of the sack of a city by Ned's assistance appealed to her with great force. She went about the house for the rest of the day subdued and quiet. Ned was puzzled at her demeanour, and had he not seen for himself that his father was progressing satisfactorily he would have thought that some relapse had taken place, some unfavourable symptom appeared. But this was clearly not the reason, and he could only fancy that now his mother's anxiety as to his father's state was in some degree abating, she was beginning to feel the loss of her father and brothers all the more.

That the request she had promised to make in his name to his father had anything to do with the matter did not enter his mind. Indeed, he had begun to regret that he had made it. Not that his intense longing to take service against the Spaniards was in any way abated, but he felt it was selfish, now that he might for the first time be of real use to his parents, for him thus to propose to embark in adventures on his own account. He had asked his mother to put the matter before his father, but he had scarce even a hope the latter would for a moment listen to the proposal. The next morning after breakfast, as he was about to start for a stroll to the wharf to have a talk with Peters, his mother said to him quietly: "Put aside your cap, Ned, your father wishes to speak to you."

She spoke so gravely that Ned ascended the stairs in some pertubation of spirit. Doubtless she had spoken to his father, and the latter was about to rate him severely for his folly in proposing to desert his duty, and to embark in so wild an adventure as that he had proposed. He was in no way reassured by the grave tone in which his father said:

"Place that chair by my bedside, Ned, and sit down; my voice is not strong and it fatigues me to speak loud. And now," he went on, when Ned with a shamefaced expression had seated himself by the bedside, "this desire that your mother tells me of to fight against the Spaniards for a time in the service of the Prince of Orange, how did it first come to you?"

"Ever since I heard the terrible story of the persecutions here," Ned replied. "I said to myself than when I came to be a man I would take revenge for these horrible murders. Since then the more I have heard of the persecutions that the people here have suffered in the cause of their religion, the more I have longed to be able to give them such aid as I could. I have spoken of it over and over again to my sisters; but I do not think that I should ever have ventured to put my desire into words, had it not been for the terrible news we learnt at Vordwyk. Now, however, that they have killed my grandfather and uncles and have wounded you, I long more than ever to join the patriots here; and of course the knowledge that many young Englishmen were coming out to Brill and Flushing as volunteers added to my desire. I said to myself if they who are English are ready to give their lives in the cause of the Hollanders, why should not I, who speak their language and am of their blood?"

"You have no desire to do great deeds or to distinguish yourself?" Captain Martin asked.

"No, father; I have never so much as thought of that. I could not imagine that I, as a boy, could be of any great service. I thought I might, perhaps, being so young, be able to be of use in passing among the Spaniards and carrying messages where a man could not get through. I thought sometimes I might perhaps carry a warning in time to enable women to escape with their children from a town that was about to be beleaguered, and I hoped that if I did stand in the ranks to face the Spaniards I should not disgrace my nation and blood. I know, father, that, it was presumptuous for me to think that I could be of any real use; and if you are against it I will, of course, as I told my mother, submit myself cheerfully to your wishes."

"I am glad to see, Ned, that in this matter you are actuated by right motives, and not moved by any boyish idea of adventure or of doing feats of valour. This is no ordinary war, my boy. There is none of the chivalry of past times in the struggle here. It is one of life and death—grim, earnest, and determined. On one side is Philip with the hosts of Spain, the greatest power in Europe, determined to crush out the life of these poor provinces, to stamp out the religion of the country, to leave not one man, woman, or child alive who refuses to attend mass and to bow the knee before the Papist images ; on the other side you have a poor people tenanting a land snatched from the sea, and held by constant and enduring labour, equally determined that they will not abjure their religion, that they will not permit the Inquisition to be established among them, and ready to give lives and homes and all in the cause of religious liberty. They have no thought of throwing off their allegiance to Spain, if Spain will but be tolerant. The Prince of Orange issues his orders and proclamations as the stadtholder and lieutenant of the king, and declares that he is warring for Philip, and designs only to repel those who, by their persecution and cruelty, are dishonouring the royal cause.

"This cannot go on for ever, and in time the Netherlands will be driven to entreat some other foreign monarch to take them under his protection. In this war there is no talk of glory. Men are fighting for their religion, their homes, their wives and families. They know that the Spaniards show neither quarter nor mercy, and that it is scarce more than a question between death by the sword and death by torture and hanging. There is no mercy for prisoners. The town that yields on good conditions is sacked and destroyed as is one taken by storm, for in no case have the Spaniards observed the conditions they have made, deeming oaths taken to heretics to be in no way binding on their consciences.

"Thus, Ned, those who embark upon this war engage in a struggle in which there is no honour nor glory, nor fame nor reward to be won, but one in which almost certain death stares them in the face, and which, so far as I can see, can end only in the annihilation of the people of this country, or in the expulsion of the Spaniards. I do not say that there is no glory to be gained ; but it is not personal glory. In itself, no cause was ever more glorious than that of men who struggle, not to conquer territory, not to gather spoil, not to gratify ambition, but for freedom, for religion, for hearth and home, and to revenge the countless atrocities inflicted upon them by their oppressors. After what I have said, do you still wish to embark upon this struggle ?"

"I do wish it, father," Ned said firmly. "I desire it above all things, if you and my mother can spare me."

Captain Martin then repeated to Ned the reasons that he had given his wife for consenting to his carrying out his wishes : the fact that there was no place for him at present on board the *Good Venture*, the oath of vengeance upon the Spaniards that he had taken, and his impression that although he himself could not carry out that oath, its weight had been transferred to his son, whose desire to take up the work he had intended to carry out, just at this moment, seemed to him to be a special design of Providence.

"Now Ned," he concluded, "you understand the reasons that sway me in giving my consent to your desire to do what you can for the cause of religion and liberty. I do not propose that you should at present actually take up arms that I question if you are strong enough to wield. I will pray the burgomaster to give you letters of introduction to the Prince, saying you are a young Englishman ready and desirous of doing all that lies in your power for the cause ; that you speak the language as a native, and will be ready to carry his messages wheresoever he may require them to be sent ; that you can be relied upon to be absolutely faithful, and have entered the cause in no light spirit or desire for personal credit or honour, but as one who has suffered great wrong in the loss of near relatives at the hands of the Spaniards, and is wishful only of giving such services as he can to the cause.

" It may be that coming with such recommendation the Prince will see some way in which he can turn your services to account. And now leave me, my boy. I am wearied with all this talking ; and although I deem that it is not my duty to withstand your wishes, it is no slight trial to see my only son embark in so terrible and perilous an adventure as this. But the cause I regard as a sacred one, and it seems to me that I have no right to keep you from entering upon it, as your mind lies that way."

Ned left the room greatly impressed with his father's words. He was glad indeed that the permission he had asked for had been granted, and that he was free to devote himself to the cause so dear to most Englishmen, and doubly so to him from his relations with the country. Sailing backwards and forwards to the various ports in the Netherlands, and able to hold intercourse with all he met, he had for years been listening to tales of atrocity and horror, until he had come to regard the Spaniards as human monsters, and to long with all his heart and strength to be able to join the oppressed people against their tyrants.

Now he had got permission to do so. But he felt more than he had done before the serious nature of the step which he was taking ; and although he did not for a moment regret the choice he had made, he was conscious of its importance and of the solemn nature of the duties he took upon himself in thus engaging in the struggle between the Netherlands and Spain. He passed the room where his mother was sitting, went over and kissed her, and then taking his cap passed out into the street and mounted the ramparts, where he could think undisturbed. His father's words had not shaken his determination, although they had depressed his enthusiasm; but as he paced up and down, with the fresh air from the sea blowing upon his cheek, the feeling of youth and strength soon sent the blood dancing through his veins again. His cheeks flushed, and his eyes brightened.

"There is honour and glory in the struggle," he said. "Did not the people, old and young, pour out to the Crusades to wrest Jerusalem from the hands of the infidels? This is a more glorious task. It is to save God's followers from destruction; to succour the oppressed; to fight for women and children as well as for men. It is a holier and nobler object than that for which the Crusaders fought. They died in hundreds of thousands by heat, by famine, thirst, and the swords of the enemy. Few of those who fought ever returned home to reap glory for their deeds ; but there was honour for those who fell. And in the same spirit in which even women and children left their homes, and went in crowds to die for the Holy Sepulchre, so will I venture my life for religion and freedom here."

An hour later he returned home ; he could see that his mother had been crying.

"Mother," he said, "I trust you will not grieve over

this. I have been thinking how the women of the early days sent their husbands and sons and lovers to fight for the Holy Sepulchre. I think that this cause is an even greater and more noble one ; and feel sure that though you may be anxious, you will not grudge me to do my best for our religion and country people."

"Truly I think it is a holy cause, my boy ; and after what your father has said, I would not if I could say nay. I can only pray that heaven will bless and keep you, and one day restore you to me. But you will not be always fighting, Ned. There is no saying how long the struggle may last ; and if I let you go, it is with the promise that at one-and-twenty at the latest you will return to us, and take your place again as your father's right hand and mine."

"I promise you, mother, that then, or if at any time before that you write and say to me come home, I will come."

"I am content with that," his mother said.

That afternoon Ned told Peters what had been decided, and the following morning the latter had a long talk with Captain Martin, who directed him to apply to the other owners of the ship to appoint him an able first mate, and also to choose one of their clerks in whom they had confidence to sail in the vessel as supercargo.

"The doctors tell me, Peters, that in two or three months I may be able to return home and to get about on crutches; but they advise me that it will be at least another four months before I can strap on a wooden leg and trust my weight to it. When I can do that, I shall see how I can get about. You heard from Ned last night that he is going to enter as a sort of volunteer under the Prince of Orange?"

"Yes, he told me, Captain Martin. He is a lad of

spirit; and if I were fifteen years younger I would go with him."

"He is young for such work yet," Captain Martin said doubtfully.

"He is a strong youth, Captain Martin, and can do a man's work. His training at sea has made him steady and cool; and I warrant me, if he gets into danger, he will get out again if there is a chance. I only hope, Captain Martin, that the brush we have had with the Spaniards will not be our last, and that we too may be in the way of striking a blow at the Spaniards."

"I hope that we may, Peters," Captain Martin said earnestly. "My mind is as much bent upon it as is Ned's; and I will tell you what must at present be known only to yourself, that I have made up mind that if I recover, and can take command of the *Good Venture* again, I will buy up the other shares, so that I can do what I like with her without accounting to any man. I need not do so much on board as I used to do, but will get you a good second mate, and will myself only direct. Then we will, as at present, trade between London and the Netherlands ; but if, as is likely enough, the Spaniards and Hollanders come to blows at sea, or the prince needs ships to carry troops to beleaguered towns, then for a time we will quit trading and will join with the *Good Venture*, and strike a blow at sea."

"That is good hearing, Captain Martin," Peters said, rubbing his hands. "I warrant me you will not find one of the crew backward at that work, and for my part I should like nothing better than to tackle a Spaniard who does not carry more than two or three times our own strength. The last fellow was a good deal too big for us, but I believe if we had stuck to him we should have beaten him in the end, big as he was."

"Perhaps we might, Peters; but the ship was not mine to risk then, and we had cargo on board. If, in the future, we meet a Spaniard when the ship is mine to venture, and our hold is clear, the *Good Venture* shall not show him her stern I warrant you, unless he be big enough to eat us."

On the following day the *Good Venture* set sail for England, and the burgomaster having received a message from Captain Martin, praying him to call upon him, paid him a visit. Captain Martin unfolded his son's plans to him, and prayed him to furnish him with a letter to the prince recommending him as one who might be trusted, and who was willing to risk his life upon any enterprise with which he might intrust him. This the burgomaster at once consented to do.

"Younger lads than he," he said, "have fought stoutly on the walls of some of our towns against the Spaniards; and since such is his wish, I doubt not he will be able to do good service. All Holland has heard how your ship beat off the *Don Pedro;* and the fact that the lad is your son, and took part in the fight, will at once commend him to the prince. All Englishmen are gladly received; not only because they come to fight as volunteers on our side, but as a pledge that the heart of England is with us, and that sooner or later she will join us in our struggle against Spain. And doubtless, as you say, the fact that the lad is by his mother's side one of us, and that he can converse in both our language and yours with equal ease, is greatly in his favour. To-morrow I will furnish him with letters to the prince, and also to two or three gentlemen of my acquaintances, who are in the prince's councils."

When the burgomaster had left, Captain Martin called Ned in.

"Now, you are going as a volunteer. Ned, and for a time,

at any rate, there must be no question of pay; you are giving your services and not selling them. In the first place you must procure proper attire, in which to present yourself to the prince; you must also purchase a helmet, breast and back pieces, with sword and pistols. As for money, I shall give you a purse with sufficient for your present needs, and a letter which you can present to any of the merchants in the seaports with whom we have trade, authorizing you to draw upon me, and praying them to honour your drafts. Do not stint yourself of money, and do not be extravagant. Your needs will be small, and when serving in a garrison or in the field you will, of course, draw rations like others. I need not give you a list of the merchants in the various towns, since you already know them, and have been with me at many of their places of business.

"In regard to your actions, I say to you do not court danger, but do not avoid it. The cause is a good one, and you are risking your life for it; but remember also that you are an only son, and there are none to fill your place if you fall. Therefore be not rash; keep always cool in danger, and if there is a prospect of escape seize it promptly. Remember that your death can in no way benefit Holland, while your life may do so; therefore do not from any mistaken sense of heroism throw away your life in vain defence, when all hope of success is over, but rather seek some means of escape by which, when all is lost, you can manage to avoid the vengeance of the Spaniards. I fear that there will be many defeats before success can be obtained, for there is no union among the various states or cities.

"Holland and Zeeland alone seem in earnest in the cause, though Friesland and Guelderland will perhaps join heartily; but these provinces alone are really Protestant,

in the other the Catholics predominate, and I fear they
will never join heartily in resistance to Spain. How this
narrow strip of land by the sea is to resist all the power of
Spain I cannot see; but I believe in the people and in
their spirit, and am convinced that sooner than fall again
into the grasp of the Inquisition they will open the sluices
and let the sea in over the country they have so hardly
won from it, and will embark on board ship and seek in
some other country that liberty to worship God in their
own way that is denied them here."

It was not necessary to purchase many articles of clothing,
for the dress of the people of Holland differed little from
that of the English. Ned bought a thick buff jerkin to
wear under his armour, and had little difficulty in buying
steel cap,'breast and back piece, sword and pistols; for the
people of Holland had not as yet begun to arm generally,
and many of the walls were defended by burghers in their
citizen dress, against the mail-clad pikemen of Spain.

Three days later Ned took a tearful farewell of his family,
and set sail in a small vessel bound for Rotterdam, where
the Prince of Orange at present was. The voyage was
made without adventure, and upon landing Ned at once
made his way to the house occupied by the prince. There
were no guards at the gate, or any sign of martial pomp.
The door stood open, and when Ned entered a page accosted him and asked him his business.

"I have letters for the prince," he said, "which I pray
you to hand to him when he is at leisure."

"In that case you would have to wait long," the page replied, "for the prince is at work from early morning until
late at night. However, he is always open of access to
those who desire to see him, therefore if you will give me
the name of the writer of the letter you bear I will inform

him, and you can then deliver it yourself." A minute later Ned was shown into the presence of the man who was undoubtedly the foremost of his age.

Born of a distinguished family, William of Orange had been brought up by a pious mother, and at the age of twelve had become a page in the family of the Emperor Charles. So great was the boy's ability, that at fifteen he had become the intimate and almost confidential friend of the emperor, who was a keen judge of merit.

Before he reached the age of twenty-one he was named commander-in-chief of the army on the French frontier. When the Emperor Charles resigned, the prince was appointed by Philip to negotiate a treaty with France, and had conducted these negotiations with extreme ability. The prince and the Duke of Alva remained in France as hostages for the execution of the treaty. Alva was secretly engaged in arranging an agreement between Philip and Henry for the extirpation of Protestantism, and the general destruction of all those who held that faith. The French king, believing that the prince of Orange was also in the secret, spoke to him one day when out hunting freely on the subject, and gave him all the details of the understanding that had been entered into for a general massacre of the Protestants throughout the dominions of France and Spain.

The Prince of Orange neither by word or look indicated that all this was new to him, and the king remained in ignorance of how completely he had betrayed the plans of himself and Philip. It was his presence of mind and reticence, while listening to this astounding relation, that gained for the Prince of Orange the title of William the Silent. Horror-struck at the plot he had discovered, the prince from that moment threw himself into the cause of

the Protestants of the Netherlands, and speedily became
the head of the movement, devoting his whole property
and his life to the object.   So far it had brought him only
trials and troubles.

His estate and that of his brothers had been spent in the
service; he had incurred enormous debts; the armies of German mercenaries he had raised had met with defeat and ruin;
the people of the Netherlands, crushed down with the apathy of despair, had not lifted a finger to assist the forces that
had marched to their aid.   It was only when, almost by an
accident, Brill had been captured by the sea beggars, that
the spark he had for so many years been trying to fan,
burst into flame in the provinces of Holland and Zeeland.

The prince had been sustained through his long and
hitherto fruitless struggle by a deep sense of religion. He
believed that God was with him, and would eventually save
the people of the Netherlands from the fate to which Philip
had doomed them.   And yet though an ardent Protestant,
and in an age when Protestants were well nigh as bigoted
as Catholics, and when the idea of religious freedom had
scarce entered into the minds of men, the prince was perfectly tolerant, and from the first insisted that in all the
provinces over which he exercised authority, the same perfect freedom of worship should be granted to the Catholics
that he claimed for the Protestants in the Catholic states
of the Netherlands.

He had not always been a Protestant.   When appointed
by Philip Stadtholder of Holland, Friesland, and Utrecht
he had been a moderate Catholic.   But his thoughts were
but little turned to religious subjects, and it was as a patriot
and a man of humane nature that he had been shocked at
the discovery that he had made, of the determination of the
kings of France and Spain to extirpate the Protestants.

He used this knowledge first to secretly urge the people of the Netherlands to agitate for the removal of the Spanish troops from the country ; and although he had secret instructions from Philip to enforce the edicts against all heretics with vigour, he avoided doing so as much as was in his power, and sent private warnings to many whom he knew to be in danger of arrest.

As Governor of the Netherlands at the age of twenty-six, he was rich, powerful, and of sovereign rank. He exercised a splendid hospitality, and was universally beloved by the whole community for the charm of his manner and his courtesy to people of all ranks. Even at this period the property which he had inherited from his father, and that he had received with his first wife, Anne of Egmont, the richest heiress of the Netherlands, had been seriously affected by his open-handed hospitality and lavish expenditure. His intellect was acknowledged to be of the highest class. He had extraordinary adroitness and capacity for conducting state affairs. His knowledge of human nature was profound. He had studied deeply, and spoke and wrote with facility Latin, French, German, Flemish, and Spanish.

The epithet Silent was in no way applicable to his general character. He could be silent when speech was dangerous, but at other times he was a most cheerful and charming companion, and in public the most eloquent orator and the most brilliant controversialist of his age. Thirteen years had passed since then, thirteen years spent in incessant troubles and struggles. The brilliant governor of Philip in the Netherlands had for years been an exile ; the careless Catholic had become an earnest and sincere Protestant ; the wealthy noble had been harassed with the pecuniary burdens he had undertaken in order to raise troops for the rescue of his countrymen.

He had seen his armies defeated, his plans overthrown, his countrymen massacred by tens of thousands, his co-religionists burnt, hung, and tortured, and it was only now that the spirit of resistance was awakening among his countrymen. But misfortune and trial had not soured his temper ; his faith that sooner or later the cause would triumph had never wavered. His patience was inexhaustible, his temper beyond proof. The incapacity of many in whom he had trusted, the jealousies and religious differences which prevented anything like union between the various states, the narrowness and jealousy even of those most faithful to the cause, would have driven most men to despair.

Upon his shoulders alone rested the whole weight of the struggle. It was for him to plan and carry out, to negotiate with princes, to organize troops, to raise money to compose jealousies, to rouse the lukewarm and appeal to the waverers. Every detail, great and small, had to be elaborated by him. So far it was not the Netherlands, it was William of Orange alone who opposed himself to the might of the greatest power in Europe.

Such was the prince to whom Ned Martin was now introduced, and it was with a sense of the deepest reverence that he entered the chamber. He saw before him a man looking ten years older than he really was ; whose hair was grizzled and thin from thought and care, whose narrow face was deeply marked by the lines of anxiety and trouble, but whose smile was as kindly, whose manner as kind and gracious as that which had distinguished it when William was the brilliant young stadt holder of the Emperor Philip.

CHAPTER VII.

A DANGEROUS MISSION.

I HEAR you have a letter for me from my good friend the burgomaster of Enkhuizen," the Prince of Orange said, as Ned with a deep reverence approached the table at which he was sitting. "He sends me no ill news, I hope?"

"No your excellency," Ned said. "It is on a matter personal to myself that he has been good enough to write to you, and I crave your pardon beforehand for occupying your time for a moment with so unimportant a subject."

The prince glanced at him keenly as he was speaking, and saw that the young fellow before him was using no mere form of words, but that he really felt embarrassed at the thought that he was intruding upon his labours. He opened the letter and glanced down it.

"Ah! you are English," he said in surprise. I thought you a countryman of mine."

"My mother is from Holland, sir," Ned replied; "and has brought me up to speak her language as well as my father's and to feel that Holland is my country as much as England."

"And you are the son of the English Captain, who, lately, as I heard, being stopped in his passage down the Zuider-Zee by the Spanish ship *Don Pedro*, defended himself so stoutly that he inflicted great loss and damage upon the Spaniard, and brought his ship into Enkhuizen without further damage than a grievous wound to himself. The burgomaster tells me that you are anxious to enter my service as a volunteer, and that you have the permission of your parents to do so. Many of your brave compatriots are already coming over; and I am glad indeed of their aid, which I regard as an omen that England will some day bestir herself on our behalf. But you look young for such rough work, young sir. I should not take you for more than eighteen."

"I am not yet eighteen, sir," Ned said, although he did not think it necessary to mention that he still wanted two years to that age. "But even children and women have aided in the defence of their towns."

"It is somewhat strange," the prince said, "that your parents should have countenanced your thus embarking in this matter at so young an age."

"The Spaniards have murdered my grandfather, three of my uncles, and an aunt; and my father would, had it not been that he is disabled by the wound he received, and which has cost him the loss of a leg, have himself volunteered," Ned replied. "But sir, if you think me too young as yet to fight in the ranks, my father thought that you might perhaps make use of me in other ways. I have sailed up every river in the Netherlands, having been for the last five years in my father's ship trading with these ports, and know their navigation and the depth of water. If you have letters that you want carried to your friends in Flanders, and would intrust them to me, I would deliver them faithfully for you whatever the risk; and being but a boy, could pass perhaps where a man would be suspected. I only ask, sir, to be put to such use as you can make of me, whatever it may be, deeming my life but of slight account in so great and good a cause."

"No man can offer more," the prince said kindly. "I like your face, young sir, and can see at once that you can be trusted, and that you have entered upon this matter in a serious spirit. Your father has proved himself to be a brave fighter and a skilful sailor, and I doubt not that you are worthy of him. Your youth is no drawback in my eyes, seeing that I myself, long before I reached your age, was mixed up in state affairs, and that the Emperor Charles, my master, did not disdain to listen to my opinions. I accept your offer of service in the name of the Netherlands; and deeming that, as you say, you may be of more service in the way of which you have spoken than were I to attach you to one of the regiments I am raising, I will for the present appoint you as a volunteer attached to my own household, and, trust me, I will not keep you long in idleness." He touched a bell and the page entered. "Take this gentleman," he said, "to Count Nieuwenar, and tell him that he is to have rank as a gentleman volunteer, and will at present remain as a member of my household, and be treated as such."

With a kindly nod he dismissed Ned, who was so affected by the kindness of manner of the prince that he could only murmur a word or two of thanks and assurances of devotion. One of the burgomaster's letters, of which Ned was the bearer, was to Count Nieuwenar, the prince's chamberlain, and when the page introduced him to that officer with the message the prince had given him, Ned handed to him the burgomaster's letter. The count ran his eye down it.

"My friend the burgomaster speaks highly in your praise, young sir," he said; "and although it needed not that since the prince himself has been pleased to appoint you to his household, yet I am glad to receive so good a report of you. All Holland and Zeeland have been talking of the

gallant fight that your father's ship made against the Spaniard; and though I hear that the Queen of England has
made remonstrances to the Spanish Ambassador as to this
attack upon an English ship, methinks that it is the Spaniards who suffered most in the affair."

"Would you kindly instruct me, sir, in the duties that
I have to perform."

"There are no duties whatever," the count said with a
smile. "There is no state or ceremony here. The prince
lives like a private citizen, and all that you have to do is to
behave discreetly, to present yourself at the hours of meals,
and to be in readiness to perform any service with which
the prince may intrust you; although for what service he
destines you, I own that I am in ignorance. But," he said
more gravely, "the prince is not a man to cumber himself
with persons who are useless to him, nor to keep about his
person any save those upon whose fidelity he is convinced
that he can rely. Therefore I doubt not that he will find
work for you to do, for indeed there is but little ease and
quiet for those who serve him. This afternoon I will find
for you an apartment, and I may tell you that although
you will have at present no duties to perform, and need
not therefore keep in close attendance, it were better that
you should never be very long absent; for when the prince
wants a thing done he wants it done speedily, and values
most those upon whom he can rely at all times of the night
and day. Return here at noon, and I will then present you
to the gentlemen and officers with whom you will associate."

On leaving the chamberlain Ned walked for some time
through the streets of Rotterdam. He scarcely noticed
where he went, so full were his thoughts of the reception
that he had met with, and the more than realization of his
hopes. The charm of manner, as well as the real kindness

of the prince, had completely captivated him, as indeed they did all who came in contact with him, and he felt that no dangers he could run, no efforts he could make would be too great if he could but win the approbation of so kind a master. He presented himself to the chamberlain at the hour named, and the latter took him to a large hall in which many officers and gentlemen were about to sit down to dinner, and introduced Ned to them as the son of the English captain who had so bravely beaten off the *Don Pedro*, and whom the Prince of Orange had received into his household in the quality of a gentleman volunteer.

Ned was well received, both on his own account and from the good-will that was entertained towards England. Although personally the Prince of Orange kept up no state and lived most simply and quietly, he still maintained an extensive household, and extended a generous hospitality more suited to his past wealth than to his present necessities. He had the habits of a great noble; and although pressed on all sides for money, and sometimes driven to make what he considered great economies in his establishment, his house was always open to his friends and adherents.

Certainly in the meal to which he sat down Ned saw little signs of economy. There was but little silver plate on the table, for the prince's jewels and plate had been pledged years before for the payment of the German mercenaries; but there was an abundance of food of all kinds, generous wine in profusion, and the guests were served by numerous pages and attendants.

On the following day the prince rode to Haarlem accompanied by his household and a hundred horsemen, for at Haarlem he had summoned a meeting of the representatives of the states that still remained faithful to him. As soon as they were settled in the quarters assigned to them Ned sallied out to make inquiries concerning the relatives with whom his aunt and cousins had taken refuge. As he knew her maiden name he had no great difficulty in learn- ing the part of the town in which her father dwelt, and knowing that the prince would at any rate for the rest of the day be wholly absorbed in important business, made his way thither, introducing himself to the burgher.

"Ah!" the latter said, "I have often heard my daughter speak of her sister-in-law who had married and settled in England. So you are her son? Well, you will find her house in the street that runs along by the city wall, near the Watergate. It was well that she happened to be laid up with illness at the time Alva's ruffians seized and mur- dered her husband and his family. She was well-nigh dis- traught for a time, and well she might be; though, indeed, her lot is but that of tens of thousands of others in this unhappy country. I would gladly have welcomed her here, but I have another married daughter who lives with me and keeps my house for me, and as she has half a dozen children the house is well-nigh full. And Elizabeth longed for quiet in her sorrow, so I established her in the little house I tell you of. I have been going to write to your father, but have put it off from time to time, for one has so much to think of in these days that one has no time for private matters. She tells me that her husband and his brothers had, foreseeing the evil times coming, sent money to England to his care, and that it has been invested in houses in London."

"I believe that is so," Ned replied; "and my father, who is at present lying sorely wounded at Enkhuizen, will, I am sure, now that he knows where my aunt is, commu- nicate with her by letter on the subject. I will give you his address at Enkhuizen, and as it is but a short journey from here you might perhaps find time to go over and see him, when he will be able to talk freely with you on the subject. Now, with your permission I will go and see my aunt."

Ned had no difficulty in finding the house indicated. He knocked at the door, and it was opened by his aunt herself. She looked up for a moment inquiringly, and then exclaimed:

"Why, it is my nephew, Edward Martin! It is nearly two years since I saw you last, and so much has happened since;" and she burst into tears.

Ned followed her into the house, where he was warmly welcomed by his two cousins—girls of fourteen and fifteen years old. He had first to explain how it was that he had come to Haarlem, and they were grieved indeed to hear what had happened to Captain Martin who was a great favourite with them.

"And so you have entered the service of the Prince of Orange?" his aunt said when he had finished his story. "Truly I wonder that your father and mother have allowed you to embark in so hopeless an enterprise."

"Not hopeless," Ned said. "Things look dark at present, but either England or France may come to our help. At any rate, aunt, if the Spanish army again sweeps over Holland and Zeeland surely you, with two girls, will not await its approach. You have friends in England. My father and mother will be only too glad to have you with them till you can make yourself a home close by. And there are the moneys sent over that will enable you to live in comfort. It will not be like going among strangers. There is quite a colony of emigrants from the Netherlands already in London. You will find plenty who can speak your language."

"All my family are here," she replied; "my father, and brothers, and sisters. I could never be happy elsewhere."

" Yes, aunt, I can understand that. But if the Spaniards come, how many of your family may be alive here a week afterwards?"

The woman threw up her hands in a gesture of despair.

" Well, we must hope for the best, aunt; but I would urge you most strongly if you hear that a Spanish army is approaching to fly to England if there be an opportunity open to you, or if not to leave the city and go to some town or village as far from here as possible."

"Haarlem is strong, and can stand a stout siege," the woman said confidently.

"I have no doubt it can, aunt. But the Spaniards are good engineers, and unless the Prince of Orange is strong enough to march to its succour, sooner or later it must fall; and you know what happens then."

"Why should they come here more than elsewhere? There are many other towns that lie nearer to them."

"That is so, aunt. But from the walls you can see the towers and spires of Amsterdam, and that city serves them as a gathering place in the heart of the country whence they may strike blows all round ; and, therefore, as you lie so close, one of the first blows may be struck here. Besides, if they take Haarlem, they cut the long strip of land that almost alone remains faithful to the prince asunder. Well, aunt, please think it over. If you doubt my words write to my mother at Enkhuizen. I warrant she will tell you how gladly she will receive you in England, and how well you may make yourself a home there. I do not know how long I am to be staying here, and I have to be in close attendance on the prince in case he may suddenly have occasion for my services, but I will come down every day for

a talk with you; and I do hope that for the sake of my
cousins, if not for your own, you will decide to leave this
troubled land for a time, and to take refuge in England,
where none will interfere with your religion, and where
you can live free from the Spaniard's cruel bigotry."

Ned remained for a fortnight without any particular
duties. When the prince was closeted with persons of importance, and he knew that there was no chance of his being
required, he spent much of his time at his aunt's. He was
beginning to feel weary of hanging about the prince's ante-
chamber doing nothing, when one day a page came up to
him and told him that the Prince required his presence.
He followed the boy to the prince's cabinet, full of hope
that he was to have an opportunity of proving that he was
in earnest in his offers of service to the cause of Holland.

"I daresay you began to think that I had forgotten you,"
the prince began when the page had retired and the curtain had fallen behind him, "but it is not so. Until to-
day I have had no occasion for your services, but have now
a mission to intrust to you. I have letters that I wish carried to Brussels and delivered to some of my friends there.
You had best start at once in the disguise of a peasant-boy.
You must sew up your despatches in your jerkin, and remember that if they are found upon you a cruel death will
surely be your fate. If you safely carry out your mission
in Brussels return with the answers you will receive by such
route as may seem best to you; for this must depend upon
the movements of the Spaniards. The chamberlain will
furnish you with what money you may require."

"Thanks, your excellency, I am provided with sufficient
means for such a journey."

"I need not tell you, my lad, to be careful and prudent.
Remember, not only is your own life at stake, but that the

interest of the country will suffer, and the lives of many
will be forfeited should you fail in your mission. You will
see that there are no names upon these letters ; only a small
private mark, differing in each case, by which you can distinguish them. Here is a paper which is a key to those
marks. You must, before you start, learn by heart the
names of those for whom the various letters are intended.
In this way, should the letters fall into the hands of the
Spaniards, they will have no clue as to the names of those
to whom they are addressed.

"This paper, on which is written, ' To the Blue Cap in
the South Corner of the Market Square of Brussels,' is intended to inclose all the other letters, and when you have
learned the marks Count Nieuwenar will fasten them up
in it and seal it with my seal. The object of doing this is,
that should you be captured, you can state that your instructions from me are to deliver the packet to a man with
a blue cap, who will meet you at the south corner of the
Market Square at Brussels, and, touching you on the
shoulder, ask ' How blows the wind in Holland?' These
are the instructions I now give you. If such a man comes
to you you will deliver the packet to him, if not you will
open it and deliver the letters. But this last does not form
part of your instructions.

" This device will not save your life if you are taken, but
it may save you from torture and others from death. For
were these unaddressed letters found upon you, you would
be put to such cruel tortures that flesh and blood could not
withstand them, and the names of those for whom these
letters are intended would be wrung from you; but inclosed
as they are to Master Blue Cap, it may be believed that
you are merely a messenger whose instructions extend no
further than the handing over the parcel to a friend of

mine in Brussels. Now, you have no time to lose. You
have your disguise to get, and these signs and the names
they represent to commit to heart. A horse will be ready
in two hours time to take you to Rotterdam, whence you
will proceed in a coasting vessel to Sluys or Axel."

At the time named Ned was in readiness. He was
dressed now as a young Flemish peasant. He had left the
chest with his clothes, together with his armour and
weapons, in the care of his aunt's father, for he hoped that
before his return she would have left the town. He could
not, however, obtain any promise that she would do so.
Her argument was, if other women could stay in Haarlem
why should she not do the same. Her friends and family
were there; and although, if the Spaniards were to besiege
the town, she might decide to quit it, she could not bring
herself to go into exile, unless indeed all Holland was conquered and all hope gone.

Ned carried a stout stick; which was a more formidable
weapon than it looked, for the knob was loaded with lead.
He hesitated about taking pistols; for if at any time he
were searched and such weapons found upon him the discovery might prove fatal, for a peasant boy certainly would
not be carrying weapons that were at that time costly and
comparatively rare. His despatches were sewn up in the
lining of his coat, and his money, beyond that required for
the present use, hidden in his big boots. A country horse
with rough trappings, such as a small farmer might ride,
was in readiness, and mounting this he rode to Rotterdam,
some thirty-five mile distant, and there put it up at a small
inn, where he had been charged to leave it.

He then walked down to the river and inquired about
boats sailing for the ports of Sluys or Axel. He was not
long in discovering one that would start the next day for

the latter place, and after bargaining with the master for a
passage returned to the inn. The next morning he set sail
soon after daybreak.   There were but three or four other
passengers, and Ned was not long before he established
himself on friendly terms with the master and the four
men that constituted the crew.

"I wonder," he said presently to the master, "that
trade still goes on between the towns of Holland and those
in the provinces that hold to Alva."

" The citizens of those towns are greatly divided in their
opinions," the captain said.   "Many would gladly rise if
they had the chance, but they lie too close to the Spanish
power to venture to do so.   Still they are friendly enough
to us; and as they have need of our goods and we of theirs,
no one hinders traffic or interferes with those who come
and go.   Most of these towns have but small Spanish garrisons, and these concern themselves not with anything
that goes on beyond maintaining the place for Spain.   It
is the Catholic magistrates appointed by Alva who manage the affairs of the towns, and as these are themselves
mostly merchants and traders their interests lie in keeping
the ports open and encouraging trade, so we come and go
unquestioned. The Spaniards have enough on their hands
already without causing discontent by restricting trade.
Besides, the duke affects to consider the rising in Holland
and Zeeland as a trifling rebellion which he can suppress
without difficulty, and it would be giving too much importance to the movement were he to close all the ports and forbid communication."

"Will you go outside or inside Walcheren?"

"Outside," the captain replied.   "It is the longest way,
but the safest.   The Spaniards hold Middleburg and Tergoes, and have lately defeated the force from Flushing that

endeavoured to capture Tergoes. There are many of our craft and some of the Spaniards in the passages, and fighting often takes place. It is better to avoid risks of trouble, although it may be a few leagues further round by Walcheren. I am ready to take my share of the fighting when it is needful, and aid in carrying the troops across from Flushing and back, but when I have goods in my hold I like to keep as well away from it as may be."

They cast anchor off Flushing for the wind was now foul, but when tide turned they again got under way and beat up the channel to Axel. No questions were asked as they drew up alongside the wharves. Ned at once stepped ashore and made his way to a small inn, chiefly frequented by sailors, near the jetty. The shades of night were just falling as they arrived, and he thought it were better not to attempt to proceed further until the following morning. He had been several times at Axel in the *Good Venture,* and was familiar with the town. The population was a mixed one, for although situated in Brabant, Axel had so much communication with the opposite shores of Holland that a considerable portion of the population had imbibed something of the spirit that animated their neighbours, and would, if opportunity offered, have gladly thrown off the authority of the officials appointed by the Spaniards.

Ned knew that as a stranger he should be viewed with great suspicion by the frequenters of the little inn, for the spy system was carried to such an extent that people were afraid to utter their sentiments even in the bosom of their own families. He therefore walked about until it was time to retire to rest, and in that way escaped alike the suspicions and questionings he might otherwise have encountered. He could easily have satisfied them as to the past—he had just arrived in the coasting smack the *Hope-*

ful from Rotterdam, and the master of the craft could, if questioned, corroborate his statement—but it would not be so easy to satisfy questioners as to the object of his coming. Why should a lad from Holland want to come to Brabant? Every one knew that work was far more plentiful in the place he had come from than in the states under the Spaniards, where the cultivators scarce dare sow crops sufficient for their own consumption, so extensive was the pillaging carried on by the Spanish troops.

These, always greatly in arrears of pay, did not hesitate to take all they required from the unfortunate inhabitants; and the latter knew that resistance or complaint was alike useless, for the soldiers were always on the verge of mutiny. Their officers had little control over them; and Alva himself was always short of money, and being unable to pay his troops was obliged to allow them to maintain themselves upon the country.

As soon as the gates were open in the morning Ned made his way to that through which the road to Brussels ran. The four or five Spanish soldiers at the gate asked no questions, and Ned passed on with a brisk step. He had gone about three miles when he heard sounds of horses' hoofs behind him, and presently two men came along. One, was by his appearance, a person of some importance, the other he took to be his clerk. Ned doffed his hat as the horse went past.

"Where are you going lad?" the elder of the two men asked.

"I am going, worshipful sir, to see some friends who live at the village of Deligen, near Brussels."

"These are evil times for travelling. Your tongue shows that you come not from Brabant."

"No sir, my relations lived at Vordwyk, hard by Amsterdam."

" Amsterdam is a faithful city ; although there, as else-where, there are men who are traitors to their king and false to their faith.   You are not one of them, I hope ?"

" I do not know," Ned said, " that I am bound to answer questions of any that ride by the highway, unless I know that they have right and authority to question me."

" I have right and authority," the man said angrily. " My name is Philip Von Aert, and I am one of the coun-cil charged by the viceroy to investigate into these mat-ters."

Ned again doffed his hat. " I know your name, worship-ful sir, as that of one who is foremost in searching out heretics.   There are few in the land, even ignorant country boys like myself, who have not heard it."

The councillor looked gratified.   " Ah ! you have heard me well spoken of ?" he said.

" I have heard you spoken of sir, well or ill, according to the sentiments of those who spoke."

" And why have you left Amsterdam to journey so far from home ?   This is a time when all men must be looked upon with suspicion until they prove themselves to be good Catholics and faithful subjects of the king, and even a boy like you may be engaged upon treasonable business.   I ask you again why are you leaving your family at Amsterdam?"

" Misfortunes have fallen upon them," Ned replied, " and they can no longer maintain me."

" Misfortunes, ah ! and of what kind ?"

" Their business no longer brings them in profit," Ned replied.   " They lived, as I told your worship, not in the town itself, but in a village near it, and in these troubled times trade is well nigh at a stand-still, and there is want at many a man's door."

" I shall stop for the night at Antwerp, where I have

business to do ; see when you arrive there that you call upon me. I must have further talk with you, for your answers do not satisfy me."

Ned bowed low.

"Very well, see that you fail not, or it will be the worse for you." So saying Von Aert put spurs to his horse, which had been walking alongside Ned as he conversed, and rode forward at a gallop.

CHAPTER VIII.

IN THE HANDS OF THE BLOOD-COUNCIL.

YOU are an evil-looking pair of scoundrels," Ned said to himself as he looked after the retreating figures of the two men. "The master I truly know by name as one of the worst instruments of the tyrant; as to the man, knave is written on his face. He is as thin as a scarecrow —he has a villainous squint and an evil smile on his face. If I had been bent on any other errand I would have given very different answers, and taken my chance of holding my own with this good stick of mine. At any rate I told them no absolute lies. The councillor will not have a chance of asking me any more questions this evening, and I only hope that he will be too busy to think any more about it. I will take the road through Ghent; it matters little which way I go, for the two roads seem to me to be of nearly equal distance."

He therefore at once left the road he was following, and struck across the fields northward until he came upon the road to Ghent, at which town he arrived soon after noon, having walked two or three and twenty miles. Fearing to be questioned he passed through the town without stopping, crossed the Scheldt and continued his way for another five miles, when he stopped at the village of Gontere. He entered a small inn.

"I wish to stop here for the night," he said, "if you have room?"

·" Room enough and to spare," the host replied. "There is no scarcity of rooms, though there is of good fare ; a party of soldiers from Ghent paid a visit to us yesterday, and have scarce left a thing to eat in the village. However, I suppose we ought to feel thankful that they did not take our lives also."

" Peter," a shrill voice cried from inside the house, "how often have I told you not to be gossipping on public affairs with strangers ? Your tongue will cost you your head presently, as I have told you a score of times."

"Near a hundred I should say, wife," the innkeeper replied. " I am speaking no treason, but am only explaining why our larder is empty, save some black bread, and some pig's flesh we bought an hour ago ; besides, this youth is scarce likely to be one of the duke's spies."

"There you are again," the woman cried angrily. " You want to leave me a widow, and your children fatherless, Peter Grantz. Was a woman ever tormented with such a man?"

"I am not so sure that it is not the other way," the man grumbled in an undertone. " Why wife," he went on, raising his voice, "who is there to say anything against us. Don't I go regularly to mass, and send our good priest a fine fish or the best cut off the joint two or three times a a week. What can I do more? Anyone would think to hear you talk that I was a heretic."

"I think you are more fool than heretic," his wife said angrily; "and that is the best hope for us. But come in, boy, and sit down; my husband will keep you gossipping at the door for the next hour if you would listen to him."

"I shall not be sorry to sit down, mistress," Ned said entering the low-roofed room. " I have walked from Axel since morning."

"That is a good long walk truly," the woman said. "Are you going on to Brussels? If so, your nearest way would have been by Antwerp."

"I took the wrong road," Ned said; "and as they told me that there was but a mile or two difference between them, I thought I might as well keep on the one I had first taken."

"You are from Holland, are you not, by your speech?" the woman asked.

"Yes; I have come from Holland," Ned replied.

"And is it true what they say, that the people there have thrown off the authority of the duke, and are going to venture themselves against all the strength of Spain?"

"Some have risen and some have not," Ned replied. "None can say what will come of it."

"You had best not say much about your coming from Holland," the woman said; "for they say that well nigh all from that province are heretics, and to be even suspected of being a heretic in Brabant is enough to cost anyone his life."

"I am not one to talk," Ned replied; "but I thank you for your caution, mistress. I have been questioned already by Philip Von Aert, and he said he would see me again; but in truth I have no intention of further intruding on him."

"He is one of the Council of Blood," the woman said, dropping her voice and looking round anxiously; and one of the most cruel of them. Beware, my lad, how you fall into his hands, for be assured he will show you no mercy, if he has reason to suspect, but in the slightest, that you are not a good Catholic and loyal to the Spaniards. Rich or poor, gentle or simple, woman or child, it is nought to him. There is no mercy for heretics, whomsoever they may be; and unless you can satisfy him thoroughly your best plan is to go back at once to Axel, and to cross to

Holland.   You do not know what they are.   There are
spies in every town and village, and were it known what I
have said to you now, little though that be, it would go
hard with me.   Women have been burned or strangled
for far less."

"I will be careful," Ned said.   "I have business which
takes me to Brussels, but when that is discharged I shall
betake me back to Holland as soon as I can."

By this time the woman, who had been standing over
the fire while she was talking, had roasted two or three
slices of pork, and these, with a piece of black bread and a
jug of ale, she placed before Ned.

Her husband, who had been standing at the door, now
came in.

"You are no wiser than I am, wife, with all your scold-
ing.   I have been listening to your talk; you have scolded
me whenever I open my lips, and there you yourself say
things ten times as dangerous."

"I say them inside the house, Peter Grantz," she retorted, "and don't stand talking at the door so that all the
village may hear me.   The lad is honest, as I can see by
his face, and if I could do aught for him I would do so."

"I should be glad if you could tell me of some little
place where I could put up in Brussels; some place where
I could stay while looking out for work, without anyone
troubling themselves as to whence I came or where I am
going, or what are my views as to religion or politics."

"That were a difficult matter," the woman replied.   "It
is not that the landlords care what party those who visit
their house belong to, but that for aught they know there
may be spies in their own household; and in these days it
is dangerous even to give shelter to one of the new religion.
Therefore, although landlords may care nothing who fre-

quent their houses, they are in a way forced to do so lest they themselves should be denounced as harbourers of heretics. Brussels has a strong party opposed to the duke; for you know that it is not those of the new religion only who would gladly see the last of the Spaniards. There are but few heretics in Brabant now, the Inquisition and the Council of Blood have made an end of most, others have fled either to France, or England, or Holland, some have outwardly conformed to the rights of the Church, and there are few indeed who remain openly separated from her, though in their hearts they may remain heretics as before.

"Still there are great numbers who long to see the old Constitution restored—to see persecution abolished, the German and Spanish troops sent packing, and to be ruled by our own laws under the viceroy of the King of Spain. Therefore in Brussels you are not likely to be very closely questioned. There are great numbers of officials, a small garrison, and a good many spies; all of these are for the duke, the rest of the population would rise to-morrow did they see a chance of success. I should say that you are more likely, being a stranger, of being suspected of being a spy than of being a heretic—that is if you are one, which I do not ask and do not want to know. The people of Brussels are not given to tumults as are those of Antwerp and Ghent, but are a quiet people going their own way. Being the capital there are more strangers resort there than to other places, and therefore people come and go without inquiry; still were I you I would, if you have any good reason for avoiding notice, prefer to lodge outside the city, entering the gates of a morning, doing what business you may have during the day, and leaving again before sunset. That way you would altogether avoid questionings, and will attract no more attention than other country people going in to sell their goods."

"Thank you, I will follow your advice," Ned said. "I have no wish to get into trouble, and being a stranger there I should have difficulty in proving that my story is a true one were I questioned."

The next morning Ned set out at daybreak, and arrived at Brussels early in the afternoon. He had determined to adopt the advice given him the evening before; and also that he would not endeavour to get a lodging in any of the villages.

"It will not take me more than a day, or at most two days, to deliver my letters," he thought to himself, "and there will be no hardship in sleeping in the fields or under a tree for a couple of nights. In that way I shall escape all notice, for people talk in villages even more than they do in towns." He had decided that he would not that day endeavour to deliver any of the letters, but would content himself with walking about the town and learning the names of the streets, so that he could set about delivering the letters without the necessity for asking many questions. When within half a mile of the town he left the road, and cutting open the lining of his jerkin took out the letters. Then he cut up a square piece of turf with his knife, scooped out a little earth, inserted the packet of letters, and then stamped down the sod above it. In another hole close to it he buried the money hidden in his boot, and then returning to the road walked on into Brussels, feeling much more comfortable now that he had for a time got rid of documents that would cost him his life, were they found upon him.

Passing through the gates, he wandered about for some hours through the streets, interested in the stir and bustle that prevailed. Mingled with the grave citizens were Spanish and German soldiers, nobles with their trains of pages and followers, deputies from other towns of Brabant and Artois, monks and priests, country people who had brought in their produce, councillors and statesmen, Spanish nobles and whining mendicants. He learnt the names of many of the streets, and marked the houses of those for whom he had letters. Some of these were nobles, others citizens of Brussels. He bought some bread and cheese in the market-place, and ate them sitting on a door-step; and having tied some food in a bundle to serve for supper, he left the town well satisfied with his discoveries.

He slept under the shelter of a hay-stack, and in the morning dug up the packet, sewed it up in its hiding-place again, and re-entered the city as soon as the gates were opened, going in with a number of market-people who had congregated there awaiting the opening of the gates. In a very short time the shops were all opened; for if people went to bed early, they were also astir early in those days. He went first towards the house of one of the burghers, and watched until he saw the man himself appear at the door of his shop ; then he walked across the street.

"The weather is clear," he said, "but the sun is nigh hidden with clouds."

The burgher gave a slight start ; then Ned went on :

"I have brought you tidings from the farm."

"Come in," the burgher said in loud tones, so that he could be heard by his two assistants in the shop. "My wife will be glad to hear tidings of her old nurse, who was ill when she last heard from her. You can reassure her in that respect, I hope?"

"Yes, she is mending fast," Ned replied, as he followed the burgher through the shop.

The man led the way upstairs, and then into a small sitting-room. He closed the door behind him.

"Now," he asked, "what message do you bring from Holland."

"I bring a letter," Ned replied ; and taking out his knife again cut the threads of the lining and produced the packet. The silk that bound it, and which was fastened by the prince's seal, was so arranged that it could be slipped off, and so enable the packet to be opened without breaking the seal. Ned took out the letters ; and after examining the marks on the corners, handed one to the burgher. The latter opened and read the contents.

"I am told," he said when he had finished, "not to give you an answer in writing, but to deliver it by word of mouth. Tell the prince that I have sounded many of my guild, and that certainly the greater part of the weavers will rise and join in expelling the Spaniards whenever a general rising has been determined upon; and it is certain that all the other chief towns will join in the movement. Unless it is general, I fear that nothing can be done. So great is the consternation that has been caused by the sack of Mechlin, the slaughter of thousands of the citizens, and the horrible atrocities upon the women, that no city alone will dare to provoke the vengeance of Alva. All must rise or none will do so. I am convinced that Brussels will do her part, if others do theirs ; although, as the capital, it is upon her the first brunt of the Spanish attack will fall. In regard to money, tell him that at present none can be collected. In the first place, we are all well nigh ruined by the exactions of the Spanish ; and in the next, however well-disposed we may be, there are few who would commit themselves by subscribing for the cause until the revolt is general and successful. Then, I doubt not, that the councillors would vote as large a subsidy as the city could afford to pay. Four at least of the members of the council of our guild can be thoroughly relied upon, and the prince can safely communicate with them. These are Gunther, Barneveldt, Hasselaer, and Buys."

"Please, repeat them again," Ned said, "in order that I may be sure to remember them rightly."

"As to general toleration," the burgher went on, after repeating the names, "in matters of religion, although there are many differences of opinion, I think that the prince's commands on this head will be complied with, and that it would be agreed that Lutherans, Calvinists, and other sects will be allowed to assemble for worship without hindrance; but the Catholic feeling is very strong, especially among the nobles, and the numbers of those secretly inclined to the new religion has decreased greatly in the past few years, just as they have increased in Holland and Zeeland, where, as I hear, the people are now well nigh all Protestants. Please assure the prince of my devotion to him personally, and that I shall do my best to further his plans, and can promise him that the Guild of Weavers will be among the first to rise against the tyranny of the Spaniards."

Ned, as he left the house, decided that the man he had visited was not one of those who would be of any great use in an emergency. He was evidently well enough disposed to the cause, but was not one to take any great risks, or to join openly in the movement unless convinced that success was assured for it. He was walking along, thinking the matter over, when he was suddenly and roughly accosted. Looking up he saw the Councillor Von Aert and his clerk; the former with an angry look on his face, the latter, who was close beside his master, and who had evidently drawn his attention to him, with a malicious grin of satisfaction.

"Hullo, sirrah," the councillor said angrily, "did I not tell you to call upon me at Antwerp?"

Ned took off his hat, and said humbly, "I should of course have obeyed your worship's order had I passed through Antwerp; but I afterwards remembered that I had cause to pass through Ghent, and therefore took that road, knowing well that one so insignificant as myself could have nothing to tell your worship that should occupy your valuable time."

"That we will see about," the councillor said grimly. "Genet, lay your hand upon this young fellow's collar. We will lodge him in safe keeping, and inquire into the matter when we have leisure. I doubt not that you were right when you told me that you suspected he was other than he seemed."

Ned glanced round; a group of Spanish soldiers were standing close by, and he saw that an attempt at escape would be hopeless. He therefore walked quietly along by the side of the clerk's horse, determining to wrest himself from the man's hold and run for it the instant he saw an opportunity. Unfortunately, however, he was unaware that they were at the moment within fifty yards of the prison. Several by-standers who had heard the conversation followed to see the result; and other passers-by, seeing Ned led by the collar behind the dreaded councillor, speedily gathered around with looks expressing no good-will to Von Aert.

The Spanish soldiers, however, accustomed to frays with the townspeople, at once drew their weapons and closed round the clerk and his captive, and two minutes later they arrived at the door of the prison, and Ned, completely taken by surprise, found himself thrust in and the door closed behind him before he had time to decide upon his best course.

"You will place this prisoner in a secure place," the councillor said. "It is a case of grave suspicion; and I will myself question him later on. Keep an eye upon him until I come again."

Ned was handed over to two warders, who conducted him to a chamber in the third storey. Here, to his dismay, one of his jailers took up his post, while the other retired, locking the door behind him. Thus the intention Ned had formed as he ascended the stairs of destroying the documents as soon as he was alone, was frustrated. The warder took his place at the window, which looked into an inner court of the prison, and putting his head out entered into conversation with some of his comrades in the yard below.

Ned regretted now that he had, before leaving the burgher, again sewn up the letters in his doublet. Had he carried them loosely about him, he could have chewed them up one by one and swallowed them ; but he dared not attempt to get at them now, as his warder might at any moment look round. The latter was relieved twice during the course of the day. None of the men paid any attention to the prisoner. The succession of victims who entered the walls of the prison only to quit them for the gallows was so rapid that they had no time to concern themselves with their affairs. Probably the boy was a heretic; but whether or not, if he had incurred the enmity of Councillor Von Aert, his doom was sealed.

It was late in the evening before a warder appeared at the door, and said that the councillor was below, and that the prisoner was to be brought before him. Ned was led by the two men to a chamber on the ground floor. Here

Von Aert, with two of his colleagues, was seated at a table, the former's clerk standing behind him.

"This is a prisoner I myself made this morning," Von Aert said to his companions. "I overtook him two miles this side of Axel, and questioned him. He admitted that he came from Holland; and his answers were so unsatisfactory that I ordered him strictly to call upon me at Antwerp, not having time at that moment to question him further. Instead of obeying, he struck off from the road and took that through Ghent; and I should have heard no more of him, had I not by chance encountered him this morning in the street here. Has he been searched?" he asked the warder.

"No, your excellency. You gave no orders that he should be examined."

"Fools!" the councillor said angrily; "this is the way you do your duty. Had he been the bearer of important correspondence he might have destroyed it by now."

"We have not left him, your excellency. He has never been alone for a moment, and had no opportunity whatever for destroying anything."

"Well, search that bundle first," the councillor said.

The bundle was found to contain nothing suspicious.

"Now, take off his doublet and boots and examine them carefully. Let not a seam or corner escape you."

Accustomed to the work, one of the warders had scarcely taken the doublet in his hand when he proclaimed that there was a parcel sewn up in the lining.

"I thought so!" Von Aert exclaimed, beaming with satisfaction at his own perspicacity. "I thought there was something suspicious about the fellow. I believe I can almost smell out a heretic or a traitor.

The councillor's colleagues murmured their admiration at his acuteness.

"What have we here?" Von Aert went on, as he examined the packet. "A sealed parcel addressed 'To the Blue Cap in the South Corner of the Market Square of Brussels.' What think you of that, my friends, for mystery and treason? Now, let us see the contents. Ah, ten letters without addresses! But I see there are marks different from each other on the corners. Ah!" he went on with growing excitement, as he tore one open and glanced at the contents, "from the arch-traitor himself to conspirators here in Brussels. This is an important capture indeed. Now, sirrah, what have you to say to this? For whom are these letters intended?"

"I know nothing of the contents of the letters, worshipful sir," Ned said, falling on his knees and assuming an appearance of abject terror. "They were delivered to me at Haarlem, and I was told that I should have five nobles if I carried them to Brussels and delivered them safely to a man who would meet me in the south corner of the Market Square of Brussels. I was to hold the packet in my hand and sling my bundle upon my stick, so that he might know me. He was to have a blue cap on, and was to touch me on the shoulder and ask me 'How blows the wind in Holland?' and that, worshipful sir, is all I know about it. I could not tell that there was any treason in the business, else not for fifty nobles would I have undertaken it."

"You lie, you young villain!" the councillor shouted. "Do you try to persuade me that the Prince of Orange would have intrusted documents of such importance to the first boy he met in the street. In the first place you must be a heretic."

"I don't know about heretics," Ned said, rising to his feet and speaking stubbornly. "I am of the religion my father taught me, and I would not pretend that I was a Catholic, not to save my life."

"There you are, you see," the councillor said triumph‑ antly to his colleagues. "Look at the obstinacy and in‑ solence of these Hollanders. Even this brat of a boy dares to tell us that he is not a Catholic. Take him away," he said to the warder, "and see that he is securely kept. We may want to question him again; but in any case he will go to the gallows to-morrow or next day."

Ned was at once led away.

"What think you?" Von Aert asked his colleagues as the door closed behin⅂ the prisoner. "Is it worth while to apply the torture to him at once to obtain from him the names of those for whom these letters were intended? It is most important for us to know. Look at this letter; it is from the prince himself, and refers to preparations mak‑ ing for a general rising."

"I should hardly think the boy would have been in‑ trusted with so important a secret," one of the other coun‑ cillors said; "for it would be well known he would be forced by torture to reveal it if these letters were to be found upon him. I think that the story he tells us is a true one, and that it is more likely they would be given him to deliver to some person who would possess the key to these marks on the letters."

"Well, at any rate no harm can be done by applying the screws," the councillor said. "If he knows they will make him speak, I warrant you."

The other two agreed.

"If you will allow me to suggest, your excellency," Genet said humbly, "that it might be the better way to try first if any such as this Blue Cap exists. The boy might be promised his life if he could prove that the story was true. Doubtless there is some fixed hour at which he was to meet this Blue Cap. We might let him go to meet him, keeping of course a strict watch over him. Then if any such man appears and speaks to him we could pounce upon him at once and wring from him the key to these marks. If no such man appears we should then know that the story was but a device to deceive, and could then obtain by some means the truth from him."

The suggestion met with approval.

"That is a very good plan, and shall be carried out. Send for the prisoner again."

Ned was brought down again.

" We see that you are young," Von Aert said, "and you have doubtless been misled in this matter, and knew not that you were carrying treasonable correspondence. We therefore are disposed to treat you leniently. At what time were you to meet this Blue Cap in the market?"

" Within an hour of sunset," Ned replied. " I am to be there at sunset and to wait for an hour; and was told that he would not fail to come in that time, but that if he did I was to come again the next day."

"It is to be hoped that he will not fail you," Von Aert said grimly, "for we shall not be disposed to wait his pleasure. To-morrow evening you will go with a packet and deliver it to the man when he comes to you. Beware that you do not try to trick us, for you will be closely watched, and it will be the worse for you if you attempt treachery. If the man comes those who are there will know how to deal with him."

"And shall I be at liberty to depart?" Ned asked doubtfully.

"Of course you will," Von Aert replied; "we should then have no further occasion for you, and you would have proved to us that your story was a true one, and that you were really in ignorance that there was any harm in carrying the packet hither."

Ned was perfectly well aware that the councillor was lying, and that even had he met the man in the blue cap he would be dragged back to prison and put to death, and that the promise meant absolutely nothing—the Spaniards having no hesitation in breaking the most solemn oaths made to heretics. He had, indeed, only asked the question because he thought that to assent too willingly to the proposal might arouse suspicion. It was the very thing he had been hoping for, and which offered the sole prospect of escape from a death by torture, for it would at least give him the chance of a dash for freedom.

He had named an hour after sunset partly because it was the hour which would have been probably chosen by those who wished that the meeting should take place unobserved, but still more because his chances of escape would be vastly greater were the attempt made after dark. The three councillors sat for some time talking over the matter after Ned had been removed. The letters had all been read. They had been carefully written, so as to give no information if they should fall into the wrong hands, and none of them contained any allusion whatever to past letters or previous negotiations.

"It is clear," Von Aert said, "that this is a conspiracy, and that those to whom these letters are sent are deeply concerned in it, and yet these letters do not prove it. Suppose that we either seize this Blue Cap or get from the boy the names of those for whom the letters are intended, they could swear on the other hand that they knew nothing whatever about them, and had been falsely accused. No doubt many of these people are nobles and citizens of good position, and if it is merely their word against the word of a boy, and that wrung from him by torture, our case would not be a strong one."

"Our case is not always strong," one of the other councillors said; "but that does not often make much difference."

"It makes none with the lower class of the people," Von
Aert agreed; "but when we have to deal with people who
have influential friends it is always best to be able to prove
a case completely. I think that if we get the names of
those for whom the letters are meant we can utilize the boy
again. We will send him to deliver the letters in person,
as I believe he was intended to do. He may receive answers to take back to Holland; but even if he does not the
fact that these people should have received such letters without at once denouncing the bearer and communicating the
contents to us, will be quite sufficient proof of their guilt."

"In that case," one of the others remarked, "the boy
must not be crippled with the torture."

"There will be no occasion for that," Von Aert said contemptuously. "A couple of turns with the thumbscrew will
suffice to get out of a boy of that age everything he knows.
Well, my friends, we will meet here to-morrow evening. I
shall go round to the Market Square with Genet to see the
result of this affair, in which I own I am deeply interested;
not only because it is most important, but because it is due
to the fact that I myself entertained a suspicion of the boy
that the discovery of the plot has been made. I will take
charge of these letters, which are for the time useless to us,
but which are likely to bring ten men's heads to the block."

As Ned sat alone in his cell during the long hours of the
following day he longed for the time to come when his
fate was to be settled. He was determined that if it lay
with him he would not be captured alive. He would mount
to the top story of a house and throw himself out of a window, or snatch a dagger from one of his guards and stab
himself, if he saw no mode of escape. A thousand times

better to die so than to expire on a gibbet after suffering atrocious tortures, which would, he knew, wring from him the names of those for whom the letters were intended.

He could bear pain as well as another; but flesh and blood could not resist the terrible agonies inflicted by the torture, and sooner or later the truth would be wrung from the most reluctant lips. Still he thought that he had a fair chance of escape. It was clear that he could not be closely surrounded by a guard, for in that case Blue Cap would not venture near him. He must, therefore, be allowed a considerable amount of liberty; and, however many men might be on watch a short distance off, he ought to be able by a sudden rush to make his way through them. There would at that hour be numbers of people in the street, and this would add to his chance of evading his pursuers.

He eat heartily of a meal that was brought him at midday, and when just at sunset the warder entered the cell and told him to follow him, he felt equal to any exertion. When he came down into the courtyard, a dozen men were gathered there, together with Von Aert and his clerk.

"Now," the councillor said sternly, "you see these men. They will be round you on all sides, and I warn you that if you attempt to escape or to give any warning sign to this Blue Cap, or to try any tricks with us of any sort, you shall be put to death with such tortures as you never dreamt of. Upon the other hand, if you carry out my orders faithfully, and hand over this packet to the man who meets you, you will be at liberty to go straight away, and to return home without molestation."

"I understand," Ned replied; "and as I cannot help myself, will do your bidding. Where are my stick and bundle? He will not know me unless I have them. I am to carry them on my shoulder."

"Ah! I forgot," the councillor said, and giving the order to one of the warders Ned's bundle and stick were brought him.

"You will stroll leisurely along," Von Aert said, "and appear natural and unconcerned. We shall be close to you, and you will be seized in an instant if we observe anything suspicious in your movements." Von Aert then took a packet from his doublet and handed it to Ned, who placed it in his belt. The prison door was opened ; three or four of the men went out, and Ned followed. It was a curious feeling to him as he walked down the street. Round him were numbers of people laughing and chatting as they went, while he, though apparently as free as they, was a prisoner with a dozen pair of eyes watching him, and his life in deadly peril.

CHAPTER IX.

IN HIDING.

AFTER five minutes' walking Ned arrived at the market-square, and passed steadily on down towards the south corner. The market was long since over, and the market folk had returned to their farms and villages, but there were a large number of people walking about. It was already growing dusk, and in another half-hour would be dark. Ned turned when he got near the corner, strolled a short distance back and then turned again, pacing backwards and forwards some thirty or forty yards. He carefully abstained from seeming to stare about. The councillor and his clerk kept within a short distance of him, the former wrapped up in a cloak with a high collar that almost concealed his face.

As to the others watching him, Ned could only guess at them. Four men he noticed, who turned whenever he did; the others he guessed were keeping somewhat further off, or were perhaps stationed at the streets leading out of the square so as to cut him off should he escape from those close to him. A few oil lamps were suspended from posts at various points in the square, and at the ends of the streets leading from it. These were lighted soon after he arrived in the square. He decided that it would not do to make for the street leading out of the south corner, as this was the one that he would be suspected of aiming for; and, moreover, men would surely be placed there to cut off

Blue Cap on his entry. He, therefore, determined to make for a somewhat narrow street, about half-way between the south and west corners.

He had followed this on the day he entered Brussels, as one of the persons to whom the letters were addressed lived in it. He knew that there were many lanes running into it, and that at the lower end several streets, branching off in various directions, met in the small square in which it terminated. Half an hour passed. It was now quite dark, and he felt that he had better delay no longer. He walked half along his beat towards the south corner, then with a sudden spring darted off. The two men walking on that side of him were some ten paces distant, and he ran straight at them. Taken by surprise, before they had time to throw back their cloaks and draw their rapiers, he was upon them.

With a blow from his leaded stick, delivered with all his strength, he struck one man to the ground, and then turning to the other struck him on the wrist as he was in the act of drawing his sword. The man uttered a loud cry of pain and rage, and Ned ran at top of his speed towards the street. He knew that he need fear no pursuit from the two men he had encountered, that those on the other side of him were some distance behind, and that as so many people intervened his pursuers would probably soon lose sight of him. Threading his way between the groups of people, who had arrested their walk at the sound of loud and sudden shouting, he approached the end of the street.

By the light of the lamp there he saw two men standing with drawn swords. Breaking suddenly into a walk he made for the house next to the street, and then turned so that he came upon the men sideways instead of from the front, at which they were expecting him. There was a

sudden exclamation from the man nearest to him; but
Ned was within two yards of him before he perceived him,
and before he was on guard the loaded stick fell with the
full sweep of Ned's arm upon his ankle, and in an instant
he was prostrate, and Ned darted at full speed down the
street with the other man in pursuit a few paces behind
him.

Before he had run far Ned found that he could gain but
little upon his pursuer, and that he must rid himself of him
if he were to have a chance of escaping. He slackened his
speed a little, and allowed the man to gain slightly upon
him. Thinking that the fugitive was within his grasp the
warder exerted himself to his utmost. Suddenly Ned sprang
into a doorway ; the man, unable to check himself, rushed
past. In a moment Ned was out again, and before the fellow could arrest his steps and turn, gave him a violent shove
behind, which hurled him on to his face with a tremendous crash, and Ned continued his way. There was a great
shouting, but it was full fifty yards away, and he felt his
hopes rise. His pursuers were now all behind him, and he
felt sure that in the darkness and the narrow streets he
should be able to evade them.

He took the first turning he came to, turned again and
again, and presently slackened his pace to a walk, convinced that for a time his pursuers must be at fault. He
was now among narrow streets inhabited by the poorer
classes. There were no lamps burning here, and he began
to wonder which way he had better take, and where he
should pass the night. It was absolutely necessary to obtain some other disguise, for he was sure that the gates
would be so carefully watched in the morning there would
be no chance whatever of his getting safely out in his present attire. Presently, through a casement on the ground-

floor, he heard the sound of low singing in a woman's voice. He stopped at once and listened. It was the air of a Lutheran hymn he had frequently heard in Holland. Without hesitation he knocked at the door, and lifting the latch entered. A woman and girl were sitting at work inside ; they looked up in surprise at seeing a stranger.

" Pardon me," he said, " but I am Protestant, and am hunted by Alva's blood-hounds. I have evaded them, and I am safe for the present ; but I know not where to go, or where to obtain a disguise. As I passed the window I heard the air of a Lutheran hymn, and knew that there were within those who would, if they could, aid me."

The woman looked reprovingly at the girl.

" How imprudent of you, Gertrude !" she said. " Not that it is your fault more than mine. I ought to have stopped you, but I did not think your voice would be heard through that thick curtain. Who are you, sir, and where do you come from?" she asked, turning to Ned.

" I come from Holland," he said, " and was the bearer of important letters from the Prince of Orange."

The woman hesitated. " I would not doubt you," she said; " but in these days one has to be suspicious of one's shadow. However, as after what you have heard our lives are in your hands, I would fain trust you; though it seems to me strange that an important mission should be intrusted to one of your age and station."

" My age was all in my favour," Ned replied. " As to my station, it is not quite what it seems; for I am a gentleman volunteer in the service of the prince, and he accepted my services thinking that I might succeed when a man would be suspected."

" I will give you shelter," the woman said quietly; " though I know that I risk my life and my danghter's in doing so. But the Lord holds us in his hands, and unless it be his will we shall not perish." So saying, she got up and barred the door.

"Now, tell me more as to how you came to fall into this peril," she said.

Ned related his adventure, and the manner in which he had effected his escape from the hands of his captors.

"You have, indeed, had an escape," the woman said. "There are few upon whom Councillor Van Aert lays his hand who ever escape from it. You have indeed shown both skill and courage in thus freeing yourself."

"There is no great courage in running away when you know that if you stay torture and death are before you," Ned replied.

"And now, what are your plans?" the woman asked.

"My only plan is to obtain a disguise in which to escape from the city. My mission is unfortunately ended by the loss of my papers, and I shall have but a sorry story to tell to the prince if I succeed in making my way back to Holland, of the utter failure I have made of the mission with which he was good enough to intrust me."

He took from his belt the packet that Von Aert had given him, and was about to throw it in the fire when his eye fell upon it. He opened it hastily, and exclaimed with delight, "Why, here are the letters! That scoundrel must have had them in his doublet, as well as the packet made up for me to carry, and he has inadvertently given me the wrong parcel. See, madam, these are the letters I told you of, and these are the marks in the corners whose meaning Von Aert was so anxious to discover. Now, if I can but obtain a good disguise I will deliver these letters before I start on my way back."

The girl, who was about fourteen years of age, spoke a

few words in a low voice to her mother. The latter glanced at Ned.

"My daughter suggests that you should disguise yourself as a woman," she said. "And indeed in point of height you might pass well, seeing that you are but little taller than myself. But I fear that you are far too widely built across the shoulders to wear my clothes."

"Yes, indeed," Ned agreed, smiling; but you are tall and slight. I could pass well enough for one of these Flemish peasant girls, for they are sometimes near as broad as they are long. Yes, indeed, if I could get a dress such as these girls wear I could pass easily enough. I am well provided with money, but unfortunately it is hidden in the ground a mile outside the gates. I only carry with me a small sum for daily use, and that of course was taken from me by my jailers."

"Be not uneasy about money," the woman said. "Like yourself, we are not exactly what we look. I am the Countess Von Harp."

Ned made a movement of surprise. The name was perfectly known to him, being that of a noble in Friesland who had been executed at Brussels a few months before by the orders of the Council of Blood.

"When my husband was murdered," the Countess Von Harp went on, "I received a warning from a friend that I and my daughter, being known to be members of the Reformed Church, would be seized. For myself I cared little; but for my daughter's sake I resolved to endeavour to escape. I knew that I should be nowhere safe in the Netherlands, and that there was little chance of a woman and girl being able to escape from the country, when upon every road we should meet with disorderly soldiery, and every town we should pass through swarmed with Alva's agents. I resolved, therefore, to stay here. An old servant took this house for me, and here I have lived ever since in the disguise you see. My servant still lives with us, and goes abroad and makes our purchases. Our neighbours are all artisans and attend to their own business. It is supposed among them that I am one who has been ruined in the troubles, and now support myself by embroidery; but in fact I am well supplied with money. When I came here I brought all my jewels with me; besides, I have several good friends who know my secret, and through whom, from time to time, money has been transmitted to me from my steward in Friesland. Our estates in Brabant have of course been confiscated, and for a time those in Friesland were also seized. But when the people rose four months ago they turned out the man who had seized them, and as he was a member of the Council of Blood he was lucky in escaping with his life. So that, you see, the cost of a peasant woman's dress is a matter that need give you no concern."

There was now a knock at the door. It was repeated. "It is my servant," the countess said. Ned at once unbarred and opened the door. The old woman gave an exclamation of astonishment at seeing a stranger.

"Come in, Magdalene." the countess said; "it is a friend. You are later than I expected."

"It is not my fault, madam," the old servant said. "I have been stopped four or five times, and questioned and made game of, by German soldiers posted at the ends of the streets; the quarter is full of them. I was going through the market-place when a sudden tumult arose, and they say a prisoner of great importance has made his escape. Councillor Von Aert was there, shouting like a madman. But he had better have held his tongue; for as soon as he was recognized the crowd hustled and beat him, and went nigh killing him, when some men with drawn swords rescued him from their hands, and with great difficulty escorted him to the town-hall. He is hated in Brussels, and it was rash of him to venture out after dark."

"This is the escaped prisoner, Magdalene." The old woman looked with surprise at Ned.

"You are pleased to joke with me, madam. This is but a boy."

"That is true, Magdalene; but he is, nevertheless, the prisoner whose escape angered the councillor so terribly, and for whom the guard you speak of are now in search."

The old servant shook her head. "Ah, madam, are you not running risks enough of detection here without adding to them that of concealing a fugitive?"

"You are right," Ned said; "and it was selfish and wrong of me to intrude myself here."

"God willed it so," the countess said. "My daughter's voice was the instrument that directed your steps here. It is strange that she should have sung that hymn just as you were passing, and that I should have heard her without checking her. The hand of God is in all these things; therefore, do not make yourself uneasy on our account. Magdalene, we have settled that he shall assume the disguise of a young peasant girl, and to-morrow you shall purchase the necessary garments."

"Yes, he might pass as a girl," the old servant agreed. "But, I pray you, let him not stay an instant in this garb. I do not think they will search the houses, for the artisans of Brussels are tenacious of their rights, and an attempt would bring them out like a swarm of bees. Still it is better that he should not remain as he is for an hour. Come with me, young sir; I will furnish you with clothes at

once.   I am not so tall as I was, but there were few taller
women in Friesland than I was when I was the countess's
nurse."

Ned could well imagine that; for Magdalene, although
now some sixty years old, was a tall, large-framed woman.
He followed her to a chamber upstairs, and was furnished
by her with all the necessary articles of dress; and in these,
as soon as, having placed an oil lamp on the table, she retired, he proceeded to array himself, and presently descended the stairs, feeling very strange and awkward in
this new attire.   Gertrude Von Harp burst into a fit of
merry laughter, and even the countess smiled.

"That will do very well, indeed," she said, "when you
have got on the Flemish head-dress, which conceals the
hair."

"I have it here, madam," Magdalene said; "but it was
useless to leave it up there for him, for he would have no
idea how to fold it rightly.   Now sit down on that stool,
sir, and I will put it on for you."

When this was done the metamorphosis was complete,
and Ned could have passed anywhere without exciting suspicion that he was other than he seemed.

"That will do all very well for the present," Magdalene
said; "but the first thing to-morrow I will go out and get
him a gown at the clothes-mart.   His face is far too young
for that dress. Moreover the head-gear is not suited to the
attire; he needs, too, a long plait of hair to hang down behind.   That I can also buy for him, and a necklace or two
of bright-coloured beads.   However, he could pass now as
my niece should anyone chance to come in.   Now I will go
upstairs and fetch down his clothes and burn them.   If a
search should be made they will assuredly excite suspicion
if found in a house occupied only by women."

"You had best not do that, Magdalene. Hide them in a bed or up one of the chimneys. When he leaves this and gets into the country he will want them again. In these times a young woman unprotected could not walk the road by herself, and dressed as a woman it would be strange for him to be purchasing male attire."

"That is true enough, madam; as you say, it will be better to hide them until he can leave, which I hope will be very shortly."

"I wish we could leave too," the countess sighed. "I am weary of this long confinement here, and it is bad for Gertrude never going out except for a short walk with you after dark."

"It would not do to attempt it," the old woman said. "The Spanish soldiers are plundering all round Ghent; the Germans are no better at Antwerp. You know what stories are reported of their doings."

"No, we could not go in that direction," the countess agreed; "but I have thought often, Magdalene, that we may possibly make our way down to Ostend. Things are much quieter on that line."

"I should be glad to give you what escort I could, madam," Ned said. "But, indeed, the times are bad for travelling; and as you are safe here as it seems for the present, I would not say a word to induce you to leave and to encounter such dangers as you might meet by the way. In a short time, I believe the greater part of the Spaniards and Germans will march against Holland, and Brabant will then be free from the knaves for a while, and the journey might be undertaken with greater safety."

"You are right," the countess said. "It was but a passing thought, and now we have waited here so long we may well wait a little longer. Now, tell us more about yourself. You speak Dutch perfectly, and yet it seems to me at times that there is some slight accent in your tones."

"I am only half Dutch," Ned replied; "my father is English." He then related the whole history of his parentage, and of the events which led him to take service with the Prince of Orange. When he had concluded the countess said:

"Your story accounts for matters which surprised me somewhat in what you first told me. The men of our Low Countries are patient and somewhat slow of action, as is shown by the way in which they so long submitted to the cruel tyranny of the Spaniards. Now they have once taken up their arms, they will, I doubt not, defend themselves, and will fight to the death, however hopeless the chances may seem against them; but they are not prompt and quick to action. Therefore the manner of your escape from the hands of those who were watching you appeared to me wonderful; but now I know that you are English, and a sailor too, I can the better understand it, for I have heard that your countrymen are quick in their decisions and prompt in action.

"They say that many of them are coming over to fight in Holland; being content to serve without pay, and venturing their lives in our cause, solely because our religion is the same and they have hatred of oppression, having long been free from exactions on the part of their sovereigns. Many of our people have taken refuge there, and I have more than once thought that if the Spaniards continued to lord it in the Netherlands I would pass across the seas with Gertrude. My jewels would sell for enough to enable us to live quietly there."

"If you should go to England, madam," Ned said earnestly. "I pray you in the first place to inquire for Mistress

Martin at Rotherhithe, which is close by the city. I can warrant you she will do all in her power to assist you, and that her house will be at your disposal until you can find a more suitable lodgment. She will know from me, if I should escape from these dangers, from how great a peril you have saved me, and if it should be that I do not return home, she will welcome you equally when she learns from your lips that you took me in here when I was pursued by the minions of the Council of Blood, and that you furnished me with a disguise to enable me to escape from them."

"Should I go to England," the countess replied, "I will assuredly visit your mother, were it only to learn whether you escaped from all the dangers of your journey; but, indeed, I would gladly do so on my own account, for it is no slight comfort on arriving as strangers in an unknown country to meet with one of one's own nation to give us advice and assistance."

For another two hours they sat and talked of England, the countess being glad, for once, to think of another subject than the sad condition of her country. Then when the clock sounded nine they retired, Magdalene insisting upon Ned occupying her chamber, while she lay down upon a settle in the room in which they were sitting. Ned slept long and heavily; he had had but little rest during the two previous nights, and the sun was high when he awoke. As soon as he began to move about there was a knock at his door and the old servant entered.

"I need not ask if you have slept well," she remarked, "for the clocks have sounded nine, and I have been back an hour from market. Here are all your things, and I warrant me that when you are dressed in them you will pass anywhere as a buxom peasant girl."

Indeed, when Ned came down stairs in the short petti-
coats, trimmed bodice, and bright kerchief pinned across the
bosom, and two rows of large blue beads round his neck, his
disguise was perfect, save as to his head. This Magdalene
again arranged for him. " Yes, you will do very well
now," she said, surveying him critically. " I have bought
a basket, too, full of eggs ; and with that on your arm you
can go boldly out and fear no detection, and can walk
straight through the city gates."

" I hope I don't look as awkward as I feel?" Ned asked
smiling.

" No, you do not look awkward at all. You had best
join a party as you go out, and separate from them when
once you are well beyond the walls."

" He must return here this evening, Magdalene," the
countess said. " He has a mission to perform, and cannot
leave until he does."

" I will set about it at once, countess, and shall get it
finished before the gates are closed. I will not on any account bring upon you the risk of another night's stay here."

" I think there will be no risk in it," the countess said
firmly ; " and for to-day at least there is sure to be a vigilant watch kept at the gates. It were best, too, that you
left before noon, for by that time most of the people from
the villages round are returning. If you are not recognized in the streets there is no risk whatever while you are
in here ; besides, we shall be anxious to know how you have
got through the day. And another reason why you had
better stay the night is that by starting in the morning you
will have the day before you to get well away, whereas if
you go at night you may well miss your road, especially if
there is no moon, and you do not know the country. Therefore I pray you urgently to come back here for to-night.

It is a pleasure to us to have a visitor here, and does us good to have a fresh subject for our thoughts. Gertrude has been doing nothing but talk about England ever since she woke."

Although Ned saw that the old servant was very reluctant that he should, as she considered, imperil her charges' safety by a longer stay, he could not refuse the invitation so warmly given. Breakfast was now placed on the table. As soon as the meal was over he prepared to start, receiving many directions from Magdalene to be sure and not take long strides, or to swing his arms too much, or to stare about, but to carry himself discreetly, as was becoming a young woman in a town full of rough foreign men.

"How do you mean to see the people to whom you have letters?" the countess asked. "Some of them, you tell me, are nobles, and it will not be easy for a peasant girl to come into their presence."

"I am told to send up the message that a person from the village of Beerholt is desirous of speaking to them, countess," Ned replied. "I believe there is no such village, but it is a sort of password; and I have another with which to address them when they see me."

"I will start with you," the servant said, "and walk with you until you are past the guards. There are many soldiers about in the quarter this morning, and I hear they are questioning every one whether they have seen aught of a country lad.

"I thank you," Ned replied, "but I would rather go alone. If I am detected harm would only come to myself, but if you were with me you would assuredly all be involved in my misfortune. I would far rather go alone. I do not feel that there is any danger of my being suspected; and if I am alone I can bandy jokes with the soldiers if they

speak to me. There is no fear that either Spanish or Germans will notice that I speak Dutch rather than Flemish.
What is the price at which I ought to offer my eggs ?"

Magdalene told him the price she generally paid to the
market women. " Of course you must ask a little more than
that, and let people beat you down to that figure."

" Now I am off, then," he said, taking up the basket.

" May God keep you in his hands !" the countess said
solemnly. " It is not only your own life that is at stake,
but the interests of our country."

" Turn round and let me take a last look at you," Magdalene said, "and be sure that everything is right. Yes,
you will pass ; but remember what I told you about your
walk."

Ned walked briskly along until he came within sight of
two soldiers standing at a point where the street branched.
He now walked more slowly, stopping here and there and
offering his eggs to women standing at their doors or going
in and out. As he thought it better to effect a sale he asked
rather lower prices than those Magdalene had given him,
and disposed of three or four dozen before he reached the
soldiers. They made no remark as he passed. He felt more
confident now, and began to enter into the spirit of his
part; and when one of a group of soldiers in front of a
wine shop made some laughing remark to him he answered
him pertly, and turned the laugh of the man's comrades
against him.

On nearing the centre of the town he began his task of
delivering the letters, choosing first those who resided in
comparatively quiet streets, so as to get rid of as many of
them as possible before he entered the more crowded thor-
oughfares, where his risk of detection would be greater.
The only persons he was really afraid of meeting were Von

Aert and his clerk. The first might not detect him, but he fel sure that if the eyes of the latter fell upon him he would recognize him. With the various burghers he had little trouble. If they were in their shops he walked boldly in, and said to them, "I am the young woman from the village of Beerholt, whom you were expecting to see;" and in each case the burgher said at once, "It is my wife who has business with you," and led the way into the interior of the house. Ned's next question: "How is the wind blowing in Holland?" was answered by his being taken into a quiet room. The letter was then produced, and in each case an answer more or less satisfactory was given.

Ned found that there were a large number of men in Brussels ripe for a revolt, but that there was no great chance of the rising taking place until the Prince of Orange had gained some marked success, such as would encourage hopes that the struggle might in the end be successful. In three or four cases there were favourable answers to the appeals for funds, one burgher saying that he and his friends had subscribed between them a hundred thousand gulden, which they would forward by the first opportunity to a banker at Leyden. One said that he found that the prince's proclamations of absolute toleration of all religions produced a bad effect upon many of his friends, for that in Brabant they were as attached as ever to the Catholic religion, and would be loth to see Lutheran and Calvinist churches opened.

"I know that the prince is desirous of wounding no one's conscience," Ned said. "But how can it be expected the Protestants of Holland and Zeeland will allow the Catholics to have churches, with priests and processions, in their midst, if their fellow religionists are not suffered to worship in their way in Brabant? The prince has already proclaimed that every province may, as at present, make its own rules. And doubtless in the provinces where the Catholic religion is dominant it will still remain so. Only he claims that no man shall be persecuted for his religion."

"It is a pity that we cannot all be of one mind," the man said doubtfully. "Were there no religious questions between the provinces they would be as one."

"That may be," Ned replied. "But in religion as in all other things, men will differ just as they do about the meats they eat and the wines they drink."

"Well, I shall do my best," the burgher said, "But I fear these religious differences will for ever stand in the way of any united action on the part of the provinces."

"I fear that it will," Ned agreed, "so long as people think it more important to enforce their neighbours' consciences than to obtain freedom for themselves."

The two last letters that Ned had to deliver were to nobles, whose mansions were situated in the Grand Square. It was not easy to obtain access here. The lackeys would probably laugh in his face did he ask them to take his message to their master. And indeed the disguise he now wore, although excellent as a protection from danger, was the worst possible as regarded his chance of obtaining an interview. By this time he had sold the greater part of his eggs, and he sat down, as if fatigued, on a door-step at a short distance from one of the mansions, and waited in the hope that he might presently see the noble with whom he had to do issue out.

In half an hour two mounted lackeys rode up to the door, one of them leading a horse. A short time afterwards a gentleman came out and mounted. He heard a bystander say to another, "There is the Count of Sluys."

Ned got up, took his basket, and as the count came along crossed the road hurriedly just in front of his horse. As he did so he stumbled and fell, and a number of his eggs rolled out on the ground. There was a laugh among the bystanders, and the count reined in his horse.

"What possessed you to run like that under my horse's feet, my poor girl?" he asked, as Ned rose and began to cry loudly. Ned looked up in his face and rapidly said: "I am the person you expect from Beerholt."

The count gave a low exclamation of surprise, and Ned went on, "How does the wind blow in Holland?" The count deliberately felt in his pouch and drew out a coin, which he handed to Ned.

"Be at my back-door in an hour's time. Say to the servant who opens it, 'I am the person expected.' He will lead you to me."

Then he rode forward, Ned pouring out voluble thanks for the coin bestowed upon him.

"You are a clever wench," a soldier standing by said to Ned laughing. "That was very artfully done, and I warrant me it is not the first time you have tried it."

"I wasn't going to carry my eggs all the way back," Ned replied in an undertone. "I suppose there are tricks in your trade as well as in mine."

The soldier laughed again, and Ned passing quickly on mingled in the crowd, and soon moved away a considerable distance from the house. An hour later he went up a side street, in which was the door used by the servants and trades-people of the count. A lackey was standing there. "I am the person expected," Ned said quietly to him. He at once led the way into the house up some back stairs and passages, along a large corridor, then opening a door he motioned to Ned to enter.

CHAPTER X.

A DANGEROUS ENCOUNTER.

THE Count of Sluys was sitting at a table covered with papers.

"You have chosen a strange disguise," he said with a smile.

"It is none of my choosing," Ned replied. "I came into the city in the dress of a peasant boy, but was arrested by Councillor Von Aert, and had I not made my escape should probably have by this time been hung."

"Are you the lad for whom such a search has been made?" the count asked in surprise. "Von Aert is so furious he can talk about nothing else, and all the world is laughing at his having been tricked by a boy. Had I known that it was the prince's messenger I should not have felt inclined to laugh; thinking that papers, that would have boded me evil if discovered, might have been found upon him."

"They were found upon me," Ned replied; "but happily I recovered them. As they were not addressed, no one was any the wiser. This is the one intended for you, sir."

The count opened and read the document, and then gave Ned a long message to deliver to the prince. It contained particulars of his interviews with several other nobles, with details as to the number of men they could put in the field, and the funds they could dispose of in aid of the rising. Ned took notes of all the figures on a slip of paper, as he had done in several other instances. The count then asked him as to his arrest and manner of escape, and laughed heartily when he found that Von Aert had himself by mistake returned the letters found upon Ned.

"I have delivered all but one," Ned said. "And that I know not how to dispose of, for it would be dangerous to play the same trick again. And, indeed, I want if possible to be out of this town to-morrow; not so much for my own sake, but because were I detected it might bring destruction upon those who are sheltering me."

"Who is this letter for?" the count asked. Ned hesitated; the noble to whom the letter was addressed was, like many others of the prince's secret adherents, openly a strong supporter of the Duke of Alva. And, indeed, many were at that time playing a double game, so as to make profit whichever side was successful in the long run.

"Perhaps it is better not to tell me," the count said, seeing Ned's hesitation, "and I am glad to see that you are so discreet. But it can be managed in this way: Take a pen and go to that other table and write the address on the letter. I will call in my servant and tell him to take it from you and to deliver it at once, and ask for a reply to the person from Beerholt. That is, if that is the password to him also. He shall deliver the reply to you, and I will give you my promise that I will never ask him afterwards to whom he took the letter."

Ned felt that this would be the best course he could adopt, and addressed the letter at once. The count touched a bell and the lackey again entered.

"Take that letter at once," the count said, motioning to the letter Ned held in his hand. "You will deliver it yourself, and ask that an answer may be given to you for the person from Beerholt. Wait for that answer and bring it back here."

After the servant had gone the count chatted with Ned as to the state of affairs in Holland, and asked him many questions about himself. It was an hour and a half before the servant returned. He was advancing with the letter to the count, when the latter motioned to him to hand it to Ned.

" Is there nothing else that I can do for you?" he asked. " How do you intend to travel back through the country? Surely not in that dress?"

" No, sir; I was thinking of procuring another."

" It might be difficult for you to get one," the count said. " I will manage that for you;" and he again touched the bell. " Philip," he said to the lackey, " I need a suit of your clothes; a quiet plain suit, such as you would use if you rode on an errand for me. Bring them here at once, and order a new suit for yourself. He is but little taller than you are," he went on when the man had retired, " and his clothes will, I doubt not, fit you. You have not got a horse, I suppose?"

" No, sir."

" Which way are you going back?"

" I shall take the Antwerp road."

" There is a clump of trees about three miles along that road," the count said. " Philip shall be there with a horse for you at any hour that you like to name."

" I thank you greatly, count. I will be there at nine in the morning. I shall sally out in my present dress, leave the road a mile or so from the town, and find some quiet place where I can put on the suit you have furnished me with, and then walk on to the wood."

" Very well; you shall find the horse there at that hour without fail. You are a brave lad, and have carried out your task with great discretion. I hope some day to see you again by the side of the Prince of Orange."

A minute later the lackey returned with a bundle containing the suit of clothes. Ned placed it in his basket.

"Good-bye, and a good journey," the count said. Ned followed the lackey, whom the count had told him had been born on his estate, and could be implicitly trusted, down the stairs, and then made his way without interruption to his lodging.

"Welcome back," the countess exclaimed, as he entered. "We have prayed for you much to-day, but I began to fear that harm had befallen you; for it is already growing dark, and I thought you would have been here two or three hours since. How have you sped?"

"Excellently well, madam. I have delivered all the letters, and have obtained answers, in all cases but one, by word of mouth. That one is in writing; but I shall commit it to heart, and destroy it at once. Then, if I am again searched, I shall not be in so perilous a position as before."

He opened the letter and read it. As he had expected, it was written with extreme caution, and in evidently a feigned hand; no names either of places or persons were mentioned. The writer simply assured "his good cousin" of his good-will, and said that owing to the losses he had had in business from the troubled times, he could not say at present how much he could venture to aid him in the new business on which he had embarked.

After reading it through, Ned threw the paper into the fire.

"He did not feel sure as to whom he was writing," he said, "and feared treachery. However, as I have obtained nine answers, I need not mind if this last be but a poor one. Now, madam, I am ready to start at half-past seven in the morning. I have been furnished with another dis-

guise to put on when I get well beyond the walls; and a
horse is to be in waiting for me at a point three miles away;
so that I hope I shall be able to make my way back without much difficulty."

Accordingly in the morning, after many thanks to the
Countess Von Harp for her kindness, and the expression of
his sincerest hope that they might meet again, either in
England or Holland, Ned started on his way.   On reaching one of the streets leading to the gate he fell in behind
a group of country people, who, having early disposed of
the produce they had brought to market, were making
their way home.   Among them was a lad of about his own
age; and on reaching the gate two soldiers at once stepped
forward and seized him, to the surprise and consternation
of himself and his friends.   The soldiers paid no heed to
the outcry, but shouted to some one in the guard-house,
and immediately a man whom Ned recognized as one of the
warders who had attended him in prison came out.

"That is not the fellow," he said, after a brief look at
the captive.   "He is about the same age, but he is much
fairer than our fellow, and in no way like him in face."

Ned did not wait to hear the result of the examination,
but at once passed on out of the gate with the country
people unconnected with the captive.   A minute or two
later the latter with his friends issued forth.   Ned kept
about half way between the two parties until he reached a
lane branching off from the road in the direction in which
he wished to go.   Following this for a mile he came into
the Ghent road, and had no difficulty in finding the place
where he had hidden his money.   Going behind a stack of
corn, a short distance away, he changed his clothes; and
pushing the female garments well into the stack, went on
his way again, well pleased to be once more in male attire.

The clothes fitted him well, and were of a sober colour, such as a trusty retainer of a noble house would wear upon a journey. He retraced his steps until again on the road to Antwerp, and followed this until he came to the clump of trees. Here the count's servant was awaiting him with two horses. He smiled as Ned came up.

"If it had not been my own clothes you are wearing, I should not have known you again, he said. "The count bade me ask you if you had need of money? If so, I was to hand you this purse."

"Give my thanks to the count," Ned replied, "and say that I am well furnished."

"Not in all respects, I think," the man said.

Ned thought for a minute.

"No," he said. "I have no arms."

The man took a brace of pistols from the holsters of his own horse and placed them in those on Ned's saddle, and then unbuckled his sword-belt and handed it to Ned.

"It is ill travelling unarmed in the Netherlands at present," he said. "What with the Spaniards and the Germans, and the peasants who have been driven to take to a robber's life, no man should travel without weapons. The count bade me give you these, and say he was sure you would use them well if there should be need."

Ned leaped into the saddle, and with sincere thanks to the man galloped off towards Antwerp. Unless ill fortune should again throw him in the way of Von Aert he now felt safe; and he had no fear that this would be the case, for they would be devoting their whole energy to the search for him in Brussels. He burst into a fit of hearty laughter as he rode along, at the thought of the fury the councillor must have been thrown into when, upon his return home, he discovered that he had given away the wrong packet of let-

ters. He would have been angry enough before at the escape of the captive he was himself watching, and the loss
thereby of the means upon which he had reckoned to discover the ownership of the letters, and so to swell the list
of victims. Still he doubtless consoled himself at the
thought that he was sure before many hours to have his
prisoner again in his power, and that, after all, annoying
as it was, the delay would be a short one indeed. But when
he took the packet from his pocket, and discovered that he
had given up the all-important documents, and had retained a packet of blank paper, he must have seen at once
that he was foiled. He might recapture the prisoner, torture him, and put him to death ; but his first step would
of course have been to destroy the precious letters, and
there would be no evidence forthcoming against those for
whom they were intended, and who were doubtless men of
considerable standing and position, and not to be assailed
upon the mere avowal extracted by torture from a boy and
unsupported by any written proofs.

" That evil-looking clerk of his will come in for a share
of his displeasure," Ned thought to himself. "I believe that
he is worse than his master, and will take it sorely to heart
at having been tricked by a boy. I should have scant
mercy to expect should I ever fall into their hands again."

Ned rode through the city of Mechlin without drawing
rein. It was but a month since that it had been the scene
of the most horrible butchery, simply because it had opened
its gates to the Prince of Orange on his forward march to
attempt the relief of Mons. A few of the prince's German
mercenaries had been left there as a garrison. These fired
a few shots when the Spanish army approached, and then
fled in the night, leaving the town to the vengeance of the
Spaniards. In the morning a procession of priests and

citizens went out to beg for pardon, but the Spaniards rushed into the town and began a sack and a slaughter that continued for three days.

The churches, monasteries, and religious houses of every kind, as well as those of the private citizens, were sacked; and the desecration of the churches by the fanatics of Antwerp, for which hundreds of heretics had been burnt to death, was now repeated a thousand-fold by the Roman Catholic soldiers of Philip. The ornaments of the altars, the chalices, curtains, carpets, gold embroidered robes of the priests, the repositories of the Host, the precious vessels used in extreme unction, the rich clothing and jewelry of the effigies of the Virgin and saints were all plundered. The property of the Catholic citizens was taken as freely as that of the Protestants; of whom, indeed, there were few in the city. Men, women, and children were murdered wholesale in the streets.

Even the ultra-Catholic Jean Richardot, member of the Grand Council, in reporting upon the events, ended his narration by saying "He could say no more, for his hair stood on end, not only at recounting, but even at remembering the scene." The survivors of the sack were moving listlessly about the streets of the ruined city as Ned rode through. Great numbers had died of hunger after the conclusion of the pillage; for no food was to be obtained, and none dare leave their houses until the Spanish and German troops had departed. Zutphen had suffered a vengeance even more terrible than that of Mechlin. Alva had ordered his son, Frederick, who commanded the army that marched against it, to leave not a single man alive in the city, and to burn every house to the ground; and the orders were literally obeyed. The garrison were first put to the sword, and then the citizens were attacked and slaughtered wholesale. Some were stripped naked and

turned out to freeze to death in the fields.   Five hundred
were tied back to back and drowned in the river.   Some
were hung up by their feet, and suffered for many hours
until death came to their relief.

Ned put up at Antwerp for the night.   The news of
the destruction of Zutphen, and of the horrors perpetrated
there, had arrived but a few hours before, and a feeling of
the most intense horror and indignation filled the inhabitants; but none dared to express what every one felt.   The
fate of Mechlin and Zutphen was as Alva had meant it to
be, a lesson so terrible, that throughout the Netherlands,
save in Holland and Zeeland alone, the inhabitants were
palsied by terror.   Had one great city set the example and
risen against the Spaniards, the rest would have followed;
but none dared be the first to provoke so terrible a vengeance.   Men who would have risked their own lives shrank
from exposing their wives and children to atrocities and
death.   It seemed that conflict was useless.   Van der Berg,
a brother-in-law of the Prince of Orange, who had been
placed by the prince as Governor of Guelderland, and
Overyssel, fled by night, and all the cities which had
raised the standard of Orange deserted the cause at
once.   Friesland, too, again submitted to the Spanish
yoke.

Ned, after putting up his horse at an hotel at Antwerp,
sauntered out into the streets.   Antwerp at that time was
one of the finest and wealthiest towns in Europe.   Its public buildings were magnificent, the town-hall a marvel of
architectural beauty.   He stood in the great square admir-
ing its beauties and those of the cathedral when he was
conscious of someone staring fixedly at him, and he could
scarce repress a start when he saw the malicious face of
Genet, the clerk of Councillor Von Aert. His first impulse
was to fly, but the square was full of burghers, with many

groups of Spanish soldiers sauntering about; he could not hope to escape.

He saw by the expression on Genet's face that as yet he was not sure of his identity. He had before seen him only as a country boy, and in his present attire his appearance was naturally a good deal changed. Still the fixed stare of the man showed that his suspicions were strongly aroused, and Ned felt sure that it would not be long before he completely recognized him. Nothing could be more unfortunate than that this man whom he had believed to be diligently searching for him in Brussels should thus meet him in the streets of Antwerp. Turning the matter over rapidly in his mind he saw but one hope of escape. He sauntered quietly up to a group of soldiers.

"My friends," he said, "do you want to earn a few crowns?"

"That would we right gladly," one of them replied, "seeing that His Gracious Majesty has forgotten to pay us for well-nigh a year."

"There is a hang-dog villain with a squint, in a russet cloak and doublet, just behind me," Ned said. "I have had dealings with him, and know him and his master to be villains. He claims that I am in debt to his master, and it may be that it is true; but I have particular reasons for objecting to be laid by the heels for it just now."

"That is natural enough," the soldier said. "I have experienced the same unpleasantness, and can feel for you."

"See here, then," Ned said. "Here are ten crowns, which is two a-piece for you. Now, I want you to hustle against that fellow, pick a quarrel with him and charge him with assaulting you, and drag him away to the guard-house. Give him a slap on the mouth if he cries out, and throw him into a cell, and let him cool his heels there till morning. That will give me time to finish my business and be off again into the country."

"That can be managed easily enough," the soldier said with a laugh. "He is an ill-favoured-looking varlet; and is, I doubt not, a pestilent heretic. It would be a pleasure to cuff him even without your honour's crowns."

"Here is the money, then," Ned said; "but above all, as I have said, do not let him talk or cry out or make a tumult. Nip him tightly by the neck."

"We know our business," the soldier said. "You can rely on us to manage your affair.'

Ned sauntered quietly on. In a minute or two he heard a loud and sudden altercation, then there was the sound of blows, and looking round he saw two of the soldiers shaking Genet violently. The man endeavoured to shout to the crowd; but one of the soldiers smote him heavily on the mouth, and then surrounding him they dragged him away. "That is very satisfactorily done," Ned said to himself, "and it is by no means likely that Master Genet will get a hearing before to-morrow morning. He will be pushed into a cell in the guard-room on the charge of brawling and insolence, and it is not probable that anyone will go near him till the morning. I certainly should like to peep in and have a look at him. His rage would be good to see; and he has been instrumental in sending such hundreds of men to prison that one would like to see how he feels now that it is his turn. Still I must not count too surely upon having time. He may possibly find some officers who will listen to his tale, although I do not think he is likely to do that; but still it would be foolish to risk it, and I will mount my horse and ride on at once."

The ostler was somewhat surprised when Ned told him that he had changed his mind, and that, instead of remaining for the night at Antwerp, he should ride forward at once. As Ned paid him handsomely for the feed the horse had had he made no remark, and Ned mounted and rode out through the town by the gate through which he had entered. Then he made a wide detour round the town, and rode on along the bank of the river until he came to a ferry. Here he crossed, and then rode on until he reached a village, where he resolved to stop the night, being now off the main roads, and therefore fairly safe from pursuit, even should Genet be able to satisfy his captors that a mistake had been made, and that those who captured him had in fact been aiding a fugitive to escape from justice.

The host of the little inn apologized for the poor fare that was set before him, on the ground of the exactions of the soldiers. " One can scarcely call one's life one's own," he grumbled. " A body of them rode into the village yesterday and stripped it clear of everything, maltreating all who ventured even to remonstrate. They came from Antwerp, I believe; but there is no saying, and even if we knew them it would be useless to make complaints."

Ned assured his host that he was very indifferent in the matter of food.

"In these days," he said, "if one can get a piece of bread one may think one's self lucky. But you have, I hope, sufficient forage for my horse."

"Yes," the landlord replied; " their horses ate as much as they could, but they could not carry off my supply of corn. Indeed the horses were pretty well laden as it was with ducks and geese. I let them have as much wine as they could drink, and of the best, so they did not trouble to go down into my cellar. If they had they would likely enough have broached all the casks and let the wine run. There is nothing that these fellows are not capable of; they seem to do mischief out of pure devilment."

Ned had scarcely finished his meal when a tramping of horses was heard outside.

"The saints protect us!" the landlord exclaimed. "Here are either these fellows coming back again, or another set doubtless just as bad."

A minute later the door opened and a party of a dozen soldiers entered.

"Wine, landlord! and your best!" a sergeant said. "Some comrades who called here yesterday told us that your tap was good, so we have just ridden over to give you a turn."

The landlord groaned.

"Gracious, sirs," he said, "I am but a poor man, and your comrades on parting forgot to settle for their wine. Another two or three such visits, and I am ruined."

A volley of impatient oaths at once broke out, and without further hesitation the terrified landlord hurried away, and returned loaded with flasks of wine, upon which the soldiers were speedily engaged.

"And who may you be, young sir?" one of them asked Ned, who was sitting at a small table apart from the rest,

"I am simply a traveller," Ned replied, "engaged upon my master's business."

"You are a likely looking young fellow too," the soldier said, "and would have made a good soldier if you had had the chance, instead of jogging about doing your lord's bidding; but I warrant me you are no better than the rest of your countrymen, and do not know one end of a sword from the other."

"I am not skilled in arms," Ned replied, "though my experience goes a little further than you say; but as you gentlemen protect the Netherlands, and we have no army of our own, I have not had the opportunity, even had I wished it, to become a soldier."

"Move over here," the soldier said, "and join us in a cup to the honour of Philip and confusion to the Prince of Orange and all traitors."

"I will join you in drinking to Philip, for in truth he is a great monarch and a powerful, and I will also drink to the confusion of all traitors whomsoever they may be."

"You are all traitors at heart," one of the Spaniards who had not before spoken, put in. "There is not a native of the Netherlands but would rise against us to-morrow."

"I think that is true speaking," said Ned quietly. "There are many traitors in the Netherlands I grant you, but there are others to whom your words can hardly apply."

"They are all the same," the soldier said angrily. "Knaves every one of them. However, before we have done with them we will reduce their number."

Ned did not reply; but having drank the glass of wine, returned to his seat, and shortly afterwards, when the soldiers began to quarrel among themselves, slipped from the room. The landlord was outside, pacing anxiously up and down.

"Are there any more of them in the village?" Ned asked.

"Not that I know of," he answered; "and to me it makes no difference. They will stay here swilling my wine all night, and in the morning like enough will set fire to my house before they ride away. I have just sent off my wife and daughters to be out of their reach. As for myself, I am half-minded to mix poison with their wine and finish with them."

"That would only bring down vengeance upon yourself," Ned said. "Some would probably escape and tell the tale. At any rate, as there are so large a number there would be sure to be inquiry when they were found to be missing, and no doubt they mentioned to some of their friends before they started where they were coming to, and inquiry would be made. You could never get rid of all their bodies. Besides, doubtless others in the village heard them ride up, and know that they have been here; so you could not escape detection. It is better to put up with them."

" Yes, if there were only these fellows; but you will see that another party will come, and another, until I am entirely ruined."

"If you think that, I would in the morning shut up my house and depart, and not return until these troubles are over."

" And then come back and find my house burned down," the innkeeper groaned.

" Better that than to see yourself gradually ruined, and perhaps lose your life," Ned said.

"There is nowhere to go to," the innkeeper said with a shake of his head.

" You might do as many others have done," Ned replied, " and go to Holland, where at least you would be safe."

" But not for long," the man said. " The army will soon be on the march in that direction, and my fate there would be worse than here. Here I am only an innkeeper to be fleeced ; there I should be regarded as a heretic to be burnt. Listen to them. They are fighting now. Do you hear my mugs crashing? I only hope that they will kill each other to the last man. I should advise you, sir, to be off at once. They may take it into their heads that you are someone it behoves them to slay, it matters not whom; and you would certainly get no sleep here to-night if you stay."

" That is true enough," Ned agreed ; " and perhaps it would be the best way for me to get on horseback again, but I know not the road, and might likely enough miss it altogether, and drown myself in one of your ditches."

" I will send my boy with you to put you on to the road," the landlord said. "I sent him out to sleep in the stables, so as to be out of the way of these desperadoes. He will walk beside your horse until you get into the main road."

Ned willingly accepted the proposal, for indeed he felt that there might be danger in remaining in the house with these drunken soldiers. He accordingly paid his reckoning, and was soon on horseback again, with the landlord's son, a boy of some ten years old, walking beside him. In half an hour they came upon a broad road.

"This," the lad said, "will take you to St. Nicholas."

Ned gave the boy a crown for his trouble, and rode slowly along. He had no idea of entering St. Nicholas, for it was now nigh eleven o'clock at night, and the arrival of a traveller at such an hour would be sure to attract attention. The night, too, was dark, and he could scarce see the road he was following. After thinking it over for some time he dismounted, led his horse a distance from the road, fastened the reins to a bush, and threw himself down on the ground to wait for daylight. The night was cold, and a fine rain was falling. Ned got up from time to time and walked about to keep himself warm, and was heartily glad when he saw the first rays of daylight in the east.

After waiting for half an hour he mounted, and after riding a few miles entered a large village. Thinking that it would be safer than at St. Nicholas, he halted there. It was still raining, and the drenched state of his clothes therefore excited no coment beyond the host's remark, "You must have started early to have got so wet?"

" Yes," he said, " I was up before daylight. I have a change of clothes in my saddle-bag, and shall be glad to

put them on.   Will you order your man to give my horse
a good rub down, and let him have a hot mash.   How far
am I from Ghent now?"

"If you have come from Antwerp, sir, you have come
just half-way."

Ned changed his clothes and had some breakfast, and
then as he sat by the fire the feeling of warmth and comfort after his long and cold night overpowered him, and he
went fast to sleep.

CHAPTER XI.

NED slept for some hours. When he woke he heard the landlord talking in loud tones in the passage outside. "I tell you, wife, it is a burning shame. Mynheer Von Bost has never done a soul harm in his life. He has always been ready to open his purse-strings in case of distress; he is a man that does not meddle in any way with politics. It is true that he does not go to mass, but that hurts no one; and there is many a ne'er-do-well in the village who never darkens the church door. If he prefers to pray in his own house and in his own way, what matter is it to anyone? His cloth-mill gives employment to half the village. What we shall do if it is shut up I am sure I don't know. But what do they care for the village. Mynheer Von Bost is a Protestant and a rich man—that is quite enough for the Blood Council; so he and his pretty young wife are to be dragged off and executed."

"What is that?" Ned asked, opening the door. "Can't the Blood Council even leave your quiet village alone?"

"They can leave nothing alone," the landlord said bitterly. "An hour ago four of their officials rode up, under one of the agents of the Council—a squint-eyed villain. They stopped at the door and asked for the house of Mynheer Von Bost, and then rode off, and half an hour afterwards one of the servants ran down into the village with the news that her master and mistress had been arrested, and that they were to be taken to Antwerp to be executed; for that, as it seems, they had already been tried without their knowing anything about it."

Ned started when he heard the landlord describe the leader of the party. This, then, accounted for Genet's presence at Antwerp; he had been sent from Brussels to arrest this cloth manufacturer. He had evidently succeeded in establishing his identity late in the evening or at early morning, and guessing that Ned would have ridden on without loss of time after setting the soldiers on to assault him, had proceeded to carry out the mission with which he was charged.

"The villagers would tear the villain limb from limb if they dared," the landlord went on.

"Why don't they dare?" Ned asked.

"Why? Why, because we should be having a troop of soldiers down here in twenty-four hours, and the village would be burnt, and every man in it, and woman too, put to death. No, no, sir; the people here would do a good deal for Mynheer Von Bost and his wife, but they won't risk everything."

"Would they risk anything, do you think?" Ned asked. "Are there half a dozen men in the village, do you think, who would strike a blow for their master, if they could do it without running the risk you speak of?"

The landlord looked at him sharply. "This is not the time, young sir, for men to speak before strangers about matters which may put their neck in danger."

"You are right," Ned said; "and I do not blame you for being discreet. I know this cross-eyed man you speak of, and know that he is the secretary of one of the most cruel and bloody of the Council; and it was but yesterday that I escaped from his hands almost by a miracle. And

I would now, if I could, baffle the villain again. I suppose they are still at his house?"

"They are. They have ordered breakfast to be prepared for them, and it may be another hour before they set out."

"My plan is this, then," Ned said. "If I could get half a dozen determined men to join me, we would go back along the road towards Antwerp three miles or so, and lie in wait until they came along, and then rescue their prisoners from them. If we could get a horse for the man to ride with his wife behind him, all the better. We could pretend to be robbers; there are plenty of starving peasants that have been driven to that, and if we attack them three miles away they would have no suspicion that the people of the village had any hand in it."

"I will see about it," the landlord said warmly. "When my son-in-law's little farm was burnt down last winter, Mynheer Van Bost advanced him money to rebuild it, and charged no interest. He lives but a quarter of a mile out of the village, and I think he will be your man, and would be able to lay his hands on the others. I will run over to him and be back in a quarter of an hour."

In the meantime Ned ordered his horse to be saddled, and when the landlord returned he was ready to start.

"My son-in-law will join you," he said. "He has two brothers whom he will bring with him. They both work in Van Bost's factory. He bids me tell you to go on for two miles, and to stop where the first road comes in on the right-hand side. They will join you there, and will then go on with you as far as you may think fit. They have got guns, so you can lie in ambush. He will bring a horse with him with a pillion. He could have got more men, but he thinks that the fewer to know the secret the better, as there may be inquiries here; and in these days none can trust his own neighbour. And now farewell, young sir. I know not who you are, but you must have a good heart to venture your life in a quarrel for people of whom you know nothing."

"I am a Protestant myself, landlord, and I have had uncles and other relations murdered by the Blood Council. Moreover I have a special feud with the chief of these villains."

So saying Ned shook the landlord's hand and rode off. He halted when he came to the point indicated. In less than half an hour he saw three men coming from the other direction. As one of them was leading a horse he at once rode on to meet them.

"We have made a detour through the fields," the young man leading the horse said. "It would not have done for anyone in the village to have seen us journeying this way."

"Quite right," Ned agreed. "There are babblers everywhere, and the fewer who know aught of a matter like this the better. Now, where had we best ambuscade?"

"There is a little wood by the roadside half a mile on, and we had best move there at once, for they may be along at any time now."

Two of the men were armed with muskets, and all three carried flails. They moved briskly forward until they got to the wood.

"You had best fasten up the horse among the trees," Ned said, "and then take your station close to the road. I will ride out from the trees as I come up and engage them in talk, so that you and your brother can take a steady aim. Don't fire until you are sure of each bringing down a man, then rush out and engage them with your flails. I will answer for their leader myself."

"We won't miss them, never fear, young sir. We have

too much practice at the ducks in the winter to miss such a mark as that."

After seeing the horse tied up, and the men take their stations behind trees, Ned went a few yards further and then waited the coming of the party with the prisoners. He had not a shadow of compunction at the fate that was about to befall these officials. They had hauled away hundreds to the gallows, and the animosity that prevailed between the two parties was so intense that neither thought of sparing the other if they fell into their hands. As for Genet, Ned felt that his own life would not be safe as long as this man lived. He might for aught he knew have other missions of the same nature as that he had just fulfilled, and he felt sure that whatever disguise he might adopt this man would detect him did they meet, and in that case not only his own life but that of many others might be sacrificed.

In about ten minutes the sound of horses' hoofs was heard. Ned waited till they came within a few paces, and then suddenly rode out from the wood. Genet, who was riding ahead of the others, reined in his horse suddenly.

"What are you doing fellow?" he began angrily, "riding out thus suddenly upon us?" Then his voice changed as he recognized Ned. "What, is it you again?" he exclaimed. "This time at least you shall not escape me."

He drew a pistol and fired. Ned was equally quick, and the two shots rang out together. Ned's cap flew from his head, the bullet just grazing his skin, while Genet fell forward on his saddle and rolled to the ground, shot through the heart. Almost at the same instant two guns were discharged from the wood, and two of the officials fell. The other two, behind whom the prisoners were strapped, set spurs to their horses; but Ned rode in front of them, and the men dashing from the trees seized the reins, " Surrender!" Ned shouted, " or you are dead men."

The two officers shouted lustily that they surrendered. but Ned had the greatest difficulty from preventing their assailants from knocking out their brains with their flails.

" There is no plunder to be obtained from them, comrades," he said loudly. " They are only poor knaves riding behind the master. Get them off their horses, and strap their hands with their own belts, and toss them in among the trees ; but you can search their pockets before you do so. I will see what their leader has got upon him."

As soon as the two prisoners were dragged away Ned addressed Mynheer Von Bost, who with his wife was standing almost bewildered by the sudden event that had freed them.

" This is no robbery, Maynheer, but a rescue. We have a horse and pillion here in the wood in readiness for you, and I should advise you to ride at once with your wife for Sluys or some other seaport, and thence take ship either into Holland or to England. Your lives will assuredly be forfeited if you remain here."

" But who are you, sir, who has done us this great service?"

" I am serving under the Prince of Orange," Ned replied; " and have been doing business for him at Brussels. I have twice narrowly escaped with my life from the hands of the leader of that party, and was in the village when they arrived and seized you. Finding how deep was the regret that so kind a master should be thus led away to execution, I determined if possible to save you, and with the aid of these three men, two of whom are workmen of yours, and the other a farmer you befriended last year when his house was burnt down, we have succeeded in doing so."

The three men now came out of the wood.

" My brave fellows," the manufacturer said, "I and my wife owe our lives to you and to this gentleman."

" You are heartily welcome, sir," the young farmer said. " You have saved me from ruin, and one good turn deserves another. I and my brothers were only too glad to join when we heard that this gentleman was determined to try to release you. If it had not been for him it would never have entered our heads till it was too late."

" May I ask your name, sir?" Von Bost said to Ned. " My wife and I would like to know to whom we owe a lifelong debt of gratitude. I will take your advice and ride at once for Sluys. I have many friends there who will conceal us and get us on board a ship. My arrangement have long been made for departure, and my capital transferred to England; but I thought I should have had sufficient notice of danger to take flight. Where can I hear of you, sir?"

" My name is Edward Martin. My father is an English captain, who lives at Rotherhithe, close by London. At present, as I said, I am in the service of the Prince of Orange; but my home is still in England. And now, sir, I think you had best be riding at once. I presume that there are by-roads by which you can avoid passing through any towns on your way to Sluys. It is better not to delay a minute, for at any moment some party or other of soldiers may come along."

The men had by this time brought out the horse. Von Bost mounted, and his wife was assisted on to the pillion behind him.

" Good-bye, good friends," he said. " God grant that no harm come to you for this kind deed."

The moment he had ridden off Ned and his companions

lifted the bodies of the three men who had fallen and carried them into the wood.

"We had best turn their pockets inside out," Ned said, "and take away everything of value upon them."

"This fellow has a well-lined purse," the young farmer said as he examined the pocket of Genet; "and here are a bundle of papers in his doublet."

"Give me the papers," Ned said, "they may be useful to me, and doubtless they contain lists of other victims whom I may be able to send warning to in time for them to escape."

"What shall we do about the horses?"

"I would take off the saddles, bridles, and accoutrements, throw them into a ditch together with the men's arms and pile a few bushes over them, then drive the horses across the fields till they reach some grazing ground near the river; the farmers there will doubtless appropriate them in time. Now, as to these two prisoners, they are the only trouble."

"You need not trouble about them," the farmer said," "we have made them safe. We are not going to risk our lives and those of our wives and families, as we should have done if we had left those fellows alive to identify us. There is sure to be a search sooner or later, and those two men would have led the party to every house within miles round, and would have been sure to recognize one or other of us. We are ready to risk our lives to save Mynheer Von Bost, but we are not willing to throw them away needlessly."

Ned could hardly blame the men, who had indeed stabbed their captives the instant they dragged them among the trees, for doubtless the risk they would have run of detection would have been great had they permitted them to live. They had now only to regain their village without observation and to keep their own secret, to be free from all risk whatever. Putting Genet's papers in his doublet Ned again mounted his horse and rode off.

Two hours later he reached St. Nicholas. He could now have ridden straight on to Bergen-op-Zoom, the port at which he hoped to be able to find a boat, but he thought that Genet's papers might contain matters upon which it might be necessary for him to act at once. He had now no fear of detection, for with the death of Genet all search for himself would be at an end. Putting up his horse at an inn he ordered a meal to be prepared at once, and calling for a flask of wine in the meantime, sat down at a table in the corner of the great parlour and examined the papers.

First there was a list of twelve names, among whom was that of Von Bost. One of these, as well as that of the manufacturer, had been crossed out. With them were official documents ordering the arrest of the persons named, together in most cases with that of their wives and one or more members of their family. Besides these was a document with the seal of the Council, ordering all magistrates and others to render every assistance required by the bearer in carrying out the duties with which he was charged.

Then there was a long list of persons resident in St. Nicholas, Sluys, and Axel, against whom denunciations of heresy or of suspected disloyalty to Philip had been laid. There was a note at the bottom of this list: "Inquire into the condition of life and probable means of each of these suspected persons."

"It is somewhat lucky for all these people," Ned said to himself, "that I happened to fall in with Mynheer Genet. The question now is how to warn them. I see there are three orders of arrest against people here, and ten names on the suspected list. At any rate I can warn them myself."

As soon as he had finished his meal Ned inquired the addresses of the three persons ordered to be arrested. They were all, as he had expected, leading men in the place; for it was the confiscation of the goods of the victims, quite as much as any question of religion or loyalty, that was at the bottom of a large proportion of the arrests and executions. The first Ned called upon was, like Von Bost, a cloth manufacturer. He was rather a pompous man, and when Ned was shown in said:

"Now, young man, my time is valuable, so let us have no useless talking. What is it you want?"

"Your time perhaps is more valuable than you think," Ned said quietly, "seeing that you have not got much of it left."

"What do you mean, sir?" the manufacturer asked angrily.

"I mean simply this," Ned replied. "That I am the bearer of an order of the Council for your arrest, and that of your wife, your son Ernest, and your daughter Mary, upon the charge of having been present and taken part in a meeting of the people of this town at which words of a treasonable character were uttered. Moreover, there is a note at the bottom of this order saying that these charges have been proved to the satisfaction of the Council, and that you are accordingly to be executed upon your arrival at Antwerp, the necessary orders having been transmitted to the governor of the prison there."

The manufacturer sank down in a chair the picture of terror.

"I have done no harm," he stammered. "I knew not when I went to the meeting what was going to be said there."

"What matters that?" Ned asked. "You have been tried and condemned, and one or other of the Council has doubt-

less obtained the grant of your property. Well, sir, I will
not frighten you longer. This is the document in question,
but fortunately I am not the person charged with this execution. I met him on the way and there was a disagree-
ment between us, and the result is that he will execute no
more orders, and his papers fell into my hands. It may be
some days before he is missed, and then doubtless someone
else will be charged to carry out the orders of which he
was the bearer. This will give you time to make preparations for flight, and I should advise you before eight-and-
forty hours are over to be on your way towards the frontier of Germany, or on board a ship at one of the ports. I
will hand you this document in order that you may con-
vince your wife and family of the danger that you are all
running, and of the urgent need of haste."

Ned left at once, before the man, who was almost stupe-
fied by the misfortune that had befallen him, had time to
utter his thanks. He then called on the other two men
against whom he bore orders of arrest. As both received
him with greater courtesy than that shown by the first he
had visited, he broke the news more gently to them, and
discussed with them the manner in which they had best
make their escape. One he found had friends and business
connections in Sluys, and doubted not that he could obtain
a passage there to Holland or England, while the other had
similar connections in Axel.

Ned handed over to them the orders for the arrest of
burghers of those towns, and these they gave him their
promise to deliver, and also either to see or to send letters
warning all the persons who were mentioned in the list of
suspected. As he was anxious to get on as soon as possible he also gave them the list of the suspected at St.
Nicholas, and these they promised also to warn; both were

profuse in their gratitude to him for having saved them from certain death. Having thus concluded his business, Ned again mounted his horse and rode for Bergen-op-Zoom, the port at which he intended, if possible, to embark for Zeeland.

Bergen-op-Zoom, an important town, lay half a mile distant from the Scheldt, and was connected with the river by a channel guarded by two forts. There had been a strong Spanish garrison here, but it had lately been weakened by the withdrawal of a large detachment to take part in the successful enterprise undertaken for the relief of Tergoes in the Island of Beveland, which was besieged by a force from Flushing. Ned had frequently been at Bergen-op-Zoom in the *Good Venture*, and knew that while the magistrates and wealthier citizens were devoted to the Spanish cause the greater portion of the inhabitants, especially the seafaring class, were patriots to a man.

He therefore went to a small inn by the water-side, where he had several times taken meals with his father when the ship was lying off from the river. Seeing his horse put up in the stable he entered the tap-room. The sailors drinking there looked somewhat surprised at the entrance of one differing much in appearance from the ordinary customers of the place. The landlord, who was leaning against his counter, did not advance to meet him; for strangers were by no means popular, and a suspicion that the new-comer was a spy would speedily empty his house. As Ned approached him he suddenly started, and was about to speak when the lad quickly placed his finger on his lip. He feared that the landlord was about to utter his name, and there might, for aught he knew, be someone there who would report it.

"How are you landlord?" he said. "It is some time

since I was here last, and I think you had almost forgotten me." The landlord took the hint.

"Yes, indeed," he said. "And how is your father? I have not seen him lately, and heard that he was not well."

"No; he has been laid up for some time, but he is mending. You see I have taken service."

"Ah, I see," the landlord said. "Well, my good wife will be glad to see you and hear about your family." So saying he led the way into a private room.

"Why, what means this, Master Martin?" he asked. "We heard here of the brave fight your father's ship made some two months since with a Spaniard in the Zuider-Zee, and that he was sorely wounded. But what means this masquerading? Surely you have not given up the sea?"

"Only for the present," Ned replied. "You know I am Dutch by my mother's side. All her family have been murdered by the Spaniards, and what with that and my father being attacked and wounded, I made up my mind to give up the sea for a time, and to help the good cause as much as I could. I have been carrying a message to Brussels and want now to get back to Rotterdam or some other seaport town. How had I best do it?"

"It is not easy," the landlord replied. "Our trade is stopped here now. The rivers swarm with craft, manned, some by the beggars of the sea, and others by fishermen; and the Spanish ships cannot come up save in great force. We have two or three of their war-ships here which go out and skirmish with our men, and do not always get the best of it. Our people did badly the other night when they let the Spaniards wade across to Tergoes. That was a bad business. But about your getting away. Let me see how it can be managed."

"I have got a horse here."

"That is bad," the landlord said. "You could put on sailor's clothes, and in the morning when I send in my guest list to the magistrate, I could put down that you had gone, but the horse would betray me. Is it a good beast?"

"Yes, it is a very good horse. It was a present to me, and I don't like parting with it. But of course I cannot - take it away."

"I will send round word to a man I know who deals in horses. He is one who will hold his tongue, especially when he sees an advantage in it. I will tell him it belonged to a man who has been here and gone away suddenly, and ask him what he will give for it, and take it quietly away after it gets dark to his own stables, and ask no questions about it. He will guess it belonged to somebody who has left secretly. Of course he won't give more than half the value of the animal; but I suppose you will not be particular about terms. Anyhow, I will do the best I can for you. When he is once out of the stables they may come and question as much as they like, but they will get nothing out of me beyond the fact that a young man came here, put up his horse, stayed the night, and left in the morning. I suppose they have no special interest in you so as to lead them to make a close inquiry?"

"None at all," Ned replied.

"That is settled then," the landlord said. "Now, as to yourself. Two of my sons are at sea, you know, and I can rig you up with some of their clothes so that you can stroll about on the wharves, and no one will suspect you of being anything but a fisherman. Then I will try and arrange with some of the sailors to take you down in a boat at night, and either put you on board the first of our craft they come upon, or land you at Flushing. Now I will take you in to my wife, and she will see about getting you a meal and making you comfortable.'

Later on the landlord came in and said that he had made a bargain for the horse.

"The beast is worth thirty crowns," he said, "but he will not give more than fifteen, and required a good deal of bargaining to raise him to that. Of course he suspected that there was something out of the way about the affair, and took advantage of it."

"That will do very well indeed," Ned said. "I did not expect to get anything for it."

"I have been having a talk too with some sailors belonging to a small craft lying at the wharf. They are most anxious to be off, for they are idle. The order that no boats were to leave was issued just after they came in. They have been six days doing nothing, and may, for aught they see, be kept here for another six months. They have been afraid to try to get away; for there are sentries all along the wall to see that none try to put out, and some guard-boats from the Spanish ships rowing backwards and forwards outside the port, both to see that no ships leave, and that none come up to harm the shipping. Still they say they have been making up their minds that they may as well stand the risk of being shot by the Spaniards as the certainty of being starved here; besides they are patriots, and know that their boats may be wanted at any time for the conveyance of troops. So when I told them that I doubted not that you would pay them well for landing you at Flushing, they agreed to make the attempt, and will try to-night. As soon as you have had your breakfast you had better join them in the tap-room, go out with them through the water-gate, and get on board their craft and lie snug there till night."

"How many men are there?" Ned asked.

"There are six altogether, but only two will be up here

presently. Here are the fifteen crowns for your horse.
That will do well to pay your passage to Flushing."

As soon as he had eaten his breakfast, Ned, now dressed
as a young fisherman, went into the tap-room with the landlord. Two sailors were sitting there."

"This is the young fellow that I was speaking to you
about," the landlord said. "He is one of us, and heart
and soul in the cause, and young though he looks has done
good service. He is ready to pay you fifteen crowns when
you land him at Flushing."

"That is a bargain," one of the men said, "and will pay
us for the week we have lost here. I should take you for
a sailor, young sir."

"I am a sailor," Ned said, and can lend a hand on board
if need be."

"Can you swim? Because if we are overhauled by the
Spaniards we shall all take to the water rather than fall
into their hands."

"Yes, I can swim," Ned said; "and agree with you
that I would rather swim than be captured. But if it is
only a boat-load that overhauls us I would try to beat them
off before giving up a craft in which I had a share."

The sailors looked rather doubtfully at the lad, and
their expression showed that they thought he was talking
boastfully.

"He means what he says," the landlord put in. "He
is the son of that English captain who beat off the great
Spanish ship *Don Pedro* in the Zuider-Zee a few weeks
ago."

The men's faces changed, and both got up and shook
hands cordially with Ned. "That was a brave affair,
young sir; and there is not a town in Holland where your

father's name is not spoken of in honour. We know the
ship well, and have helped load her before now; and now
we know who you are, recognize your face. No wonder
you want to get out of Bergen-op-Zoom. Why, if I had
known it had been you we would have been glad enough
to take you to Flushing without charging you a penny,
and will do so now—will we not, comrade ?—if it presses
you in any way to pay us ?"

"Not at all," Ned said. "I am well supplied with
money; and since you are risking your boat, as well as
your lives, it is only fair that I should pay my share. I
can afford the fifteen crowns well enough, and indeed it is
but the price of a horse that was given to me."

"Well, if it will not hurt you we will not say any more
about it," the sailor replied; "seeing that we have had a
bad time of it lately, and have scarce money enough left
between us to victual us until we get home. But had it been
otherwise, we would have starved for a week rather than
had it said that we made hard terms with the son of the
brave Captain Martin when he was trying to escape from
the hands of the Spaniards."

"Now, lads, you had better be off at once," the landlord interrupted. "It is time I sent in my report to the
town-hall; and like enough men will be down here asking
questions soon after, so it were best that Master Martin
were on board your craft at once. Good-bye, young sir.
Tell your worthy father that I am glad indeed to have been
able to be of some slight service to his son, and I trust that
it will not be very long before we see the last of the Spaniards, and that we shall then have his ship alongside the
wharves again."

Ned shook hands heartily with the landlord, who had refused to accept any payment whatever from him, and then

started with the two sailors. They made their way down
to the inner haven, and then went on board the boat, a
craft of about ten tons burden which was lying alongside.
The wharves had a strange and deserted appearance. When
Ned had last been there some fifty or sixty vessels of different sizes had been lying alongside discharging or taking in cargo, while many others lay more out in the stream.
Now there were only a dozen boats of about the same size
as that on which they embarked, all, like it, arrested by
the sudden order that no vessels should leave the port.

There were no large merchantmen among them, for trade
had altogether ceased, save when a strong convoy of French,
Spanish, or German ships arrived. For with Flushing in
the hands of the patriots, and the sea swarming with the
craft of the beggars, foreign vessels bound for ports in the
hands of the Spaniards did not dare singly to approach the
mouth of the Scheldt. Ned received a hearty welcome
from the other sailors when they learned from their skipper and his companion who he was, and before he had been
ten minutes on board they asked him to give them the full
details of the fight off Enkhuizen, and how it was that the
Spaniards thus interfered with an English ship.

Ned told them the story, and the sailors when he had finished had each some tale to tell of oppression and cruelty
to friends or relatives on the part of the Spaniards. When
they had finished their mid-day meal, which was the hearti-
est the sailors had enjoyed for some days, for the landlord
when making the bargain had paid them five crowns in advance, and the empty larder had been accordingly replen-
ished, the skipper said to Ned, "I think that it will be
just as well you did something, in case the magistrates
should take it into their heads to send down to search the
craft along the wharves. The landlord said that they might

make inquiries as to what had become of the man who stayed last night at his inn. You may be sure he did not put down in his guest list a description which would help them much in their search for you, should they make one, still they keep a pretty sharp look-out over us, and if they search at all are likely to come to try here to begin with."

"I am quite ready to do anything you may set me to," Ned said.

"Then we will get the boat out, and row off and bait our hooks and try for fish; we have caught a few every day since we have been here. And, indeed, if it were not for the fish the men in most of the boats here would be starving."

"That will do capitally," Ned said. "Anyhow it will be an amusement to me."

The boat was pulled up alongside, Ned and four of the men got into it and rowed down the port into the Old Haven, and out between the two forts guarding the entrance into the Scheldt, then dropping their grapnel, baited some lines and began to fish. As boats from all the other craft lying by the shore were engaged in the same work, either with line or net, this was natural enough, and they did not return until evening was falling, by which time they had captured a considerable number of fish.

"We have had more luck than we have had all the week," one of the men said as they rowed back. "Sometimes we have only got just enough for ourselves, to-day when we don't want them we have caught enough to sell for two or three guilders; for fish are scarce now in the town and fetch good prices. However, they will come in handy for our voyage."

When they came alongside the skipper told them that three hours before two of the city constables had come along, and had inquired of him whether he had seen aught of a tall man of some thirty years of age, dressed in sober clothes, and with the appearance of a retainer in some good family. He had assured them he had seen none at all answering that description, and, indeed, that no one beside himself and his crew had been on the wharf that day. They had nevertheless come on board and searched the cabin, but finding nothing suspicious, and hearing that the rest of the crew, four men and a boy, were engaged in fishing, they had gone off without further question.

" Where do the guard-boats ply?" Ned asked presently.

" A mile or two above the forts, and as much below; for, you see, vessels can come up either passage from the sea. It is the longest round by Walcheren, but far easier and freer from sand-banks. Vessels from the west generally take the Walcheren passage; but those from the east, and coasters who know every foot of the river, come by the eastern Scheldt."

" Which way do you think of going?"

" That by Flushing, if we have the choice. We pass several towns in the possession of the Spaniards, and were the beggars to come up they would probably take the other channel. And I have noticed that there are always two row-boats in the river to the east, and only one to the west. Our greatest difficulty will be in passing the two war-ships anchored at the mouth of the port, under the guns of the forts. Once fairly out into the Scheldt we may think ourselves safe, for the river is so wide that unless by grievous ill-chance we are not likely to be seen on a dark night, such as this will be, by the row-boats. Our real danger is in getting through the two forts, and the ships at the mouth of this port.

" There is a vigilant watch kept at the forts ; but there are not likely to be any sentries placed on the walls at the entrance of this inner haven, or on that running along by Old Haven down to the forts. We will start as soon as the tide turns, and drift down with it. We will get out a pole or two to keep our course down the centre till we get near the forts, and must then let her drift as she will, for a splash in the water or the slightest sound would call the attention of the sentries there, and if the alarm were given the boats of the two ships outside would have us to a certainty. I think the night is going to be most favourable. The clouds are low, and I have felt a speck or two of mist ; it will come on faster presently, and it will want keen eyes to see five yards away when the night falls. Luckily there is not a breath of wind at present ; and I hope there will not be until we are fairly out, otherwise we should be sure to drift ashore on one side or the other as we go down the channel."

CHAPTER XII.

BEFORE throwing off the warps from the shore the captain gave each man his orders. Two were to stand with fenders, in case the boat drifted either against another craft or against the wall. Two were to take the long poles used for punting. An old sail had been torn up into strips and wrapped round these, with a pad of old rope at the end, so that they could push off from the wall without noise. Not a word was to be spoken in case of their being hailed, nor was there to be the slightest movement on board unless the use of the fenders or poles were required. Lastly, all took off their boots.

It was half an hour after the turn of tide when the warps were thrown off. The tide in the inner port was so sluggish that it was absolutely necessary to pole the boat along until she got out into what was known as the Old Haven, which was the cut leading down from the town to the river.

The work was noiselessly done; and Ned, standing at the bow beside the skipper, scarce heard the slightest sound. The night was fortunately very dark, and looking intently he could hardly make out the outline of the shore on either side. In a quarter of an hour they emerged from the inner port. On their left hand the wall of the fortifications connecting the town with the north fort at the mouth of the haven rose high above them, but its outline could be seen against the sky. The captain had told the men poling to take her sharp round the corner, and keep her along as close as possible to the foot of the wall, as she was far less likely to be observed by any sentry who might be there than she would be if kept out in the centre of the cut.

Very slowly the boat drifted along her course, assisted occasionally by the men pushing with their poles against the foot of the wall that rose a few feet from them, while those with the fenders stood in readiness to place them in position should the ship approach so close to the wall as to render contact probable. The captain was now at the tiller, the way given her by the poles being sufficient to enable him to keep her on her course close to the wall. Another quarter of an hour and they were at the end of the wall, for the forts at the entrance were detached. They were now approaching the most dangerous portion of the passage; they were no longer sheltered in the shadow, but must go along openly. It was, however, improbable that there would be sentries on the face of the fort looking towards the town, and Ned, accustomed as he was to keep watch on deck at night, could scarce make out the low shore a few yards away, and felt pretty confident that the eyes of the sleepy sentries would not be able to pierce the gloom.

The men had ceased poling now, only giving an occasional push to keep her head straight and prevent her from swinging round. Presently a sailor standing next to Ned touched his arm and pointed to the right, and straining his eyes he could dimly make out a dark mass looming in that direction.

Unlike the wall they had left, the forts stood at a little distance back from the water, and Ned was sure that as he could scarce make out the outline of the one nearest to them, no one upon its wall could distinguish the tracery of the masts and rigging of the boat. The mist had thickened since they had started, and coming on heavier just at this point the fort was presently entirely obscured.

Another twenty minutes passed. They must be now, Ned knew, in the course of the river; and he began to think that the danger was all over, when a dark object suddenly appeared from the mist, close at hand. In another moment there was a shock, and then a long grinding motion as the boat swept along by the side of a large ship. Following the shock came a sharp challenge from the darkness above, followed by other shouts. Obedient to the orders they had received, no sound was heard from the smack. Each man stooped low under the bulwarks. Two or three shots rang out from the ship, and there was a hail in Dutch—"Stop, or we will sink you."

Ned knew that this was an idle threat. The vessel was lying head to the tide, and only a small gun or two in the stern could be brought to bear, and already the ship was lost to sight in the mist. There was much shouting and noise heard astern, and then the creaking of blocks. Ned made his way aft.

"The game is up," the skipper said. "They will be alongside in a few minutes. Dark as it is they cannot miss us. They will know that we must have drifted straight down. We must take to the boats and row for it."

"I should say, captain," Ned said, "we had best take to the boat and row off for a short distance, and then wait. As likely as not they may think when they board her that she has simply drifted out from the town, having been carelessly moored. In that case they may let drop her anchor and return to their ship."

"That is a happy thought," the captain said; and running forward he told the crew to take the boat at once.

"I have another idea, captain," Ned said, just as they

were about to push off. "As we saw when we were passing the ship we are drifting stern foremost. If we can fasten a long line to her stern we can hang on to it. They will not be able to see us if we are twenty fathom astern. Then, if they anchor, and, as is likely enough, leave two or three men on board, we can haul ourselves noiselessly up with the rope and board her."

"Capital!" the captain replied. "I was wondering how we should find her again in the dark. That would be the very thing."

He sprang on board again, fastened a light line to the rudder, and dropped down into the boat again.

"Now, back her astern, lads, very gently. I can hear their oars."

In a minute the captain gave orders to cease rowing, for the line had tightened. The Spanish ship was showing a bright light in her stern. This acted as a guide to the boats, and in two or three minutes after the crew had left the smack two large boats full of soldiers came alongside. Those in the little boat, lying but fifty or sixty yards away, could hear every word that was spoken. First came a volley of angry exclamations of disappointment as the Spaniards found that they had been called from their beds only to capture an empty little coaster. As Ned had expected, they speedily came to the conclusion that having been carelessly fastened up alongside the wharves, without anyone being left in charge, she had drifted out with the tide.

"It would serve them right if we were to set her alight," one of the officers said.

"We had best not to do that," another replied. "It might cause an alarm in the town; and, besides, boats are wanted. We had better drop her anchor, and leave four men on board to take care of her. In the morning the knaves to whom she belongs will come out to claim her; and I warrant you the captain will punish them sharply for the trouble they have given us."

This opinion prevailed. A minute later a splash was heard in the water, and in a very short time the line connecting the boat with the smack tightened, and those on board knew that she had been brought up by her anchor. There was a good deal of noise and trampling of feet as the Spaniards took their place in the boats again, and then the heavy splashing of many oars as they started to row back against the tide to their own vessel.

The captain wrung Ned's hand.

"You have saved the boat for us, young sir, for we should never have found her again; and if we had, those on board would have heard us rowing up to them, and would have given the alarm. Now we have only to wait for a bit, and then haul ourselves up and overpower the Spaniards."

"I doubt if we could do that without noise," Ned replied. "At any rate it would be very dangerous while their ship is lying so close. I should say the best plan will be to wait, as you say, till the Spaniards have settled themselves comfortably, then to haul up to her and push the boat along by her side, fending her off carefully so as to make no noise until we reach the bow, then we can cut the cable and let her drift. The tide is running strong now, and in half an hour she will be over a mile down the river, and there will be no fear of a shout being heard on board the ship, and we can then board her and tackle the Spaniards."

"That will certainly be the best way," the captain agreed. "Nothing could be better. Well, we will give them half an hour to settle themselves in the cabin. They will not stay on deck many minutes in the wet."

The sound of voices on board the smack soon ceased.

After waiting half an hour to give the Spaniards time if not to go to sleep to become drowsy, the captain and one of his men began to pull upon the line. Presently the dark mass could be seen ahead, and they were soon up to her.

Very carefully they passed the boat alongside, taking pains to prevent her touching. When they reached the bow the captain grasped the cable, and with two or three cuts with his knife severed it. Then the boat was pushed off from the ship and gently paddled away to the full length of the line. Another half hour and they again drew alongside, and noiselessly climbed on to the deck. The men armed themselves with belaying-pins, and Ned took his pistols from the belt beneath his jacket. Then they quietly approached the door. There was a light burning within.

The cabin was astern, and built upon the deck, and was used by the skipper himself and by any passengers he might be carrying, the crew living in the fo'castle. The doors, which opened outwards, were noiselessly closed, for two of the Spaniards were sitting up playing cards, and there was no chance of taking the party so much by surprise as to capture them without noise. The instant the doors were closed a heavy coil of rope was thrown against them. There was a loud exclamation in the cabin, and a moment later a rush to the door. This, however, did not yield. Then a window in the side was thrown open and a head was thrust out, and there was a loud shout of "Treachery! Help!"

A moment later a heavy belaying-pin fell on the head, and it disappeared. Then there was a loud explosion as an arquebus was fired, the bullet crashing through the door.

"It is a good thing we are well on our way," the skipper said. "We must be two miles from the Spanish ship now;

and even if they hear the report they will not think it has anything to do with us. Besides, if they did, they could never find us."

Some more ropes had now been piled against the door, and there was no fear of its being burst open. Two men were posted at the windows on each side of the cabin with swords, for weapons had now been fetched from the fo'castle.

"Now," the captain said, "let us get up the sails. There is but little wind, but I think there is enough to give us steerage-way and prevent us from drifting on to the sand-banks."

"I suppose we are well beyond the guard-boats now, captain?" Ned asked.

"Oh, yes; they are not more than half a mile below the forts. Besides, I should think they have not been out; for they would know that when the tide once turned no craft could come up from below. Yes, we are quite safe as far as they are concerned."

Sail was soon made; and though there was scarce wind enough to belly out the canvas, the boat began to move slowly through the water, as was shown by her answering her helm. The discharge of the arquebus in the cabin was continued from time to time.

"You may as well cease that noise," the captain shouted to them. "Your ship is miles away; and unless you want your throats cut you had better keep yourselves quiet. You know the beggars are not to be trifled with."

The soldiers ceased firing. They had, indeed, already concluded, from the fact that the boats did not come to their rescue, that the vessel must somehow have got far from their ship. The name of the terrible beggars filled them with alarm, for they knew that they showed no mercy. They had not the least idea as to the number of their captors, and gave themselves up for lost. An hour

THE SPANISH SOLDIERS ALLOWED TO LEAVE THE SHIP.

later the captain dropped the second anchor, and brought up in the stream.

"We must wait till morning," he said. It is no use getting away from the Spaniards to be cast ashore; and there is no saying in what part of the river we may be at present, though we must certainly be six or seven miles below Bergen."

Towards morning the mist cleared off, and the wind began to freshen.

"I think it will blow hard before long," the captain said; "and as it is from the south-west, it will soon carry us out of the river. Now, what had we better do with those fellows in the cabin?"

"I should say the best plan, captain, would be to bring the boat alongside, and tell them that if they will leave their arms behind them, and come out one by one, they may take to it and row ashore. That if they refuse, we shall open the door and give them no quarter."

"That would be the best plan," the captain agreed, and going to one of the windows offered these terms to the Spaniards. The men had prepared for the worst, and had determined to sell their lives as dearly as possible. So convinced were they that the beggars would show no quarter that they were at first incredulous.

"It is a trick to get us to give up our arms," one said.

"It is not," the captain replied. "I swear to you on the word of a sailor that we will respect the terms and allow you to depart unarmed. We don't want to throw away three or four lives merely for the pleasure of cutting your throats."

After a consultation between themselves the soldiers accepted the terms. Ned placed himself at one of the windows to see that the arms were laid aside before the men issued out. Then the coils of rope were removed, and the door opened, the sailors taking their place there in case the Spaniards at the last moment should catch up their arms. This, however, they had no idea of doing, and were indeed far more afraid of treachery than were their captors. One by one they issued out, passed between the line of sailors to the bulwark, and got into the boat. It was still dark, and they could not tell that the group of men at the cabin door were all those on board. As soon as the last was in, the rope was thrown off and the boat dropped astern.

"It will be light enough to see the shore in half an hour," the captain said as they drifted away, "and then you cand land where you like."

"It would be awkward if they happen to light upon some town," Ned said, "and so bring out boats to cut us off."

"There is no fear of that," the captain replied. "Tergoes is the only place down here in which they have a garrison, and that lies some miles away yet. Besides, we shall get under way as soon as we can make out the shore. They have only two oars on board, and are not likely to know very much about rowing; besides, we shall make out the shore from deck before they will from the boat."

"Of course you will not go round by Flushing now? It will be shorter for you to go straight out to sea through the islands."

"Yes, and less dangerous. There may be ships at Tergoes and on the east side of Walcheren, as they still hold Middleburg."

"The sooner we are out to sea the better, and it will of course suit you also," Ned replied. "I only wanted to put ashore at Flushing in order to take another boat there for Rotterdam, so that I shall save one day, if not two, if you sail there direct."

In another half hour it was light enough to make out the shore. The anchor was again weighed in and the boat got under way. They were now off the end of the Island of St. Anna, and leaving South Beveland behind them turned up the channel called the Kype, between the Islands of North Beveland and Duveland. Here they passed many fishing smacks and coasting vessels, for they were now in the heart of Zeeland, and far beyond reach of the Spaniards. They were frequently hailed, and were greeted with shouts of applause when they told how they had given the Spaniards the slip and made their escape from Bergen. Two hours later they were out at sea, and before sunset entered the port of Rotterdam. Finding, when he landed that the Prince of Orange had that day returned from a trip to Haarlem and some other towns, where he had been engaged in raising the spirits of the citizens, inciting them to resistance, and urging them that it was necessary to make a common effort against the enemy, and not to allow the town to be taken piecemeal, Ned at once made his way to the house he occupied. As he entered one of the pages hurried up to him. "What do you want?" he asked. "The prince is ready to give audience to all who have important business, but it is too much that he should be intruded upon by sailor lads."

"You do not remember me!" Ned laughed. "Your memory is a short one, Master Hans."

"I did not, indeed!" the page exclaimed. "Who would have thought of seeing you dressed as a sailor boy? The prince will be glad to see you; for the first question he asked when he crossed the threshold this afternoon was whether you had returned."

He hurried away, and returned a minute later with word that the prince would see Ned at once.

"Well, my brave lad, so you have returned," the prince said as Ned entered. "I have blamed myself many times for letting you go upon so dangerous a mission, and I am glad indeed to see that you have safely returned, even if you have failed altogether touching the matter on which you went."

"I thought more of the honour than of the danger of the mission you intrusted to me, your excellency," Ned replied, "and am happy to say that I have fulfilled it successfully, and have brought you back messages by word of mouth from all, save one, of those to whom your letters were addressed."

"Say you so!" the prince exclaimed in tones of satisfaction. "Then you have indeed done well. And how fared it with you on your journey? Did you deliver the letters and return here without suspicion falling upon you?"

"No, sir. I have run some slight risk and danger owing to an unfortunate meeting with Councillor Von Aert, who was of a more suspicious nature than his countrymen in general; but I will not occupy your excellency's time by talking about myself, but will deliver the various messages with which I am charged."

He then went through the particulars of his interviews with each of the nine persons he had visited, and gave the contents of the letter, word for word, he had received from the tenth, excusing himself for not having brought the message by word of mouth, owing to the difficulty of obtaining a private audience with him. He also produced the paper upon which he had jotted down all the particulars of the men and money that had been confided to him.

"Your news might be better, and worse," the prince said when he had concluded. "Some of these men doubtless are, as they say, zealous in the cause, others are not to

be largely trusted in extremities. The money they promise is less than I had hoped. Promises are cheaper than
gold, and even here in Holland, where all is at stake, the
burghers are loth to put their hands in their pockets, and
haggle over their contributions as if they were to be spent
for my pleasure instead of their own safety. It is pitiful
to see men so fond of their money-bags. The numbers of
the men who can be relied upon to rise are satisfactory, and
more even than I had hoped for; for in matters like this a
man must proceed cautiously, and only sound those upon
whom he feels sure beforehand he can rely. The worst of
it is, they are all waiting for each other. One will move if
another will move, but none will be first. They will move
if I get a victory. But how can I win a victory when I
have no army nor money to raise one, and when each city
will fight only in its own defence, and will not put a man
under arms for the common cause?"

As the prince was evidently speaking to himself rather
than to him, Ned remained silent. "Please to write all
the particulars down that you have given me," the prince
went on, "that I may think it over at my leisure. And
so you could not see the Count of Coeverden? Was he
more difficult of access than he of Sluys?"

"I do not know that he was, sir," Ned replied; "but my
attire was not such as to gain me an entrance into ante-
chambers."

"No, I did not think of that," the prince said. "You
should have taken with you a suit of higher quality. I
forgot when I agreed that you should, for safety, travel as
a country lad, that in such a dress you could hardly gain
an entrance into the palace of nobles; and of course it
would have excited surprise for one so attired to try to purchase such clothes as would have enabled you to boldly enter."

"I might possibly have managed as a peasant lad," Ned replied with a smile; "but having been detected in that attire, and being eagerly sought for by Von Aert's agents, I was at the time dressed as a peasant woman, and could think of no possible excuse upon which I might obtain an audience with the count."

"No, indeed," the prince said smiling. "I must hear your story with all its details; but as it is doubtless somewhat long, I must put it off until later. After the evening meal you shall tell us your adventures before I betake myself to my work."

Ned retired to his own room and resumed the attire he usually wore. After supper he was sent for by the prince, with whom he found the chamberlain and three or four of his principal officers.

"Now, young sir, tell us your story," the prince said. "Do not fear of its being long. It is a rest to have one's mind taken off the affairs of state. I have already told these gentlemen what valuable services you have rendered to the cause we all have at heart, and they, like myself, wish to know how you fared, and how you escaped the danger you referred to at the hands of Von Aert."

Thus requested, Ned gave a full account of his journey, and of the adventures he had met with in Brussels and on his way back.

"What think you, sirs," the prince asked when Ned had concluded his story. "It seems to me that this lad has shown a courage, a presence of mind, and a quickness of decision that would be an honour to older men. The manner in which he escaped from the hands of Von Aert, one of the craftiest as well as of the most cruel of the Council of Blood, was excellent; and had he then, after obtaining his disguise escaped at once from the city, I for one should assuredly not have blamed him, and I consider he showed a rare devotion in continuing to risk his life to deliver my letters. Then, again, the quickness with which he contrives to carry out his scheme for saying a word to the Count of Sluys was excellent; and though he takes no credit to himself, I doubt not that the escape of the boat, after falling foul of the Spanish ship, was greatly due to him. I think, sirs, you will agree with me that he has the makings of a very able man in him, and that henceforth we can safely intrust him with the most delicate as well as the most perilous missions."

There was a general cordial agreement.

"I am free to aver that you are right and that I am wrong, prince," the chamberlain said. "I know that you seldom fail in your judgment of character, and yet it seemed to me, if you will not mind my saying so, that it was not only rash but wrong to risk the lives of our friends in Brussels upon the chances of the discretion of the lad. I now see you were right, for there are few indeed who, placed as he was, would have carried out his mission as skilfully and well as he has done."

"By the way," the prince said, "I would beg you to seek out the captain of the boat in which you came here, and bid him come to me this time to-morrow evening. I would fain hear from him somewhat further details as to how you escaped from the Spaniards, for I observed that in this matter you were a little reticent as to your share in it. He may be able to tell me, too, more about the strength of the Spanish garrisons in Bergen and its neighborhood than you can do."

For the next fortnight Ned was employed carrying messages from the prince to various towns and ports. Alva was at Amsterdam, and the army under his son, Don

Frederick, was marching in that direction on their way from Zutphen. They came down upon the little town of Naarden on the coast of the Zuider-Zee. A troop of a hundred men was sent forward to demand its surrender. The burghers answered that they held the town for the king and the Prince of Orange, and a shot was fired at the troopers. Having thus committed themselves, the burghers sent for reinforcements and aid to the Dutch towns, but none were sent them, and when the Spaniards approached on the 1st of December they sent out envoys to make terms. The army marched forward and encamped a mile and a half from the town.

A large deputation was sent out and was met by General Romero, who informed them that he was commissioned on the part of Don Frederick to treat with them. He demanded the keys, and gave them a solemn pledge that the lives and properties of all the inhabitants should be respected. The gates were thrown open, and Romero with five hundred soldiers entered. A sumptuous feast was prepared for them by the inhabitants. After this was over the citizens were summoned by the great bell to assemble in the church that was used as a town hall. As soon as they assembled the soldiers attacked them and killed them all. The town was then set on fire, and almost every man, woman, and child killed. Don Frederick forbade that the dead should be burried, and issued orders forbidding anyone, on pain of death, to give shelter to the few fugitives who had got away. The few houses which had escaped the flames were levelled to the ground, and Naarden ceased to exist.

Great as the horrors perpetrated at Zutphen had been, they were surpassed by the atrocities committed at Naarden. The news of this horrible massacre, so far from frightening the Hollanders into submission, nerved them to even more strenuous resistance. Better death in whatsoever form it came than to live under the rule of these foul murderers. With the fall of Naarden there remained only the long strip of land facing the sea, and connected at but a few points with the mainland, that remained faithful to the cause of freedom. The rest of the Netherlands lay cowed beneath the heel of the Spaniards. Holland alone and a few of the islands of Zeeland remained to be conquered.

The inhabitants of Holland felt the terrible danger; and Bossu, Alva's stadtholder, formally announced that the system pursued at Mechlin, Zutphen, and Naarden was the deliberate policy of the government, and that man, woman and child would be exterminated in every city which opposed the Spanish authority. The day after the news arrived of the fall of Naarden, Ned received a letter from his father, saying that the *Good Venture* was again at Enkhuizen, and that she would in two days start for Haarlem with a fleet of Dutch vessels; that he himself had made great progress in the last six weeks, and should return to England in her; and that if Ned found that he could get away for a day or two he should be glad to see him.

The prince at once gave Ned permission to leave, and as he had an excellent horse at his service he started the next morning at daybreak and arrived at Enkhuizen before nightfall. He was received with great joy by his family, and was delighted to find his father looking quite himself again, " Yes, thanks to good nursing and good food, my boy, I feel almost strong and well enough to take my post at the helm of the *Good Venture* again. The doctor tells me that in another couple of months I shall be able to have a wooden leg strapped on, and to stump about again. That was a rare adventure you had at Brussels, Ned; and you must give us a full account of it presently. In the morning you must come on board the vessel, Peters and the crew will be all glad to see you again."

Ned stayed two days with his family. On the evening of the second day he said to his father: "I should like to make the trip to Haarlem and back, father, in the *Good Venture*. It may be that the Spaniards will sally out from Amsterdam and attack it. Last time we had to run away, you know, but if there is a sea-fight I should like to take my part in it."

"Very well, Ned, I have no objection; but I hardly think that there will be a fight. The Spaniards are too strong, and the fleet will start so as to pass through the strait by night."

"Well, at any rate I should like to be on board the *Good Venture* again if only for the sail down and back again," Ned said. "They are to sail at three o'clock to-morrow, so that if the wind is fair they will pass the strait at night and anchor under the walls of Haarlem in the morning. I suppose they will be two days discharging their cargo of food and grain, and one reason why I want to go is that I may if possible persuade my aunt and the two girls to return with me and to sail for England with you. All think that Haarlem will be the next place besieged, and after what has taken place in the other towns it would be madness for my aunt to stop there."

"I quite agree with you, Ned. The duke is sure to attack Haarlem next. If he captures it he will cut Holland in two and strike a terrible blow at the cause. Your mother shall write a letter to-night to her sister-in-law urging her to come with us, and take up her abode in England till these troubles are over. She can either dwell with us, or, if she would rather, we can find her a cottage hard by. She will be well provided with money, for I have at home a copy of your grandfather's will signed by him leaving all his property to such of his relatives as may survive him.

"His three sons are dead; your mother and Elizabeth are therefore his heirs, and the money he transmitted to England is in itself sufficient to keep two families in comfort. What proportion of it was his and what belonged to his sons now matters not, seeing that your mother and aunt are the sole survivors of the family. As you say, it is madness for her to remain in Holland with her two girls. Were I a burgher of that town I would send my family away to Leyden or Dort and stay myself to defend the walls to the last, but I do not believe that many will do so. Your countrymen are obstinate people, Sophie, and I fear that few will send their families away."

Upon the following afternoon Ned started with the little fleet. The wind was fair and light, and they reached the mouth of the strait leading from the Zuider-Zee to Haarlem. Then suddenly the wind dropped and the vessels cast anchor. For the two or three days previous the weather had been exceedingly cold, and with the fall of the wind the frost seemed to increase in severity, and Ned, who had been pacing the deck with Peters chatting over what had happened since they last met, was glad to go into the cabin, where the new first mate and supercargo had retired as soon as the anchor was let go. They sat talking for a couple of hours until a sailor came in, and said that they were hailed by the nearest ship. They all went on deck. Ned shouted to know what was the matter.

"Do you not see the water is freezing? By morning we shall be all frozen up hard and fast."

This was startling news indeed, for they were now in full sight of Amsterdam, and would, if detained thus, be open to an attack across the ice.

CHAPTER XIII.

THE SIEGE OF HAARLEM.

THERE was much shouting in the little fleet as the news spread that the sea was freezing. Boats were lowered and rowed from ship to ship, for the ice was as yet no thicker than window glass. Ned went from the *Good Venture* to the craft round which most of the boats were assembling to hear what was decided. He returned in a few minutes.

"They are all of opinion that it is hopeless for us to get out of this. We could tow the vessels a short distance, but every hour the ice will thicken. They concluded that anchors shall be got up, and that the ships all lie together as close as they can pack."

"What will be the use of that ?" Peters asked. "If we are to be frozen up it makes no difference that I can see, whether we are together or scattered as at present."

"The idea is," Ned said, "if we are packed together we can defend ourselves better than if scattered about, and what is more important still, we can cut through the ice and keep a channel of open water round us."

"So we could," Peters agreed. "Let us to work then. Which ship are we to gather round?"

"The one I have just left, Peters; she is lying nearly in the centre."

For the next two hours there was much bustle and hard work. Thin as the ice was it yet greatly hindered the operation of moving the ships. At last they were all packed

closely together; much more closely than would be possible in these days, for the bowsprits, instead of running
out nearly parallel with the water-line, stood up at a sharp
angle, and the vessels could therefore be laid with the bow
of one touching the stern of that in advance. As there was
now no motive for concealment, lamps were shown and
torches burned. There were thirty craft in all, and they
were arranged in five lines closely touching each other.
When all was done the crews retired to rest. There was
no occasion to keep watch, for the ice had thickened so
fast that boats could not now force their way through it,
while it would not before morning be strong enough to
bear the weight of armed men walking across it.

"This is a curious position," Ned said, as he went on
deck next morning. "How long do you think we are likely
to be kept here, Peters?"

"Maybe twenty-four hours, maybe three weeks, lad.
These frosts when they set in like this seldom last less than
a fortnight or three weeks. What do you think of our
chances of being attacked?"

"I should say they are sure to attack us. The whole
Spanish army is lying over there in Amsterdam, and as
soon as the ice is strong enough to bear them you will see
them coming out. How strong a force can we muster?"

"There are thirty craft," Peters replied; "and I should
think they average fully fifteen men each—perhaps twenty.
They carry strong crews at all times, and stronger than
usual now."

"That would give from five to six hundred men. I suppose all carry arms?"

"Oh, yes. I do not suppose that there is a man here who
has not weapons of some kind, and most of them have arquebuses. It will take a strong force to carry this wooden fort."

It was still freezing intensely, and the ice was strong enough to bear men scattered here and there, although it would not have sustained them gathered together. Towards the afternoon the captain judged that it had thickened sufficiently to begin work, and fifty or sixty men provided with hatchets got upon the ice and proceeded to break it away round the vessels. After a couple of hours a fresh party took their places, and by nightfall the ships were surrounded by a belt of open water, some fifteen yards wide. A meeting of the captains had been held during the day, and the most experienced had been chosen as leader, with five lieutenants under him. Each lieutenant was to command the crews of six ships. When it became dark five boats were lowered. These were to row round and round the ships all night so as to keep the water from freezing again. The crews were to be relieved once an hour, so that each ship would furnish a set of rowers once in six hours. Numerous anchors had been lowered when the ships were first packed together, so as to prevent the mass from drifting when tide flowed or ebbed, as this would have brought them in contact with one side or the other of the ice around them. The next morning the ice was found to be five inches thick, and the captains were of opinion that the Spaniards might now attempt an attack upon them.

"Their first attack will certainly fail," Ned said, as they sat at breakfast. "They will be baffled by this water belt round us. However, they will come next time with rafts ready to push across it, and then we shall have fighting in earnest."

The lieutenant under whom the crew of the *Good Venture* were placed, came down while they were at breakfast to inquire how many arquebuses there were on board.

"We have ten," the captain said.

"As I suppose you have no men who skate on board, I

should be glad if you will hand them over to me."

"What does he say?" the first mate asked in surprise upon this being translated to him. "What does he mean by asking if we have any men who skate, and why should we give up our guns is we can use them ourselves?" Ned put the questions to the lieutenant.

"We are going to attack them on the ice as they come out," he replied. "Of course all our vessels have skates on board; in winter we always carry them, as we may be frozen up at any time. And we shall send out as many men as can be armed with arquebuses; those who remain on board will fight the guns."

"That is a capital plan," Ned said; "and the Spanish, who are unaccustomed to ice, will be completely puzzled. It is lucky there was not a breath of wind when it froze, and the surface is as smooth as glass. Well, there will be nine arquebuses for you, sir; for I have been out here two winters and have learnt to skate, so I will accompany the party, the other nine arquebuses with ammunition we will hand over to you."

A look-out at one of the mastheads now shouted that he could make out a black mass on the ice near Amsterdam, and believed that it was a large body of troops. Every preparation had already been made on board the ships for the fight. The *Good Venture* lay on the outside tier facing Amsterdam, having been placed there because she carried more guns than any of the other vessels, which were for the most part small, and few carried more than four guns, while the armament of the *Good Venture* had, after her fight with the *Don Pedro*, been increased to ten guns. The guns from the vessels in the inner tiers had all been shifted on to those lying outside, and the wooden fort literally bristled with cannon.

A quarter of an hour after the news that the Spaniards were on their way had been given, three hundred men with arquebuses were ferried across the channel, and were dis-embarked on to the ice. They were divided into five companies of sixty men each, under the lieutenants; the captain remained to superintend the defence of the ships. The Dutch sailors were as much at home on their skates as upon dry land, and in high spirits started to meet the enemy. It was a singular sight to see the five bodies of men gliding away across the ice. There was no attempt at formation or order; all understood their business, for in winter it was one of their favourite sports to fire at a mark while skating at a rapid pace.

It was two miles from the spot where the ships lay frozen —up to Amsterdam. The Spaniards, a thousand strong, had traversed about a third of the distance when the skaters approached them. Keeping their feet with the utmost difficulty upon the slippery ice, they were astonished at the rapid approach of the Dutchmen. Breaking up as they approached, their assailants came dashing along at a rapid pace, discharged their arquebuses into the close mass of the Spaniards, and then wheeled away at the top of their speed, reloaded and again swept down to fire.

Against these tactics the Spaniards could do little. Unsteady as they were on their feet the recoil of their heavy arquebuses frequently threw them over, and it was impossible to take anything like an accurate aim at the flying figures that passed them at the speed of a galloping horse. Nevertheless they doggedly kept on their way, leaving the ice behind them dotted with killed and wounded. Not a gun was discharged from on board the ships until the head of the Spanish column reached the edge of the water, and discovered the impassable obstacle that lay between them and the vessels.   Then the order was given to fire, and the head of the column was literally swept away by the discharge.

The commander of the Spaniards now gave the order for a retreat.   As they fell back the guns of the ships swept their ranks, the musketeers harassed them on each flank, the ice, cracked and broken by the artillery fire, gave way under their feet, and many fell through and were drowned, and of the thousand men who left Amsterdam less than half regained that city.   The Spaniards were astonished at this novel mode of fighting, and the despatches of their officers gave elaborate descriptions of the strange append-anges that had enabled the Hollanders to glide so rapidly over the ice.   The Spaniards were, however, always ready to learn from a foe, Alva immediately ordered eight thousand pairs of skates, and the soldiers were kept hard at work practicing until they were able to make their way with fair rapidity over the ice.

The evening after the fight a strong wind suddenly sprang up from the south-west, and the rain descended in torrents. By morning the ice was already broken up, the guns were hastily shifted to the vessels to which they belonged, the ships on the outside tiers cast off from the others, and before noon the whole were on their way back towards Enkhuizen, which they reached without pursuit by the Spanish vessels; for at nine in the morning the wind changed suddenly again, the frost set in as severely as before, and the Spaniards in the port of Amsterdam were unable to get out.   This event caused great rejoicing in Holland, and was regarded as a happy omen for the coming contest.

After remaining another day with his family, Ned mounted his horse and rode to Haarlem. The city lay at the narrowest point of the narrow strip of land facing the German

Ocean, and upon the shore of the shallow lake of the same name. Upon the opposite side of this lake, ten miles distant, stood the town of Amsterdam. The Lake of Haarlem was separated from the long inlet of the Zuider-Zee called the Y by a narrow strip of land, along which ran the causeway connecting the two cities. Half-way along this neck of land there was a cut, with sluice works, by which the surrounding country could be inundated. The port of Haarlem on the Y was at the village of Sparendam, where there was a fort for the protection of the shipping.

Haarlem was one of the largest cities of the Netherlands; but it was also one of the weakest. The walls were old, and had never been formidable. The extent of the defences made a large garrison necessary; but the force available for the defence was small indeed. Upon his way towards Haarlem Ned learnt that on the night before, the 10th of December, Sparendam had been captured by the Spaniards. A secret passage across the flooded and frozen meadows had been shown to them by a peasant, and they had stormed the fort, killed three hundred men, and taken possession of the works and village. Thus Haarlem was at once cut off from all aid coming from the Zuider-Zee.

Much disquieted by the news, Ned rode on rapidly and entered the town by a gate upon the southern side; for, as he approached, he learned that the Spaniards had already appeared in great force before the city. He rode at once to his aunt's house, hoping to find that she had already left the town with the girls. Leaping from his horse he entered the door hurriedly, and was dismayed to find his aunt seated before the fire knitting.

"My dear aunt!" he exclaimed, "do you know that the Spaniards are in front of the town? Surely to remain here with the two girls is madness!"

" Every one else is remaining, why should not I, Ned?"
his aunt asked calmly.

" Other people have their houses and their businesses,
aunt, but you have nothing to keep you here. You know
what has happened at Zutphen and Naarden. How can
you expose the girls, even if you are so obstinate yourself,
to such horrors?"

" The burghers are determined to hold out until relief
comes, nephew."

"Ay, if they can," Ned replied. " But who knows
whether they can. This is madness, aunt. I beseech you
come with me to your father, and let us talk over the matter with him; and in the morning, if you will not go, I
will get two horses and mount the girls on them, and ride
with them to Leyden—that is, if by the morning it is not
already too late. It would be best to proceed at once."

Dame Plomaert reluctantly yielded to the energy of her
nephew, and accompanied him to the house of her father;
but the weaver was absent on the walls, and did not return until late in the evening. Upon Ned's putting the
case to him, he at once agreed that it would be best both
for her and the girls to leave.

" I have told her so twenty times already," he said; "but
Elizabeth was always as obstinate as a mule. Over and
over again she has said she would go; and having said that
has done nothing. She can do no good by stopping here;
and there are only three more mouths to feed. By all
means, lad, get them away the first thing in the morning.
If it be possible I would say start to-night, dark as it is;
but the Spanish horse may be all round the city, and you
might ride into their arms without seeing them."

Ned at once sallied out, and without much difficulty
succeeded in bargaining for three horses; for few of the

inhabitants had left, and horses would not only be of no use during the siege, but it would be impossible to feed them. Therefore their owners were glad to part with them for far less than their real value. When he reached the house he found that his aunt had made up three bundles with clothes and what jewelry she had, and that she was ready to start with the girls in the morning.

Before daybreak Ned went out to the walls on the south side, but as the light broadened out discovered that it was too late. During the night heavy reinforcements had arrived to Don Frederick from Amsterdam, and a large force was already facing the west side of the city.

With a heavy heart he returned to his aunt's with the news that it was too late, for that all means of exit was closed. Dame Plomaert took the news philosophically. She was a woman of phlegmatic disposition, and objected to sudden movement and changes, and to her it seemed far less terrible to await quietly the fortunes of the siege than to undergo the fatigues of a journey on horseback and the uncertainty of an unknown future.

"Well, nephew" she said placidly, "if we cannot get away, we cannot; and it really saves a world of trouble. But what are you going to do yourself? for I suppose if we cannot get away, you cannot."

"The way is open across the lake," Ned replied, "and I shall travel along the ice to the upper end and then over to Leyden, and obtain permission from the prince to return here by the same way; or if not, to accompany the force he is raising there, for this will doubtless march at once to the relief of the town. Even now, aunt, you might make your escape across the ice."

"I have not skated since I was fifteen years old," the good woman said placidly; "and at my age and weight I am certainly not going to try now, Ned. Just imagine me upon skates!"

Ned could not help smiling, vexed as he was. His aunt was stout and portly, and he certainly could not imagine her exerting herself sufficiently to undertake a journey on skates!"

"But the girls can skate," he urged.

"The girls are girls," she said decidedly; "and I am not going to let them run about the world by themselves. You say yourself that reinforcements will soon start. You do not know our people, nephew. They will beat off the Spaniards. Whatever they do, the city will never be taken. My father says so, and every one says so. Surely they must know better than a lad like you!"

Ned shrugged his shoulders in despair, and went out to see what were the preparations for defence. The garrison consisted only of some fifteen hundred German mercenaries and the burgher force. Ripperda, the commandant of the garrison, was an able and energetic officer. The towns-people were animated by a determination to resist to the end. A portion of the magistracy had, in the first place, been anxious to treat, and had entered into secret negotiations with Alva, sending three of their number to treat with the Duke at Amsterdam. One had remained there; the other two on their return were seized, tried, and executed; and Sainte Aldegonde, one of the prince's ministers, had been dispatched by him to make a complete change in the magistracy.

The total force available for the defence of the town was not, at the commencement of the siege, more than 3000 men, while over 30,000 Spaniards were gathering round its walls, a number equal to the entire population of the city.

The Germans under Count Overstein, finally took up their

encampment in the extensive grove of trees that spread between the southern walls and the shore of the lake.

The Spaniards, under Don Frederick, faced the north walls, while the Walloons and other regiments closed it in on the east and west. But these arrangements occupied some days; and the mists which favored their movements were not without advantage to the besieged. Under cover of the fog supplies of provisions and ammunition were brought by men and women and even children, on their heads or in sledges down the frozen lake, and in spite of the efforts of the besiegers introduced into the city.

Ned was away only two days. The prince approved of his desire to take part in the siege, and furnished him with letters to the magistrates promising reinforcements, and to Ripperda recommending Ned as a young gentleman volunteer of great courage and quickness, who had already performed valuable service for the cause. His cousins were delighted to see him back. Naturally they did not share in their mother's confidence as to the result of the siege, and felt in Ned's presence a certain sense of security and comfort. The garrison, increased by arrivals from without and by the enrolment of every man capable of bearing arms, now numbered a thousand pioneers, three thousand fighting men, and three hundred fighting women.

The last were not the least efficient portion of the garrison. All were armed with sword, musket, and dagger, and were led by Kanau Hasselaer, a widow of distinguished family, who at the head of her female band took part in many of the fiercest fights of the siege, both upon and without the walls.

The siege commenced badly. In the middle of December the force of some 3500 men assembled at Leyden set out under the command of De la Marck, the former admiral of the sea beggars. The troops were attacked on their march by the Spaniards, and a thousand were killed, a number taken prisoners, and the rest routed.

Among the captains was a brave officer named Van Trier, for whom De la Marck offered two thousand crowns and nineteen Spanish prisoners. The offer was refused. Van Trier was hanged by one leg until he was dead, upon one of the numerous gibbets erected in sight of the town; in return for which De la Marck at once executed the nineteen Spaniards. On the 18th of December Don Frederick's batteries opened fire upon the northern side, and the fire was kept up without intermission for three days. As soon as the first shot was fired, a crier going round the town summoned all to assist in repairing the damages as fast as they were made.

The whole population responded to the summons. Men, women, and children brought baskets of stones and earth, bags of sand and beams of wood, and these they threw into the gaps as fast as they were made. The churches were stripped of all their stone statutes, and these too were piled in the breaches. The besiegers were greatly horrified at what they declared to be profanation; a complaint that came well from men who had been occupied in the wholesale murder of men, women, and children, and in the sacking of the churches of their own religion. Don Frederick anticipated a quick and easy success. He deemed that this weakly fortified town might well be captured in a week by an army of 30,000 men, and that after spending a few days slaughtering its inhabitants, and pillaging and burning the houses, the army would march on against the next town, until ere long the rebellion would be stamped out, and Holland transformed into a desert.

At the end of three days' cannonade the breach, in spite

of the efforts of the besieged, was practicable, and a strong storming party led by General Romero advanced against it. As the column was seen approaching the church bells rang out the alarm, the citizens caught up their arms, and men and women hurried to the threatened point. As they approached the Spaniards were received with a heavy fire of musketry; but with their usual gallantry the veterans of Spain pressed forward and began to mount the breach. Now they were exposed not only to the fire of the garrison, but to the missiles thrown by the burghers and women. Heavy stones, boiling oil, and live coals were hurled down upon them; small hoops smeared with pitch and set on fire were dexterously thrown over their heads, and after a vain struggle, in which many officers were killed and wounded, Romero, who had himself lost an eye in the fight, called off his troops and fell back from the breach, leaving from three to four hundred dead behind him, while but a half dozen of the townsmen lost their lives.

Upon the retreat of the Spaniards the delight in the city was immense; they had met the pikemen of Spain and hurled them back discomfited, and they felt that they could now trust themselves to meet further assaults without flinching.

To Ned's surprise his aunt, when the alarm bells rung, had sallied out from her house accompanied by the two girls. She carried with her half a dozen balls of flax, each the size of her head. These had been soaked in oil and turpentine, and to each a stout cord about two feet long was attached. The girls had taken part in the work of the preceding day, but when she reached the breach she told them to remain in shelter while she herself joined the crowd on the walls flanking the breach, while Ned took part in the front row of its defenders. Frau Plomaert was slow, but she was strong when she chose to exert herself, and when the conflict was at its thickest she lighted the balls at the fires over which caldrons of oil were seething, and whirling them round her head sent them one by one into the midst of the Spanish column.

"Three of them hit men fairly in the face," she said to one of her neighbours, "so I think I have done my share of to-day's work."

She then calmly descended the wall, joined her daughters and returned home, paying no attention to the din of the conflict at the breach, and contended that she had done all that could be expected of her. On reaching home she bade the girls take to their knitting as usual, while she set herself to work to prepare the mid-day meal.

A few days later the Prince of Orange sent from Sassenheim, a place on the southern extremity of the lake, where he had now taken up his head-quarters, a force of 2000 men, with seven guns and a convoy of wagons with ammunition and food towards the town, under General Batenburg. This officer had replaced De la Marck, whose brutal and ferocious conduct had long disgraced the Dutch cause, and whom the prince, finding that he was deaf alike to his orders and the dictates of humanity, had now deprived of his commission. Batenburg's expedition was no more fortunate than that of De la Marck had been.

On his approach to the city by night a thick mist set in, and the column completely lost its way. The citizens had received news of its coming, and the church bells were rung and cannon fired to guide it as to its direction; but the column was so helplessly lost, that it at last wandered in among the Spaniards, who fell upon them, slew many and scattered the rest—a very few only succeeding in entering the town. Batenburg brought off, under cover of the mist, a remnant of his troops, but all the provisions and ammunition were lost.

The second in command, De Koning, was among those captured. The Spaniards cut off his head and threw it over the wall into the city, with a paper fastened on it bearing the words: "This is the head of Captain De Koning, who is on his way with reinforcements for the good city of Haarlem." But the people of Haarlem were now strung up, both by their own peril and the knowledge of the atrocities committed by the Spaniards in other cities, to a point of hatred and fury equal to that of the foes, and they retorted by chopping off the heads of eleven prisoners and throwing them into the Spanish camp. There was a label on the barrel with these words, "Deliver these heads to Duke Alva in payment of his tenpenny tax, with one additional head for interest."

The besieged were not content to remain shut up in the walls, but frequently sallied out and engaged in skirmishes with the enemy. Prisoners were therefore often captured by one side or the other, and the gibbets on the walls and in the camp were constantly occupied.

Ned as a volunteer was not attached to any special body of troops, Ripperda telling him to act for himself and join in whatever was going on as he chose. Consequently he took part in many of the skirmishes outside the walls, and was surprised to find how fearlessly the burghers met the tried soldiers of Spain, and especially at the valour with which the corps of women battled with the enemy.

In strength and stature most of the women were fully a match for the Walloon troops, and indeed for the majority of the Spaniards; and they never feared to engage any body of troops of equal numerical strength.

"Look here, aunt," Ned said to Frau Plomaert upon the

day after the failure of Batenburg's force to relieve the town, "you must see for yourself now that the chances are that sooner or later the town will be captured. We may beat off all the assaults of the Spaniards, but we shall ere long have to fight with an even more formidable foe within the town. You know that our stock of provisions is small, and that in the end unless help comes we must yield to famine. The prince may possibly throw five thousand armed men into the town, but it is absolutely impossible that he can throw in any great store of provisions, unless he entirely defeats the Spaniards; and nowhere in Holland can he raise an army sufficient for that.

"I think, aunt, that while there is time we ought to set to work to construct a hiding-place, where you and the girls can remain while the sack and atrocities that will assuredly follow the surrender of the town are taking place."

"I shall certainly not hide myself from the Spaniards," Frau Plomaert said stoutly.

"Very well, aunt, if you choose to be killed on your own hearth-stone of course I cannot prevent it; but I do say that you ought to save the girls from these horrors if you can."

"That I am ready to do," she said. "But how is it to be managed?"

"Well, aunt, there is your wood-cellar below. We can surely construct some place of concealment there. Of course I will do the work, though the girls might help by bringing up baskets of earth and scattering them in the streets." Having received a tacit permission from his aunt, Ned went down into the wood-cellar, which was some five feet wide by eight feet long. Like every place about a Dutch house it was whitewashed, and was half full of wood. Ned climbed over the wood to the further end.

"This is where it must be," he said to the girls who had

followed him. "Now, the first thing to do is to pile the wood so as to leave a passage by which we can pass along. I will get a pick and get out the bricks at this corner."

"We need only make a hole a foot wide, and it need not be more than a foot high," Lucette, the elder, said. "That will be sufficient for us to squeeze through."

"It would, Lucette; but we shall want more space for working, so to begin with we will take away the bricks up to the top. We can close it up as much as we like afterwards. There is plenty of time, for it will be weeks before the city is starved out. If we work for an hour a day we can get it done in a week."

Accordingly the work began, the bricks were removed, and with a pick and shovel Ned dug into the ground beyond, while the girls carried away the earth and scattered it in the road. In a fortnight a chamber, five feet high, three feet wide, and six feet long had been excavated. Slats of wood, supported by props along the sides, held up the roof. A quantity of straw was thrown in for the girls to lie on. Frau Plomaert came down from time to time to inspect the progress of the work, and expressed herself well pleased with it.

"How are you going to close the entrance, Ned?" she asked.

"I propose to brick it up again three feet high, aunt. Then when the girls and you have gone in—for I hope that you will change your mind at the last—I will brick up the rest of it, but using mud instead of mortar, so that the bricks can be easily removed when the time comes, or one or two can be taken out to pass in food; and then replaced as before. After you are in I will whitewash the whole cellar, and no one would then guess the wall had ever been disturbed. I shall leave two bricks out in the bottom row of all to give air. They will be covered over by the wood. However hard up we get for fuel we can leave enough to cover the floor at that end a few inches deep. If I can I will pierce a hole up under the boards in the room above this, so as to give a free passage of air."

" If the Spaniards take away the wood, as they may well do, they will notice that the two bricks are gone," Mrs. Plomaert objected.

" We can provide for that, aunt, by leaving two bricks inside, whitewashed like the rest, to push into the holes if you hear anyone removing the wood. There is only the light that comes in at the door, and it would never be noticed that the two bricks were loose."

"That will do very well," Mrs. Plomaert said. " I thought at first that your idea was foolish, but I see that it will save the girls if the place is taken. I suppose there will be plenty of time to brick them up after they have taken refuge in it."

" Plenty of time, aunt. We shall know days before if the city surrenders to hunger. I shall certainly fight much more comfortably now that I know that whatever comes Lucette and Annie are safe from the horrors of the sack."

CHAPTER XIV.

THE FALL OF HAARLEM.

AFTER the terrible repulse inflicted upon the storming party, Don Frederick perceived that the task before him was not to be accomplished with the ease and rapidity he had anticipated, and that these hitherto despised Dutch heretics had at last been driven by despair to fight with a desperate determination that was altogether new to the Spaniards. He therefore abandoned the idea of carrying the place by assault, and determined to take it by the slower and surer process of a regular siege. In a week his pioneers would be able to drive mines beneath the walls; an explosion would then open a way for his troops. Accordingly the work began, but the besieged no sooner perceived what was being done than the thousand men who had devoted themselves to this work at once began to drive counter mines.

Both parties worked with energy, and it was not long before the galleries met, and a desperate struggle commenced under ground. Here the drill and discipline of the Spaniards availed them but little. It was a conflict of man to man in narrow passages, with such light only as a few torches could give. Here the strength and fearlessness of death of the sturdy Dutch burghers and fishermen more than compensated for any superiority of the Spaniards in the management of their weapons. The air was so heavy and thick with powder that the torches gave but a feeble light, and the combatants were well nigh stifled by the fumes of sulphur, yet in the galleries which met men fought night and day without intermission. The places of those who retired exhausted, or fell dead, were filled by others impatiently waiting their turn to take part in the struggle. While the fighting continued the work went on also. Fresh galleries were continually being driven on both sides, and occasionally tremendous explosions took place as one party or the other sprung their mines; the shock sometimes bringing down the earth in passages far removed from the explosions, and burying the combatants beneath them; while yawning pits were formed where the explosions took place, and fragments of bodies cast high in the air. Many of the galleries were so narrow and low that no arms save daggers could be used, and men fought like wild beasts, grappling and rolling on the ground, while comrades with lanterns or torches stood behind waiting to spring upon each other as soon as the struggle terminated one way or the other.

For a fortnight this underground struggle continued, and then Don Frederick—finding that no ground was gained, and that the loss was so great that even his bravest soldiers were beginning to dread their turn to enter upon a conflict in which their military training went for nothing, and where so many hundreds of their comrades had perished —abandoned all hopes of springing a mine under the walls, and drew off his troops. A month had already elapsed since the repulse of the attack on the breach; and while the fight had been going on underground a steady fire had been kept up against a work called a ravelin, protecting the gate of the Cross. During this time letters had from time to time been brought into the town by carrier-pigeons, the prince urging the citizens to persevere, and holding out hopes of relief.

These promises were to some extent fulfilled on the 28th of January, when 400 veteran soldiers, bringing with them 170 sledges laden with powder and bread, crossed the frozen lake and succeeded in making their way into the city. The time was now at hand when the besieged foresaw that the ravelin of the Cross gate could not much longer be defended. But they had been making preparations for this contingency. All through the long nights of January, the non-combatants, old men, women and children, aided by such of the fighting men as were not worn out by their work on the walls or underground, laboured to construct a wall in the form of a half moon on the inside of the threatened point. None who were able to work were exempt, and none wished to be exempted, for the heroic spirit burned brightly in every heart in Haarlem.

Nightly Ned went down with his aunt and cousins and worked side by side with them. The houses near the new work were all levelled in order that the materials should be utilized for the construction of the wall, which was built of solid masonry. The small stones were carried by the children and younger girls in baskets, the heavier ones dragged on hand sledges by the men and women. Although constitutionally adverse to exertion, Frau Plomaert worked sturdily, and Ned was often surprised at her strength; for she dragged along without difficulty loaded sledges, which he was unable to move, throwing her weight on to the ropes that passed over her shoulders, and toiling backwards and forwards to and from the wall for hours, slowly but unflinchingly.

It seemed to Ned that under these exertions she visibly decreased in weight from day to day, and indeed the scanty supply of food upon which the work had to be done was ill calculated to support the strength of those engaged upon such fatiguing labor. For from the commencement of the siege the whole population had been rationed, all the provisions in the town had been handed over to the authorities for equal division, and every house, rich and poor, had been rigorously searched to see that none were holding back supplies for their private consumption. Many of the cattle and horses had been killed and salted down, and a daily distribution of food was made to each household according to the number of mouths it contained.

Furious at the successful manner in which the party had entered the town on the 28th January, Don Frederick kept up for the next few days a terrible cannonade against the gates of the Cross and of St. John, and the wall connecting them. At the end of that time the wall was greatly shattered, part of St. John's gate was in ruins, and an assault was ordered to take place at midnight. So certain was he of success that Don Frederick ordered the whole of his forces to be under arms opposite all the gates of the city, to prevent the population making their escape. A chosen body of troops were to lead the assault, and at midnight these advanced silently against the breach. The besieged had no suspicion that an attack was intended, and there were but some forty men, posted rather as sentries than guards, at the breach.

These, however, when the Spaniards advanced, gave the alarm, the watchers in the churches sounded the tocsin, and the sleeping citizens sprang from their beds, seized their arms, and ran towards the threatened point. Unawed by the overwhelming force advancing against them the sentries took their places at the top of the breach, and defended it with such desperation that they kept their assailants at bay until assistance arrived, when the struggle assumed a more equal character. The citizens defended themselves by the same means that had before proved successful, boiling oil and pitch, stones, flaming hoops, torches, and missiles of all kinds were hurled down by them upon the Spaniards, while the garrison defended the breach with sword and pike.

Until daylight the struggle continued, and Philip then ordered the whole of his force to advance to the assistance of the storming party. A tremendous attack was made upon the ravelin in front of the gate of the Cross. It was successful, and the Spaniards rushed exultingly into the work, believing that the city was now at their mercy. Then, to their astonishment, they saw that they were confronted by the new wall, whose existence they had not even suspected. While they were hesitating a tremendous explosion took place. The citizens had undermined the ravelin and placed a store of powder there; and this was now fired, and the work flew into the air, with all the soldiers who had entered.

The retreat was sounded at once, and the Spaniards fell back to their camp, and thus a second time the burghers of Haarlem repulsed an assault by an overwhelming force under the best generals of Spain. The effect of these failures was so great that Don Frederick resolved not to risk another defeat, but to abandon his efforts to capture the city by sap or assault, and to resort to the slow but sure process of famine. He was well aware that the stock of food in the city was but small and the inhabitants were already suffering severely, and he thought that they could not hold out much longer.

But greatly as the inhabitants suffered, the misery of the army besieging them more than equalled their own. The intense cold rendered it next to impossible to supply so large a force with food, and small as were the rations of the inhabitants, they were at least as large and more regularly delivered than those of the troops. Moreover, the citizens who were not on duty could retire to their comfortable houses; while the besiegers had but tents to shelter them from the severity of the frosts. Cold and insufficient food brought with them a train of disease, and great numbers of the soldiers died.

The cessation of the assaults tried the besieged even more than their daily conflicts had done, for it is much harder to await death in a slow and tedious form than to face it fighting. They could now fully realize the almost hopeless prospect. Ere long the frost would break up, and with it the chances of obtaining supplies or reinforcements across the frozen lake would be at an end.

It was here alone that they could expect succour, for they knew well enough that the prince could raise no army capable of cutting its way through the great beleaguering force. In vain did they attempt to provoke or anger the Spaniards into renewing their attacks. Sorties were constantly made. The citizens gathered on the walls, and with shouts and taunts of cowardice challenged the Spaniards to come on; they even went to the length of dressing themselves in the vestments of the churches, and contemptuously carrying the sacred vessels in procession, in hopes of infuriating the Spaniards into an attack. But Don Frederick and his generals were not to be moved from their purpose.

The soldiers, suffering as much as the besiegers, would gladly have brought matters to an issue one way or the other by again assaulting the walls; but their officers restrained them, assuring them that the city could not hold out long, and that they would have an ample revenge when the time came. Life in the city was most monotonous now. There was no stir of life or business; no one bought or sold; and except the men who went to take their turn as sentries on the wall, or the women who fetched the daily ration for the family from the magazines, there was no occasion to go abroad. Fuel was getting very scarce, and families clubbed together and gathered at each others houses by turns, so that one fire did for all.

But at the end of February their sufferings from cold came to an end, for the frost suddenly broke up; in a few days the ice on the lake disappeared, and spring set in. The remaining cattle were now driven out into the fields under the walls to gather food for themselves. Strong guards went with them, and whenever the Spaniards endeavored to come down and drive them off, the citizens flocked out and fought so desperately that the Spaniards ceased to molest them ; for as one of those present wrote, each captured bullock cost the lives of at least a dozen soldiers.

Don Frederick himself had long since become heartily weary of the siege, in which there was no honor to be gained, and which had already cost the lives of so large a number of his best soldiers. It did not seem to him that the capture of a weak city was worth the price that had to be paid for it, and he wrote to his father urging his views, and asking permission to raise the siege. But the duke thought differently, and despatched an officer to his son with this message: " Tell Don Frederick that if he be not decided to continue the siege until the town be taken, I shall no longer consider him my son. Should he fall in the siege I will myself take the field to maintain it, and when we have both perished, the duchess, my wife, shall come from Spain to do the same."

Inflamed by this reply Don Frederick recommenced active operations, to the great satisfaction of the besieged. The batteries were reopened, and daily contests took place. One night, under cover of a fog, a party of the besieged marched up to the principal Spanish battery, and attempted to spike the guns. Every one of them was killed round the battery, not one turning to fly. "The citizens," wrote Don Frederick, "do as much as the best soldiers in the world could do."

As soon as the frost broke up, Count Bossu, who had been building a fleet of small vessels in Amsterdam, cut a breach through the dyke and entered the lake, thus entirely cutting off communications. The Prince of Orange on his part was building ships at the other end of the lake, and was doing all in his power for the relief of the city. He was anxiously waiting the arrival of troops from Germany or France, and doing his best with such volunteers as he could raise. These, however, were not numerous; for the Dutch, although ready to fight to the death for the defence of their own cities and families, had not yet acquired a national spirit, and all the efforts of the prince failed to induce them to combine for any general object.

His principal aim now was to cut the road along the dyke which connected Amsterdam with the country round it. Could he succeed in doing this, Amsterdam would be as completely cut off as was Haarlem, and that city, as well as the Spanish army, would speedily be starved out. Alva himself was fully aware of this danger, and wrote to the king: "Since I came into this world I have never been in such anxiety. It they should succeed in cutting off communication along the dykes we should have to raise the siege of Haarlem, to surrender, hands crossed, or to starve."

The prince, unable to gather sufficient men for this at-

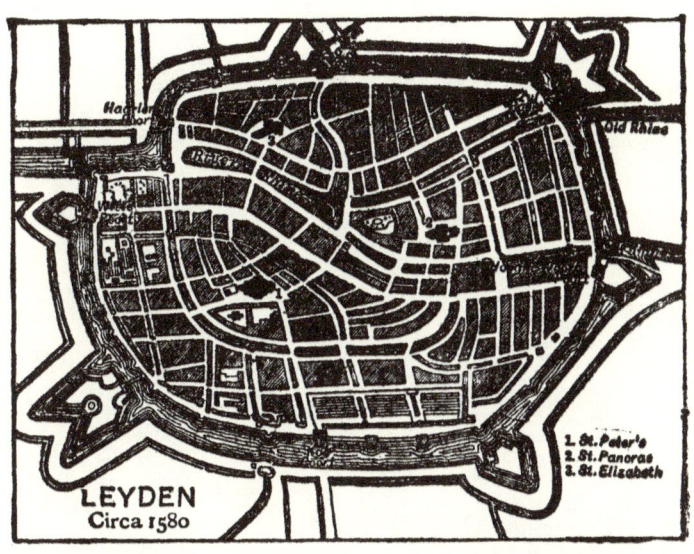

LEYDEN
Circa 1580

1. St. Peter's
2. St. Pancras
3. St. Elizabeth

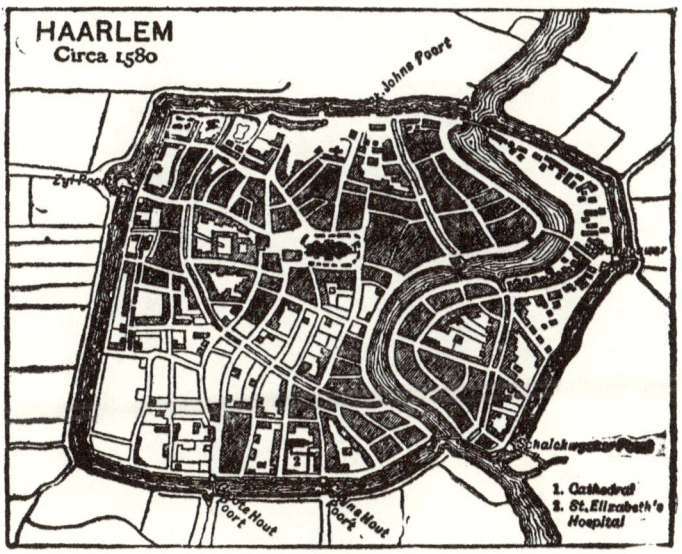

HAARLEM
Circa 1580

1. Cathedral
2. St. Elizabeth's
Hospital

tempt, sent orders to Sonoy, who commanded the small
army in the north of Holland, to attack the dyke between
the Diemar Lake and the Y, to open the sluices, and break
through the dyke, by which means much of the country
round Haarlem would be flooded.   Sonoy crossed the Y in
boats, seized the dyke, opened the sluices, and began the
work of cutting it through.   Leaving his men so engaged,
Sonoy went to Edam to fetch up reinforcements.   While
he was away a large force from Amsterdam came up, some
marching along the causeway and some in boats.

A fierce contest took place, the contending parties fighting partly in boats, partly on the slippery causeway, that
was wide enough but for two men to stand abreast, partly
in the water.   But the number of the assailants was too
great, and the Dutch, after fighting gallantly, lost heart
and retired just as Sonoy, whose volunteers from Edam
had refused to follow him, arrived alone in a little boat.
He tried in vain to rally them, but was swept away by the
rush of fugitives, many of whom were, however, able to
gain their boats and make their retreat, thanks to the
valour of John Haring of Horn, who took his station on
the dyke, and, armed with sword and shield, actually
kept in check a thousand of the enemy for a time long
enough to have enabled the Dutch to rally had they been
disposed to do so.   But it was too late ; and they had
enough of fighting.   However, he held his post until many
had made good their retreat, and then, plunging into the
sea, swam off to the boats and effected his escape. A braver
feat of arms was never accomplished.

Some hundreds of the Dutch were killed or captured. All
the prisoners were taken to the gibbets in the front of
Haarlem, and hung, some by the neck and some by the
heels, in view of their countrymen, while the head of one

of their officers was thrown into the city. As usual this act of ferocity excited the citizens to similar acts. Two of the old board of magistrates belonging to the Spanish party, with several other persons, were hung, and the wife and daughter of one of them hunted into the water and drowned.

In the words of an historian, "Every man within and without Haarlem seemed inspired by a spirit of special and personal vengeance." Many, however, of the more gentle spirits were filled with horror at these barbarities and the perpetual carnage going on. Captain Curey for example, one of the bravest officers of the garrison, who had been driven to take up arms by the sufferings of his countrymen, although he had naturally a horror of bloodshed, was subject to fits of melancholy at the contemplation of these horrors. Brave in the extreme, he led his men in every sortie, in every desperate struggle. Fighting without defensive armour he was always in the thick of the battle, and many of the Spaniards fell before his sword. On his return he invariably took to his bed, and lay ill from remorse and compunction till a fresh summons for action arrived, when, seized by a sort of frenzy, he rose and led his men to fresh conflicts.

On the 25th March a sally was made by a thousand of the besieged. They drove in all the Spanish outposts, killed eight hundred of the enemy, burnt three hundred tents, and captured seven cannons, nine standards, and many wagon loads of provisions, all of which they succeeded in bringing into the city.

The Duke of Alva, who had gone through nearly sixty years of warfare, wrote to the king that "never was a place defended with such skill and bravery as Haarlem," and that "it was a war such as never before was seen or heard of in any land on earth." Three veteran Spanish regiments now reinforced the besiegers, having been sent from Italy to aid in overcoming the obstinate resistance of the city. But the interest of the inhabitants was now centred rather on the lake than upon the Spanish camp. It was from this alone that they could expect succour, and it now swarmed with the Dutch and Spanish vessels, between whom there were daily contests.

On the 28th of May the two fleets met in desperate fight. Admiral Bossu had a hundred ships, most of considerable size. Martin Brand, who commanded the Dutch, had a hundred and fifty, but of much smaller size. The ships grappled with each other, and for hours a furious contest raged. Several thousands of men were killed on both sides, but at length weight prevailed and the victory was decided in favour of the Spaniards. Twenty-two of the Dutch vessels were captured and the rest routed. The Spanish fleet now sailed towards Haarlem, landed their crews, and joined by a force from the army, captured the forts the Dutch had erected and had hitherto held on the shore of the lake, and through which their scanty supplies had hitherto been received.

From the walls of the city the inhabitants watched the conflict, and a wail of despair rose from them as they saw its issue. They were now entirely cut off from all hope of succour, and their fate appeared to be sealed. Nevertheless they managed to send a message to the prince that they would hold out for three weeks longer in hopes that he might devise some plan for their relief, and carrier-pigeons brought back word that another effort should be made to save them. But by this time the magazines were empty. Hitherto one pound of bread had been served out daily to each man and half a pound to each woman, and on this alone they had for many weeks subsisted; but the flour was now exhausted, and henceforth it was a battle with starvation.

Every living creature that could be used as food was slain and eaten. Grass and herbage of all kinds were gathered and cooked for food, and under cover of darkness parties sallied out from the gates to gather grass in the fields. The sufferings of the besieged were terrible. So much were they reduced by weakness that they could scarce drag themselves along the streets, and numbers died from famine.

During the time that the supply of bread was served out Ned had persuaded his aunt and the girls to put by a morsel of their food each day.

" It will be the only resource when the city surrenders," he said. " For four or five days at least the girls must remain concealed, and during that time they must be fed. If they take in with them a jar of water and a supply of those crusts, which they can eat soaked in the water, they can maintain life."

And so each day, as long as the bread lasted, a small piece was put aside until a sufficient store was accumulated to last the two girls for a week. Soon after the daily issue ceased Frau Plomaert placed the bag of crusts into Ned's hands.

"Take it away and hide it somewhere," she said; " and do not let me know where you have put it, or we shall assuredly break into it and use it before the time comes. I do not think now that, however great the pressure, we would touch those crusts; but there is no saying what we may do when we are gnawed by hunger. It is better, anyhow, to put ourselves out of the way of temptation."

During the long weeks of June Ned found it hard to keep the precious store untouched. His aunt's figure had shrunk to a shadow of her former self, and she was scarce able to cross the room. The girls' cheeks were hollow and bloodless with famine, and although none of them ever asked him to break in upon the store, their faces pleaded more powerfully than any words could have done; and yet they were better off than many, for every night Ned either went out from the gates or let himself down by a rope from the wall and returned with a supply of grass and herbage.

It was fortunate for the girls that there was no necessity to go out of doors, for the sights there would have shaken the strongest. Men, women, and children fell dead by scores in the streets, and the survivors had neither strength nor heart to carry them away and bury them. On the 1st of July the burghers hung out a flag of truce, and deputies went out to confer with Dou Frederick. The latter, however, would grant no terms whatever, and they returned to the city. Two days later a tremendous cannonade was opened upon the town, and the walls broken down in several places, but the Spaniards did not advance to the assault, knowing that the town could not hold out many days longer.

Two more parleys were held, but without result, and the black flag was hoisted upon the cathedral town as a signal of despair; but soon afterwards a pigeon flew into the town with a letter from the prince, begging them to hold out for two days longer, as succour was approaching. The prince had indeed done all that was possible. He assembled the citizens of Delft in the market-place, and said that if any troops could be gathered he would march in person at their head to the relief of the city. There were no soldiers to be obtained; but 4000 armed volunteers from the various Dutch cities assembled, and 600 mounted troops. The

prince placed himself at their head, but the magistrates
and burghers of the towns would not allow him to hazard
a life so indispensable to the existence of Holland, and the
troops themselves refused to march unless he abandoned
his intention. He at last reluctantly consented, and handed
over the command of the expedition to Baron Batenburg.

On the 8th of July at dusk the expedition set out from
Sassenheim, taking with them four hundred wagon loads
of provisions and seven cannon. They halted in the woods,
and remained till midnight. Then they again marched
forward, hoping to be able to surprise the Spaniards and
make their way through before these could assemble in force.
The agreement had been made that signal fires should
be lighted and that the citizens should sally out to assist
the relieving force as it approached. Unfortunately two
pigeons with letters giving the details of the intended expedition had been shot while passing over the Spanish
camp, and the besiegers were perfectly aware of what was
going to be done. Opposite the point at which the besieged
were to sally out the Spaniards collected a great mass of
green branches, pitch, and straw. Five thousand troops
were stationed behind it, while an overwhelming force was
stationed to attack the relieving army.

When night fell the pile of combustibles was lighted, and
gave out so dense a smoke that the signal fires lighted by
Batenburg were hidden from the townspeople. As soon as
the column advanced from the wood they were attacked by
an overwhelming force of the enemy. Batenburg was killed
and his troops utterly routed, with the loss, according to
the Dutch account, of from five to six hundred, but of
many more according to Spanish statements. The besieged,
ranged under arms, heard the sound of the distant conflict,
but as they had seen no signal fires believed that it was

only a device of the Spaniards to tempt them into making a sally, and it was not until morning when Don Frederick sent in a prisoner with his nose and ears cut off to announce the news, that they knew that the last effort to save them had failed.

The blow was a terrible one, and there was great commotion in the town. After consultation the garrison and the able-bodied citizens resolved to issue out in a solid column, and to cut their way through the enemy or perish. It was thought that if the women, the helpless, and infirm alone remained in the city they would be treated with greater mercy after all the fighting men had been slain. But as soon as this resolution became known the women and children issued from the houses with loud cries and tears. The burghers were unable to withstand their entreaties that all should die together, and it was then resolved that the fighting men should be formed into a hollow square, in which the women, children, sick, and aged should be gathered, and so to sally out, and either win a way through the camp or die together.

But the news of this resolve reached the ears of Don Frederick. He knew now what the burghers of Haarlem were capable of, and thought that they would probably fire the city before they left, and thus leave nothing but a heap of ashes as a trophy of his victory. He therefore sent a letter to the magistrates, in the name of Count Overstein, commander of the German forces in the besieging army, giving a solemn assurance that if they surrendered at discretion no punishment should be inflicted except upon those who, in the judgment of the citizens themselves, had deserved it.

At the moment of sending the letter Don Frederick was in possession of strict orders from his father not to leave a man alive of the garrison, with the exception of the Germans, and to execute a large number of the burghers. On the receipt of this letter the city formally surrendered on the 10th of July. The great bell was tolled, and orders were issued that all arms should be brought to the town hall, that the women should assemble in the cathedral and the men in the cloister of Zyl. Then Don Frederick with his staff rode into the city. The scene which met their eyes was a terrible one. Everywhere were ruins of houses which had been set on fire by the Spanish artillery, the pavement had been torn up to repair the gaps in the walls, unburied bodies of men and women were scattered about the streets, while those still alive were mere shadows scarcely able to maintain their feet.

No time was lost in commencing the massacre. All the officers were at once put to death. The garrison had been reduced during the siege from 4000 to 1800. Of these the Germans—600 in number—were allowed to depart. The remaining 1200 were immediately butchered, with at least as many of the citizens. Almost every citizen distinguished by service, station, or wealth was slaughtered, and from day to day five executioners were kept constantly at work. The city was not sacked, the inhabitants agreeing to raise a great sum of money as a ransom.

As soon as the surrender was determined upon, Ned helped his cousins into the refuge prepared for them, passed in the bread and water, walled up the hole and whitewashed it, his aunt being too weak to render any assistance. Before they entered he opened the bag and took out a few crusts.

"You must eat something now, aunt," he said. "It may be a day or two before any food is distributed, and it is no use holding on so long to die of hunger when food is almost in sight. There is plenty in the bag to last the girls for a week. You must eat sparingly, girls,—not because there is not enough food, but because after fasting so long it is necessary for you at first to take food in very small quantities."

The bread taken out was soaked, and it swelled so much in the water that it made much more than he had expected. He therefore divided it in half, and a portion made an excellent meal for Ned and his aunt, the remainder being carefully put by for the following day.

An hour or two after eating the meal Frau Plomaert felt so much stronger that she was able to obey the order to go up to the cathedral. Ned went with the able-bodied men to the cloisters. The Spaniards soon came among them, and dragged off numbers of those whom they thought most likely to have taken a prominent part in the fighting, to execution. As they did not wish others from whom money could be wrung to escape from their hands, they presently issued some food to the remainder. The women, after remaining for some hours in the cathedral, were suffered to depart to their homes, for their starving condition excited the compassion even of the Spaniards; and the atrocities which had taken place at the sacks of Mechlin, Zutphen and Naarden, were not repeated in Haarlem.

The next day the men were also released; not from any ideas of mercy, but in order that when they returned to their homes the work of picking out the better class for execution could be the more easily carried on. For three days longer the girls remained in their hiding, and were then allowed to come out, as Ned felt now that the danger of a general massacre was averted.

"Now, Ned," his aunt said, "you must stay here no

longer. Every day we hear proclamations read in the streets that all sheltering refugees and others not belonging to the town will be punished with death; and, as you know, every stranger caught has been murdered."

This they had heard from some of the neighbours. Ned himself had not stirred out since he returned from the cloisters; for his aunt had implored him not to do so, as it would only be running useless risk.

"I lfear, she went on, "that they have searched many houses for fugitives and it is probable the hunt may become even more strict; therefore I think, Ned, that for our sake as well as your own you had better try to escape."

"I quite agree with you, aunt. Now that the worst is over, and I know that you and the girls are safe, no good purpose could be served by my staying; and being both a stranger and one who has fought here, I should certainly be killed if they laid hands on me. As to escaping, I do not think there can be any difficulty about that. I have often let myself down from the walls, and can do so again; and although there is a strict watch kept at the gates to prevent any from leaving until the Spaniards' thirst for blood is satisfied, there can be no longer any vigilant watch kept up by the troops encamped outside, and I ought certainly to be able to get through them at night. It will be dark in a couple of hours, and as soon as it is so I will be off."

The girls burst into tears at the thought of Ned's departure. During the seven long months that the siege had lasted he had been as a brother to them—keeping up their spirits by his cheerfulness, looking after their safety, and as far as possible after their comfort, and acting as the adviser and almost as the head of the house. His aunt was almost equally affected, for she had come to lean entirely upon him and to regard him as a son.

"It is best that it should be so, Ned; but we shall all miss you sorely. It may be that I shall follow your advice and come over to England on a long visit. Now that I know you so well it will not seem like going among strangers, as it did before; for although I met your father and mother whenever they came over to Vordwyk, I had not got to know them as I know you. I shall talk the matter over with my father. Of course everything depends upon what is going to happen in Holland."

Ned did not tell his aunt that her father had been one of the first dragged out from the cloisters for execution, and that her sister, who kept house for him, had died three days previous to the surrender. His going away was grief enough for her for one day, and he turned the conversation to other matters until night fell, when, after a sad parting, he made his way to the walls, having wound round his waist the rope by which he had been accustomed to lower himself.

The executions continued in Haarlem for two days after he had left, and then the five executioners were so weary of slaying that the three hundred prisoners who still remained for execution were tied back to back and thrown into the lake.

CHAPTER XV.

IT was fortunate for Ned that the watch round the city had relaxed greatly when he started from it. The soldiers were discontented at the arrangement that had been made for the city to pay an immense sum of money to escape a general sack. They were all many months in arrear of their pay. They had suffered during the siege, and they now considered themselves to be cheated of their fair reward. The sum paid by the city would go into the hands of the duke; and although the soldiers were promised a share of the prize-money, the duke's necessities were so great that it was probable little of the money would find its way into the hands of the troops.

A sack upon the other hand was looked upon as a glorious lottery. Every one was sure to gain something. Many would obtain most valuable prizes of money or jewelry. No sooner, therefore, had Haarlem surrendered than a mutinous spirit began to show itself among the troops; they became slack in obeying the orders of their officers, refused to perform their duties, and either gathered in bodies to discuss their wrongs or sulked in their tents. Thus the work of keeping a vigilant watch round the walls by night, to prevent the escape of the victims selected to satiate the vengence of Don Frederick, was greatly relaxed.

After lowering himself from the walls Ned proceeded with great caution. On reaching the spot where he ex-

NED OVERHEARS THE MUTINEERS.

pected to meet with a cordon of sentries, he was surprised at finding everything still and quiet. Unaware of the state of things in the camp, and suspecting that some device had perhaps been hit upon with the view of inducing men to try to escape from the city, he redoubled his precautions, stopping every few paces to listen for the calls of the sentries, or a heavy tread, or the clash of arms. All was silent, and he continued his course until close to the camps of some of the German regiments. Incredible as it seemed to him, it was now evident that no sentries had been posted. He saw great fires blazing in the camps, and a large number of men standing near one of them; they were being addressed by a soldier standing upon a barrel.

Keeping in the shadow of the tents, Ned made his way close up to the group, and the similarity of the German language to the Dutch enabled him to gather without difficulty the meaning of the speaker's words. He was recounting to the soldiers the numberless toils and hardships through which they had passed in the service of Spain, and the ingratitude with which they were treated.

" They pretend they have no money!" he exclaimed," it is not true. Spain has the wealth of the Indies at her back, and yet she grudges us our pay for the services we have faithfully rendered her. Why should we throw away our lives for Spain? What do we care whether she is mistress of this wretched country or not? Let us resolve, brethren, to be moved neither by entreaties or threats, but to remain fast to the oath we and our Spanish comrades have sworn, that we will neither march a foot nor lift an arm until we have received our pay; and not only our pay, but our share of the booty they have stolen from us."

The shouts of approval that greeted the speech showed that the speaker's audience was thoroughly in accord with him. Ned waited to hear no further orations, he understood now the withdrawal of the sentries. It was another of the mutinies that had so frequently broken out among the Spanish forces in the Netherlands. Making his way out through the other side of the camp he proceeded on his journey. The news was important, for if the mutiny continued it would give the Prince of Orange time to prepare for the forward march of the enemy. He passed several other camps, but observed everywhere the same slackness of discipline and the absence of military precaution.

All night he pushed forward without stopping, and as soon as the gates of Leyden were opened he entered. Upon inquiring he found that the prince was at Delft, and hiring a horse he at once rode there. The prince received him with real pleasure.

"And so you have escaped safe and sound from the siege, Master Martin? Truly your good fortune is wonderful. I am glad indeed to see you. Tell me how goes it in Haarlem. Rumours reached me that there, as at other towns, they have broken their oaths, and are massacring the whole population."

"It is not so bad as that, sir," Ned replied. "They put to death numbers of the principal citizens and all refugees they could discover in the city, but there has been no regular sack. The women have not been ill treated, and although five executioners were kept busily at work there has been nothing like a general massacre."

"Thank God for that," the prince said piously. "That has eased my mind. I feared that the horrors of Zutphen and Naarden had been re-enacted."

"I have another piece of good news to give you, sir. As I passed through their camps, I learned that all the troops, German as well as Spanish, are in open mutiny, and have

sworn that they will neither march nor fight until they receive all arrears of pay."

"That is good news indeed!" the prince exclaimed. "It
will give us breathing time, of which we are sadly in need.
Were the Spaniards to march forward now, they could
sweep over Holland, for I could not put a thousand men
in the field to withstand them. And now, Master Martin,
what shall I do for you? You have received as yet no reward whatever for the great service you rendered us by the
successful carrying out of your mission to Brussels, to say
nothing of the part you have borne in the defence of Haarlem. I know that you joined us from pure love of our
cause and hatred of Spanish tyranny, still that is no reason why I should not recognize your services. If you
would like it, I would gladly appoint you to the command
of a company of volunteers."

"I thank you greatly, your highness," replied Ned;
but I am far too young to command men, and pray
that you will allow me to remain near your person,
and to perform such service as you may think me capable of."

"If that be your wish, it shall be so for the present,"
the prince replied; "and it is pleasant to me in these
days, when almost every noble in the Netherlands puts a
price on his services, and when even the cities bargain for
every crown-piece they advance, to find one who wants
nothing. But now you need rest. When I am more at
leisure you shall furnish me with further details of what
took place inside Haarlem during the siege."

The long defence of Haarlem, the enormous expenditure which it had cost, both in money and life, for no less
than 10,000 soldiers had fallen in the assault or by disease,
induced Alva to make another attempt to win back the

people of Holland, and three days after Ned's return a proclamation was sent to every town.

He adopted an affectionate tone: "Ye are well aware," began the address," that the king has over and over again manifested his willingness to receive his children, in however forlorn a condition the prodigals might return. His majesty assures you once more that your sins, however black they may have been, shall be forgiven and forgotten in the plenitude of royal kindness, if you will repent and return in season to his majesty's embrace. Notwithstanding your manifold crimes, his majesty still seeks, like a hen calling her chickens, to gather you all under the parental wing."

This portion of the document, which was by the order of the magistrates affixed to the doors of the town halls, was received with shouts of laughter by the citizens, and many were the jokes as to the royal hen and the return of the prodigals. The conclusion of the document afforded a little further insight into the affectionate disposition of the royal bird. "If," continued the proclamation, "ye disregard these offers of mercy, and receive them with closed ears as heretofore, then we warn you that there is no rigour or cruelty, however great, which you are not to expect, by laying waste, starvation, and the sword. In such manner that nowhere shall remain a relic of that which at present exists, but his majesty will strip bare and utterly depopulate the land, and cause it to be inhabited again by strangers, since otherwise his majesty would not believe that the will of God and of his majesty had been accomplished."

This proclamation produced no effect whatever; for the people of Holland were well aware that Philip of Spain would never grant that religious toleration for which they

were fighting, and they knew also that no reliance whatever could be placed in Spanish promises or oaths. For a
month Alva was occupied in persuading the troops to return to their duty, and at last managed to raise a sufficient
sum of money to pay each man a portion of the arrears
due to him, and a few crowns on account of his share of
the ransom paid by Haarlem. During this breathing-time
the Prince of Orange was indefatigable in his endeavours
to raise a force capable of undertaking the relief of such
towns as the Spaniards might invest.

   This, however, he found well nigh impossible. The
cities were all ready to defend themselves, bnt in spite of
the danger that threatened they were chary in the extreme
in contributing money for the common cause, nor would
the people enlist for service in the field. Nothing had
occurred to shake the belief of the invincibility of the
Spanish soldiery in fair fight in the open, and the disasters
which had befallen the bodies of volunteers who had endeavoured to relieve Haarlem, effectually deterred others
from following their example. The prince's only hope,
therefore, of being able to put a force into the field, rested
upon his brother Louis, who was raising an army of mercenaries in Germany.

   He had little assurance, however, that relief would
come from this quarter, as the two armies he had himself
raised in Germany had effected absolutely nothing. His
efforts to raise a fleet were more successful. The hardy
mariners of Zeeland were ready to fight on their own ele-
ment, and asked nothing better than to meet the Spaniards
at sea. Nevertheless money had to be raised for the purchase of vessels, stores, artillery, and ammunition. Ned
was frequently despatched by the prince with letters to
magistrates of the chief towns, to nobles and men of influ-

ence, and always performed his duties greatly to the prince's satisfaction.

As soon as the Duke of Alva had satisfied the troops, preparations began for a renewal of hostilities, and the prince soon learnt that it was intended that Don Frederick should invade Northern Holland with 16,000 men, and that the rest of the army, which had lately received further reinforcements, should lay siege to Leyden. The prince felt confident that Leyden could resist for a time, but he was very anxious as to the position of things in North Holland. In the courage and ability of Sonoy, the Lieutenant-governor of North Holland, the prince had entire confidence; but it was evident by the tone of his letters that he had lost all hope of being able to defend the province, and altogether despaired of the success of their cause. He had written in desponding tones at the utterly insufficient means at his disposal for meeting the storm that was about to burst upon the province, and had urged that unless the prince had a good prospect of help, either from France or England, it was better to give up the struggle, than to bring utter destruction upon the whole people.

The letter in which the prince answered him has been preserved, and well illustrates the lofty tone of his communications in this crisis of the fate of Holland. He reprimanded with gentle but earnest eloquence the despondency and want of faith of his lieutenant and other adherents. He had not expected, he said, that they would have so soon forgotten their manly courage. They seemed to consider the whole fate of the country attached to the city of Haarlem. He took God to witness that he had spared no pains, and would willingly have spared no drop of his blood to save that devoted city.

"But as, notwithstanding our efforts," he continued,

"it has pleased God Almighty to dispose of Haarlem according to his divine will, shall we, therefore, deny and deride his holy word? Has his Church, therefore, come to naught? You ask if I have entered into a firm treaty with any great king or potentate, to which I answer that before I ever took up the cause of the oppressed Christians in these provinces I had entered into a close alliance with the King of kings; and I am firmly convinced that all who put their trust in him shall be saved by his Almighty hand. The God of armies will raise up armies for us to do battle with our enemies and his own."

In conclusion he detailed his preparations for attacking the enemy by sea as well as by land, and encouraged his lieutenant and the population of the northern province to maintain a bold front before the advancing foe. That Sonoy would do his best the prince was sure; but he knew how difficult it is for one who himself regards resistance as hopeless to inspire enthusiasm in others, and he determined to send a message to cheer the people of North Holland, and urge them to resist to the last, and to intrust it to one who could speak personally as to the efforts that were being made for their assistance, and who was animated by a real enthusiasm in the cause.

It was an important mission; but after considering the various persons of his household, he decided to intrust it to the lad who had showed such courage and discretion in his dangerous mission to Brussels. A keen observer of character, the prince felt that he could trust the young fellow absolutely to do his best at whatever risk to himself. He had believed when he first joined him that Ned was some eighteen years of age, and the year that had since elapsed with its dangers and responsibilities had added two or three years to his appearance.

It was the fashion in Holland to entirely shave the face, and Ned's smooth cheeks were therefore no sign of youth. Standing over the average height of the natives of Holland, with broad shoulders and well-set figure, he might readily pass as a man of three and four and twenty. The prince accordingly sent for the lad.

"I have another mission for you, Master Martin; and again a dangerous one. The Spaniards are on the point of marching to lay siege to Alkmaar, and I wish a message carried to the citizens, assuring them that they may rely absolutely upon my relieving them by breaking down the dykes. I wish you on this occasion to be more than a messenger. In these despatches I have spoken of you as one Captain Martin, who possesses my fullest confidence. You would as you say be young to be a captain of a company of fighting men, but as an officer attached to my household you can bear that rank as well as another.

" It will be useful, and will add to your influence and authority, and I have therefore appointed you to the grade of captain, of which by your conduct you have proved yourself to be worthy. Your mission is to encourage the inhabitants to resist to the last, to rouse them to enthusiasm if you can, to give them my solemn promise that they shall not be deserted, and to assure them that if I cannot raise a force sufficient to relieve them I will myself come round and superintend the operation of cutting the dykes and laying the whole country under water. I do not know whether you will find the lieutenant-governor in the city, but at any rate he will not remain there during the siege, as he has work outside. But I shall give you a letter recommending you to him, and ask him to give you his warmest support."

The prince then took off the gold chain he wore round

his neck, and placed it upon Ned. "I give you this in the first place, Captain Martin, in token of my esteem and of my gratitude for the perilous service you have already rendered; and secondly, as a visible mark of my confidence in you, and as a sign that I have intrusted you with authority to speak for me. Going as you now do, it will be best for you to assume somewhat more courtly garments in order to do credit to your mission. I have given orders that these shall be prepared for you, and that you shall be provided with a suit of armour, such as a young noble would wear. All will be prepared for you this afternoon. At six o'clock a ship will be in readiness to sail, and this will land you on the coast at the nearest point to Alkmaar. Should any further point occur to you before evening, speak to me freely about it."

Ned retired depressed rather than elated at the confidence the prince reposed in him, and at the rank and dignity he had bestowed upon him. He questioned, too, whether he had not done wrong in not stating at once when the prince had, on his first joining him, set down his age at over eighteen, that he was two years under that age, and he hesitated whether he ought not even now to go to him and state the truth. He would have done so had he not known how great were the labours of the prince, and how incessantly he was occupied, and so feared to upset his plans and cause him fresh trouble. "Anyhow," he said to himself at last, "I will do my best; and I could do no more if I were nineteen instead of seventeen. The prince has chosen me for this business, not because of my age, but because he thought I could carry it out; and carry it out I will, if it be in my power."

In the afternoon a clothier arrived with several suits of handsome material and make, but of sober colours, such as

a young man of good family would wear, and an armourer
brought him a morion and breast and back pieces of steel,
handsomely inlaid with gold.   When he was alone he attired himself in the quietest of his new suits, and looking
at himself in the mirror burst into a fit of hearty laughter.

"What in the world would my father and mother and
the girls say were they to see me pranked out in such attire as this? They would scarce know me, and I shall
scarce know myself for some time.   However, I think I
shall be able to play my part as the prince's representative better in these than I should have done in the dress I
started in last time, or in that I wore on board the *Good
Venture.*"

At five o'clock Ned paid another visit to the prince, and
thanked him heartily for his kindness towards him, and
then received a few last instructions. On his return to his
room he found a corporal and four soldiers at the door.
The former saluted.

"We have orders, Captain Martin, to place ourselves
under your command for detached duty.   Our kits are already on board the ship; the men will carry down your
mails if they are packed."

"I only take that trunk with me," Ned said, pointing to the one that contained his new clothes; "and there
is besides my armour, and that brace of pistols."

Followed by the corporal and men, Ned now made his
way down to the port, where the captain of the little vessel received him with profound respect.   As soon as they
were on board the sails were hoisted, and the vessel ran
down the channel from Delft through the Hague to the
sea.   On the following morning they anchored soon after
daybreak.   A boat was lowered, and Ned and the soldiers
landed on the sandy shore.   Followed by them he made

his way over the high range of sand-hills facing the sea, and then across the low cultivated country extending to Alkmaar. He saw parties of men and women hurrying northward along the causeways laden with goods, and leading in most instances horses or donkeys, staggering under the weights placed upon them.

"I think we are but just in time, corporal. The population of the villages are evidently fleeing before the advance of the Spaniards. Another day and we should have been too late to get into the town."

Alkmaar had been in sight from the time they had crossed the dunes, and after walking five miles they arrived at its gates.

"Is the lieutenant-governor in the town?" Ned asked one of the citizens.

"Yes, he is still here," the man said. "You will find him at the town-hall."

There was much excitement in the streets. Armed burghers were standing in groups, women were looking anxiously from doors and casements; but Ned was surprised to see no soldiers about, although he knew that the eight hundred whom the prince had despatched as a garrison must have arrived there some days before. On arriving at the town-hall he found the general seated at table. In front of him were a group of elderly men whom he supposed to be the leading citizens, and it was evident by the raised voices and angry looks, both of the old officer and of the citizens, that there was some serious difference of opinion between them.

"Whom have we here?" Sonoy asked as Ned approached the table.

"I am a messenger, sir, from the prince. I bear these despatches to yourself, and have also letters and messages from him to the citizens of Alkmaar."

"You come at a good season," the governor said snortly, taking the despatches, "and if anything you can say will soften the obstinacy of these good people here, you will do them and me a service."

There was silence for a few minutes as the governor read the letters Ned had brought him.

"My good friends," he said at last to the citizens, "this is Captain Martin, an officer whom the prince tells me stands high in his confidence. He bore part in the siege of Haarlem, and has otherwise done great service to the state; the prince commends him most highly to me and to you. He has sent him here in the first place to assure you fully of the prince's intentions on your behalf. He will especially represent the prince during the siege, and from his knowledge of the methods of defence at Haarlem, of the arrangements for portioning out the food and other matters, he will be able to give you valuable advice and assistance. As you are aware, I ride in an hour to Enkhuizen in order to superintend the general arrangement for the defence of the province, and especially for affording you aid, and I am glad to leave behind me an officer who is so completely in the confidence of the prince. He will first deliver the messages with which he is charged to you, and then we will hear what he says as to this matter which is in dispute between us."

The passage of Ned with his escort through the street had attracted much attention, and the citizens had followed him into the hall in considerable numbers to hear the message of which he was no doubt the bearer. Ned took his place by the side of the old officer, and facing the crowd began to speak. At other times he would have been diffident in addressing a crowded audience, but he felt that he must justify the confidence imposed on him, and knowing the preparations that were being made by the prince, and his intense anxiety that Alkmaar should resist to the end, he began without hesitation, and speedily forgot himself in the importance of the subject.

"Citizens of Alkmaar," he began, "the prince has sent me specially to tell what there is in his mind concerning you, and how his thoughts, night and day, have been turned towards your city. Not only the prince, but all Holland are turning their eyes towards you, and none doubt that you will show yourselves as worthy, as faithful, and as steadfast as have the citizens of Haarlem. You fight not for glory, but for your liberty, for your religion, for the honour and the lives of those dear to you; and yet your glory and your honour will be great indeed if this little city of yours should prove the bulwark of Holland, and should beat back from its walls the power of Spain. The prince bids me tell you that he is doing all he can to collect an army and a fleet.

"In the latter respect he is succeeding well. The hardiest seamen of Holland and Zeeland are gathering round him, and have sworn that they will clear the Zuider-Zee of the Spaniards or die in the attempt. As to the army, it is, as you know, next to impossible to gather one capable of coping with the host of Spain in the field; but happily you need not rely solely upon an army to save you in your need. Here you have an advantage over your brethren of Haarlem. There it was impossible to flood the land round the city; and the dykes by which the food supply of the Spaniards could have been cut off were too strongly guarded to be won, even when your noble governor himself led his forces against them.

"But it is not so here. The dykes are far away, and the Spaniards cannot protect them. Grievous as it is to the prince to contemplate the destruction of the rich country

288   THE PRINCE'S PROMISE.

your fathers have won from the sea, he bids me tell you that he will not hesitate; but that, as a last resource, he pledges himself that he will lay the country under water and drown out the Spaniards to save you. They have sworn, as you know, to turn Holland into a desert—to leave none alive in her cities and villages. Well, then; better a thousand times that we should return it to the ocean from which we won it, and that then, having cast out the Spaniards, we should renew the labours of our fathers, and again recover it from the sea."

A shout of applause rang through the hall.

"But this," Ned went on, "is the last resource, and will not be taken until nought else can be done to save you. It is for you first, to show the Spaniards how the men of Holland can fight for their freedom, their religion, their families, and their homes. Then, when you have done all that men can do, the prince will prove to the Spaniards that the men of Holland will lay their country under water rather than surrender."

"Does the prince solemnly bind himself to do this?" one of the elder burghers asked.

"He does; and here is his promise in black and white, with his seal attached."

"We will retire, and let you have our answer in half an hour."

Ned glanced at the governor, who shook his head slightly.

"What! is there need of deliberation?" Ned asked in a voice that was heard all over the hall. "To you, citizens at large, I appeal. Of what use is it now to deliberate? Have you not already sent a defiant answer to Alva? Are not his troops within a day's march of you? Think you that, even if you turn traitors to your country and to your

prince, and throw open the gates, it would save you now?
Did submission save Naarden? How many of you, think
you, would survive the sack? and for those who did so,
what would life be worth? They would live an object of
reproach and scoffing among all true Hollanders, as the
men of the city who threatened what they dared not perform, who were bold while Alva was four days' march
away, but who cowered like children when they saw the
standards of Spain approaching their walls. I appeal to
you, is this a time to hesitate or discuss? I ask you now,
in the name of the prince, are you true men or false? Are
you for Orange or Alva? What is your answer?"

A tremendous shout shook the hall.

"We will fight to the death! No surrender! Down with
the council!" and there were loud and threatening shouts
against some of the magistrates. The governor now rose:

"My friends," he said. "I rejoice to hear your decision;
and now there is no time for idle talk. Throw open the
gates, and call in the troops whom the prince has sent to
your aid, and whom your magistrates have hitherto
refused to admit. Choose from among yourself six men
upon whom you can rely to confer with me and with the
officer commanding the troops. Choose good and worshipful men, zealous in the cause. I will see before I leave to-
day that your magistracy is strengthened. You need now
men of heart and action at your head. Captain Martin,
who has been through the siege of Haarlem, will deliberate
with twelve citizens whom I will select as to the steps to be
taken for gathering the food into magazines for the
public use, for issuing daily rations, for organizing the
women as well as the men for such work as they are fit.
There is much to be done, and but little time to do it, for
to-morrow the Spaniard will be in front of your walls."

In an hour's time the 800 troops marched in from Egmont Castle and Egmont Abbey, where they had been
quartered while the citizens were wavering between resistance and submission.   Four of the citizens, who had
already been told off for the purpose, met them at the
gate and alloted them quarters in the various houses.
Governor Sonoy was already in deliberation with the six
men chosen by the townspeople to represent them. He had
at once removed from the magistracy an equal number of
those who had been the chief opponents of resistance; for
here, as in other towns, the magistrates had been appointed
by the Spaniards.

Ned was busy conferring with the committee, and explaining to them the organization adopted at Haarlem. He
pointed out that it was a first necessity that all the men
capable of bearing arms should be divided into companies
of fifty, each of which should select its own captain and
lieutenant; that the names of the women should be in-
scribed, with their ages, that the active and able-bodied
should be divided into companies for carrying materials to
the walls, and aiding in the defence when a breach was attacked; and that the old and feeble should be made useful
in the hospitals and for such other work as their powers
admitted.   All children were to join the companies to
which their mothers belonged, and to help as far as they
could in their work.   Having set these matters in train,
Ned rejoined the governor.

"I congratulate you, Captain Martin, upon the service
you have rendered to-day. Your youth and enthusiasm
have succeeded where my experience failed. You believe
in the possibility of success, and thus your words had a
ring and fervour which were wanting in mine, fearing, as
I do, that the cause is a lost one. I wondered much when

you first presented yourself that the prince should have given his confidence to one so young. I wonder no longer. The prince never makes a mistake in his instruments, and he has chosen well this time.

"I leave the city to-night, and shall write to the prince from Enkhuizen telling him how you have brought the citizens round to a sense of their duty; and that whereas, at the moment of your arrival I believed the magistrates would throw open the gates to-morrow, I am now convinced the city will resist till the last. In military matters the officer in command of the troops will of course take the direction of things; but in all other matters you, as the prince's special representative, will act as adviser of the burghers. I wish that I could stay here and share in the perils of the siege. It would be far more suitable to my disposition than arguing with pig-headed burghers, and trying to excite their enthusiasm when my own hopes have all but vanished."

The officer commanding the garrison now entered, and the governor introduced Ned to him.

"You will find in Captain Martin, one who is in the prince's confidence, and has been sent here as his special representative, and able coadjutor. He will organize the citizens as they were organized at Haarlem; and while you are defending the walls he will see that all goes on in good order in the town, that there is no undue waste in provisions, that the breaches are repaired as fast as made, that the sick and wounded are well cared for, and that the spirits of the townspeople are maintained."

"That will indeed be an assistance," the officer said courteously. "These details are as necessary as the work of fighting; and it is impossible for one man to attend to them and to see to his military work."

"I shall look to you, sir, for your aid and assistance," Ned said modestly. "The prince is pleased to have a good opinion of me ; but I am young and shall find the responsibility a very heavy one, and can only hope to maintain my authority by the aid of your assistance."

"I think not that you will require much aid, Captain Martin," the governor said. "I marked you when you were speaking, and doubt not that your spirit will carry you through all difficulties."

That night was a busy one in Alkmaar. Few thought of sleeping, and before morning the lists were all prepared, the companies mustered, the officers chosen, posts on the walls assigned to them, and every man, woman, and child in Alkmaar knew the nature of the duties they would be called upon to perform. Just before midnight the governor left.

"Farewell, young man," he said to Ned ; "I trust that we may meet again. Now that I have got rid of the black sheep among the magistracy I feel more hopeful as to the success of the defence."

"But may I ask, sir, why you did not dismiss them before ?"

"Ah ! you hardly know the burghers of these towns," Sonoy said, shaking his head. "They stand upon their rights and privileges, and if you touch their civic officers they are like a swarm of angry bees. Governor of North Holland as I am, I could not have interfered with the magistracy even of this little town. It was only because at the moment the people were roused to enthusiasm, and because they regarded you as the special representative of the prince, that I was able to do so. Now that the act is done they are well content with the change, especially as I have appointed the men they themselves chose to the vacant places. It was the same thing at Enkhuizen—I could do nothing; and it was only when Sainte Aldegonde came with authority from the prince himself that we were able to get rid of Alva's creatures. Well, I must ride away. The Spaniards are encamped about six miles away, and you may expect to see them soon after daybreak."

It was indeed early in the morning that masses of smoke were seen rising from the village of Egmont, telling the citizens of Alkmaar that the troopers of Don Frederick had arrived. Alkmaar was but a small town, and when every man capable of bearing arms was mustered they numbered only about 1300, besides the 800 soldiers. It was on the 21st of August that Don Frederick with 16,000 veteran troops appeared before the walls of the town, and at once proceeded to invest it, and accomplished this so thoroughly that Alva wrote, "It is impossible for a sparrow to enter or go out of the city." There was no doubt what the fate of the inhabitants would be if the city were cap. tured. The duke was furious that what he considered his extraordinary clemency in having executed only some 2400 persons at the surrender of Haarlem should not have been met with the gratitude it deserved.

"If I take Alkmaar," he wrote to the king, "I am resolved not to leave a single person alive; the knife shall be put to every throat. Since the example of Haarlem has proved to be of no use, perhaps an example of cruelty will bring the other cities to their senses."

CHAPTER XVI.

FRIENDS IN TROUBLE.

WITHIN the little town of Alkmaar all went on quietly. While the Spaniards constructed their lines of investment and mounted their batteries, and then laboured continually at strengthening their walls, the women and children carried materials, all the food was collected in magazines, and rations served out regularly. A carpenter named Peter Van der Mey managed to make his way out of the city a fortnight after the investment began with letters to the Prince and Sonoy, giving the formal consent of all within the walls for the cutting of the dykes when it should be necessary; for, according to the laws of Holland, a step that would lead to so enormous a destruction of property could not be undertaken, even in the most urgent circumstances, without the consent of the population.

At daybreak on the 18th of September a heavy cannonade was opened against the walls, and after twelve hours' fire two breaches were made. Upon the following morning two of the best Spanish regiments which had just arrived from Italy led the way to the assault, shouting and cheering as they went, and confident of an easy victory. They were followed by heavy masses of troops.

Now Ned was again to see what the slow and somewhat apathetic Dutch burghers could do when fairly aroused to action. Every man capable of bearing a weapon was upon the walls, and not even in Haarlem was an attack received with more coolness and confidence. As the storming parties approached they were swept by artillery and musketry, and as they attempted to climb the breaches, boiling water, pitch and oil, molten lead and unslacked lime were poured upon them. Hundreds of tarred and blazing hoops were skilfully thrown on to their necks, and those who in spite of these terrible missiles mounted the breach, found themselves confronted by the soldiers and burghers, armed with axe and pike, and were slain or cast back again.

Three times was the assault renewed, fresh troops being ever brought up and pressing forward, wild with rage at their repulses by so small a number of defenders. But each was in turn hurled back. For four hours the desperate fight continued. The women and children showed a calmness equal to that of the men, moving backwards and forwards between the magazines and the ramparts with supplies of missiles and ammunition to the combatants. At nightfall the Spaniards desisted from the attack and fell back to their camp, leaving a thousand dead behind them; while only twenty-four of the garrison and thirteen of the burghers lost their lives.

A Spanish officer who had mounted the breach for an instant, and, after being hurled back, almost miraculously escaped with his life, reported that he had seen neither helmet nor harness as he looked down into the city—only some plain-looking people, generally dressed like fishermen. The cannonade was renewed on the following morning, and after 700 shots had been fired and the breaches enlarged, a fresh assault was ordered. But the troops absolutely refused to advance. It seemed to them that the devil, whom they believed the Protestants worshipped, had protected the city, otherwise how could a handful of townsmen and fishermen have defeated the invincible soldiers of Spain, outnumbering them eight-fold.

In vain Don Frederick and his generals entreated and stormed. Several of the soldiers were run through the body, but even this did not intimidate the rest into submission, and the assault was in consequence postponed. Already, indeed, there was considerable uneasiness in the Spanish camp. Governor Sonoy had opened many of the dykes, and the ground in the neighbourhood of the camp was already feeling soft and boggy. It needed but that two great dykes should be pierced to spread the inunda-- tion over the whole country. The carpenter who had soon after the commencement of the siege carried out the despatches had again made his way back.

He was the bearer of the copy of a letter sent from the prince to Sonoy, ordering him to protect the dykes and sluices with strong guards, lest the peasants, in order to save their crops, should repair the breaches. He was directed to flood the whole country at all risks rather than to allow Alkmaar to fall. The prince directed the citizens to kindle four great beacon-fires as soon as it should prove necessary to resort to extreme measures, and solemnly promised that as soon as the signal was given an inundation should be created which would sweep the whole Spanish army into the sea.

The carpenter was informed of the exact contents of his despatches, so that in case of losing them in his passage through the Spanish camp he could repeat them by word of mouth to the citizens. This was exactly what happened. The despatches were concealed in a hollow stick, and this stick the carpenter, in carrying out his perilous undertaking, lost. As it turned out it was fortunate that he did so. The stick was picked up in the camp and discovered to be hollow. It was carried to Don Frederick, who read the despatches, and at once called his officers together.

Alarmed at the prospect before them, and already heartily sick of a siege in which the honour all fell to their opponents, they agreed that the safety of an army of the picked troops of Spain must not be sacrificed merely with the hope of obtaining possession of an insignificant town. Orders were therefore given for an immediate retreat, and on the 8th of October the siege was raised and the troops marched back to Amsterdam.

Thus for the first time the Spaniards had to recoil before their puny adversaries. The terrible loss of life entailed by the capture of Haarlem had struck a profound blow at the haughty confidence of the Spaniards, and had vastly encouraged the people of Holland. The successful defence of Alkmaar did even more. It showed the people that resistance did not necessarily lead to calamity, that the risk was greater in surrender than in defiance, and, above all, that in their dykes they possessed means of defence that, if properly used, would fight for them even more effectually than they could do for themselves.

Ned had taken his full share in the labours and dangers of the siege. He had been indefatigable in seeing that all the arrangements worked well and smoothly, had slept on the walls with the men, encouraged the women, talked and laughed with the children, and done all in his power to keep up the spirits of the inhabitants. At the assault on the breaches he had donned his armour and fought in the front line as a volunteer under the officer in command of the garrison.

On the day when the Spaniards were seen to be breaking up their camps and retiring, a meeting was held in the town-hall, after a solemn thanksgiving had been offered in the church, and by acclamation Ned was made a citizen of the town, and was presented with a gold chain as a token of the gratitude of the people of Alkmaar. There was nothing more for him to do here, and as soon as the Spaniards had broken up their camp he mounted a horse and rode to Enkhuizen, bidding his escort follow him at once on foot.

He had learned from the carpenter who had made his way in, that the fleet was collected, and that a portion of them from the northern ports under Admiral Dirkzoon had already set sail, and the whole were expected to arrive in a few days in the Zuider-Zee. As he rode through the street on his way to the burgomaster's his eye fell upon a familiar face, and he at once reined in his horse.

"Ah! Peters," he exclaimed, "is it you? Is the *Good Venture* in port?"

Peters looked up in astonishment. The voice was that of Ned Martin, but he scarce recognized in the handsomely dressed young officer the lad he had last seen a year before.

"Why, it is Master Ned, sure enough!" he exclaimed, shaking the lad's hand warmly. "Though if you had not spoken I should have assuredly passed you. Why, lad, you are transformed. I took you for a young noble with your brave attire and your gold chain; and you look years older than when I last saw you. You have grown into a man; but though you have added to your height and your breadth your cheeks have fallen in greatly, and your colour has well nigh faded away."

"I have had two long bouts of fasting, Peters, and have but just finished the second. I am Captain Martin now, by the favour of the Prince of Orange. How are they at home? and how goes it with my father?"

"He is on board, Master Ned. This is his first voyage,

and right glad we are, as you may guess, to have him back again; and joyful will he be to see you. He had your letter safely that you wrote after the fall of Haarlem, and it would have done you good if you had heard the cheers in the summer-house when he read it out to the captains there. We had scarce thought we should ever hear of you again."

"I will put up my horse at the burgomaster's, Peters, and come on board with you at once. I must speak to him first for a few minutes. A messenger was sent off on horseback last night the moment the road was opened to say that the Spaniards had raised the siege of Alkmaar; but I must give him a few details."

"So you have been there too? The guns have been firing and the bells ringing all the day, and the people have been well nigh out of their minds with joy. They had looked to the Spaniards coming here after they had finished with Alkmaar, and you may guess how joyful they were when the news came that the villains were going off beaten."

A quarter of an hour later Ned leapt from the quay on to the deck of the *Good Venture*. His father's delight was great as he entered the cabin, and he was no less astonished than Peters had been at the change that a year had made in his appearance.

"Why, Ned," he said, after they had talked for half an hour, "I fear you are getting much too great a man ever to settle down again to work here."

"Not at all, father," Ned laughed. "I have not the least idea of remaining permanently here. I love the sea, and I love England and my home, and nothing would tempt me to give them up. I cannot leave my present work now. The prince has been so kind to me that even if I wished it I could not withdraw from his service now.

But I do not wish. In another year, if all the Dutch cities prove as staunch as Haarlem and Alkmaar have done, the Spaniards will surely begin to see that their task of subduing such a people is a hopeless one. At any rate I think that I can then very well withdraw myself from the work and follow my profession again. I shall be old enough then to be your second mate, and to relieve you of much of your work."

"I shall be glad to have you with me," Captain Martin said. "Of course I still have the supercargo, but that is not like going ashore and seeing people one's self. However, we can go on as we are for a bit. You have been striking a blow for freedom, lad, I mean to do my best to strike one to-morrow or next day."

"How is that, father?"

"Bossu's fleet of thirty vessels are cruising off the town, and they have already had some skirmishes with Dirkzoon's vessels; but nothing much has come of it yet. The Spaniards, although their ships are much larger and heavily armed, and more numerous too than ours, do not seem to have any fancy for coming to close quarters; but there is sure to be a fight in a few days. There is a vessel in port which will go out crowded with the fishermen here to take part in the fight; and I am going to fly the Dutch flag for once instead of the English, and am going to strike a blow to pay them off for the murder of your mother's relations, to say nothing of this," and he touched his wooden leg. "There are plenty of men here ready and willing to go, and I have taken down the names of eighty who will sail with us; so we shall have a strong crew, and shall be able to give good account of ourselves."

"Can I go with you, father?" Ned asked eagerly.

"If you like, lad. It will be tough work, you know; for

the Spaniards fight well, that cannot be denied. But as you stood against them when they have been five to one in the breaches of Haarlem and Alkmaar, to say nothing of our skirmish with them, you will find it a novelty to meet them when the odds are not altogether against us."

The next day, the 11th of October, the patriot fleet were seen bearing down with a strong easterly breeze upon the Spaniards, who were cruising between Enkhuizen and Horn. All was ready on board the *Good Venture* and her consort. The bells rang, and a swarm of hardy fishermen came pouring on board. In five minutes the sails were hoisted, and the two vessels, flying the Dutch flag, started amidst the cheers of the burghers on the walls to take their share in the engagement. They came up with the enemy just as Dirkzoon's vessels engaged them, and at once joined in the fray.

The patriot fleet now numbered twenty-five vessels against the thirty Spaniards, most of which were greatly superior in size to their opponents. The Dutch at once manœuvred to come to close quarters, and the Spaniards, who had far less confidence in themselves by sea than on land, very speedily began to draw out of the fight. The *Good Venture* and a Dutch craft had laid themselves alongside a large Spanish ship, and boarded her from both sides. Ned and Peters, followed by the English sailors, clambered on board near the stern, while the Dutch fishermen, most of whom were armed with heavy axes, boarded at the waist.

The Spaniards fought but feebly, and no sooner did the men from the craft on the other side pour in and board her than they threw down their arms. Four other ships were taken, and the rest of the Spanish vessels spread their sails and made for Amsterdam, hotly pursued by the Dutch fleet. One huge Spanish vessel alone, the *Inquisition*, a name that was in itself an insult to the Dutch, and which was by far the largest and best manned vessel in the two fleets, disdained to fly. She was the admiral's vessel, and Bossu, who was himself a native of the Netherlands, although deserted by his fleet, refused to fly before his puny opponents.

The Spaniards in the ships captured had all been killed or fastened below, and under charge of small parties of the Dutch sailors the prizes sailed for Enkhuizen. The ship captured by the *Good Venture* had been the last to strike her flag, and when she started under her prize crew there were three smaller Dutch ships besides the *Good Venture* on the scene of the late conflict. With a cheer, answered from boat to boat, the four vessels sailed towards the *Inquisition*. A well directed broadside from the Spaniards cut away the masts out of one of them, and left her in a sinking condition. The other three got alongside and grappled with her.

So high did she tower above them that her cannon were of no avail to her now, and locked closely together the sailors and soldiers fought as if on land.

It was a life and death contest. Bossu and his men, clad in coats of mail, stood with sword and shield on the deck of the *Inquisition* to repel all attempts to board. The Dutch attacked with their favourite missiles—pitch hoops, boiling oil, and molten lead. Again and again they clambered up the lofty sides of the *Inquisition* and gained a momentary footing on her deck, only to be hurled down again into their ships below. The fight began at three o'clock in the afternoon and lasted till darkness. But even this did not terminate it; and all night Spaniards and Dutchmen grappled in deadly conflict. All this time the vessels were drifting as the winds and tide took them, and at last grounded on a shoal called The Neck, near Wyde-

ness. Just as morning was breaking John Haring of Horn
—the man who had kept a thousand at bay on the
Diemar Dyke, and who now commanded one of the vessels—gained a footing on the deck of the *Inquisition*
unnoticed by the Spaniards, and hauled down her colours;
but a moment later he fell dead, shot through the body.
As soon as it was light the country people came off in
boats and joined in the fight, relieving their compatriots
by carrying their killed and wounded on shore. They
brought fresh ammunition as well as men, and at eleven
o'clock Admiral Bossu, seeing that further resistance was
useless, and that his ship was aground on a hostile
shore, his fleet dispersed and three-quarters of his soldiers
and crew dead or disabled, struck his flag and surrendered
with 300 prisoners.

He was landed at Horn, and his captors had great
difficulty in preventing him from being torn to pieces
by the populace in return for the treacherous massacre
at Rotterdam, of which he had been the author.

During the long fight Ned Martin behaved with great
bravery. Again and again he and Peters had led the
boarders, and it was only his morion and breast-piece that
had saved him many times from death. He had been
wounded several times, and was so breathless and hurt by
his falls from the deck that at the end he could no longer
even attempt to climb the sides of the Spanish vessel. Captain Martin was able to take no part in the melee. He had
at the beginning of the fight taken up his post on the taff-
rail, and, seated there, had kept up a steady fire with a musket against the Spaniards as they showed themselves above.

As soon as the fight was over the *Good Venture* sailed
back to Enkhuizen. Five of her own crew and thirty-
eight of the volunteers on board her had been killed, and

there was scarcely a man who was not more or less severely wounded. The English were received with tremendous acclamation by the citizens on their arrival in port, and a vote of thanks was passed to them at a meeting of the burghers in the town-hall.

Ned sailed round in the *Good Venture* to Delft and again joined the Prince of Orange there, and was greatly commended for his conduct at Alkmaar, which had been reported upon in the most favourable terms by Sonoy. On learning the share that the *Good Venture* had taken in the sea-fight, the prince went on board and warmly thanked Captain Martin and the crew, and distributed a handsome present among the latter. Half an hour after the prince returned to the palace he sent for Ned.

"Did you not say," he asked, "that the lady who concealed you at Brussels was the Countess Von Harp?"

"Yes, your highness. You have no bad news of her, I hope?"

"I am sorry to say that I have," the prince replied. "I have just received a letter brought me by a messenger from a friend at Maastricht. He tells me among other matters that the countess and her daughter were arrested there two days since. They were passing through in disguise, and were, it was supposed, making for Germany, when it chanced that the countess was recognized by a man in the service of one of the magistrates. It seems he had been born on Von Harp's estate, and knew the countess well by sight. He at once denounced her, and she and her daughter and a woman they had with them were thrown into prison. I am truly sorry, for the count was a great friend of mine, and I met his young wife many times in the happy days before these troubles began."

Ned was greatly grieved when he heard of the danger to

which the lady who had behaved so kindly to him was exposed, and an hour later he again went into the prince's study.

" I have come in to ask, sir, if you will allow me to be absent for a time?"

" Certainly, Captain Martin," the prince replied. " Are you thinking of paying a visit to England?"

" No, sir. I am going to try if I can do anything to get the Countess Von Harp out of the hands of those who have captured her."

" But how are you going to do that?" the prince asked in surprise. " It is one thing to slip out of the hands of Alva's minions as you did at Brussels, but another thing altogether to get two women out of prison."

" That is so," Ned said; " but I rely much, sir, upon the document which I took a year since from the body of Von Aert's clerk, and which I have carefully preserved ever since. It bears the seal of the Blood Council, and is an order to all magistrates to assist the bearer in all ways that he may require. With the aid of that document I may succeed in unlocking the door of the prison."

" It is a bold enterprise," the prince said, " and may cost you your life. Still I do not say it is impossible."

" I have also," Ned said, " some orders for the arrest of prisoners. These are not sealed, but bear the signature of the president of the council. I shall go to a scrivener and shall get him to copy one of them exactly, making only the alteration that the persons of the Countess Von Harp, her daughter, and servant are to be handed over to my charge for conveyance to Brussels. Alone, this document might be suspected; but, fortified as I am by the other with the seal of the council, it may pass without much notice."

" Yes, but you would be liable to detection by any one who has known this man Genet."

"There is a certain risk of that," Ned replied; "and if anyone who knew him well met me I should of course be detected. But that is unlikely. The man was about my height, although somewhat thinner. His principal mark was a most evil squint that he had, and that anyone who had once met him would be sure to remember. I must practise crossing my eyes in the same manner when I present my papers."

The prince smiled. "Sometimes you seem to me a man, Martin, and then again you enter upon an undertaking with the light-heartedness of a boy. However, far be it from me to hinder your making the attempt. It is pleasant, though rare, to see people mindful of benefits bestowed upon them, and one is glad to see that gratitude is not altogether a lost virtue. Go, my lad; and may God aid you in your scheme. I will myself send for a scrivener at once and give him instructions; it may well be that he would refuse to draw up such a document as that you require merely on your order.

"Leave the order for arrest with me, and I will bid him get a facsimile made in all respects. You will require two or three trusty men with you to act as officials under your charge. I will give you a letter to my correspondent in Maastricht begging him to provide some men on whom he can rely for this work. It would be difficult for you, a stranger in the town, to put your hand upon them."

The next morning Ned, provided with the forged order of release, started on his journey. He was disguised as a peasant, and carried a suit of clothes similar in cut and fashion to those worn by Genet. He went first to Rotterdam, and bearing west crossed the river Lek, and then struck the Waal at Gorichen, and there hired a boat and proceeded up the river to Nymegen. He then walked across to Grave, and again taking boat proceeded up the Maas, past Venlo and Roermond to Maastricht. He landed a few miles above the town, and changed his peasant clothes for the suit he carried with him.

At a farmhouse he succeeded in buying a horse, saddle, and bridle. The animal was but a poor one, but it was sufficiently good for his purpose, as he wanted it not for speed, but only to enable him to enter the city on horseback. Maastricht was a strongly fortified city, and on entering its gates Ned was requested to show his papers. He at once produced the document bearing the seal of the Council. This was amply sufficient, and he soon took up his quarters at an inn. His first step was to find the person for whom he bore the letter from the prince. The gentleman, who was a wealthy merchant, after reading the missive and learning from Ned the manner in which he could assist him, at once promised to do so.

"You require three men, you say, dressed as officials in the employment of the Council. The dress is easy enough, for they bear no special badge or cognizance, although generally they are attired in dark green doublets and trunks and red hose. There will be no difficulty as to the men themselves. The majority of the townsmen are warmly affected to the patriotic cause, and there are many who are at heart Protestants; though, like myself, obliged to abstain from making open confession of their faith. At any rate, I have three men at least upon whom I can absolutely rely. Their duty, you say, will be simply to accompany you to the prison and to ride with you with these ladies until beyond the gates. They must, of course, be mounted, and must each have pillions for the carriage of the prisoners behind them. Once well away from the town they will scatter, leave their horses at places I shall

appoint, change their clothes, and return into the city.
What do you mean to do with the ladies when you have
got them free?"

"I do not know what their plans will be, or where they
will wish to go," Ned said. "I should propose to have a
vehicle with a pair of horses awaiting them two miles outside the town. I should say that a country cart would be
the least likely to excite suspicion. I would have three
peasant's dresses there with it. I do not know that I can
make further provision for their flight, as I cannot say
whether they will make for the coast, or try to continue
their journey across the frontier."

"You can leave these matters to me," the merchant
said; "the cart and disguises shall be at the appointed
spot whenever you let me know the hour at which you will
be there. You must give me until noon to-morrow to
make all the arrangements."

"Very well, sir," Ned said. "I am greatly obliged to you,
and the prince, who is a personal friend of the countess,
will, I am sure, be greatly pleased when he hears how
warmly you have entered into the plans for aiding her
escape. I will present myself to the magistrates to-
morrow at noon, and obtain from them the order upon the
governor of the prison to hand the ladies over to me. If I
should succeed I will go straight back to my inn. If you
will place someone near the door there to see if I enter,
which if I succeed will be about one o'clock, he can bring
you the news. I will have my horse brought round at two,
and at that hour your men can ride up and join me, and I
will proceed with them straight to the prison."

CHAPTER XVII.

A T twelve o'clock on the following day Ned went to the town-hall, and on stating that he was the bearer of an order from the Council, was at once shown into the chamber in which three of the magistrates were sitting.

"I am the bearer of an order from the Council for the delivery to me of the persons of the Countess Von Harp, her daughter, and the woman arrested in company with them for conveyance to Brussels, there to answer the charges against them. This is the order of the Council with their seal, ordering all magistrates to render assistance to me as one of their servants. This is the special order for the handing over to me of the prisoners named."

The magistrates took the first order, glanced at it and at the seal, and perfectly satisfied with this gave but a casual glance at that for the transferring of the prisoners.

"I think you were about a year since with Councillor Von Aert?" one of the magistrates said. Ned bowed. "By the way, did I not hear that you were missing, or that some misfortune had befallen you some months since? I have a vague recollection of doing so."

"Yes. I was sorely maltreated by a band of robber peasants who left me for dead, but as you see I am now completely recovered."

"I suppose you have some men with you to escort the prisoners?" one of the magistrates asked.

"Assuredly," Ned replied. "I have with me three men, behind whom the women will ride."

The magistrates countersigned the order upon the governor of the prison to hand over the three prisoners, and gave it with the letter of the Council to Ned. He bowed and retired.

"I should not have remembered him again," the magistrate who had been the chief speaker said after he had left the room, "had it not been for that villainous cast in his eyes. I remember noticing it when he was here last time, and wondered that Von Aert should like to have a man whose eyes were so crossways about him; otherwise I do not recall the face at all, which is not surprising seeing that I only saw him for a minute or two, and noticed nothing but that abominable squint of his."

Ned walked back to his inn, ordered his horse to be saddled at two o'clock, and partook of a hearty meal. Then paying his reckoning he went out and mounted his horse. As he did so three men in green doublets and red hose rode up and took their places behind him. On arriving at the prison he dismounted, and handing his horse to one of his followers entered.

"I have an order from the Council, countersigned by the magistrates here, for the delivery to me of three prisoners."

The warder showed him into a room.

"The governor is ill," he said, "and confined to his bed; but I will take the order to him."

Ned was well pleased with the news, for he thought it likely that Genet might have been there before on similar errands, and his person be known to the governor. In ten minutes the warder returned.

"The prisoners are without," he said, "and ready to depart."

Pulling his bonnet well down over his eyes, Ned went out into the courtyard.

"You are to accompany me to Brussels, countess," he said gruffly. "Horses are waiting for you without."

The countess did not even glance at the official who had thus come to convey her to what was in all probability death, but followed through the gate into the street. The men backed their horses up to the block of stone used for mounting. Ned assisted the females to the pillions, and when they were seated mounted his own horse and led the way down the street. Many of the people as they passed along groaned or hooted, for the feeling in Maastricht was strongly in favour of the patriot side, a feeling for which they were some years later to be punished by the almost total destruction of the city, and the slaughter of the greater portion of its inhabitants.

Ned paid no attention to these demonstrations, but quickening his horse into a trot rode along the street and out of the gate of the city. As the road was a frequented one, he maintained his place at the head of the party until they had left the city nearly two miles behind them. On arriving at a small cross-road one of the men said: "This is the way, sir, it is up this road that the cart is in waiting." Ned now reined back his horse to the side of that on which the countess was riding.

"Countess," he said, "have you forgotten the English lad you aided a year ago in Brussels?"

The countess started.

"I recognize you now, sir," she said coldly; "and little did I think at that time that I should next see you as an officer of the Council of Blood."

Ned smiled.

"Your mistake is a natural one, countess; but in point

of fact I am still in the service of the Prince of Orange, and have only assumed this garb as a means of getting you and your daughter out of the hands of those murderers. I am happy to say that you are free to go where you will; these good fellows are like myself disguised, and are at your service. In a few minutes we shall come to a cart which will take you wheresoever you like to go, and there are disguises similar to those with which you once fitted me out in readiness for you there."

The surprise of the countess for a moment kept her silent; but Gertrude, who had overheard what was said, burst into exclamations of delight.

"Pardon me for having doubted you," the countess exclaimed much affected.

"No pardon is required, countess. Seeing that the prison authorities handed you over to me, you could not but have supposed that I was as I seemed, in the service of the Council."

Just at this moment they came upon a cart drawn up by the roadside. Ned assisted the countess and her daughter to alight, and while he was rendering similar assistance to the old servant, mother and daughter threw themselves into each other's arms, and wept with delight at this unexpected delivery that had befallen them. It was some time before they were sufficiently recovered to speak.

"But how do you come here?" the Countess asked Ned, "and how have you effected this miracle?"

Ned briefly related how he had heard of their captivity, and the manner in which he had been enabled to effect their escape.

"And now, countess," he said, "the day is wearing on, and it is necessary that you should at once decide upon your plans. Will you again try to make to the German

frontier   or   to   the   sea-coast,   or   remain   in   hiding
here ? "

" We cannot make for Germany without again crossing
the Maas," the countess said, " and it is a long way to the
sea-coast.   What say you, Magdalene?"

" I think," the old woman said, " that you had best
carry out the advice I gave before.   It is little more than
twelve miles from here to the village where, as I told you,
I have relations living.   We can hire a house there, and
there is no chance of your being recognized.   I can send a
boy thence to Brussels to fetch the jewels and money you
left in charge of your friend the Count Von Dort there."

" That will certainly be the best way, Magdalene.   We
can wait there until either there is some change in the
state of affairs, or until we can find some safe way of
escape.   It is fortunate, indeed, that I left my jewels in
Brussels, instead of taking them with me as I had at
first intended.   It will hardly be necessary, will it," she
asked Ned, " to put on the disguises, for nothing in the
world can be simpler than our dresses at present?"

" You had certainly best put the peasant cloaks and
caps on.   Inquiries are sure to be made all through the
country when they find at Maastricht how they have been
tricked.   Three peasant women in a cart will attract no
attention whatever, even in passing through villages; but,
dressed as you are now, some one might notice you and recall it if inquiries were made."

The three men who had aided in the scheme had ridden
off as soon as the cart was reached, and Ned, being anxious
that the party should be upon their way, and desirous, too,
of avoiding the expressions of gratitude of the three women, hurried them into the cart.   It was not necessary for
them to change their garments, as the peasants cloaks com-

pletely enveloped them, and the high head-dresses quite changed their appearance.

"Do not forget, countess, I hope some day to see you in England," Ned said as they took their seats.

"I will not forget," the countess said; "and only wish that at present I was on my way thither."

After a warm farewell, and seeing the cart fairly on its way, Ned mounted his horse and rode north-west. He slept that night at Heerenthals, and on the following night at Bois-le-Duc. Here he sold his horse for a few crowns, and taking boat proceeded down the Dommel into the Maas, and then on to Rotterdam. On his arrival at Delft he was heartily welcomed by the prince; who was greatly pleased to hear that he had, without any accident or hitch, carried out successfully the plan he had proposed to himself. Three weeks later the prince heard from his correspondent at Maastricht. The letter was cautiously worded, as were all those interchanged, lest it should fall into the hands of the Spanish.

"There has been some excitement here. A week since a messenger arrived from Brussels with orders that three female prisoners confined here should be sent at once to Brussels; but curiously enough it was found that the three prisoners in question had been handed over upon the receipt of a previous order. This is now pronounced to be a forgery, and it is evident that the authorities have been tricked. There has been much search and inquiry, but no clue whatever has been obtained as to the direction taken by the fugitives, or concerning those engaged in this impudent adventure."

Alva's reign of terror and cruelty was now drawing to an end. His successor was on his way out, and the last days of his administration were embittered by the failure of his plans, the retreat of his army from before Alkmaar, and the naval defeat from the Zuider-Zee. But he continued his cruelties to the end. Massacres on a grand scale were soon carried on, and a nobleman named Uitenhoove, who had been taken prisoner, was condemned to be roasted to death before a slow fire, and was accordingly fastened by a chain to a stake, around which a huge fire was kindled; he suffered in slow torture a long time until despatched by the executioner with a spear, a piece of humanity that greatly angered the duke.

Alva had contracted an enormous amount of debt, both public and private, in Amsterdam, and now caused a proclamation to be issued that all persons having demands upon him were to present their claims on a certain day. ·On the previous night he and his train noiselessly took their departure. The heavy debts remained unpaid, and many opulent families were reduced to beggary. Such was the result of the confidence of the people of Amsterdam in the honour of their tyrant.

On the 17th of November Don Louis de Requesens, Grand Commander of St. Jago, Alva's successor, arrived in Brussels; and on the 18th of December the Duke of Alva left. He is said to have boasted, on his way home, that he had caused 18,000 inhabitants of the provinces to be executed during the period of his government. This was, however, a mere nothing to the number who had perished in battle, siege, starvation, and massacre. After the departure of their tyrant the people of the Netherlands breathed more freely, for they hoped that, under their new governor, there would be a remission in the terrible agony they had suffered; and for a time his proclamations were of a conciliatory nature. But it was soon seen that there was no change in policy. Peace was to be given only on the condition of all Protestants recanting or leaving their country.

The first military effort of the new governor was to endeavour to relieve the city of Middleburg, the capital of the Island of Walcheren, which had long been besieged by the Protestants. Mondragon the governor was sorely pressed by famine, and could hold out but little longer, unless rescue came. The importance of the city was felt by both parties. Requesens himself went to Bergen-op-Zoom, where seventy-five ships were collected under the command, nominally, of Admiral de Glimes, but really under that of Julian Romero, while another fleet of thirty ships was assembled at Antwerp, under D'Avila, and moved down towards Flushing, there to await the arrival of that of Romero. Upon the other hand, the Prince of Orange collected a powerful fleet under the command of Admiral Boisot, and himself paid a visit to the ships, and assembling the officers roused them to enthusiasm by a stirring address.

On 20th of January the *Good Venture* again entered the port of Delft; and hearing that a battle was expected in a few days, Captain Martin determined to take part in it. As soon as he unloaded his cargo he called the crew together and informed them of his determination, but said that as this was no quarrel of theirs, any who chose could remain on shore until his return.

But Englishmen felt that the cause of Holland was their own, and not a single man on board availed himself of this permission. Ned informed the Prince of Orange of his father's intention, and asked leave to accompany him.

"Assuredly you may go if you please," the prince said; "but I fear that, sooner or later, the fortune of war will deprive me of you, and I should miss you much. Moreover almost every sailor in port is already in one or other of

Boisot's ships; and I fear that, with your weak crew, you would have little chance if engaged with one of these Spanish ships full of men."

"We have enough to work our cannon, sir," Ned said; "besides, I think we may be able to beat up some volunteers. There are many English ships in port waiting for cargoes, which come in but slowly, and I doubt not that some of them will gladly strike a blow against the Spaniards."

Ned and Peters accordingly went round among the English vessels, and in the course of two hours had collected a hundred volunteers. In those days every Englishman regarded a Spaniard as a natural enemy. Drake and Hawkins, and other valiant captains, were warring fiercely against them in the Indian seas, and officers and men in the ships in Delft were alike eager to join in the forthcoming struggle against them.

The *Good Venture* had, flying the Dutch flag, joined Boisot's fleet at Romerswael, a few miles below Bergen, on the 27th of January; and when the Hollanders became aware of the nationality of the vessel which had just joined them, they welcomed them with tremendous cheers. Two days later the fleet of Romero were seen coming down the river in three divisions. When the first of the Spanish ships came near they delivered a broadside, which did considerable execution among the Dutch fleet. There was no time for further cannonading. A few minutes later the fleets met in the narrow channel, and the ships grappling with each other, a hand to hand struggle began.

The fighting was of the most desperate character; no quarter was asked or given on either side, and men fought with fury hand to hand upon decks slippery with blood. But the combat did not last long. The Spaniards had

little confidence in themselves on board ship. Their discipline was now of little advantage to them, and the savage
fury with which the Zeelanders fought shook their courage. Fifteen ships were speedily captured and 1200 Spaniards slain, and the remainder of the fleet, which, on
account of the narrowness of the passage had not been
able to come into action, retreated to Bergen.

Romero himself, whose ship had grounded, sprang out
of a port-hole and swam ashore, and landed at the very
feet of the Grand Commander, who had been standing all
day upon the dyke in the midst of a pouring rain, only to
be a witness of the total defeat of his fleet. Mondragon
now capitulated, receiving honourable conditions. The
troops were allowed to leave the place with their arms, amu-
nition and personal property, and Mondragon engaged
himself to procure the release of Sainte Aldegonde and
four other prisoners of rank, or to return and give himself up as a prisoner of war.

Requesens, however, neither granted the release of the
prisoners, nor permitted Mondragon to return. It was
well for these prisoners that Bossu was in the hands of the
prince. Had it not been for this they would have all been
put to death.

With the fall of Middleburg the Dutch and Zeelanders
remained masters of the entire line of sea-coast, but upon
land the situation was still perilous. Leyden was closely
invested, and all communication by land between the
various cities suspended. The sole hope that remained
was in the army raised by Count Louis.

He had raised 3000 cavalry and 6000 infantry, and, ac-
companied by the prince's other two brothers, crossed the
Rhine in a snow-storm and marched towards Maastricht.
The Prince of Orange had on his part with the greatest

difficulty raised 6000 infantry, and wrote to Count Louis to move to join him in the Isle of Bommel after he had reduced Maastricht. But the expedition, like those before it, was destined to failure. A thousand men deserted, seven hundred more were killed in a night surprise, and the rest were mutinous for their pay. Finally, Count Louis found himself confronted by a force somewhat inferior in numbers to his own.

But the Spanish infantry were well disciplined and obedient, those of Louis mere mercenaries and discontented; and although at first his cavalry gained an advantage, it was a short one, and after a fierce action his army was entirely defeated. Count Louis, finding that the day was lost, gathered a little band of troopers, and with his brother, Count Henry, and Christopher, son of the Elector Palatine, charged into the midst of the enemy. They were never heard of more. The battle terminated in a horrible butchery. At least 4000 men were either killed on the field, suffocated in the marshes, drowned in the river, or burned in the farmhouses in which they had taken refuge. Count Louis, his brother, and friend probably fell on the field, but stripped of their clothing, disfigured by wounds and the trampling of horses, their bodies were never recognized.

The defeat of the army and the death of his two brave brothers was a terrible blow to the Prince of Orange. He was indeed paying dear for his devotion to his country. His splendid fortune had been entirely spent, his life had been one of incessant toil and anxiety, his life had been several times threatened with assassination, he had seen his every plan thwarted. Save on the sandy slip of coast by the ocean, the whole of the Netherlands was still prostrate beneath the foot of the Spaniard; and now he had lost two of his brothers. England and France had alternately encouraged and stood aloof from him, and after all these efforts and sacrifices the prospects of ultimate success were gloomy in the extreme.

Fortunately the Spaniards were not able to take full advantage of their victory over the army of Count Louis. They differed from the German mercenaries inasmuch that while the latter mutinied before they fought, the Spaniards fought first and mutined afterwards. Having won a great battle, they now proceeded to defy their generals. Three years' pay were due to them, and they took the steps that they always adopted upon these occasions. A commander called the "Eletto" was chosen by acclamation, a board of councillors was appointed to assist and control him, while the councillors were narrowly watched by the soldiers. They crossed the Maas and marched to Antwerp.

An offer was accordingly made of ten months' arrears in cash, five months in silks and woollen cloths, and the rest in promises to be fulfilled within a few days. The Eletto declared that he considered the terms satisfactory, whereupon the troops at once deposed him and elected another. Carousing and merry-making went on at the expense of the citizens, and after suffering for some weeks from the extortions and annoyance of the soldiers, the 400,000 crowns demanded by Requesens were paid over, and the soldiers received all their pay due either in money or goods. A great banquet was held by the whole mass of soldiery, and there was a scene of furious revelry. The soldiers arrayed themselves in costumes cut from the materials they had just received. Broadcloths, silks, satins, and gold-embroidered brocades were hung in fantastic drapery over their ragged garments, and when the banquet was finished gambling began.

But when they were in the midst of their revelry the sound of cannon was heard. Boisot had sailed up the Scheldt to attack the fleet of D'Avila, which had hastened up to Antwerp for refuge after the defeat of that of Romero. There was a short and sharp action, and fourteen of the Spanish ships were burnt or sunk. The soldiers swarmed down to the dyke and opened a fire of musketry upon the Dutch. They were, however, too far off to effect any damage, and Boisot, with a few parting broadsides, sailed triumphantly down the river, having again struck a heavy blow at the naval power of Spain.

The siege of Leyden had been raised when Count Louis crossed the Rhine, the troops being called in from all parts to oppose his progress. The Prince of Orange urged upon the citizens to lose no time in preparing themselves for a second siege, to strengthen their walls, and, above all, to lay in stores of provisions. But, as ever, the Dutch burghers, although ready to fight and to suffer when the pinch came, were slow and apethetic unless in face of necessity; and in spite of the orders and entreaties of the prince, nothing whatever was done, and the Spaniards when they returned before the city on the 26th of May, after two months' absence, found the town as unprepared for resistance as it had been at their first coming, and that the citizens had not even taken the trouble to destroy the forts that they had raised round it.

Leyden stood in the midst of broad and fruitful pastures reclaimed from the sea; around were numerous villages, with blooming gardens and rich orchards. Innumerable canals cut up the country, and entering the city formed its streets. These canals were shaded with trees, crossed by a hundred and forty-five bridges. Upon an artificial elevation in the centre of the city rose a ruined tower of great antiquity, assigned either to the Saxons before they crossed to England or with greater probability to the Romans.

The force which now appeared before the town consisted of 8000 Walloons and Germans, commanded by Valdez. They lost no time in taking possession of the Hague, and all the villages and forts round Leyden. Five hundred English volunteers under command of Colonel Chester abandoned the fort of Valkenberg which had been intrusted to them and fled towards Leyden. Not as yet had the English soldiers learnt to stand before the Spaniards, but the time was ere long to come when, having acquired confidence in themselves, they were to prove themselves more than a match for the veterans of Spain. The people of Leyden refused to open their gates to the fugitives, and they surrendered to Valdez. As at that moment a mission was on the point of starting from Requesens to Queen Elizabeth, the lives of the prisoners were spared, and they were sent back to England.

CHAPTER XVIII.

THE SIEGE OF LEYDEN.

THE Spaniards had no sooner appeared before Leyden than they set to work to surround it with a cordon of redoubts. No less than sixty-two, including those left standing since the last siege, were erected and garrisoned, and the town was therefore cut off from all communication from without. Its defenders were few in number, there being no troops in the town save a small corps composed of exiles from other cities, and five companies of burgher guard. The walls, however, were strong, and it was famine rather than the foe that the citizens feared. They trusted to the courage of the burghers to hold the walls and to the energy of the Prince of Orange to relieve them.

The prince, although justly irritated by their folly in neglecting to carry out his orders, sent a message by a pigeon to them, encouraging them to hold out, and reminding them that the fate of their country depended upon the issue of this siege. He implored them to hold out for at least three months, assuring them that he would within that time devise means for their deliverance. The citizens replied, assuring the prince of their firm confidence in their own fortitude and his exertions.

On the 6th of June the Grand Commander issued what was called a pardon, signed and sealed by the king. In it he invited all his erring and repentant subjects to return to his arms, and accept a full forgiveness for their past offence upon the sole condition that they should once more enter the Catholic Church. A few individuals mentioned by name were alone excluded from this amnesty. But all Holland was now Protestant, and its inhabitants were resolved that they must not only be conquered but annihilated before the Roman Church should be re-established on their soil. In the whole province but two men came forward to take advantage of the amnesty. Many Netherlanders belonging to the king's party sent letters from the camp to their acquaintances in the city exhorting them to submission, and imploring them "to take pity upon their poor old fathers, their daughters, and their wives;" but the citizens of Leyden thought the best they could do for these relatives was to keep them out of the clutches of the Spaniards.

At the commencement of the siege the citizens gathered all their food into the magazines, and at the end of June the daily allowance to each full-grown man was half a pound of meat and half a pound of bread, women and children receiving less.

The prince had his headquarters at Delft and Rotterdam, and an important fortress called the Polderwaert between these two cities secured him the control of the district watered by the rivers Yssel and Maas. On the 29th of June the Spaniards attacked this fort, but were beaten off with a loss of 700 men. The prince was now occupied in endeavouring to persuade the Dutch authorities to permit the great sluices at Rotterdam, Schiedam, and Delft-Haven to be opened. The damage to the country would be enormous; but there was no other course to rescue Leyden, and with it the whole of Holland, from destruction.

It was not until the middle of July that his eloquent appeals and arguments prevailed, and the estates consented to his plan.   Subscriptions were opened in all the Dutch towns for maintaining the inhabitants of the district that was to be submerged until it could be again restored, and a large sum was raised, the women contributing their plate and jewelry to the furtherance of the scheme.   On the 3rd of August all was ready, and the prince himself superintended the breaking down of the dykes in sixteen places, while at the same time the sluices at Schiedam and Rotterdam were opened and the water began to pour over the land.

While waiting for the water to rise, stores of provisions were collected in all the principal towns, and 200 vessels of small draught of water gathered in readiness.   Unfortunately no sooner had the work been done than the prince was attacked by a violent fever, brought on by anxiety and exertion.

On the 21st of August a letter was received from the town saying that they had now fulfilled their original promise, for they had held out two months with food and another month without food.   Their bread had long been gone, and their last food, some malt cake, would last but four days. After that was gone there was nothing left but starvation.

Upon the same day they received a letter from the prince, assuring them that the dykes were all pierced and the water rising upon the great dyke that separated the city from the sea.   The letter was read publicly in the market-place, and excited the liveliest joy among the inhabitants.   Bands of music played in the streets, and salvos of cannon were fired.   The Spaniards became uneasy at seeing the country beyond them gradually becoming covered with water, and consulted the country people and the royalists in their camp, all of whom assured them that the enterprise of the prince was an impossibility, and that the water would never reach the walls.

The hopes of the besieged fell again, however, as day after day passed without change; and it was not until the 1st of September, when the prince began to recover from his fever, and was personally able to superintend the operations, that these began in earnest. The distance from Leyden to the outer dyke was fifteen miles; ten of these were already flooded, and the flotilla, which consisted of more than 200 vessels, manned in all with 2500 veterans, including 800 of the wild sea beggars of Zeeland, renowned as much for their ferocity as for nautical skill, started on their way, and reached without difficulty the great dyke called the Land-scheiding. Between this town and Leyden were several other dykes, all of which would have to be taken. All these, besides the 62 forts, were defended by the Spanish troops, four times the number of the relieving force.

Ned had been in close attendance upon the prince during his illness, and when the fleet was ready to start requested that he might be allowed to accompany it. This the prince at once granted, and introduced him to Admiral Boisot.

"I shall be glad if you will take Captain Martin in your own ship," he said. "Young as he is he has seen much service, and is full of resource and invention. You will, I am sure, find him of use; and he can act as messenger to convey your orders from ship to ship."

The prince had given orders that the Land-scheiding, whose top was still a foot and a half above water, should be taken possession of at all hazard, and this was accomplished by surprise on the night of the 10th. The Spaniards stationed there were either killed or driven off, and the Dutch fortified themselves upon it. At daybreak the

Spaniards stationed in two large villages close by advanced to recover the important position, but the Dutch, fighting desperately, drove them back with the loss of some hundreds of men. The dyke was at once cut through and the fleet sailed through the gap.

The admiral had believed that the Land-scheiding once cut, the water would flood the country as far as Leyden, but another dyke, the Greenway, rose a foot above water three-quarters of a mile inside the Land-scheiding. As soon as the water had risen over the land sufficiently to float the ships, the fleet advanced, seized the Greenway, and cut it. But as the water extended in all directions, it grew also shallower, and the admiral found that the only way by which he could advance was by a deep canal leading to a large mere called the Fresh Water Lake.

This canal was crossed by a bridge, and its sides were occupied by 3000 Spanish soldiers. Boisot endeavoured to force the way but found it impossible to do so, and was obliged to withdraw. He was now almost despairing. He had accomplished but two miles, the water was sinking rather than rising owing to a long-continued east wind, and many of his ships were already aground. On the 18th, however, the wind shifted to the north-west, and for three days blew a gale. The water rose rapidly, and at the end of the second day the ships were all afloat again.

Hearing from a peasant of a comparatively low dyke between two villages Boisot at once sailed in that direction. There was a strong Spanish force stationed here; but these were seized with a panic and fled, their courage unhinged by the constantly rising waters, the appearance of the numerous fleet, and their knowledge of the reckless daring of the wild sailors. The dyke was cut, the two villages with their fortifications burned, and the fleet moved on to

North Aa. The enemy abandoned this position also, and fled to Zoetermeer, a strongly fortified village a mile and a quarter from the city walls. Gradually the Spanish army had been concentrated round the city as the water drove them back, and they were principally stationed at this village and the two strong forts of Lammen and Leyderdorp, each within a few hundred yards of the town.

At the last-named post Valdez had his headquarters, and Colonel Borgia commanded at Lammen. The fleet was delayed at North Aa by another dyke, called the Kirkway. The waters, too, spreading again over a wider space, and diminished from the east wind again setting in, sank rapidly, and very soon the whole fleet was aground; for there were but nine inches of water, and they required twenty to float them. Day after day they lay motionless. The Prince of Orange, who had again been laid up with the fever, rose from his sick-bed and visited the fleet. He encouraged the dispirited sailors, rebuked their impatience, and after reconnoitring the ground issued orders for the immediate destruction of the Kirkway, and then returned to Delft.

All this time Leyden was suffering horribly. The burghers were aware that the fleet had set forth to their relief, but they knew better than those on board the obstacles that opposed its progress. The flames of the burning villages and the sound of artillery told them of its progress until it reached North Aa, then there was a long silence, and hope almost deserted them. They knew well that so long as the east wind continued to blow there could be no rise in the level of the water, and anxiously they looked from the walls and the old tower for signs of a change. They were literally starving, and their misery far exceeded even that of the citizens of Haarlem.

A small number of cows only remained; and of these a

few were killed every day, and tiny morsels of meat distributed, the hides and bones being chopped up and boiled. The green leaves were stripped from the trees, and every herb gathered and eaten. The mortality was frightful, and whole families died together in their houses from famine and plague; for pestilence had now broken out, and from six to eight thousand people died from this alone. Leyden abandoned all hope, and yet they spurned the repeated summonses of Valdez to surrender. They were fully resolved to die rather than to yield to the Spaniards. From time to time, however, murmurs arose among the suffering people, and the heroic burgomaster, Adrian Van der Werf, was once surrounded by a crowd and assailed by reproaches.

He took off his hat and calmly replied to them: "I tell you I have made an oath to hold the city, and may God give me strength to keep it. I can die but once—either by your hands, the enemy's, or by the hand of God. My own fate is indifferent to me; not so that of the city intrusted to my care. I know that we shall all starve if not soon relieved; but starvation is preferable to the dishonoured death which is the only alternative. Your menaces move me not. My life is at your disposal. Here is my sword; plunge it into my breast and divide my flesh among you. Take my body to appease your hunger; but expect no surrender so long as I remain alive.

Still the east wind continued, until stout Admiral Boisot himself almost despaired. But on the night of the 1st of October a violent gale burst from the north-west. The water was piled up high upon the southern coast of Holland, and sweeping furiously inland poured through the ruined dykes, and in twenty-four hours the fleet was afloat again. At midnight they advanced in the midst of the storm and darkness. Some Spanish vessels that had been brought up to aid the defenders were swept aside and sunk.

The fleet, sweeping on past half-submerged stacks and farmhouses, made its way to the fresh water mere. Some shallows checked it for a time, but the crews sprang overboard into the water, and by main strength hoisted their vessels across them. Two obstacles alone stood between them and the city—the forts of Zoeterwoude and Lammen, the one five hundred, the other but two hundred and fifty yards from the city. Both were strong and well supplied with troops and artillery, but the panic which had seized the Spaniards extented to Zoeterwoude. Hardly was the fleet in sight in the grey light of the morning when the Spaniards poured out from the fortress, and spread along a road on the dyke leading in a westerly direction towards the Hague.

The waves, driven by the wind, were beating on the dyke, and it was crumbling rapidly away, and hundreds sank beneath the flood. The Zeelanders drove their vessels up alongside, and pierced them with their harpoons, or, plunging into the waves, attacked them with sword and dagger. The numbers killed amounted to not less than a thousand; the rest effected their escape to the Hague. Zoeterwoude was captured and set on fire, but Lammen still barred their path. Bristling with guns, it seemed to defy them either to capture or pass it on their way to the city.

Leyderdorp, where Valdez with his main force lay, was a mile and a half distant on the right, and within a mile of the city, and the guns of the two forts seemed to render it next to impossible for the fleet to pass on. Boisot, after reconnoitring the position, wrote despondently to the prince that he intended if possible on the following morning to carry the fort, but if unable to do so, he said, there would be nothing for it but to wait for another gale of wind to still further raise the water, and enable him to make a wide circuit and enter Leyden on the opposite side. A pigeon had been despatched by Boisot in the morning informing the citizens of his exact position, and at nightfall the bur gomaster and a number of citizens gathered at the watch-tower.

"Yonder," cried the magistrate, pointing to Lammen, "behind that fort, are bread and meat and brethren in thousands. Shall all this be destroyed by Spanish guns, or shall we rush to the aid of our friends?"

"We will tear the fortress first to fragments with our teeth and nails," was the reply; and it was resolved that a sortie should be made against Lammen at daybreak, when Boisot attacked it on the other side. A pitch-dark night set in, a night full of anxiety to the Spaniards, to the fleet, and to Leyden. The sentries on the walls saw lights flitting across the waters, and in the dead of night the whole of the city wall between two of the gates fell with a loud crash. The citizens armed themselves and rushed to the breach, believing that the Spaniards were on them at last; but no foe made his appearance.

In the morning the fleet prepared for the assault. All was still and quiet in the fortress, and the dreadful suspicion that the city had been carried at night, and that all their labour was in vain, seized those on board. Suddenly a man was seen wading out from the fort, while at the same time a boy waved his cap wildly from its summit. The mystery was solved. The Spaniards had fled panic-stricken in the darkness. Had they remained they could have frustrated the enterprise, and Leyden must have fallen; but the events of the two preceding days had shaken their courage. Valdez retired from Leyderdorp and ordered Colonel Borgia to evacuate Lammen.

Thus they had retreated at the very moment that the fall of the wall sapped by the flood laid bare a whole side of the city for their entrance. They heard the crash in the darkness, and it but added to their fears, for they thought that the citizens were sallying out to take some measures which would further add to the height of the flood. Their retreat was discovered by the boy, who, having noticed the procession of lights in the darkness, became convinced that the Spaniards had retired, and persuaded the magistrates to allow him to make his way out to the fort to reconnoitre. As soon as the truth was known the fleet advanced, passed the fort, and drew up alongside the quays.

These were lined by the famishing people, every man, woman, and child having strength to stand having come out to greet their deliverers. Bread was thrown from all the vessels among the crowd as they came up, and many died from too eagerly devouring the food after their long fast. Then the admiral stepped ashore, followed by the whole of those on board the ships. Magistrates and citizens, sailors and soldiers, women and children, all repaired to the great church and returned thanks to God for the deliverance of the city. The work of distributing food and relieving the sick was then undertaken. The next day the prince, in defiance of the urgent entreaties of his friends, who were afraid of the effects of the pestilential air of the city upon his constitution enfeebled by sickness, repaired to the town.

Shortly afterwards, with the advice of the States, he granted the city as a reward for its suffering a ten days' annual fair, without tolls or taxes, and it was further resolved that a university should, as a manifestation of the gratitude of the people of Holland, be established within its walls. The fiction of the authority of Philip was still maintained, and the charter granted to the university was, under the circumstances, a wonderful production. It was drawn up in the name of the king, and he was gravely made to establish the university as a reward to Leyden for rebellion against himself.

"Considering," it said, "that during these present wearisome wars within our provinces of Holland and Zeeland, all good instruction of youth in the sciences and literary arts is likely to come into entire oblivion; considering the difference of religion; considering that we are inclined to gratify our city of Leyden, with its burghers, on account of the heavy burden sustained by them during this war with such faithfulness, we have resolved—after ripely deliberating with our dear cousin William Prince of Orange, stadtholder—to erect a free public school, and university," &c. So ran the document establishing this famous university, all needful regulations for its government being intrusted by Philip to his above-mentioned dear cousin of Orange.

Ned Martin was not one of those who entered Leyden with Boisot's relieving fleet. His long watching and anxiety by the bedside of the prince had told upon him, and he felt strangely unlike himself when he started with the fleet. So long as it was fighting its way forward the excitement kept him up; but the long delay near the village of Aa, and the deep despondency caused by the probable failure of their hopes of rescuing the starving city, again brought on an attack of the fever that had already seized him before starting, and when the Prince of Orange paid his visit to the fleet Boisot told him the young officer he had recommended to him was down with a fever, which was, he believed, similar to that from which the prince himself was but just recovering.

The prince at once ordered him to be carried on board his own galley, and took him back with him to Delft.

Here he lay for a month completely prostrated. The prince several times visited him personally, and, as soon as he became in some degree convalescent, said to him :

"I think we have taxed you too severely, and have worked you in proportion to your zeal rather than to your strength. The surgeon says that you must have rest for a while, and that it will be well for you to get away from our marshes for a time. For two years you have done good and faithful service, and even had it not been for this fever you would have a right to rest, and I think that your native air is the best for you at present. With the letters that came to me from Flushing this morning is one from your good father, asking for news of you. His ship arrived there yesterday, and he has heard from one of those who were with Boisot that you have fallen ill; therefore, if it be to your liking, I will send you in one of my galleys to Flushing."

"I thank your excellency much." Ned said. "Indeed for the last few days I have been thinking much of home and longing to be back. I fear that I shall be a long time before I shall be fit for hard work again here."

"You will feel a different man when you have been a few hours at sea," the prince said kindly. "I hope to see you with me again some day. There are many of your countrymen, who, like yourself, have volunteered in our ranks and served us well without pay or reward, but none of them have rendered better service than you have done. And now farewell. I will order a galley to be got in readiness at once. I leave myself for Leyden in half an hour. Take this, my young friend, in remembrance of the Prince of Orange; and I trust that you may live to hand it down to your descendants as a proof that I appreciated your good services on behalf of a people struggling to be free."

So saying he took off his watch and laid it on the table

by Ned's bedside, pressed the lad's hand, and retired. He felt it really a sacrifice to allow this young Englishman to depart. He had for years been a lonely man, with few confidants and no domestic pleasures. He lived in an atmosphere of trouble, doubt and suspicion. He had struggled alone against the might of Philip, the apathy of the western provinces, the coldness and often the treachery of the nobles, the jealousies and niggardliness of the Estates, representing cities each of which thought rather of itself and its privileges than of the general good; and the company of this young Englishman, with his frank utterances, his readiness to work at all times, and his freedom from all ambitious or self-interested designs, had been a pleasure and relief to him, and he frequently talked to him far more freely than even to his most trusted counsellors.

Ever since the relief of Alkmaar Ned had been constantly with him, save when despatched on missions to the various towns, or to see that the naval preparations were being pushed on with all speed; and his illness had made a real blank in his little circle. However, the doctors had spoken strongly as to the necessity for Ned's getting away from the damp atmosphere of the half-submerged land, and he at once decided to send him back to England, and seized the opportunity directly the receipt of Captain Martin's letter informed him that the ship was at Flushing.

An hour later four men entered with a litter; the servants had already packed Ned's mails, and he was carried down and placed on board one of the prince's vessels. They rowed down into the Maas, and then hoisting sail proceeded down the river, kept outside the islands to Walcheren, and then up the estuary of the Scheldt to Flushing. It was early morning when they arrived in port. Ned was carried upon deck, and soon made out the

Good Venture lying a quarter of a mile away.   He was at
once placed in the boat and rowed alongside.   An exclamation from Peters, as he looked over the side and saw Ned
lying in the stern of the boat, called Captain Martin out
from his cabin.

"Why, Ned, my dear boy!" he exclaimed, as he looked
over the side; "you seem in grievous state indeed."

"There is not much the matter with me, father.   I
have had fever, but am getting over it, and it will need
but a day or two at sea to put me on my feet again.   I
have done with the war at present, and the prince has
been good enough to send me in one of his own galleys to
you."

"We will soon get you round again, never fear, Master
Ned," Peters said as he jumped down into the boat to aid
in hoisting him on board.   "No wonder the damp airs of
this country have got into your bones at last.   I never can
keep myself warm when we are once in these canals.   If
it wasn't for their schiedam I don't believe the Dutchmen
could stand it themselves."

Ned was soon lifted on board, and carried into the cabin
aft.   The *Good Venture* had already discharged her cargo,
and, as there was no chance of filling up again at Flushing,
sail was made an hour after he was on board, and the vessel put out to sea.   It was now early in November, but although the air was cold the day was fine and bright, and
as soon as the vessel was under weigh Ned was wrapped up
in cloaks and laid on a mattress on deck, with his head well
propped up with pillows.

"One seems to breathe in fresh life here, father," he
said.   "It is pleasant to feel the motion and the shock of
the waves after being so long on land.   I feel stronger already, while so long as I was at Delft I did not seem to gain

from one day to the other. I hope we sha'n't make too rapid a voyage; I don't want to come home as an invalid."

"We shall not make a fast run of it unless the wind changes, Ned. It blows steadily from the west at present, and we shall be lucky if we cast anchor under a week in the Pool."

"All the better, father. In a week I shall be on my legs again unless I am greatly mistaken."

Ned's convalescence was indeed rapid, and by the time they entered the mouth of the Thames he was able to walk from side to side of the vessel, and as the wind still held from the west it was another four days before they dropped anchor near London Bridge. Ned would have gone ashore in his old attire; but upon putting it on the first day he was able to get about, he found he had so completely outgrown it that he was obliged to return to the garments he had worn in Holland.

He was now more than eighteen years of age, and nearly six feet in height. He had broadened out greatly, and the position he had for the last year held as an officer charged with authority by the prince had given him a manner of decision and authority altogether beyond his years. As he could not wear his sailor dress he chose one of the handsomest of those he possessed. It consisted of maroon doublet and trunks, slashed with white, with a short mantle of dark green, and hose of the same colour; his cap was maroon in colour, with small white and orange plumes, and he wore a ruff round his neck. Captain Martin saluted him with a bow of reverence as he came on deck.

"Why, Ned, they will think that I am bringing a court gallant with me. Your mother and the girls will be quite abashed at all this finery."

"I felt strange in it myself at first," Ned laughed; "but

of course I am accustomed to it now. The prince is not one who cares for state himself, but as one of his officers I was obliged to be well dressed; and, indeed, this dress and the others I wear were made by his orders and presented to me. Indeed I think I am very moderate in not decking myself out with the two gold chains I have—the one a present from his highness, the other from the city of Alkmaar—to say nothing of the watch set with jewels that the prince gave me on leaving."

Ned's mother and the girls were on the look-out, for the *Good Venture* had been noticed as she passed. Ned had at his father's suggestion kept below in order that he might give them a surprise on his arrival.

"I verily believe they won't know you," he said as they approached the gate. "You have grown four inches since they saw you last, and your cheeks are thin and pale instead of being round and sunburnt. This, with your attire, has made such a difference that I am sure anyone would pass you in the street without knowing you."

Ned hung a little behind while his mother and the girls met his father at the gate. As soon as the embraces were over Captain Martin turned to Ned and said to his wife:

"My dear, I have to introduce an officer of the prince who has come over for his health to stay a while with us. This is Captain Martin."

Dame Martin gave a start of astonishment, looked incredulously for a moment at Ned, and then with a cry of delight threw herself into his arms.

"It really seems impossible that this can be Ned," she said, as, after kissing his sisters, he turned to her. "Why, husband, it is a man!"

"And a very fine one, too, wife. He tops me by two inches; and as to his attire, I feel that we must all smarten up to be fit companions to such a splendid bird. Why, the girls look quite awed at him!"

"But you look terribly pale, Ned, and thin," his mother said; "and you were so healthy and strong."

"I shall soon be healthy and strong again, mother. When I have got out of these fine clothes, which I only put on because I could not get into my old ones, and you have fed me up for a week on good English beef, you will see that there is no such great change in me after all."

"And now let us go inside," Captain Martin said; "there is a surprise for you there." Ned entered, and was indeed surprised at seeing his Aunt Elizabeth sitting by the fire, while his cousins were engaged upon their needlework at the window. They, too, looked for a moment doubtful as he entered; for the fifteen months since they had last seen him, when he left them at the surrender of Haarlem, had changed him much, and his dress at that time had been very different to that he now wore. It was not until he exclaimed "Well, aunt, this is indeed a surprise!" that they were sure of his identity, and they welcomed him with a warmth scarcely less than his mother and sisters had shown.

Elizabeth Plomaert was not of a demonstrative nature; but although she had said little at the time, she had felt deeply the care and devotion which Ned had exhibited to her and her daughters during the siege, and knew that had it not been for the supplies of food, scanty as they were, that he nightly brought in, she herself, and probably the girls, would have succumbed to hunger.

"When did you arrive, aunt?" Ned asked, when the greetings were over.

"Four months ago, Ned. Life was intolerable in Haarlem owing to the brutal conduct of the Spanish soldiers. I was a long time bringing myself to move. Had it not

been for the girls I should never have done so. But things
became intolerable; and when most of the troops were removed at the time Count Louis advanced, we managed to
leave the town and make our way north.   It was a terrible
journey to Enkhuizen; but we accomplished it, and after
being there a fortnight took passage in a ship for England,
and, as you see, here we are."

CHAPTER XIX.

A FEW days after Ned's return home his aunt and cousins moved into a house close by, which they had taken a short time before; dame Plomaert's half of the property, purchased with the money that had been transmitted by her father-in-law and his sons to England, being ample to keep them in considerable comfort. Just as Ned was leaving Delft some despatches had been placed in his hands for delivery upon his arrival in London to Lord Walsingham. The great minister was in attendance upon the queen at Greenwich, and thither Ned proceeded by boat on the morning after his arrival. On stating that he was the bearer of despatches from the Prince of Orange Ned at once obtained an audience, and bowing deeply presented his letters to the queen's counsellor. The latter opened the letter addressed to himself, and after reading a few words said:

"Be seated, Captain Martin. The prince tells me that he sends it by your hand, but that as you are prostrate by fever you will be unable to deliver it personally. I am glad to see that you are so far recovered."

Ned seated himself, while Lord Walsingham continued the perusal of his despatches.

"The prince is pleased to speak in very high terms of you, Captain Martin," he said; "and tells me that as you are en-

tirely in his confidence you will be able to give me much information besides that that he is able to write."

He then proceeded to question Ned at length as to the
state of feeling in Holland, its resources and means of resistance, upon all of which points Ned replied fully.   The
interview lasted nearly two hours, at the end of which
time Lord Walsingham said:

"When I hand the letter inclosed within my own to the
queen I shall report to her majesty very favourably as to
your intelligence, and it may possibly be that she may
desire to speak to you herself, for she is deeply interested
in this matter; and although circumstances have prevented
her showing that warmth for the welfare of Holland that
she feels, she has no less the interest of that country at
heart, and will be well pleased to find that one of her subjects has been rendering such assistance as the prince is
pleased to acknowledge in his letter to me.   Please, therefore, to leave your address with my secretary in the next room
in order that I may communicate with you if necessary."

Two days later one of the royal servants brought a
message that Captain Martin was to present himself on
the following day at Greenwich, as her majesty would
be pleased to grant him an audience.   Knowing that
the queen loved that those around her should be bravely attired, Ned dressed himself in the suit that he had
only worn once or twice when he had attended the prince
to meetings of the Estates.

It was of puce-coloured satin slashed with green, with
a short mantle of the same material, with the cape embroidered in silver.   The bonnet was to match, with a
small white feather.   He placed the chain the prince
had given him round his neck, and with an ample ruff
and manchets of Flemish lace, and his rapier by his

side, he took his place in the boat, and was rowed to Greenwich. He felt some trepidation as he was ushered in. A page conducted him to the end of the chamber, where the queen was standing with Lord Walsingham at her side. Ned bowed profoundly, the queen held out her hand, and bending on one knee Ned reverently placed it to his lips.

"I am gratified, Captain Martin," she said, "at the manner in which my good cousin, the Prince of Orange, has been pleased to speak of your services to him. You are young indeed, sir, to have passed through such perilous adventures; and I would fain hear from your lips the account of the deliverance of Leyden, and of such other matters as you have taken part in."

The queen then seated herself, and Ned related modestly the events at Leyden, Haarlem, Alkmaar, and the two sea-fights in which he had taken part. The queen several times questioned him closely as to the various details.

"We are much interested," she said, "in these fights, in which the burghers of Holland have supported themselves against the soldiers of Spain, seeing that we may ourselves some day have to maintain ourselves against that power. How comes it, young sir, that you came to mix yourself up in these matters? We know that many of our subjects have crossed the water to fight against the Spaniards; but these are for the most part restless spirits, who are attracted as much, perhaps, by a love of adventure as by their sympathy with the people of the Netherlands."

Ned then related the massacre of his Dutch relations by the Spaniards, and how his father had lost a leg while sailing out of Antwerp.

"I remember me now," the queen said. "The matter was laid before our council, and we remonstrated with the Spanish ambassador, and he in turn accused our seamen of having first sunk a Spanish galley without cause or reason. And when not employed in these dangerous en- terprises of which you have been speaking, do you say that you have been in attendance upon the prince himself? He speaks in his letter to my Lord Walsingham of his great confidence in you. How came you first, a stranger and a foreigner, to gain the confidence of so wise and prudent a prince?"

"He intrusted a mission to me of some slight peril, your majesty, and I was fortunate enough to carry it out to his satisfaction."

"Tell me more of it," the queen said. "It may be that we ourselves shall find some employment for you, and I wish to know upon what grounds we should place confi- dence in you. Tell me fully the affair. I am not pressed for time, and love to listen to tales of adventure."

Ned thus commanded related in full the story of his mission to Brussels.

"Truly the prince's confidence was well reposed in you," she said, when Ned had finished. "You shall hear from us anon, Captain Martin. Since you know Holland so well, and are high in the confidence of the prince, we shall doubtless be able to find means of utilizing your services for the benefit of the realm."

So saying she again extended her hand to Ned, who, after kissing it, retired from the audience-chamber delight- ed with the kindness and condescension of Elizabeth. When he had left, the queen said to Lord Walsingham.

"A very proper young officer, Lord Walsingham; and one of parts and intelligence as well as of bravery. Me- thinks we may find him useful in our communications with the Prince of Orange; and from his knowledge of the people we may get surer intelligence from him of the state of feeling there with regard to the alliance they are proposing with us, and to their offers to come under our protection, than we can from our own envoy. It is advisable, too, at times to have two mouthpieces: the one to speak in the public ear, the other to deliver our private sentiments and plans."

"He is young for so great a responsibility," Lord Walsingham said hesitatingly.

"If, the Prince of Orange did not find him too young to act in matters in which the slightest indiscretion might bring a score of heads to the block, I think that we can trust him, my lord. In some respects his youth will be a distinct advantage. Did we send a personage of age and rank to Holland it might be suspected that he had a special mission from us, and our envoy might complain that we were treating behind his back; but a young officer like this could come and go without attracting observation, and without even Philip's spies suspecting that he was dabbling in affairs of state."

At this time, indeed, the queen was, as she had long been, playing a double game with the Netherlands. Holland and Zeeland were begging the prince to assume absolute power. The Prince of Orange, who had no ambition whatever for himself, was endeavouring to negotiate with either England or 'France to take the Estates under their protection. Elizabeth, while jealous of France, was unwilling to incur the expenditure in men and still more in money that would be necessary were she to assume protection of Holland as its sovereign under the title offered to her of Countess of Holland; and yet, though unwilling to do this herself, she was still more unwilling to see France step in and occupy the position offered to her, while, above all, she shrank from engaging at present in a life-and-death struggle with Spain.

Thus, while ever assuring the Prince of Orange of her good-will, she abstained from rendering any absolute assistance, although continuing to hold out hopes that she would later on accept the sovereignty offered.

For the next three weeks Ned remained quietly at home. The gatherings in the summer-house were more largely attended than ever, and the old sailors were never tired of hearing from Ned stories of the sieges in Holland.

It was a continual source of wonder to them how Will Martin's son, who had seemed to them a boy like other boys, should have gone through such perilous adventures, should have had the honour of being in the Prince of Orange's confidence, and the still greater honour of being received by the queen and allowed to kiss her hand. It was little more than two years back that Ned had been a boy among them, never venturing to give his opinion unless first addressed, and now he was a young man, with a quiet and assured manner, and bearing himself rather as a young noble of the court than the son of a sea-captain like themselves.

It was all very wonderful, and scarce seemed to them natural, especially as Ned was as quiet and unaffected as he had been as a boy, and gave himself no airs whatever on the strength of the good fortune that had befallen him. Much of his time was spent in assisting his aunt to get her new house in order, and in aiding her to move into it. This had just been accomplished when he received an order to go down to Greenwich and call upon Lord Walsingham. He received from him despatches to be delivered to the Prince of Orange, together with many verbal directions for the prince's private ear. He was charged to ascertain as far as possible the prince's inclinations towards a French alliance, and what ground he had for encouragement from the French king.

"Upon your return, Captain Martin, you will render me an account of all expenses you have borne, and they will, of course, be defrayed."

"My expenses will be but small, my lord," Ned replied; "for it chances that my father's ship sails to-morrow for Rotterdam, and I shall take passage in her. While there I am sure that the prince, whose hospitality is boundless, will insist upon my staying with him, as his guest; and indeed, it seems to me that this would be best so, for having so long been a member of his household it will seem to all that I have but returned to resume my former position."

The public service in the days of Queen Elizabeth was not sought for by men for the sake of gain. It was considered the highest honour to serve the queen; and those employed on embassies, missions, and even in military commands spent large sums, and sometimes almost beggared themselves in order to keep up a dignity worthy of their position, considering themselves amply repaid for any sacrifices by receiving an expression of the royal approval. Ned Martin therefore returned home greatly elated at the honourable mission that had been intrusted to him. His father, however, although also gratified at Ned's reception at court and employment in the queen's service, looked at it from the matter-of-fact point of view.

"It is all very well, Ned," he said, as they were talking the matter over in family conclave in the evening; "and I do not deny that I share in the satisfaction that all these women are expressing. It is a high honour that you should be employed on a mission for her majesty, and there are scores of young nobles who would be delighted to be employed in such service; but you see, Ned, you are not a young noble, and although honour is a fine thing, it will buy neither bread nor cheese. If you were the heir to

great estates you would naturally rejoice in rendering services which might bring you into favour at court, and win
for you honour and public standing; but you see you are the
son of a master-mariner, happily the owner of his own ship
and of other properties which are sufficient to keep him in
comfort, but which will naturally at the death of your
mother and myself go to the girls, while you will have the
Good Venture and my shares in other vessels. But these
are businesses that want looking after, and the income
would go but a little way to support you in a position at
court. You have now been two years away from the sea.
That matters little; but if you were to continue in the royal
service for a time you would surely become unfitted to return to the rough life of a master-mariner. Fair words
butter no parsnip, Ned. Honour and royal service empty
the purse instead of filling it. It behoves you to think
these matters over."

"I am surprised at you, Will," Dame Martin said. "I
should have thought that you would have been proud of
the credit and honour that Ned is winning. Why, all our
neighbours are talking of nothing else!"

All our neighbors will not be called upon, wife, to pay
for Master Ned's support, to provide him with courtly garments, and enable him to maintain a position which will
do credit to his royal mistress. I am proud of Ned, as
proud as anyone can be, but that is no reason why I should
be willing to see him spend his life as a needy hanger-on of
the court rather than as a British sailor, bearing a good
name in the city, and earning a fair living by honest trade.
Ned knows that I am speaking only for his own good.
Court favor is but an empty thing, and our good queen is
fickle in her likings, and has never any hesitation in dis-
avowing the proceedings of her envoys. When a man has

broad lands to fall back upon he can risk the cost of court favour, and can go into retirement assured that sooner or later he will again have his turn.   But such is not Ned's position.   I say not that I wish him at once to draw back from this course; but I would have him soberly think it over and judge whether it is one that in the long run is likely to prove successful."

Mrs. Martin, her sister-in-law, and the four girls looked anxiously at Ned.   They had all, since the day that he was first sent for to Greenwich, been in a high state of delight at the honour that had befallen him, and his father's words had fallen like a douche of cold water upon their aspirations.

"I fully recognize the truth of what you say, father," he said, after a pause, "and will think it deeply over, which I shall have time to do before my return from Holland. Assuredly it is not a matter to be lightly decided.   It may mean that this royal service may lead to some position of profit as well as honour; although now, as you have put it to me, I own that the prospect seems to me to be a slight one, and that where so many are ready to serve for honour alone, the chance of employment for one requiring money as well as honour is but small.   However, there can be no need for instant decision.   I am so fond of the sea that I am sure that, even if away from it for two or three years, I should be ready and willing to return to it.   I am as yet but little over eighteen, and even if I remained in the royal service until twenty-one I should still have lost but little of my life, and should not be too old to take to the sea again.

"In time I shall see more plainly what the views of Lord Walsingham are concerning me, and whether there is a prospect of advancement in the service.   He will know that I cannot afford to give my life to the queen's service without pay, not being, as you say, a noble or a great land-owner."

"That is very well spoken, Ned," his father said. "There is no need·in any way for you to come to any resolution on the subject at present; I shall be well content to wait until you come of age. As you say, by that time you will see whether this is but a brief wind of royal favour, or whether my Lord Walsingham designs to continue you in the royal service and to advance your fortunes. I find that I am able to get on on board a ship better than I had expected, and have no wish to retire from the sea at present; therefore there will be plenty of time for you to decide when you get to the age of one and twenty. Nevertheless this talk will not have been without advantage, for it will be far better for you not to have set your mind altogether upon court service; and you will then, if you finally decide to return to the sea, not have to suffer such disappointment as you would do had you regarded it as a fixed thing that some great fortune was coming to you. So let it be an understood thing, that this matter remain entirely open until you come to the age of twenty-one.

Ned accordingly went backwards and forwards to Holland for the next two years, bearing letters and messages between the queen and the Prince of Orange.

There was some pause in military operations after the relief of Leyden. Negotiations had for a long time gone on between the King of Spain, acting by Royal Commissioners, on the one side, and the prince and the Estates on the other. The Royal Commissioners were willing in his name to make considerable concessions, to withdraw the Spanish troops from the country, and to permit the Estates-general to assemble; but as they persisted that all heretics should either recant or leave the provinces, no possible agreement could be arrived at, as the question of re-

ligion was at the bottom of the whole movement.
During the year 1575 the only military operation of importance was the recovery by the Spaniards of the Island
of Schouwen, which, with its chief town Zierickzee, was
recovered by a most daring feat of arms—the Spaniards
wading for miles through water up to the neck on a wild
and stormy night, and making their way across in spite of
the efforts of the Zeelanders in their ships. Zierickzee indeed resisted for many months, and finally surrendered
only to hunger; the garrison obtaining good terms from the
Spaniards, who were so anxious for its possession that to
obtain it they were even willing for once to forego their
vengeance for the long resistance it had offered.

In March, 1576, while the siege was still going on, Requesens died suddenly of a violent fever, brought on partly by
anxiety caused by another mutiny of the troops. This
mutiny more than counterbalanced the advantage gained
by the capture of the Island of Schouwen, for after taking
possession of it the soldiers engaged in the service at once
joined the mutiny and marched away into Brabant.

The position of Holland had gone from bad to worse, the
utmost efforts of the population were needed to repair the
broken dykes and again recover the submerged lands. So
bare was the country of animals of all kinds, that it had
become necessary to pass a law forbidding for a considerable period the slaughter of oxen, cows, calves, sheep, or
poultry. Holland and Zeeland had now united in a con-
federacy, of which the prince was at the head, and by an
Act of Union in June, 1575, the two little republics became
virtually one. Among the powers and duties granted to
the prince he was to maintain the practice of the reformed
evangelical religion, and to cause to cease the exercise of
all other religions contrary to the Gospel. He was, how-

ever, not to permit that inquisition should be made into any man's belief or conscience, or that any man by cause thereof should suffer trouble, injury, or hinderance.

Upon one point only the prince had been peremptory, he would have no persecution. In the original terms he had been requested to surpress "the Catholic religion," but had altered the words into "religion at variance with the Gospel." Almost alone, at a time when every one was intolerant, the Prince of Orange was firmly resolved that all men should have liberty of conscience.

Holland suffered a great loss when Admiral Boisot fell in endeavouring to relieve Zierickzee. The harbour had been surrounded by the Spaniards by a submerged dyke of piles of rubbish. Against this Boisot drove his ship, which was the largest of his fleet. He did not succeed in breaking through. The tide ebbed and left his ship aground, while the other vessels were beaten back. Rather than fall into the hands of the enemy, he and 300 of his companions sprang overboard and endeavoured to effect their escape by swimming, but darkness came on before he could be picked up, and he perished by drowning.

The mutiny among the Spanish regiments spread rapidly, and the greater part of the German troops of Spain took part in it. The mutineers held the various citadels, throughout the country, and ravaged the towns, villages, and open country. The condition of the people of Brabant was worse than ever. Despair led them to turn again to the provinces which had so long resisted the authority of Spain, and the fifteen other states, at the invitation of the prince, sent deputies to Ghent to a general congress, to arrange for a close union between the whole of the provinces of the Netherlands.

Risings took place in all parts of the country, but they

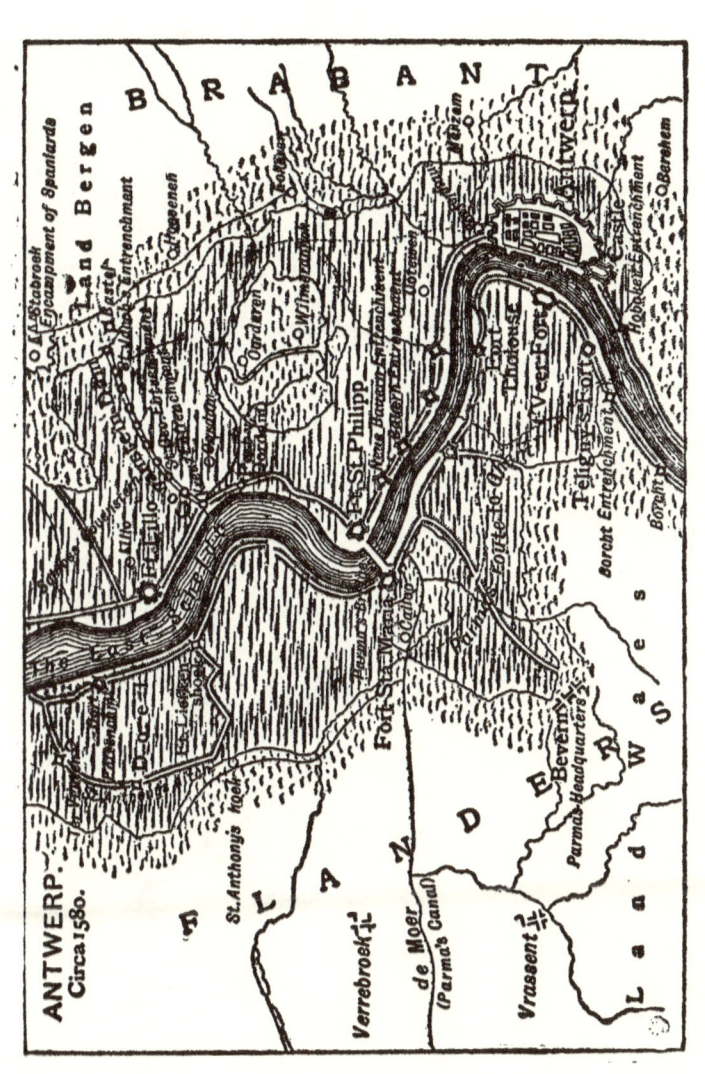

ANTWERP.
Circa 1580.

were always repressed by the Spaniards; who, though in open mutiny against their king and officers, had no idea of permitting the people of the Netherlands to recover the liberty that had at the cost of so much blood been wrung from them. Maastricht drove out its garrison; but the Spaniards advanced against the town seized a vast number of women, and placing these before them advanced to the assault. The citizens dared not fire, as many of their own wives or sisters were among the women; the town was therefore taken, and a hideous massacre followed.

Ned Martin had now been two years engaged upon various missions to Holland, and Lord Walsingham himself acknowledged to his mistress that her choice of the young officer had been a singularly good one. He had conducted himself with great discretion, his reports were full and minute, and he had several times had audiences with the queen, and had personally related to her matters of importance concerning the state of Holland, and the views of the prince and the Estates-general. The congress at Ghent, and the agitation throughout the whole of the Netherlands, had created a lively interest in England, and Ned received orders to visit Ghent and Antwerp, and to ascertain more surely the probability of an organization of the provinces into a general confederation.

When he reached Ghent he found that the attention of the citizens was for the time chiefly occupied with the siege of the citadel, which was held by a Spanish garrison, and he therefore proceeded to Antwerp. This was at the time probably the wealthiest city in Europe. It carried on the largest commerce in the world, its warehouses were full of the treasures of all countries, its merchants vied with princes in splendour. The proud city was dominated, however, by its citadel, which had been erected not for the purpose of external defence but to overawe the town.

The governor of the garrison, D'Avila, had been all along recognized as one of the leaders of the mutiny. The town itself was garrisoned by Germans who still held aloof from the mutiny, but who had been tampered with by him. The governor of the city, Champagny, although a sincere Catholic, hated the Spaniards, and had entered into negotiations with the prince. The citizens thought at present but little of the common cause, their thoughts being absorbed by fears of their own safety, threatened by the mutinous Spanish troops who had already captured and sacked Alost, and were now assembling with the evident intention of gathering for themselves the rich booty contained within the walls of Antwerp.

As they approached the town, a force of 5000 Walloon infantry and 1200 cavalry were despatched from Brussels to the aid of its sister city. No sooner, however, did this force enter the town than it broke into a mutiny, which was only repressed with the greatest difficulty by Champagny. It was at this moment that Ned entered the city. He at once communicated with the governor, and delivered to him some messages with which he had been charged by the Prince of Orange, whom he had visited on his way.

"Had you arrived three days since I could have discussed these matters with you," the governor said; "but as it is we are hourly expecting attack, and can think of nothing but preparations for defence. I shall be glad if you can assist me in that direction. Half the German garrison are traitors, the Walloons who have just entered are in no way to be relied upon, and it is the burghers themselves upon whom the defence of the town must really fall. They are now engaged in raising a rampart facing the citadel. I am at once proceeding thither to superintend the work."

Ned accompanied the governor to the spot and found twelve thousand men and women labouring earnestly to erect a rampart, constructed of bales of goods, casks of earth, up-turned wagons, and other bulky objects. The guns of the fortress opened upon the workers, and so impeded them that night fell before the fortifications were nearly completed. Unfortunately it was bright moonlight, and the artillerymen continued their fire with such accuracy that the work was at last abandoned, and the citizens retired to their homes. Champagny did all that was possible. Aided by some burghers and his own servants, he planted what few cannon there were at the weakest points; but his general directions were all neglected, and not even scouts were posted.

In the morning a heavy mist hung over the city, and concealed the arrival of the Spanish troops from all the towns and fortresses in the neighbourhood. As soon as it was fairly daylight the defenders mustered. The Marquis of Havré claimed for the Walloons the post of honour in defence of the lines facing the citadel; and 600 men were disposed here, while the bulk of the German garrison were stationed in the principal squares.

At ten o'clock the mutineers from Alost marched into the citadel, raising the force there to 5000 veteran infantry and 600 cavalry.

Ned had been all night at work assisting the governor, He had now laid aside his ordinary attire, and was clad in complete armour. He was not there to fight; but there was clearly nothing else to do, unless indeed he made his escape at once to the fleet of the Prince of Orange, which was lying in the river. This he did not like doing until it was clear that all was lost. He had seen the Dutch burghers beat back the most desperate assaults of the Spanish troops, and assuredly the Walloons and Germans, who, without counting the burghers, considerably exceeded the force of the enemy, ought to be able to do the same.

Just before daybreak he made his way down to the quays, ascertained the exact position of the fleet, and determined how he had best get on board. He chose a small boat from among those lying at the quay, and removed it to the foot of some stairs by a bridge. He fastened the head rope to a ring and pushed the boat off, so that it lay under the bridge, concealed from the sight of any who might pass along the wharves. Having thus prepared for his own safety, he was making his way to join the governor when a woman came out from a house in a quiet street. As she met him he started.

"Why, Magdalene!" he exclaimed, "is it you?" What are you doing in Antwerp? Is the countess here?"

The woman looked at him in surprise.

"Don't you remember me, Magdalene? the boy you dressed up as a girl at Brussels, and whom you last saw at Maastricht?"

"Bless me!" the old servant exclaimed, "is it you, sir? I should never have known you again."

"Three years make a great deal of difference," Ned laughed; "and it is more than that now since we last met."

"Please to come in, sir; the countess will be right glad to see you, and so will Miss Gertrude. They have talked of you hundreds of times, and wondered what had become of you." She opened the door again with the great key, and led the way into the house.

"Mistress," she said, showing the way into the parlour, "here is a visitor for you." The countess and her daughter had, like every one else in Antwerp, been up all night, and rose from her seat by the fire as the young officer entered. He took off his helmet and bowed deeply.

"What is your business with me?" the countess asked, seeing that he did not speak.

"I have not come exactly upon business, countess," he replied, "but to thank you for past kindnesses."

"Mother, it is the English boy!" exclaimed the young lady sitting upon the other side of the fire, rising from her seat. "Surely, sir, you are Master Edward Martin?"

"Your eyes are not in fault, Fraulein. I am Edward Martin."

"I am glad, indeed, to see you, sir," the countess said. "How often my daughter and I have longed for the time when we might again meet you to tell you how grateful we are for the service you did us. I wonder now that I did not recognize you; but you have changed from a lad into a man. You must remember it is more than four years since we were together at Brussels. As for the meeting near Maastricht, it was such a short one; and I was so full of joy at the thought that Gertrude and I had escaped the fearful danger hanging over us that I scarce noticed your appearance, nor had we any time to talk then. We received the letter you wrote after leaving us at Brussels, from the Hague, telling us that you had arrived there safely. But since you did us that service at Maastricht we have never heard of you."

"I had not your address," Ned replied. "And even had I known where you were I should not have dared to write; for there was no saying into whose hands the letter might not fall. But, countess, excuse me if I turn to other matters, for the time presses sorely. You know that the city will be attacked to-day."

"So every one says," the countess replied. "But surely you do not think that there is any danger. The Walloons and Germans should be able alone to hold the barricades, and behind them are all the citizens."

"I put little faith in the Walloons," Ned said shortly; "and some of the Germans we know have been bribed. I would rather that all were out of the way, and that it were left to the burghers alone to defend the barricades. I have seen how the citizens of the Netherlands can fight at Haarlem and Alkmaar. As for these Walloons, I have no faith in them. I fear, countess, that the danger is great; and if the Spaniards succeed in winning their way into the town, there is no mercy to be expected for man, woman, or child. I consider that it would be madness for you to stay here."

" But what are we to do, sir?" the countess asked.

" The only way, madam, is to make your way on board the prince's fleet. I am known to many of the officers, and can place you on board at once. If you wait until the Spaniards enter it will be too late. There will be a wild rush to the river, and the boats will be swamped. If the attack fails, and the Spaniards retire from before the city, you can if you choose return to shore, though I should say that even then it will be better by far to go to Rotterdam or Delft; unless you decide to do as you once talked about, to find a refuge for a time in England."

"I will accept your offer gladly, sir," the countess said. "I have long been looking for some way to leave the city. But none can go on board the ships without a pass, and I have not dared to ask for one. Not for worlds would I expose my daughter to the horrors of a sack. Can we go at once?"

"Yes, madam, I have everything in readiness, and would advise no delay."

"I have nothing that I need mind leaving behind. I am, as you see, more comfortable here than I was at Brussels; but I am still forced to keep in concealment. In five minutes we shall be ready."

CHAPTER XX.

THE "SPANISH FURY."

IN a very short time the countess and her daughter returned to the room where Ned was awaiting them. Each carried a hand-bag.

"We are ready now," the countess said. "I have my jewels and purse. As for the things we leave behind, they are scarce worth the taking by the Spaniards."

Locking the door of the house behind them the three women accompanied Ned down to the river-side. He took the first boat that came to hand and rowed them down to the fleet, which was moored a quarter of a mile below the town. He passed the first ship or two, and then rowed to one with whose captain he was acquainted.

"Captain Enkin," he said, "I have brought on board two ladies who have long been in hiding, waiting an opportunity of being taken to Holland—the Countess Von Harp and her daughter. I fear greatly that Antwerp will fall to-day, and wish, therefore, to place them in safety before the fight begins. Before sunset, unless I am mistaken, you will have a crowd of fugitives on board."

"I am very pleased, madam," the captain said, bowing to the countess, "to receive you, and beg to hand over my cabin for your use. The name you bear is known to all Dutchmen; and even were it not so, anyone introduced to me by my good friend Captain Martin would be heartily welcome. Are you going to return on shore?" he asked Ned.

"Yes, I must do so," Ned replied. "I promised the governor to stand by him to the last; and as he has scarce a soul on whom he can rely, it is clearly my duty to do so. It is not for me to shirk doing my duty as long as I can, because I fear that the day will go against us."

"You will have difficulty in getting off again if the Spaniards once enter the city," the captain said. "There will be such a rush to the boats that they will be swamped before they leave the shore."

"I have a boat hidden away in which I hope to bring off the governor with me," Ned replied. "As to myself, I can swim like a fish."

"Mind and get rid of your armour before you try it. All the swimming in the world could not save you if you jumped in with all that steel mail on you."

"I will bear it in mind," Ned said. "Good-bye, countess. Good-bye, Fraulein Gertrude. I trust to see you at nightfall, if not before."

"That is a very gallant young officer," Captain Enkin said as the two ladies sat watching Ned as he rowed to the shore.

"You addressed him as Captain Martin?" the countess said.

"Yes, he has been a captain in the prince's service fully three years," the sailor said; "and fought nobly at Alkmaar, at the naval battle on the Zuider-Zee, and in the sea-fight when we drove Romero's fleet back in Bergen. He stands very high in the confidence of the prince, but I do not think he is in our service now. He is often with the prince, but I believe he comes and goes between England and Holland, and is, men say, the messenger by whom private communications between the queen of England and the prince are chiefly carried."

"He is young to have such confidence reposed in him," the countess said.

"Yes, he is young," Captain Enkin replied. "Not, I suppose, beyond seven and eight and twenty. He was a captain and high in the prince's confidence when I first knew him three years ago, so he must surely have been four and five and twenty then; and yet, indeed, now you speak of it, methinks he is greatly bigger now than he was then. I do not think he was much taller than I am, and now he tops me by nigh a head. But I must surely be mistaken as to that, for the prince would scarcely place his confidence in a mere lad."

The countess made no reply, though she exchanged a quiet smile with her daughter. They knew that Ned could not be much more than twenty. He was, he had said, about three years older than Gertrude, and she had passed seventeen but by a few months.

Ned, on returning to shore, tied up the boat and then proceeded to the palace of the governor. A servant was holding a horse at the door.

"The governor ordered this horse to be ready and saddled for you, sir, when you arrived, and begged you to join him at once in the market-place, where he is telling off the troops to their various stations."

Leaping on the horse, Ned rode to the market-place, and at once placed himself under orders of the governor.

"There is nothing much for you to do at present," Champagny said. "The troops are all in their places, and we are ready when they deliver the assault."

It was not until eleven o'clock that the Spaniards advanced to the attack—3000 of them, under their Eletto, by the street of St. Michael; the remainder with the Germans, commanded by Romero, by that of St. George. No

sooner did the compact masses approach the barricades
than the Walloons, who had been so loud in their boasts
of valour, and had insisted upon having the post of danger, broke and fled, their commander, Havrè, at their
head; and the Spaniards, springing over the ramparts,
poured into the streets.

"Fetch up the Germans from the exchange!" Champagny shouted to Ned; and leaping his horse over a garden wall, he himself rode to another station and brought
up the troops there, and led them in person to bar the
road to the enemy, trying in vain to rally the flying Wal-
lons he met on the way. For a few minutes the two parties of Germans made a brave stand; but they were unable
to resist the weight and number of the Spaniards, who
bore them down by sheer force. Champagny had fought
gallantly in the mêlée, and Ned, keeping closely beside
him, had well seconded his efforts; but when the Germans
were borne down they rode off, dashing through the streets
and shouting to the burghers everywhere to rise in defence of their homes.

They answered to the appeal. The bodies already collected at the exchange and cattle market moved forward,
and from every house the men poured out. The Spanish
columns had already divided, and were pouring down the
streets with savage cries. The German cavalry of Havrè
under Van Eude at once deserted, and joining the Spanish
cavalry fell upon the townsmen. In vain the burghers
and such of the German infantry as remained faithful
strove to resist their assailants. Although they had been
beaten off in their assaults upon breaches, the Spaniards
had ever proved themselves invincible on level ground;
and now, inspired alike by the fury for slaughter and the
lust for gold, there was no withstanding them.

Round the exchange some of the bravest defenders made a rally, and burghers and Germans, mingled together, fought stoutly until they were slain.

There was another long struggle round the town-hall, one of the most magnificent buildings in Europe; and for a time the resistance was effective, until the Spanish cavalry and the Germans under the traitor Van Eude charged down upon the defenders. Then they took refuge in the buildings, and every house became a fortress, and from window and balcony a hot fire was poured into the square. But now a large number of camp-followers who had accompanied the Spaniards came up with torches, which had been specially prepared for firing the town, and in a short time the city hall and other edifices in the square were in flames.

The fire spread rapidly from house to house and from street to street, until nearly a thousand buildings in the most splendid and wealthy portion of the city were in a blaze.

In the street behind the town-hall a last stand was made. Here the margrave of the city, the burgomasters, senators, soldiers, and citizens fought to the last, until not one remained to wield a sword. When resistance had ceased the massacre began. Women, children, and old men were killed in vast numbers, or driven into the river to drown there.

Then the soldiers scattered on the work of plunder. The flames had already snatched treasures estimated at six millions from their grasp, but there was still abundance for all. The most horrible tortures were inflicted upon men, women, and children to force them to reveal the hiding-places, where they were supposed to have concealed their wealth, and for three days a pandemonium reigned in the city. Two thousand five hundred had been slain, double that number burned and drowned. These are the lowest estimates, many placing the killed at very much higher figures.

Champagny had fought very valiantly, joining any party of soldiers or citizens he saw making a defence. At last, when the town-hall was in flames and all hope over, he said to Ned, who had kept throughout the day at his side: "It is no use throwing away our lives. Let us cut our way out of the city."

"I have a boat lying in readiness at the bridge," Ned said. "If we can once reach the stairs we can make our way off to the fleet."

As they approached the river they saw a Spanish column crossing the street ahead of them. Putting spurs to their horses they galloped on at full speed, and bursting into it hewed their way through and continued their course, followed, however, by a number of the Spanish infantry.

"These are the steps!" Ned exclaimed, leaping from his horse.

Champagny followed his example. The Spaniards were but twenty yards behind.

"If you pull on that rope attached to the ring a boat lying under the bridge will come to you," Ned said. "I will keep them back till you are ready."

Ned turned and faced the Spaniards, and for two or three minutes kept them at bay. His armour was good, and though many blows struck him he was uninjured, while several of the Spaniards fell under his sweeping blows. They fell back for a moment, surprised at his strength; and at this instant the governor called out that all was ready.

Ned turned and rushed down the steps. The governor

was already in the boat. Ned leaped on board, and with a
stroke of his sword severed the head rope. Before the
leading Spaniards reached the bottom of the steps the boat
was a length away. Ned seated himself, and seizing the
oars rowed down the river. Several shots were fired at
them from the bridge and wharves as they went, but they
passed on uninjured. Ned rowed to the admiral's ship
and left the governor there, and then rowed to that of
Captain Enkin.

"Welcome back," the captain said heartily. "I had begun to fear that ill had befallen you. A few fugitives
came off at noon with the news that the Spaniards had entered the city and all was lost. Since then the roar of
musketry, mingled with shouts and yells, has been unceas-
ing, and that tremendous fire in the heart of the city told
its own tale. For the last three hours the river has been
full of floating corpses; and the conntess and her daughter,
who until then had remained on deck, retired to pray in
their cabin. The number of fugitives who have reached
the ships is very small. Doubtless they crowded into such
boats as there were and sank them. At any rate, but few
have made their way out, and those chiefly at the beginning
of the fight. Now we had best let the ladies know you are
here, for they have been in the greatest anxiety about you."

Ned went to the cabin door and knocked. "I have returned, countess."

In a moment the door opened. "Welcome back, indeed, Captain Martin," she said. "We had begun to fear
that we should never see you again. Thankful indeed am
I that you have escaped through this terrible day. Are
you unhurt?" she asked, looking at his bruised and dented
armour and at his clothes, which were splashed with blood.

"I have a few trifling cuts," he replied, "but nothing

worth speaking of. I am truly thankful, countess, that you and your daughter put off with me this morning."

"Yes, indeed," the countess said. "I shudder when I think what would have happened had we been there in the city. What a terrible sight it is!"

"It is, indeed," Ned replied.

The shades of night had now fallen, and over a vast space the flames were mounting high, and a pall of red smoke, interspersed with myriads of sparks and flakes of fire, hung over the captured city. Occasional discharges of guns were still heard, and the shrieks of women and the shouts of men rose in confused din. It was an immense relief to all on board when an hour later the admiral, fearing that the Spaniards might bring artillery to bear upon the fleet, ordered the anchors to be weighed, and the fleet to drop down a few miles below the town.

After taking off his armour, washing the blood from his wounds and having them bound up, and attiring himself in a suit lent him by the captain until he should get to Delft, where he had left his valise, Ned partook of a good meal, for he had taken nothing but a manchet of bread and a cup of wine since the previous night. He then went into the cabin and spent the evening in conversation with the countess and her daughter, the latter of whom had changed since they had last met to the full as much as he had himself done. She had then been a girl of fourteen—slim and somewhat tall for her age, and looking pale and delicate from the life of confinement and anxiety they had led at Brussels, and their still greater anxiety at Maastricht. She was now budding into womanhood. Her figure was lissom and graceful, her face was thoughtful and intelligent, and gave promise of rare beauty in another year or two. He learned that they had remained for a time in the village to which they had first gone, and had then moved to another a few miles away, and had there lived quietly in a small house placed at their disposal by one of their friends. Here they had remained unmolested until two months before, when the excesses committed throughout the country by the mutinous soldiery rendered it unsafe for anyone to live outside the walls of the town. They then removed to Antwerp, where there was far more religious toleration than at Brussels; and the countess had resumed her own name, though still living in complete retirement in the house in which Ned had so fortunately found her.

"The times have altered with me for the better," the countess said. "The Spaniards have retired from that part of Friesland where some of my estates are situated, and those to whom Alva granted them have had to fly. I have a faithful steward there, and since they have left he has collected the rents and has remitted to me such portions as I required, sending over the rest to England to the charge of a banker there. As it may be that the Spaniards will again sweep over Friesland, where they still hold some of the principal towns, I thought it best, instead of having my money placed in Holland, where no one can foresee the future, to send it to England, where at least one can find a refuge and a right to exercise our religion."

"I would that you would go there at once, countess; for surely at present Holland is no place for two unprotected ladies. Nothing would give my mother greater pleasure than to receive you until you can find a suitable home for yourselves. My sisters are but little older than your daughter, and would do all in their power to make her at home. They too speak your language, and there are thousands of your compatriots in London."

"What do you say, Gertrude?" the countess asked. "But I know that your mind has been so long made up that it is needless to question you."

"Yes, indeed, mother, I would gladly go away anywhere from here, where for the last six years there has been nothing but war and bloodshed. If we could go back and live in Friesland among our own people in safety and peace I should be delighted to do so, but this country is as strange to us as England would be. Our friends stand aloof from us, and we are ever in fear either of persecution or murder by the Spanish soldiers. I should be so glad to be away from it all; and, as Captain Martin says, there are many of our own people in London, that it would scarce feel a strange land to us.

"You have said over and over again that you would gladly go if you could get away, and now that we can do so, surely it will be better and happier for us than to go on as we have done. Of course it would be better in Holland than it has been here for the last four years, because we should be amongst Protestants; but we should be still exposed to the dangers of invasion and the horrors of sieges."

"It is as my daughter says, Captain Martin; our thoughts have long been turning to England as a refuge. In the early days of the troubles I had thought of France, where so many of our people went, but since St. Bartholomew it has been but too evident that there is neither peace nor safety for those of the religion there, and that in England alone can we hope to be permitted to worship unmolested. Therefore, now that the chance is open to us, we will not refuse it. I do not say that we will cross at once. We have many friends at Rotterdam and Delft, and the prince held my husband in high esteem in the happy days before the troubles; therefore I shall tarry there for a while, but it will be for a time only. It will not be long before the Spanish again resume their war of conquest; besides, we are sick of the tales of horror that come to us daily, and long for calm and tranquility, which we cannot hope to obtain in Holland. Had I a husband or brothers I would share their fate whatever it was, but being alone and unable to aid the cause in any way it would be folly to continue here and endure trials and risks. You say that you come backwards and forwards often, well then in two months we shall be ready to put ourselves under your protection and to sail with you for England."

The next morning the admiral despatched a ship to Rotterdam with the news of the fate of Antwerp, and Ned obtained a passage in her for himself, the ladies, and servant, and on arriving at Rotterdam saw them bestowed in comfortable lodgings. He then, after an interview with the prince, went on board a ship just leaving for England, and upon his arrival reported to the minister, and afterwards to the queen herself, the terrible massacre of which he had been a witness in Antwerp.

The Spanish fury, as the sack of Antwerp was termed, vastly enriched the soldiers, but did small benefit to the cause of Spain. The attack was wanton and unprovoked. Antwerp had not risen in rebellion against Philip, but had been attacked solely for the sake of plunder; and all Europe was shocked at the atrocities that had taken place, and at the slaughter, which was even greater than the massacre in Paris on the eve of St. Bartholomew. The queen remonstrated in indignant terms, the feeling among the Protestants in Germany was equally strong, and even in France public feeling condemned the act.

In the Netherlands the feeling of horror and indignation

was universal. The fate that had befallen Antwerp might be that of any other sister city. Everywhere petitions were signed in favour of the unity of all the Netherlands under the Prince of Orange. Philip's new governor, Don John, had reached the Netherlands on the very day of the sack of Antwerp, and endeavoured to allay the storm of indignation it had excited by various concessions; but the feeling of unity, and with it of strength, had grown so rapidly that the demands of the commissioners advanced in due proportion, and they insisted upon nothing less than the restoration of their ancient constitution, the right to manage their internal affairs, and the departure of all the Spanish troops from the country.

Don John parleyed and parried the demands, and months were spent in unprofitable discussions, while all the time he was working secretly among the nobles of Brabant and Flanders, who were little disposed to see with complacency the triumph of the democracy of the towns and the establishment of religious toleration. Upon all other points Don John and his master were ready to yield. The Spanish troops were sent away to Italy, the Germans only being retained. The constitutional rights would all have been conceded, but on the question of religious tolerance Philip stood firm. At last, seeing that no agreement would ever be arrived at, both parties prepared again for war.

The Queen of England had lent £100,000 on the security of the cities, and the pause in hostilities during the negotiations had not been altogether wasted in Holland. There had been a municipal insurrection in Amsterdam; the magistrates devoted to Philip had been driven out, and to the great delight of Holland, Amsterdam, its capital, that had long been a stronghold of the enemy, a gate through which he could at will pour his forces, was restored to it

In Antwerp, and several other of the cities of Brabant and Flanders, the citizens razed the citadels by which they had been overawed; men, women, and children uniting in the work, tearing down and carrying away the stones of the fortress that had worked them such evil.

Antwerp had at the departure of the Spanish troops been again garrisoned by Germans, who had remained inactive during this exhibition of the popular will. The Prince of Orange himself had paid a visit to the city, and had, at the invitation of Brussels, proceeded there, and had received an enthusiastic reception, and for a time it seemed that the plans for which so many years he had struggled were at last to be crowned with success. But his hopes were frustrated by the treachery of the nobles and the cowardice of the army the patriots had engaged in their service.

Many of the Spanish troops had been secretly brought back again, and Don John was preparing for a renewal of the war.

Unknown to the Prince of Orange, numbers of the nobles had invited the Archduke Mathias, brother of the Emperor Rudolph of Germany, to assume the government. Mathias, without consultation with his brother, accepted the invitation and journeyed privately to the Netherlands. Had the Prince of Orange declared against him he must at once have returned to Vienna, but this would have aroused the anger of the emperor and the whole of Germany. Had the prince upon the other hand abandoned the field and retired into Holland, he would have played into the hands of his adversaries. Accordingly he received Mathias at Antwerp with great state, and the archduke was well satisfied to place himself in the hands of the most powerful man in the country.

The prince's position was greatly strengthened by the queen instructing her ministers to inform the envoy of the Netherlands that she would feel compelled to withdraw all succour of the states if the Prince of Orange was deprived of his leadership, as it was upon him alone that she relied for success. The prince was thereupon appointed Ruward of Brabant, a position almost analogous to that of dictator. Ghent, which was second only in importance to Antwerp, rose almost immediately, turned out the Catholic authorities, and declared in favour of the prince. A new act of union was signed at Brussels, and the Estates-general passed a resolution declaring Don John to be no longer governor or stadtholder of the Netherlands. The Prince of Orange was appointed lieutenant-general for Mathias, and the actual power of the latter was reduced to a nullity, but he was installed at Brussels with the greatest pomp and ceremony.

Don John, who had by this time collected an army of 20,000 veterans at Namur, and had been joined by the Prince of Parma, a general of great vigour and ability, now marched against the army of the Estates, of which the command had been given to the nobles of the country in the hope of binding them firmly to the national cause.

The patriot army fell back before that of the Spaniards, but were soon engaged by a small body of cavalry. Alexander of Parma came up with some 1200 horse, dashed boldly across a dangerous swamp, and fell upon their flank. The Estates cavalry at once turned and fled, and Parma then fell upon the infantry, and in the course of an hour not only defeated but almost exterminated them, from 7000 to 8000 being killed, and 600 taken prisoners, the latter being executed without mercy by Don John. The loss of the Spaniards was only about ten men. This

extraordinary disproportion of numbers, and the fact that
1200 men so easily defeated a force ten times more numerous, completely dashed to the ground the hopes of the
Netherlands, and showed how utterly incapable were its
soldiers of contending in the field with the veterans of Spain.

The battle was followed by the rapid reduction of a
large number of towns, most of which surrendered without resistance as soon as the Spanish troops approached.
In the meantime the Estates had assembled another army,
which was joined by one composed of 12,000 Germans under Duke Casimir. Both armies were rendered inactive
by want of funds, and the situation was complicated by the
entry of the Duke Alençon, the brother of the King of
France, into the Netherlands. Don John, the hero of the
battle of Lepanto, who had shown himself on many battle-
fields to be at once a great commander and a valiant soldier, was prostrate by disease, brought on by vexation,
partly at the difficulties he had met with since his arrival
in the Netherlands, partly at the neglect of Spain to furnish him with money with which he could set his army,
now numbering 30,000, in motion, and sweep aside all resistance. At this critical moment his malady increased,
and after a week's illness he expired, just two years after
his arrival in the Netherlands.

He was succeeded at first temporarily and afterwards
permanently by Alexander of Parma, also a great commander, and possessing far greater resolution than his
unfortunate predecessor.

The two years had been spent by Edward Martin in almost incessant journeyings between London and the Netherlands. He now held, however, a position much superior
to that which he had formerly occupied. The queen, after
hearing from him his account of the sack of Antwerp and

his share in the struggle, had said to the Secretary, "I think that it is only just that we should bestow upon Captain Martin some signal mark of our approbation at the manner in which he has for two years devoted himself to our service, and that without pay or reward, but solely from his loyalty to our person, and from his good-will towards the state. Kneel, Captain Martin." The queen took the sword that Walsingham handed to her, and said, "Rise, Sir Edward Martin. You will draw out, Mr. Secretary, our new knight's appointment as our special envoy to the Prince of Orange; and see that he has proper appointments for such a post. His duties will, as before, be particular to myself and the prince, and will not clash in any way with those of our envoy at the Hague."

The delight of Ned's mother and sisters when he returned home and informed them of the honour that the queen had been pleased to bestow upon him was great indeed. His father said:

"Well, Ned, I must congratulate you with the others; though I had hoped to make a sailor of you. However, circumstances have been too much for me. I own that you have been thrust into this work rather by fortune than design; and as it is so I am heartily glad that you have succeeded. It seems strange to me that my boy should have become Sir Edward Martin, an officer in the service of her majesty, and I say frankly that just at present I would rather that it had been otherwise. But I suppose I shall get accustomed to it in time, and assuredly none but myself will doubt for a moment that you have gained greatly by all this honour and dignity."

Queen Elizabeth, although in some respects parsimonious in the extreme, was liberal to her favourites, and the new-made knight stood high in her liking. She loved to

have good-looking men about her; and without being actually handsome, Ned Martin, with his height and breadth
of shoulder, his easy and upright carriage, his frank, open
face and sunny smile, was pleasant to look upon. He had
served her excellently for two years, had asked for no re-
wards or favours, but had borne himself modestly, and
been content to wait. Therefore the queen was pleased to
order her treasurer to issue a commission to Sir Edward
Martin, as her majesty's special envoy to the Prince of
Orange, with such appointments as would enable him handsomely to support his new dignity and his position as her
representative.

Even Captain Martin was now bound to confess that Ned
had gained profit as well as honour. He did indeed warn
his son not to place too much confidence in princes; but
Ned replied, "I do not think the queen is fickle in her
likes and dislikes, father. But I rely not upon this, but
on doing my duty to the state for further employmen . I
have had extraordinary good fortune, too; and have, without any merit save that of always doing my best, mounted
step by step from the deck of the *Good Venture* to knight-
hood and employment by the state. The war appears to
me to be as far from coming to an end as it did six years
ago; and if I continue to acquit myself to the satisfaction
of the lord treasurer and council, I hope that at its conclusion I may be employed upon such further work as I am
fitted for."

"You speak rightly, Ned; and I am wrong to feel anxiety about your future when you have already done so well.
And now, Ned, you had best go into the city and order
from some tailor who supplies the court such suits as are
fitting to your new rank. The queen loves brave dresses
and bright colours, and you must cut as good a figure as

the rest. You have been somewhat of an expense to me these last two years; but that is over now, and I can well afford the additional outlay to start you worthily. What was good enough for Captain Martin is not good enough for Sir Edward Martin; therefore stint not expense in any way. I should not like that you should not hold your own with the young fops of the court."

It was well that Ned had provided himself with a new outfit, for he was not sent abroad again for more than a month, and during that time he was almost daily at court, receiving from the royal chamberlain a notification that the queen expected to see him at all entertainments. At the first of these Lord Walsingham introduced him to many of the young nobles of the court, speaking very highly of the services he had rendered ; and as the queen was pleased to speak often to him and to show him marked favour, he was exceedingly well received, and soon found himself at his ease.

He was, nevertheless, glad when the order came for him to proceed again to Holland with messages to the Prince of Orange. Upon his arrival there he was warmly congratulated by the prince.

"You have well earned your rank," the prince said. "I take some pride to myself in having so soon discovered that you had good stuff in you. There are some friends of yours here who will be glad to hear of the honour that has befallen you. The Countess Von Harp and her daughter have been here for the last six weeks. I have seen them several times, and upon each occasion they spoke to me of their gratitude for the services you have rendered them. One of my pages will show you where they are lodging. They are about to proceed to England, and I think their decision is a wise one, for this country is at present no place for unprotected women."

The countess and her daughter were alike surprised and pleased when Ned was announced as Sir Edward Martin. And when a fortnight later Ned sailed for England, they took passage in the same ship. Ned had sent word to his mother by a vessel that sailed a week previously that they would arrive with him, and the best room in the house had been got in readiness for them, and they received a hearty welcome from Ned's parents and sisters. They stayed a fortnight there and then established themselves in a pretty little house in the village of Dulwich. One of Ned's sisters accompanied them to stay for a time as Gertrude's friend and companion.

Whenever Ned returned home he was a frequent visitor at Dulwich, and at the end of two years his sisters were delighted but not surprised when he returned one day and told them that Gertrude Von Harp had accepted him. The marriage was not to take place for a time; for Ned was still young, and the countess thought it had best be delayed. She was now receiving a regular income from her estates; for it had been a time of comparative peace in Holland, and that country was increasing fast in wealth and prosperity.

Alexander of Parma had by means of his agents corrupted the greater part of the nobility of Flanders and Brabant, had laid siege to Maastricht, and, after a defence even more gallant and desperate than that of Haarlem, and several terrible repulses of his soldiers, had captured the city and put the greater part of its inhabitants—men and women—to the sword. After vain entreaties to Elizabeth to assume the sovereignty of the Netherlands, this had been offered to the Duke of Anjou, brother of the King of France.

The choice appeared to be a politic one, for Anjou was

at the time the all but accepted suitor of Queen Elizabeth, and it was thought that the choice would unite both powers in defence of Holland. The Duke, however, speedily proved his incapacity. Irritated at the smallness of the authority granted him, and the independent attitude of the great towns, he attempted to capture them by force. He was successful in several places; but at Antwerp, where the French thought to repeat the Spanish success and to sack the city, the burghers gathered so strongly and fiercely that the French troops employed were for the most part killed, those who survived being ignominiously taken prisoners.

Anjou retired with his army, losing a large number of men on his retreat by the bursting of a dyke and the flooding of the country. By this time the Prince of Orange had accepted the sovereignty of Holland and Zeeland, which was now completely separated from the rest of the Netherlands. After the flight of Anjou he received many invitations from the other provinces to accept their sovereignty; but he steadily refused, having no personal ambition, and knowing well that no reliance whatever could be placed upon the nobles of Brabant and Flanders.

CHAPTER XXI.

THE SIEGE OF ANTWERP.

ON the 10 of July, 1584, a deep gloom was cast over all Holland and England, by the assassination of the Prince of Orange. Many attempts had been made upon his life by paid agents of the King of Spain. One had been nearly successful, and the prince had lain for weeks almost at the point of death. At last the hatred of Philip and Parma gained its end, and the prince fell a victim to the bullet of an assassin, who came before him disguised as a petitioner. His murderer was captured, and put to death with horrible tortures, boasting of his crime to the last. It was proved beyond all question that he, as well as the authors of the previous attempts, was acting at the instigation of the Spanish authorities, and had been promised vast sums in the event of his success.

Thus died the greatest statesmen of his age; a pure patriot, a disinterested politician, a great orator, a man possessing at once immense talent, unbounded perseverance, a fortitude under misfortunes beyond proof, and an unshakeable faith in God. But terrible as was the blow to the Netherlands, it failed to have the effect which its instigators had hoped from it. On the very day of the murder the Estates of Holland, then sitting at Delft, passed a resolution "to maintain the good cause, with God's help, to the uttermost, without sparing gold or blood." The prince's eldest son had been kidnapped from school in

Leyden by Philip's orders, and had been a captive in Spain for seventeen years under the tutorship of the Jesuits. Maurice, the next son, now seventeen years old, was appointed head of the States Council.

But the position of the Netherlands was still well-nigh desperate. Flanders and Brabant lay at the feet of the Spaniards. A rising which had lately taken place had been crushed. Bruges had surrendered without a blow. The Duke of Parma, with 18,000 troops, besides his garrisons, was threatening Ghent, Mechlin, Brussels, and Antwerp, and was freely using promises and bribery to induce them to surrender. Dendermonde and Vilvoorde both opened their gates, the capitulation of the latter town cutting the communication between Brussels and Antwerp. Ghent followed the example and surrendered without striking a blow, and at the moment of the assassination of the Prince of Orange Parma's army was closing round Antwerp.

Sir Edward Martin was at Antwerp, where he had gone by the queen's order, when he received the news of the murder of the prince, whom he had seen a few days before. He was filled with grief and horror at the loss of one who had been for six years his friend, and whom he regarded with enthusiastic admiration. It seemed to him at first that with the death of the prince the cause of the Netherlands was lost, and had the former attempts of Philip's emissaries upon the prince's life been successful such a result would no doubt have followed; but the successful defence of their cities, and the knowledge they had gained that the sea could be made to fight for them, had given the people of Holland strength and hope. Their material resources, too, were larger than before, for great numbers of the Protestants from the other provinces had emigrated there, and had added alike to their strength and wealth. At first, however, the news caused something like despair in Antwerp. Men went about depressed and sorrowful, as if they had lost their dearest friend; but Sainte Aldegonde, who had been appointed by the prince to take charge of the defence of Antwerp, encouraged the citizens, and their determination to resist returned. Unfortunately there had already been terrible blundering. William de Blois, Lord of Treslong and Admiral of the fleet of Holland and Zeeland, had been ordered to carry up to the city provisions and munitions of war sufficient to last for a year, the money having been freely voted by the States-general of these provinces.

But Treslong disobeyed the orders, and remained week after week at Ostend drinking heavily and doing nothing else. At last the States, enraged at his disobedience, ordered him to be arrested and thrown into prison; but this was too late to enable the needed stores to be taken up to Antwerp. The citizens were under no uneasiness. They believed that it was absolutely impossible to block the river, and that, therefore, they could at all times receive supplies from the coast. On both sides of the river below the town the land was low and could at any time be laid under water, and Sainte Aldegonde brought the Prince of Orange's instructions that the great dyke, called the Blauwgaren, was to be pierced. This would have laid the country under water for miles, and even the blocking of the river would not have prevented the arrival of ships with provisions and supplies.

Unfortunately Sainte Aldegonde's power was limited. The Butchers' Guild rose against the proposal, and their leaders appeared before the magistrates and protested against the step being carried out. Twelve thousand cattle grazed upon the pastures which would be submerged; and the destruction of farms, homesteads, and orchards would be terrible. As to the blocking up of the river, the idea was absurd, and the operation far beyond the power of man. The butchers were supported by the officers of the militia, who declared that were the authorities to attempt the destruction of the dyke the municipal soldiery would oppose it by force.

Such was the state of things when the only man whom the democracy would listen to and obey fell by the assassin's knife, and his death and the obstinate stupidity of the burghers of Antwerp sealed the fate of the city. Sainte Aldegonde had hailed the arrival of Elizabeth's envoy, and consulted with him as to the steps to be taken for the defence of the city. He himself did not believe in the possibility of the river being stopped. It was nearly half a mile in width and sixty feet in depth, with a tidal rise and fall of eleven feet. Ned agreed with the governor or burgomaster—for this was Sainte Aldegonde's title—that the work of blocking this river seemed impossible, but his reliance upon the opinion of the prince was so great that he did what he could towards persuading the populace to permit the plans to be carried out. But Elizabeth had so often disappointed the people of the Netherlands that her envoy possessed no authority, and the magistrates, with whom were the ward masters, the deans of all the guilds, the presidents of chambers and heads of colleges, squabbled and quarrelled amongst themselves, and nothing was done.

The garrison consisted only of a regiment of English under Colonel Morgan and a Scotch regiment under Colonel Balfour, but these were in a state of indiscipline, and a mutiny had shortly before broken out among them. Many of the troops had deserted to Parma and some had returned home, and it was not until Morgan had beheaded Captain Lee and Captain Powell that order was restored among them. Beside these were the burgher militia, who were brave and well trained but insubordinate, and ready on every occasion to refuse obedience to authority.

The first result of the general confusion which prevailed in Antwerp was the Herenthals was allowed to fall without assistance. Had this small but important city been succoured it would have enabled Antwerp to protract its own defence for some time.

The veteran Mondragon as he took possession remarked, "Now it is easy to see that the Prince of Orange is dead;" and indeed it was only under his wise supervision and authority that anything like concerted action between the cities, which were really small republics, was possible.

Quietly but steadily the Duke of Parma established fortified posts at various points on both banks of the Lower Scheldt, thereby rendering its navigation more difficult, and covering in some degree the spot where he intended to close the river. Nine miles below the city were two forts—Lillo and Liefkenshoek—one on either side of the stream. The fortifications of Lillo were complete, but those of Liefkenshoek were not finished when Parma ordered the Marquis of Richebourg to carry it by assault. It was taken by surprise, and the eight hundred men who composed its garrison were all killed or drowned. This first blow took place on the very day the Prince of Orange was killed.

Lillo was garrisoned by Antwerp volunteers, called the Young Bachelors, together with a company of French under Captain Gascoigne, and 400 Scotch and Englishmen under Colonel Morgan. Mondragon was ordered to take the place at any cost. He took up his position with 5000

men at the country house and farm of Lillo a short distance from the fort, planted his batteries and opened fire.
The fort responded briskly, and finding that the walls
were little injured by his artillery fire Mondragon tried to
take it by mining. Teligny, however, run counter mines,
and for three weeks the siege continued, the Spaniards
gaining no advantage and losing a considerable number of
men. At last Teligny made a sortie, and a determined
action took place without advantage on either side. The
defenders were then recalled to the fort, the sluice gates
were opened, and the waters of the Scheldt, swollen by a
high tide, poured over the country. Swept by the fire of
the guns of the fort and surrounded by the water, the
Spaniards were forced to make a rapid retreat; struggling
breast high in the waves.

Seeing the uselessness of the siege the attempt to capture
Lillo was abandoned, having cost the Spaniards no less
than two thousand lives. Parma's own camp was on the
opposite side of the river, at the villages of Beveren, Kalloo, and Borght, and he was thus nearly opposite to Antwerp, as the river swept round with a sharp curve. He had
with him half his army, while the rest were at Stabroek on
the opposite side of the river, nearly ten miles below Antwerp. Kalloo stood upon rising ground, and was speedily
transformed into a bustling town. From this point an
army of men dug a canal to Steeken, a place on the river
above Antwerp twelve miles from Kalloo, and as soon as
Ghent and Dendermonde had fallen, great rafts of timber,
fleets of boats laden with provisions, munitions, building
materials, and every other requisite for the great undertaking Parma had in view were brought to Kalloo.

To this place was brought also by Parma's orders the
shipwrights, masons, ropemakers, sailors, boatmen, bakers,

brewers, and butchers of Flanders and Brabant, and work went on unceasingly. But while the autumn wore on the river was still open; and in spite of the Spanish batteries on the banks the daring sailors of Zeeland brought up their ships laden with corn to Antwerp, where the price was already high. Had this traffic been continued Antwerp would soon have been provisioned for a year's siege; but the folly and stupidity of the municipal authorities put a stop to it, for they enacted that, instead of the high prices current for grain, which had tempted the Zeelanders to run the gauntlet of the Spanish batteries, a price but little above that obtainable in other places should be given. The natural result was, the supply of provisions ceased at once.

"Did you ever see anything like the obstinacy and folly of these burghers?" Sainte Aldegonde said in despair to Ned, when, in spite of his entreaties, this suicidal edict had been issued. "What possible avail is it to endeavour to defend a city which seems bent on its own destruction?"

"The best thing to do," Ned replied in great anger, "would be to surround the town-hall with the companies of Morgan's regiment remaining here, and to hang every one of these thick-headed and insolent tradesmen."

"It would be the best way," Sainte Aldegonde agreed, "if we had also a sufficient force to keep down the city. These knaves think vastly more of their own privileges than of the good of the State, or even of the safety of the town. Here, as in Ghent, the people are divided into sections and parties, who, when there is no one else to quarrel with, are ever ready to fly at each other's throats. Each of these leaders of guilds and presidents of chambers considers himself a little god, and it is quite enough if anyone else expresses an opinion for the majority to take up at once the opposite view."

"I looked in at the town-hall yesterday," Ned said, "and such an uproar was going on that no one could be heard to speak. Twenty men were on their feet at once, shouting and haranguing, and paying not the slightest attention to each other; while the rest joined in from time to time with deafening cries and yells. Never did I see such a scene. And it is upon such men as these that it rests to decide upon the measures to be taken for the safety of the city!"

"Ah, if we had but the prince here among us again for a few hours there would be some hope," Sainte Aldegonde said; "for he would be able to persuade the people that in times like these there is no safety in many counsellors, but that they must be content for the time to obey one man."

On the Flemish side of the river the sluices had been opened at Saftingen. The whole country there, with the exception of the ground on which Kalloo and the other villages stood, was under water. Still the Blauwgaren dyke, and an inner dyke called the Kowenstyn, barred back the water, which, had it free course, would have turned the country into a sea and given passage to the fleets of Zeeland. Now that it was too late, those who had so fiercely opposed the plan at first were eager that these should be cut. But it was now out of their power to do so. The Lord of Kowenstyn, who had a castle on the dyke which bore his name, had repeatedly urged upon the Antwerp magistracy the extreme importance of cutting through this dyke, even if they deferred the destruction of the outer one. Enraged at their obstinacy and folly, and having the Spanish armies all round him, he made terms with Parma, and the Spaniards established themselves firmly along the bank, built strong redoubts upon it, and stationed five thousand men there.

As the prince had forseen, the opening of the Saftingen sluice had assisted Parma instead of adding to his difficulties; for he was now no longer confined to the canal, but was able to bring a fleet of large vessels, laden with cannon and ammunition, from Ghent down the Scheldt, and in through a breach through the dyke of Borght to Kalloo. Sainte Aldegonde, in order to bar the Borght passage, built a work called Fort Teligny upon the dyke, opposite that thrown up by the Spaniards, and in the narrow passage between them constant fighting went on between the Spaniards and patriots. Still the people of Antwerp felt confident, for the Scheldt was still open, and when food became short the Zeeland fleet could at any time sail up to their assistance. But before the winter closed in Parma commenced the work for which he had made such mighty preparations.

Between Kalloo and Oordam, on the opposite side, a sand bar had been discovered, which somewhat diminished the depth of the stream and rendered pile-driving comparatively easy. A strong fort was erected on each bank and the work of driving in the piles began. From each side a framework of heavy timber, supported on these massive piles, was carried out so far that the width of open water was reduced from twenty-four to thirteen hundred feet, and strong block-houses were erected upon each pier to protect them from assault. Had a concerted attack been made by the Antwerp ships from above, and the Zeeland fleet from below, the works could at this time have been easily destroyed. But the fleet had been paralysed by the insubordination of Treslong, and there was no plan or concert; so that although constant skirmishing went on, no serious attack was made.

The brave Teligny, one night going down in a row-boat

to communicate with the Zeelanders and arrange for joint
action, was captured by the Spanish boats, and remained
for six years in prison. His loss was a very serious blow to
Antwerp and to the cause. On the 13th of November
Parma sent in a letter to Antwerp, begging the citizens to
take compassion on their wives and children and make
terms. Parma had none of the natural blood-thirstiness
of Alva, and would have been really glad to have arranged
matters without further fighting; especially as he was
almost without funds, and the attitude of the King of
France was so doubtful that he knew that at any moment
his plans might be overthrown.

The States in January attempted to make a diversion in
favour of Antwerp by attacking Bois-le-Duc, a town from
which the Spaniards drew a large portion of their supplies.
Parma, although feeling the extreme importance of this
town, had been able to spare no men for its defence; and
although it was strong, and its burghers notably brave and
warlike, it seemed that it might be readily captured by
surprise. Count Hohenlohe was entrusted with the
enterprise, and with 4000 infantry and 200 cavalry advanced
towards the place. Fifty men, under an officer who knew
the town, hid at night near the gate, and when in the morning the portcullis was lifted rushed in, overpowered the
guard, and threw open the gate, and Hohenlohe, with his
200 troopers and 500 pikemen, entered.

These at once, instead of securing the town, scattered to
plunder. It happened that forty Spanish lancers and
thirty foot soldiers had come into the town the night before to form an escort for a convoy of provisions. They
were about starting when the tumult broke out. As Hohenlohe's troops thought of nothing but pillage, time was
given to the burghers to seize their arms; and they, with

the little body of troops, fell upon the plunderers, who, at the sight of the Spanish uniforms, were seized with a panic. Hohenlohe galloped to the gate to bring in the rest of the troops; but while he was away one of its guards, although desperately wounded at its capture, crawled to the ropes which held up the portcullis and cut them with his knife. Thus those within were cut off from their friends. Many of them were killed, others threw themselves from the walls into the moat, and very few of those who had entered made their escape.

When Hohenlohe returned with 2000 fresh troops and found the gates shut in his face, he had nothing to do but to ride away, the enterprise having failed entirely through his own folly and recklessness; for it was he himself who had encouraged his followers to plunder. Had he kept them together until the main force entered, no resistance could have been offered to him, or had he when he rode out to fetch reinforcements left a guard at the gate to prevent its being shut, the town could again have been taken. Parma himself wrote to Philip acknowledging that "Had the rebels succeeded in their enterprise, I should have been compelled to have abandoned the siege of Antwerp."

But now the winter, upon which the people in Antwerp had chiefly depended for preventing the blocking of the stream, was upon the besiegers. The great river, lashed by storms into fury, and rolling huge masses of ice up and down with the tide, beat against the piers, and constantly threatened to carry them away. But the structure was enormously strong. The piles had been driven fifty feet into the river bed, and withstood the force of the stream, and on the 25th of February the Scheldlt was closed.

Parma had from the first seen that it was absolutely impossible to drive piles across the deep water between the piers, and had prepared to connect them with a bridge of boats. For this purpose he had constructed thirty-two great barges, each sixty-two feet in length, and twelve in breadth. These were moored in pairs with massive chains and anchors, the distance between each pair being twenty-two feet. All were bound together with chains and timbers and a roadway protected by a parapet of massive beams was formed across it. Each boat was turned into a fortress by the erection of solid wooden redoubts at each end, mounting heavy guns, and was manned by thirty-two soldiers and four sailors. The forts at the end of the bridge each mounted ten great guns, and twenty armed vessels with heavy pieces of artillery were moored in front of each fort. Thus the structure was defended by 170 great guns.

As an additional protection to the bridge, two heavy rafts, each 1250 feet long, composed of empty barrels, heavy timbers, ships' masts, and woodwork bound solidly together, were moored at some little distance above and below the bridge of boats. These rafts were protected by projecting beams of wood tipped with iron, to catch any vessels floating down upon them. The erection of this structure was one of the most remarkable military enterprises ever carried out.

Now that it was too late the people of Antwerp bitterly bewailed their past folly, which had permitted an enterprise that could at any moment have been interrupted to be carried to a successful issue.

But if something like despair seized the citizens at the sight of the obstacle that cut them off from all hope of succour, the feelings of the great general whose enterprise and ability had carried out the work were almost as depressed. His troops had dwindled to the mere shadow of an army, the cavalry had nearly disappeared, the garrisons in the various cities were starving, and the burghers had no food either for the soldiers or themselves.

The troops were two years behindhand in their pay. Parma had long exhausted every means of credit, and his appeals to his sovereign for money met with no response. But while in his letters to Philip he showed the feelings of despair which possessed him, he kept a smiling countenance to all else. A spy having been captured, he ordered him to be conducted over every part of the encampment. The forts and bridge were shown to him, and he was requested to count the pieces of artillery, and was then sent back to the town to inform the citizens of what he had seen.

At this moment Brussels, which had long been besieged, was starved into surrender, and Parma was reinforced by the troops who had been engaged in the siege of that city. A misfortune now befell him similar to that which the patriots had suffered at Bois-le-Duc. He had experienced great inconvenience from not possessing a port on the sea coast of Flanders, and consented to a proposal of La Motte, one of the most experienced of the Walloon generals, to surprise Ostend. On the night of the 29th of March, La Motte, with 2000 foot and 1200 cavalry, surprised and carried the old port of the town. Leaving an officer in charge of the position, he went back to bring up the rest of his force. In his absence the soldiers scattered to plunder. The citizens roused themselves, killed many of them, and put the rest to flight, and by the time La Motte returned with the fresh troops the panic had become so general that the enterprise had to be abandoned.

The people of Antwerp now felt that unless some decisive steps were taken their fate was sealed. A number of armed vessels sailed up from Zeeland, and, assisted by a detach ment from Fort Lillo, suddenly attacked and carried Fort Liefkenshoek, which had been taken from them at the commencement of the siege, and also Fort St. Anthony lower down the river. In advancing towards the latter fort they disobeyed Sainte Aldegonde's express orders, which were that they should, after capturing Liefkenshock, at once follow the dyke up the river to the point where it was broken near the fort at the end of the bridge, and should there instantly throw up strong works.

Had they followed out these orders they could from this point have battered the bridge, and destroyed this barrier over the river. But the delay caused by the attack on the Fort St. Anthony was fatal, for at night Parma sent a strong body of soldiers and sappers in boats from Kalloo to the broken end of the dyke, and these before morning threw up works upon the very spot where Sainte Aldegonde had intended the battery for the destruction of the bridge to be erected. Nevertheless the success was a considerable one. The possession of Lillo and Liefkenshoek restored to the patriots the command of the river to within three miles of the bridge, and enabled the Zeeland fleet to be brought up at that point.

Another blow was now meditated. There was in Antwerp an Italian named Gianobelli, a man of great science and inventive power. He had first gone to Spain to offer his inventions to Philip, but had met with such insolent neglect there that he had betaken himself in a rage to Flanders, swearing that the Spaniards should repent their treatment of him. He had laid his plans before the Council of Antwerp, and had asked from them three ships of a hundred and fifty, three hundred and fifty, and five hundred tons respectively, besides these he wanted sixty flat-bottomed scows. Had his request been complied with it is certain that Parma's bridge would have been utterly destroyed; but the leading men were building a great ship or floating castle of their own design, from which they expected such great things that they christened it the End of the War. Gianobelli had warned them that this ship would certainly turn out a failure. However, they persisted, and instead of granting him the ships he wanted, only gave him two small vessels of seventy and eighty tons.

Although disgusted with their parsimony on so momentous an occasion, Gianobelli set to work with the aid of two skilful artisans of Antwerp to fit them up.

In the hold of each vessel a solid flooring of brick and mortar a foot thick was first laid down. Upon this was built a chamber of masonry forty feet long, three and a half feet wide, and as many high, and with side walls five feet thick. This chamber was covered with a roof six feet thick of tombstones placed edgeways, and was filled with a powder of Gianobelli's own invention. Above was piled a pyramid of millstones, cannon-balls, chain-shot, iron hooks, and heavy missiles of all kinds, and again over these were laid heavy marble slabs. The rest of the hold was filled with paving-stones.

One ship was christened the *Fortune*, and on this the mine was to be exploded by a slow match, cut so as to explode at a calculated moment. The mine on board the *Hope* was to be started by a piece of clock-work, which at the appointed time was to strike fire from a flint. Planks and woodwork were piled on the decks to give to the two vessels the appearance of simple fire-ships. Thirty-two small craft, saturated with tar and turpentine and filled with inflammable materials, were to be sent down the river in detachments of eight every half hour, to clear away if possible the raft above the bridge and to occupy the attention of the Spaniards.

The 5th of April, the day after the capture of the Lief-kenshoek, was chosen for the attempt. It began badly. Admiral Jacobzoon, who was in command, instead of send-ing down the fire-boats in batches as arranged, sent them all off one after another, and started the two mine ships immediately afterwards. As soon as their approach was discovered, the Spaniards, who had heard grave rumours that an attack by water was meditated, at once got under arms and mustered upon the bridge and forts. Parma himself, with all his principal officers, superintended the arrangements. As the fleet of small ships approached they burst into flames. The Spaniards silently watched the ap-proaching danger, but soon began to take heart again. Many of the boats grounded on the banks of the river be-fore reaching their destination, others burned out and sank, while the rest drifted against the raft, but were kept from touching it by the long projecting timbers, and burned out without doing any damage.

Then came the two ships. The pilots as they neared the bridge escaped in boats, and the current carried them down, one on each side of the raft, towards the solid ends of the bridge. The *Fortune* came first, but grounded near the shore without touching the bridge. Just as it did so the slow match upon deck burnt out. There was a faint ex-plosion, but no result; and Sir Ronald Yorke, the man who had handed over Zutphen, sprang on board with a party of volunteers, extinguished the fire smouldering on deck, and thrusting their spears down into the hold, en-deavoured to ascertain the nature of its contents. Finding it impossible to do so they returned to the bridge.

The Spaniards were now shouting with laughter at the impotent attempt of the Antwerpers to destroy the bridge, and were watching the *Hope*, which was now following her consort. She passed just clear of the end of the raft, and struck the bridge close to the block-house at the commencement of the floating portion. A fire was smouldering on her deck, and a party of soldiers at once sprang on board to extinguish this, as their comrades had done the fire on board the *Fortune*. The Marquis of Richebourg, standing on the bridge, directed the operations. The Prince of Parma was standing close by, when an officer named Vega, moved by a sudden impulse, fell on his knees and implored him to leave the place, and not to risk a life so precious to Spain. Moved by the officer's entreaties Parma turned and walked along the bridge. He had just reached the entrance to the fort when a terrific explosion took place.

The clock-work of the *Hope* had succeeded better than the slow match in the *Fortune*. In an instant she disappeared, and with her the block-house against which she had struck, with all its garrison, a large portion of the bridge, and all the troops stationed upon it. The ground was shaken as if by an earthquake, houses fell miles away, and the air was filled with a rain of mighty blocks of stone, some of which were afterwards found a league away. A thousand soldiers were killed in an instant, the rest were dashed to the ground, stunned and bewildered. The Marquis of Richebourg and most of Parma's best officers were killed. Parma himself lay for a long time as if dead, but presently recovered and set to work to do what he could to repair the disaster.

The Zeeland fleet were lying below, only waiting for the signal to move up to destroy the rest of the bridge and carry succour to the city; but the incompetent and cowardly Jacobzoon rowed hastily away after the explosion, and the rocket that should have summoned the Zeelanders was never sent up. Parma moved about among his troops, restoring order and confidence, and as the night went on and no assault took place he set his men to work to collect drifting timbers and spars, and make a hasty and temporary restoration, in appearance at least, of the ruined portion of the bridge.

It was not until three days afterwards that the truth that the bridge had been partially destroyed, and that the way was open, was known at Antwerp. But by this time it was too late. The Zeelanders had retired ; the Spaniards had recovered their confidence, and were hard at work restoring the bridge. From time to time fresh fire-ships were sent down ; but Parma had now established a patrol of boats, which went out to meet them and towed them to shore far above the bridge. In the weeks that followed Parma's army dwindled away from sickness brought on by starvation, anxiety, and overwork; while the people of Antwerp were preparing for an attack upon the dyke of Kowenstyn. If that could be captured and broken, Parma's bridge would be rendered useless, as the Zeeland fleet could pass up over the submerged country with aid.

Parma was well aware of the supreme importance of this dyke. He had fringed both its margins with breast-works of stakes, and had strengthened the whole body of the dyke with timber-work and piles. Where it touched the great Scheldt dyke a strong fortress called the Holy Cross had been constructed under the command of Mondragon, and at the further end, in the neighbourhood of Mansfeldt's headquarters, was another fort called the Stabroek, which commanded and raked the whole dyke.

On the body of the dyke itself were three strong forts a mile apart, called St. James, St. George, and the Fort

of the Palisades. Several attacks had been made from
time to time, both upon the bridge and dyke, and at daybreak on the 7th of May a fleet from Lillo, under Hohenlohe, landed five hundred Zeelanders upon it between St.
George's and Fort Palisade. But the fleet that was to
have come out from Antwerp to his assistance never arrived; and the Zeelanders were overpowered by the fire
from the two forts and the attacks of the Spaniards, and
retreated, leaving four of their ships behind them, and
more than a fourth of their force.

Upon the 26th of the same month the grand attack,
from which the people of Antwerp hoped so much, took
place. Two hundred vessels were ready. A portion of
these were to come up from Zeeland, under Hohenlohe;
the rest to advance from Antwerp, under Sainte Aldegonde.
At two o'clock in the morning the Spanish sentinels saw
four fire-ships approaching the dyke. They mustered
reluctantly, fearing a repetition of the previous explosion,
and retired to the fort. When the fire-ships reached the
stakes protecting the dyke, they burned and exploded,
but without effecting much damage. But in the meantime a swarm of vessels of various sizes were seen approaching. It was the fleet of Hohenlohe, which had been sailing and rowing from ten o'clock on the previous night.

Guided by the light of the fire-ships they approached
the dyke, and the Zeelanders sprang ashore and climed up.
They were met by several hundred Spanish troops, who, as
soon as they saw the fire-ships burnt out harmlessly, sallied
out from their forts. The Zeelanders were beginning to
give way when the Antwerp fleet came up on the other
side, headed by Sainte Aldegonde. The new arrivals
sprang from their boats and climbed the dyke. The Spaniards were driven off, and three thousand men occupied all

the space between Fort George and the Palisade Fort.

With Sainte Aldegonde came all the English and Scotch troops in Antwerp under Balfour and Morgan, and many volunteers, among whom was Ned Martin. With Hohenlohe came Prince Maurice, William the Silent's son, a lad of eighteen. With woolsacks, sandbags, planks, and other materials the patriots now rapidly entrenched the position they had gained, while a large body of sappers and miners set to work with picks, mattocks, and shovels, tearing down the dyke. The Spaniards poured out from the forts; but Antwerpers, Dutchmen, Zeelanders, Scotchmen, and Englishmen met them bravely, and a tremendous conflict went on at each end of the narrow causeway.

Both parties fought with the greatest obstinacy, and for an hour there was no advantage on either side. At last the patriots were victorious, drove the Spaniards back into their two forts, and following up their success attacked the Palisade Fort. Its outworks were in their hands when a tremendous cheer was heard. The sappers and miners had done their work. Salt water poured through the broken dyke, and a Zeeland barge, freighted with provisions, floated triumphantly into the water beyond, now no longer an inland sea. Then when the triumph seemed achieved another fatal mistake was made by the patriots. Sainte Aldegonde and Hohenlohe, the two commanders of the enterprise, both leaped on board, anxious to be the first to carry the news of the victory to Antwerp, where they arrived in triumph, and set all the bells ringing and bonfires blazing.

For three hours the party on the dyke remained unmolested. Parma was at his camp four leagues away, and in ignorance of what had been done, and Mansfeldt could send no word across to him. The latter held a council of war, but it seemed that nothing could be done. Three thousand men were entrenched on the narrow dyke, covered by the guns of a hundred and sixty Zeeland ships. Some of the officers were in favor of waiting until nightfall; but at last the advice of a gallant officer, Camillo Capizucca, colonel of the Italian Legion, carried the day in favour of an immediate assault, and the Italians and Spaniards. marched together from Fort Stabroek to the Palisade Fort, which was now in extremity.

They came up in time, drove back the assailants, and were preparing to advance against them when a distant shout from the other end of the dyke told that Parma had arrived there. Mondragon moved from the Holy Cross to Fort George; and from that fort and from the Palisade the Spaniards advanced to the attack of the patriots' position. During the whole war no more desperate encounter took place than that upon the dyke, which was but six paces wide. The fight was long and furious. Three times the Spaniards were repulsed with tremendous loss; and while the patriot soldiers fought, their pioneers still carried on the destruction of the dyke.

A fourth assault was likewise repulsed, but the fifth was more successful. The Spaniards believed that they were led by a dead commander who had fallen some months before, and this superstitious belief inspired them with fresh courage. The entrenchment was carried, but its defenders fought as obstinately as before on the dyke behind it. Just at this moment the vessels of the Zeelanders began to draw off. Many had been sunk or disabled by the fire that the forts had maintained on them; and the rest found the water sinking fast, for the tide was now ebbing.

The patriots, believing that they were deserted by the fleet, were seized with a sudden panic; and, leaving the

dyke, tried to wade or swim off to the ships. The Spaniards
with shouts of victory persued them. The English and
Scotch were the last to abandon the position they had held
for seven hours, and most of them were put to the sword.
Two thousand in all were slain or drowned, the remainder
succeeded in reaching the ships on one side or other of the
dyke.

Ned Martin had fought to the last. He was standing
side by side with Justinius of Nassau, and the two sprang
together into a clump of high rushes, tore off their heavy
armour and swam out to one of the Zeeland ships, which
at once dropped down the river and reached the sea.
Ned's mission was now at an end, and he at once returned to England.

The failure of the attempt upon the Kowenstyn dyke
sealed the fate of Antwerp. It resisted until the middle
of June; when finding hunger staring the city in the face,
and having no hope whatever of relief, Sainte Aldegonde
yielded to the clamour of the mob and opened negotiations.

These were continued for nearly two months. Parma
was unaware that the town was reduced to such an extremity, and consented to give honourable terms. The
treaty was signed on the 17th of August. There was to
be a complete amnesty for the past. Royalist absentees
were to be reinstated in their positions. Monasteries and
churches to be restored to their former possessors. The
inhabitants of the city were to practice the Catholic
religion only, while those who refused to conform were
allowed two years for the purpose of winding up their
affairs. All prisoners, with the exception of Teligny,
were to be released. Four hundred thousand florins were
to be paid by the city as a fine, and the garrison were to
leave the town with arms and baggage, and all honours of war.

The fall of Antwerp brought about with it the entire submission of Brabant and Flanders, and henceforth the war was continued solely by Zeeland, Holland, and Friesland.

The death of the Prince of Orange, and the fall of Antwerp, marked the conclusion of what may be called the first period of the struggle of the Netherlands for freedom. It was henceforth to enter upon another phase. England, which had long assisted Holland privately with money, and openly by the raising of volunteers for her service, was now about to enter the arena boldly and to play an important part in the struggle, which, after a long period of obstinate strife, was to end in the complete emancipation of the Netherlands from the yoke of Spain.

Sir Edward Martin married Gertrude von Harp soon after his return to England. He retained the favour of Elizabeth to the day of her death, and there were few whose counsels had more influence with her. He long continued in the public service, although no longer compelled to do so as a means of livelihood; for as Holland and Zeeland freed themselves from the yoke of Spain, and made extraordinary strides in wealth and prosperity, the estates of the countess once more produced a splendid revenue, and this at her death came entirely to her daughter. A considerable portion of Sir Edward Martin's life, when not actually engaged upon public affairs, was spent upon the broad estates which had come to him from his wife.

THE END.